MW01538812

The Affair
at Cloud Bay

John —
It'll be fun again
some day.
Let's go fishin'.
Regards —
Douglas

The Affair
at Cloud Bay

Douglas Terrel

Copyright © 2011 by Douglas Terrel
All rights reserved
Printed in the United States of America

For Barbara, and for Elaine.
Thank you for the support and patience.

The Affair
at Cloud Bay

1

Two months after their first coupling Mary Archer told her husband she was pregnant. Old Henry forked a potato into his mouth. He shoved his empty bowl aside and grunted.

"That's that."

Mary Archer didn't have the courage to ask what he meant but the weeks swelled into months and she found out. The man's own living seed repulsed him. She lived on abused hope through all the foul months she carried Tom, sure that when she'd emptied her womb – like moving her bowels – Old Henry would return to his usual form. That wasn't much more than a rutting shove and a sweaty collapse but it was all she knew and all she ever expected. She was doomed to disappointment in even that.

She had spread herself shortly after he'd arrived in town, walking, his thin bedroll tied with a rope and slung over his shoulder. It had been early 1904; times were bad, at least locally, and she'd needed a man to support her. When she took Old Henry behind the machine shop and showed what she was willing to trade for that support he shrugged agreement and they were married in the church of indifference.

Old Henry had been a merchant seaman and a hard rock miner and he'd been to far bright places but not even exposure to horizons beyond the scraggy hills of Outcrop had added any vision to his character. Shortly after his arrival in the shabby little

Washington town a southbound rumor passed through saying he'd killed a Chinaman on a ship up in the Inland Passageway but nobody pressed him to say it was true. Nobody cared. He told the Outcrop hiring man he'd learned tunneling in Alaska, knew what he needed to know, "...And I kin show it." The company put him on and sent him down. Work in the mine was hard and common and ended with itself but it was the fruit of Old Henry's attitudes and aspirations. The black dust in his pores and in his soul went as deep as the veins in the rocky earth.

Baby Tom Archer didn't need a slap on the fanny. He was born shrieking and continued without cease for eighty-four days. The high-pitched wails, clenched face and tight little fists killed whatever small affection his mother might've had for the howling creature she'd spawned. Old Henry spent most of his time elsewhere, couldn't stand to be around the two-room house with its resounding clapboard walls. Probably that saved the child.

The town's medicine man couldn't find a physical reason for baby Tom's endless scream and finally gave Mary Archer a bottle of codeia and a tiny dropper. After the baby had been a month on the drops without spontaneous improvement, whimpering even from the deep shadows of drugged unconsciousness, the doctor had second thoughts and terminated his prescription. The screaming continued hour after unrelenting hour.

Neighbors were sympathetic at first. Then they complained to each other, then to Old Henry and finally to his boss in the mine. There was nothing Mary Archer could do to stop the noise. Even when she forced her swollen pap into Tom's face he moaned and trembled and when he'd gasped away the dryness in his throat he shoved away and threw back his head, fighting her frantic efforts to plug him with her nipple, twisting, pushing, shrieking. Resolution grew. She'd kill him. She planned the smothering. She knew nobody in the stone-hearted town would accuse her. But she couldn't make herself do it even when her husband pushed her.

Then one morning Tom just stopped.

She'd buried his noise in the dark root cellar, had wrapped him in blankets against the damp. She was washing diapers when she noticed the sound of the silence. She stood, shitty yellow suds on her forearms, her head canted. She could hear the throb of her own life. She stood a minute more, listening, wiping her wrists on her dress. She could walk out, stand in the yard, find something to do, something to keep her distracted until the screaming creature in the cellar was cold and stiff. Had it turned over and wrapped a corner of the blanket around its neck? Was it dead? Her hopes lashed her to the cellar door, the silence a writ. She put her ear to the wood.

There wasn't any noise. Not a wail or sniffle, not a happy gurgling, nothing that forecast the future. She opened the small door, ducked into the cellar and in the faint light coming through the doorway, looked at her baby.

Tom looked back, his heavy black eyebrows crunched together, one thumb clutched in his other fist, his feet poked through a fold in the covers. He blinked at her, then looked around at the cellar as if he'd just awakened from a long, confusing sleep.

She and Old Henry and all the neighbors feared the silence was temporary and lived at the ends of their nerves for days but as the period lengthened they relaxed. Mary Archer even hoped her husband would use her again in bed. He would, but only the other way.

****

Old Henry had been to China. It had been in the last month of 1900. He'd crewed on a fetid ship steaming into the corrupt mouth of the Yangtze to load humans. His interests had been avaricious and carnal and the Shanghai voyage promised whole satisfaction. The crew would split high stakes if they could successfully deliver the illegal cargo they thrust aboard in Shanghai, and nobody cared how the coolies below decks were used on the long voyage east.

Many of the men crammed into the holds of the slaver had been young, almost boys. They'd arrived from every drainage in China, flushed by desperation and ignorance from the interior until the scums of the sordid coastal city caught them. Some had been sold half a dozen times on their way to the slaver. Some arrived in wooden yokes, others voluntarily, even eagerly. Hong Deng Wei was one of those who presented himself, more or less.

****

His hamlet was a timid cluster of huts where two rivers rushed together, a score of mud brick buildings huddled behind a screen of small trees. At the exact V of the rivers an eddy swirled and where the two waters mated there was abundant food: fish of several kinds and small freshwater shrimp, and crayfish. Frogs growled in the reeds. Scrawny chickens scratched through scrubby vegetable plots. In other places, where the commercial measurement of time was important, it was the spring of 1900. By the river junction it was only The Year the Outlaws Arrived.

Deng Wei was almost a man, wiry and quick, with strong hands. As an infant he'd been strapped tightly to a board carried to his mother's chores, and those years had flattened the back of his forming skull. Below his bright eyes and wide nose a smile waited, always ready for its chance against the serious frowns of youth. He was different that way, willing to expose his feelings on his face, and that willingness would alter his life.

It was windless and hot the afternoon the Mongol outlaws pushed through the small trees, past the old sleeping sentry and into the hamlet. They pointed their grim faces everywhere, their suspicions cocked, then they relaxed and disarmed themselves. Their rest lengthened to a stay and days droned into weeks.

Deng Wei wasn't opposed to them at first, but that attitude didn't last long. He'd been the only bachelor to court the one local girl of marrying age. Now there were seven more. Eight, if the old outlaw with one arm was counted. The girl counted even that one.

But that wasn't all. The intruders told stories that carried Deng Wei far beyond the half-day journeys of his own experience, tales that compelled him even more than the knotted roiling in the wrinkled sack between his legs. Uncountable people crammed together in swarms of swirling confusion like the tadpoles in the rushes. Mountains that stabbed the sky. Humped-back animals. Dancing women. Deng Wei knew they were just vying for recognition with their shining lies but still he hovered, listening, trying to see with his mind.

One morning he spoke to the girl. She ignored him, walked on, her face averted. Deng Wei kicked dust at a strutting rooster and flung stones at a cur, cursed the girl and her suitors. He couldn't sleep, wasn't hungry. He tormented his sisters and brother until his mother drove him off. He couldn't even find solace along the banks of the river. The water seemed to taunt him, flowing past like the moments of his life.

Before the outlaws arrived his future had been as vague and unconsidered as the world beyond the screen of trees, his stunted imagination choked by the shielding woods and the thickets of his own ignorance. Now, as if the newcomers had felled the trees and distance had burst through like light, the future was suddenly exposed in all its urgency, blinding in its commanding mystery. His thoughts blurred with his simple, ignorant fantasies.

Finally, driven by the whips of his own frustrations, Deng Wei marched to the eddy, caught a log, dragged it to where the current flowed straight. He threw both his arms over it and shoved off. He had nothing to take with him. He didn't leave anything behind.

The river was the Hwang and he followed it, sometimes riding on its back when he found a boat ride, sometimes walking along its flanks, often drifting in the current the way he'd started. Hunger ate at the lining of his stomach but he was a good forager and he didn't need much to keep him alive, and he had no sense of taste or knowledge of luxury driving him to acquisition. When the river became a lake he chose the western shore because by then summer was ending and he liked the warmth in his face as the sun rose across the water on the chilly mornings. He followed the river again when it abandoned the lake to plummet through white-topped mountain wilderness onto the great alluvial plain of the Honan. He heard about fighting to the north, so he turned south. He eventually crossed the Yangtze on a rickety boat at Nanking, earning his fare by carrying loads up from the ferry. There was trouble in that city and talk in the markets about political change but he didn't understand any of that and cared less.

He was looking for something to eat along a riverside street in Nanking when suddenly he was confronted by eight ragged children with heavy sticks and hungry eyes, an impressment gang. He turned to run but they were too close. One of them hit him from behind, just below his ear. As he started to fall another whacked him on the thigh. Sticks pounded his kidneys. He struggled but the urchins confounded him with their sticks, poking at him, thumping him from behind when he rolled to meet an attack, aiming at his face when he grabbed. They were all over him but always out of reach, jabbing, pounding. Almost unconscious from the blows, he felt himself being dragged into the dark of an alley like a writhing worm pulled into a spider's hole. In cramping pain, unable to fight back, he screamed. They hit him again and gagged him with alley dirt.

Another gang heard the scuffles and came running, yelling, raising their own sticks, and while the two groups fought Deng Wei rolled into an open sewer and pulled himself away, slithering with frightened rats into the river. The heavy brown water washed the filth from his limbs and the sewage from his mouth.

When he drifted into the seaport of Shanghai the population was bundled for winter. He needed clothes – his were rags – and he needed real food, but when he tried to steal a sack of rice – he should have carried it easily – he was too weak to run with it. He had to throw it down to get away. Without friends or family he was prey to every predator and bloodsucker in the teeming city. Corpses were a common sight; he knew he was close to becoming one of them.

In desperation he sought out the Street of the Hongs, near a large temple where bald nuns moved up and down wide stairs. He stood in the middle of the narrow, crowded street, with the stenches and the noise and the people trading and pushing their way past, and he planted his feet against the jostle and raised both his arms straight to the sky and at the top of his voice he proclaimed, "I am Hong Deng Wei and I claim the honorable Hong family as my own."

He looked around. Nobody had noticed.

He raised his arms again, fingers splayed to show the emptiness of his life, and he shouted, "I am Hong Deng Wei and I claim the generous Hong family as my own."

And again. And again, each time altering only the adjective with which he blessed his family name. Before long his feet and calves were bruised and slashed from the passage of other feet and the hubs of pushcart wheels. His kidneys ached, tenderized from the thuds of hundreds of elbows. His voice was a squeak and he could barely lift his arms. But at nightfall he still stood, feet planted, croaking his allegiance. He was prepared to die there, had no choice, really.

Finally a young boy came and stood in front of him, looked up into his face. "Come with me, honorable Uncle with the flat head," the boy said, and walked quickly away. Deng Wei followed, reeling.

The boy led him to a substantial house of fired brick near the wharf end of the street. Colorful dragons hunched protectively against devils at the corners of its well-formed roof. A more prosaic protection – a high wall with spiked iron along the top – shielded the house and its inhabitants from the devilment of humans.

Deng Wei bent his stiffened body through a tiny gate. A guard closed it behind him, locked it with a heavy bar. A cheerful light and the plinking of a stringed instrument flowed from the house. Deng Wei stopped and stared... the aromas – he almost fainted. The boy tugged his tattered sleeve. "Come, Curious Uncle." Deng Wei glanced at the gate guard standing at his post, then followed the boy to the rear of the house. There were several small buildings there: servants' quarters and utility houses. A kitchen. A washroom. A trussed, gagged pig struggled for a moment when the boy and Deng Wei passed, then lay still again. The smell of rice with pungent fish sauce darted into Deng Wei's nose and rumbled around in his empty belly. There were servants washing clothes, cleaning things, chopping foods, but they didn't even look up as he passed. Only the pig followed him with its eyes, as if their fates were somehow linked.

The boy led him into a low, vapor-filled building with charcoal cooking fires at each side of the door. In the light of a bowl-lamp Deng Wei could see a hearth where water bubbled in a sooted kettle. At the other end of the small building a stone sink clutched the wall, draining into an open gutter. A mossy pipe spit noisy water. On his left an old round table and two stools cowered suspiciously against the wall. "Wash there, Dirty Uncle, and sit here, Hungry Uncle."

Deng Wei did as he was told and when he was seated the boy went out without another word. An ancient hag appeared at the threshold like a crooked witch. She was carrying a wooden tray. On it was the most sumptuous meal Deng Wei had seen in weeks. Months. Perhaps ever. He started up to show his respect. She showed her gums and came toward him. "Sit down, Great Grandson, sit down and eat." The hairless crone pressed the sticks into his hand, pushed the rice bowl toward him. "Eat, eat."

He scooped and shoveled, stoking himself.

****

Outcrop was a blunt grey manifestation of America's need for energy. Its mine gave up a poor coal but even after the cost of dragging it to the surface there was enough left to keep the dingy community alive in the wooded west-central Washington hills. Beneath the ground men hacked away their lives in the humid darkness; above, among the poor houses and the stolid hopelessness, women trudged through theirs in peasant drudgery.

Tom Archer was allowed to age like the porch was left to rot. His concerns, if he had any, died unsolicited and unexpressed. He was a quiet child, as if he'd expended every sound in his cells during those wailing infant days. When he learned to crawl it was from his wooden box to the end of the splintered boards that formed the front stoop. Unheralded, even unnoticed, he learned to walk pulling himself through the dust along the weathered pickets of the fence and his world was the unraked dirt of the small yard. It'd be years before he learned to talk.

When his father slumped out in the early mornings, his carbon lamp strapped to his helmet, his black lunch box almost a burden, Tom was allowed to leave his bed – first the box and later a straw-filled pallet – in the small alcove behind the stove. When he'd eaten what was left of his father's breakfast he went outside to the yard. He played with whatever he found there. If it rained or snowed he played in the fine dust under the porch. There wasn't much trouble he could cause in the yard. If he wanted to eat filth, or kill a cat, that was up to him. His days passed unvaried.

2

For four days and nights Hong Deng Wei stayed at the walled house, eating when he was told to eat, speaking occasionally with the servants, trying to make himself useful in little ways. They talked with him at times in their work but told him nothing. When he got in the way they shooed him. He did help kill the pig and was rewarded with a small cup of blood sauce with his rice that night. He felt his strength returning and began to feel as if his fortune lurked just around the corner. But when he wandered toward the front of the house once the gate guard showed a short fighting stick and ordered him back.

The old hag seemed taken with him and on the second day of his stay she caught his elbow as he passed. "Wait, Great Grandson. Let me see you." She peered with weepy eyes at his forehead, studied the shallow traces of lines on his hands and on his face.

"What do you see?" he asked.

She was silent, studying his brows, turning his chin with a gnarly finger to see his ear. As her glance passed over his throat she flashed her eyes at his, but briefly, said nothing, went on with her study.

"What? Can you see my fortune?"

"I see some things, yes," she croaked. "But isn't it better not to know everything?"

"But tell me something. Tell me something good," he implored.

"I see a fortune and a woman and a son. I see the woman weep. It isn't for me to say what's good or bad, Great Grandson, only to see." She finished and knuckled him in the chest. "Enough, Child. Earn your meal. Rub an old woman's legs…"

On the fourth day the gate guard summoned him summarily and turned him over to a house guard who passed him to a butler, who showed him into a high-ceilinged room with dark enameled furniture. A small recessed altar smoked on the wall at the back of the room, joss sticks sending tendrils of fragrance into the shadowed corners. Against another wall a tall chest decorated with crowds of carved figures loomed like a bulky, tattooed bodyguard. The floor was polished tile, cold beneath Deng Wei's bare feet. A brazier with white-encrusted charcoal warmed the feet of the man who sat in the center of the room. The low marble table beside the man's chair reflected the deep purple of his quilted robe. He held a rolled paper in his hands and was reading when Deng Wei was led in. Deng Wei had no idea what to expect.

The master looked up. He wore a small smile but Deng Wei could tell it was a fake; in the corners of the man's face Deng Wei saw cruelty. He bowed deeply from the waist – he'd seen the man's wall, clear evidence of his power.

The master's voice bounced off the shiny surfaces of the room. "Well, Hong Deng Wei, so you've called on the venerable Family of Hong to receive you. And has it? Has the honorable, the exalted, the beneficent Family of Hong opened its arms to you?" His questions rose in octave and volume.

Deng Wei's fear broke out like sweat. He bowed deeply again, quickly, several times. "Yes, Master."

Now the queries came soft and cunning, like entreaties from a clever woman. "And might I now amuse myself, now that you've enjoyed the hospitality of the House of Hong, now that you've

12

feasted and rested in these walls of Hong? Might I now pose a contest to you?"

Deng Wei didn't have the slightest idea what the man meant but he was cowed by the very real power exhibited all around him. He didn't know how else to respond so he bowed again. "Yes, Master."

"Good, good," the man in the purple robe said happily. "Then here it is, and I'll tell you, my fattened, frightened nephew with the long string of adjectives, if you win, I'll put you on your way to your fortune." He suddenly scowled and the voice sucked like mud at the cold soles of Deng Wei's fear. "But if you fail I'll have the queue cut off your flat northern head and stuffed in your mouth. I'll have you stripped and whipped and carried back to the Street of the Hongs in a pig basket. You'll have no family, no name." Again his voice rose. "Do you agree?"

Deng Wei trembled. He looked around. There wasn't any way out. He knew the man could do what he said. He bowed again and his throat quivered when he replied this time. "Yes, Master."

"So then, here it is." The man rubbed the palms of his hands together. "As you stood in the street with your arms raised, beseeching the Family Hong, you were very capable in wailing the virtues of the Family. I have that on the good authority of the money changer outside whose door you stood, and he remembers *everything.*

"Now here's your challenge; let's hear a further virtue of this esteemed family – a virtue *you did not name in the street. Quickly now!*" He clapped his hands twice and another man was hustled in by the butler. The newcomer bowed and the man in the purple robe clapped his hands again. "Quickly, Hong Deng Wei, we're waiting! *A new virtue!*"

This time the room trembled to the madman's screech and Deng Wei's brain boggled. His thoughts whirled as he tried to remember the words he'd used in the market but the bouncing madman distracted him and his feeble list shattered and he tried to start again but he'd been in the street so long… It was *impossible!* The purple robe rose in front of his swimming vision, the rant increasing in pitch and volume… He clamped his hands to his ears, shutting out the noise, and then he threw his arms up and thrust his fingers toward the sky as he had in the street and words came to him and with his eyes still squeezed tightly shut he screamed, "The *pig-eating* Hong Family! *I claim the pig-eating Hong Family as my own!*"

Silence swooped into the room like sudden darkness. Sweat stood out on Deng Wei's forehead and on his lip and ran down the small of his back. He felt his sphincter open and his bladder leaked a hot trickle down his leg. He shuddered, then hung his head. From in front of him there was a snort. He raised his head.

The man was standing, stooped, both hands on the polished armrests of his massive chair. His purple robe shimmered. He snorted again and flopped back into the chair. He snorted again, and again, and again, and the snorts were linked together until he was clutching himself, trying to speak. "Pig-eating…"

Deng Wei looked sheepishly at the money changer, who shrugged, then at the massive butler, who probably knew what was going to happen but wouldn't say.

Finally the laughter gave way to chortles, then to deep chuckles until the master, his face as purple as his robe, caught his breath and looked at Deng Wei. "Pig-eating. A virtue! Well, my most distant relative, you've met the challenge. Pig-eating Hong Family…" He tittered, shaking his head, then straightened his demeanor, sat back. "And so you'll have it. Your fortune." He spoke to the butler. "The ship's leaving on tomorrow's tide for Ala-sa-ja. Give him clothing and some coins to jingle in his purse and ensure he's on that steamer with the others. Add his name to the voucher." He waved his hand, finished with them, and as Deng Wei shuffled dumbly to the door behind the butler his dazed ears

14

heard the man in the chair chuckling softly. "Venerable *pig-eating* Hongs, honorable *pig-eating* Hongs…"

****

Tom Archer drew a picture of a pig in the dirt, rubbed it out, drew a tree, rubbed it out, drew other pictures. It was what he did during his days.

At six o'clock without regard for the season of the sun he was permitted in the house. After supper, the only span of time he ever spent near his parents, he could sit on the floor against the wall by the stove if he wanted, listening to the whines of their talk, and, later, to the strange quick grunts from their bedroom, or he could scoot into his small alcove behind the stove. It didn't matter as long as he didn't make noise. There was nothing to read in the house: nobody capable of making sense of scribbles lived there. Old Henry spoke fewer than twenty words a year to him. Even the occasional crushing death of a neighbor in the mine was just more proof that devils ruled and, "…it don't need no talk."

****

Hong Deng Wei had never seen a foreign devil so he wasn't prepared for the shock of it. He started his day full of confidence. He had new clothes, and cloth slippers on his feet, almost new. He wore a withered amulet on a string around his neck – the crone had pressed it on him – and in a small purse tied to the cord inside his trousers he carried four thin coins. He didn't have any idea what they'd buy but he felt important. "Come on, it's time to go," he told the butler's nephew, who'd take him to the ship. He'd heard about people who were wealthy, supposedly, because they received gold from relatives who'd gone to the Devil Land. That place couldn't be any further than he'd already come.

Then he arrived at the wharf and his sense of urgency dried up. The dock teemed where the steamship was tied and though he knew the press of crowded markets, this was different. Malignant. Greedy. Scores of men stood in groups along the dock, herded by men with short whips tied to their wrists. The whip men were *all* foreign devils! He started to draw back but the butler's big nephew pushed him forward.

Some of the herded men clutched small bags or baskets of belongings. Others had nothing but the clothes they wore. Long queues danced along every spine. The noise was deafening, everybody yelling at once in a dozen dialects. On the outskirts of the crowd where he stood resisting the efforts of the nephew to push him forward there were other men saying goodbye to wailing women and holding clutches of children of all ages and it suddenly became clear that the ridiculous foreigners carried whips to *discourage the unprivileged* from crowding aboard and overturning the ship. There were already more men standing in lines than could possibly ride on that one vessel and he wondered how many would actually be allowed aboard. Prodded by that thought, his courage gathered and his resolve to be among the fortunate set, Deng Wei pushed forward, almost leaving the nephew behind.

Hawkers closed in, tugging at his clothes, pulling his fingers, pinching his elbow, distracting him. They shouted their wares in his face and in his ears, staggering him. He felt hands tugging toward his purse and struck out, knocking two of the vendors aside and driving the rest an arm's length away, but they persisted. "Chicken eggs, Cousin, you've got to have chicken eggs for your journey."

"A quilt, Cousin, for your bed."

"Baskets to carry your gold?"

Dried ducks, opened at the breast and pressed flat like toads under the wheel of a cart. Bamboo joints filled with rice and bean paste. Leaves rolled tightly around spiced meat, heads of cabbage strung together like floppy green beads. Something made Deng Wei's stomach turn.

A man shoved steamed bread at him with one hand and groped for his purse with the other – Deng Wei whirled away and pressed on. Someone snatched at his tunic and it tore. His head began to ache and he pushed on toward the tall stacks of the ship – all he could see now except the sea of hawkers.

All at once he was through the melee and the suddenness of his escape propelled him forward, tripping, almost falling. He saved himself by catching hold of a table in his path and when he recovered his balance he was looking into the eyes of a hairy foreign devil, seated not a spit away. They were blue! His throat contracted and he jumped back and tried to turn to plunge back into the maelstrom of vendors but the nephew was there, crowding him.

The barbarian laughed and *gold* flashed in his teeth! Deng Wei leaned forward to stare and the barbarian stopped his laugh and bared his teeth. It was true! Ala-sa-ja *was* the land of gold! Then the foreigner slammed his lips shut and shouted incomprehensibly to a gentle-looking young man standing beside him, a Chinese with no queue. The young man yelled at the nephew standing behind Deng Wei, "Is this part of the Hong consignment?" The nephew nodded. "Then put his name on this contract and get him over to that group there." He pointed to a group of men being counted by the barbarians with whips.

In seconds it was done. Deng Wei was pushed toward the ship and when he turned the nephew was gone, only his head and shoulders visible as he fought his way back through the crowd. Deng Wei hadn't spoken more than two or three times with him but still something tore as he watched the man disappear. Like a last touch with something precious. Then he was shoved rudely and all at once Deng Wei knew he was no longer among the hospitable, pig-eating Family of Hong.

His head pounded. The pale sun and the heat of the massed bodies seemed to have raised his own temperature. The concentrated stink of the river, the stench of the crowd and of the piles of garbage and the oily smoke of the steamer's coal fire crawled up his nostrils and gagged him. He swooned, almost passed out, was caught and half-shoved, half-carried up a steep plank and through a small door, down a steep ladder, through a dark passageway. Pushed along, pushing along the man in front, stumbling through another small door and almost tumbling into a great hole but catching the ladder, stepping on fingers, his own crushed from above. Head pounding. Terrible stench, a sewer. Dark and airless. Shoving. The edge of a platform struck his thigh and another his forehead and he was crawling back into a dark space, following, followed until he was jammed on all sides and even in the pitch dark everything went blacker and he knew nothing.

****

The captain had modified the internal spaces of his small ship after seeing a schematic of a schooner that had taken slaves to Carolina. It wasn't necessary that his passengers have room to sit up. By crowding them on their sides spoon-like in close layers he could get more of them into the hold and make the voyage pay. But over the days that followed, the cramping was eased. Each time the men went on deck to eat and to gasp the clean air into their lungs a few bodies were dropped overboard. That was to be expected, and the captain had allowed for it.

The men were fed rice and when fish were caught they ate rice that smelled vaguely of fish. For the first two weeks they also had some cabbage but then it stank too much to eat and after they'd picked out the worms and eaten them they threw the slimy, putrid leaves overboard. Many of the men were seasick from the moment the ship began to move but after Deng Wei recovered from the first day's illness he was healthy, if hungry, for the rest of the trip.

As the ship steamed closer to its destination the weather worsened, growing colder, and fully clothed corpses weren't thrown overboard any more. Finally it snowed so hard nothing was visible, not even the slowly rolling sea.

One night a word rustled among the men. Muttering became declaration and then exclamation as they all rushed from the platforms to the ladders, up into the narrow passageways, pushing and shoving to get through the little doors and onto the deck, over to the rails. *"Land!"* someone had said, "Land!"

But they couldn't see any land in the dark night and as more of them crowded to the side of the ship, trying to see, the vessel began to list. More men pushed toward the rail. The deck canted, began to rise… "Hey, you coolies, get back, get away…" Tragedy was averted only when the barbarians flailed in with short clubs and whips, driving them back. Finally the ship leveled and as the excitement died most of the men returned, shivering, to the filth-encrusted but warmer platforms below. Hong Deng Wei was one of those who stayed on deck, his back against a warm steam casing, his eyes peeled for the first-light sight of land. He knew it was there, just so close. He could smell it.

A late, sickly dawn revealed snow-covered forests and twisting, misted fjords. Then it was dark again, even the sun shunning this frozen, barbarian land. Deng Wei watched the coast slip by and shivered, hugging himself and backing up more firmly against the casing. He didn't know what waited for him out there on that land, but whatever it was, he knew it wasn't warmth.

****

Until he went to school, Tom Archer never ventured beyond the fence of his yard. It wasn't permitted. The gate was latched. He didn't hear about Christmas or the written word or friendship until he went to school. He didn't know what a birthday was until he'd lived through six of them. When he finally started school he knew only words he'd heard his parents use and so had a vocabulary of about a hundred stunted lamentations, complaints, curses and combatives.

Once in a while a neighbor woman would visit his mother. While they muttered together in the house Tom and her son would be thrust together in the yard like wary creatures dropped into the same cage. The two small boys watched each other silently, drew pictures with sticks in the dirt, rubbed them out, did it again. They didn't know what else to do.

****

Hong Deng Wei was grossly ignorant and ill-equipped. He didn't own anything but his inadequate clothes. He had no idea where he was or what he faced. He didn't even know he was indentured. But he wasn't stupid. He'd foraged during his short life and had taken nothing but his own resourcefulness through China's desperate, dangerous landscape. He'd used his wits. He'd taken advantage of situations when he saw opportunities to feed or shelter himself, and of people when they barred the door to opportunity. But if he'd hurt others along the way it was only in passing and without malice. He'd occasionally exchanged pride for a meal, and had lived more than once with his hunger hanging on the edge of common sense. But he'd survived in times when millions perished.

He wasn't afraid. He'd thrown his arms over a log and had floated down a mysterious river for the sheer sake of going. His sense of adventure was primordial, his willingness to endure, eternal. Now as he sat with his knees pulled to his chest, his kidneys pressed against the steam casing, he tried to think about his situation but the thoughts were hard to hold. The future was a black unknown and only the cold made it real.

The whistle shrieked, shattering his concentration. He stood as other coolies began to cluster on the deck, all talking excitedly but careful to stay away from the rail where the whip-men stood. He was resigned: wherever he was, he had arrived. Whatever fortune or misfortune waited for him must already be there in those dark, frozen forests.

Under thick, malevolent skies the ship eased slowly through a narrow channel. An island brooded on the left and close, steep continental mountains loomed on the right. Between the base of the mountains and the frozen beach of the channel stretched a flat area a tired man could explore in much less than half a day. A small round hill squatted petulantly in the center of the flat, with a ramshackle little settlement clustered in the dirty snow around it. All the trees on and around the little hill had been cut down. Smoke squirted from the chimneys of the crude houses. As the ship dropped its anchor Deng Wei could see a jagged canyon cutting into the wall of the mountains beyond the little round hill. A snow-banked stream wriggled from the canyon. Gentler, rolling land – an island – formed the other bank of the channel, extending as far as Deng Wei could see in the cold mist. There were only a few scattered buildings on that side of the water.

He heard other coolies say it but he didn't say it himself until he heard one of the barbarians make the sound, then it was real to him and he listened for the word again. Alaska. He mouthed the word himself. *Ala-sa-ja.*

****

Tom Archer's father was mean and slum tough and his raging temper lived among them like a loosely chained beast. Only the boy's quickness kept him relatively uninjured. The slightest annoyance or insubordination from Tom or his mother would prod the temper out, snarling into their midst where it slashed and clubbed at will until Old Henry wearied. Black-grained fists thudded on cowered shoulders. When the temper was finished Old Henry would harness it and drag it back to its black lair somewhere in the bowels of his brain.

Tom and his mother suffered together, but unequally. She said it was him, Tom, "...that makes your father that way, God damn the jisim that made you, boy."

Tom shouldered his bruises and licked his cuts and hid beneath the house in the dirt, ducking his head, holding his hurts; when he was older he'd flee through heaped slag to the sanctuary of the school building. Later – when he knew about such things – he'd realize he should have killed his father with something blunt, or something sharp. By the time he knew that, his barren life was sprinkled with the seeds of madness, and now those seeds lay dormant and waiting for the heat of events to germinate them.

3

Hong Deng Wei's new master was on the shore waiting, fretting, close to the broken ice that crowded the channel, wanting to row out and carry the coolies ashore himself. He paced. He raised his arms, slapped them down against his long fur coat. "Would you please stop wasting time and just put the coolies ashore," he wailed toward the ship. He turned to his assistant, a woman bundled in layers of clothes. "What's the blasted delay now? You'd think they weren't tired of being at sea." She didn't respond and he turned roughly away.

The steamship whistle pierced the cold air and Kevin Aspin whirled at the sound, eyes fixed on the mountain slopes hulking close behind. He jerked the flaps of his cap away from his ears and strained to hear but only the high-pitched echo of the whistle came rumbling down from somewhere up in the clouds. After a few moments he relaxed, put the ear flaps back down and barked at the figure behind him, who hadn't moved. "Stupid son of a bitch is going to get us all rubbed out and hasn't even got sense enough to know it. Just lucky it's early in the season." He turned and glanced once more at the avalanche slopes behind him and then began running in place, beating his arms, chanting in small puffs of condensed breath, "Come on, come on, come on…"

This cargo of coolies was Kevin Aspin's first and only venture in slave trading. He'd come to lower Alaska – Southeast –

the previous spring to make a quick fortune in the Canyon of Gold but by the time he arrived the whole place was a quilt of claims. All the likely spots had been staked and laid out with pieces of twine, and tempers pounded the miner whose shovel cut into the gravel on the wrong side of a string. Kevin had staked a claim high up in the bowl of the canyon but it was a poor place and had produced nothing.

Desperation inspired him. He was hungry and his rumbling belly convinced him food was valuable, even more than gold. He quit shoveling gravel and took up his rifle, borrowed a small boat and rowed the fifty yards across the channel to the island. Deer Island, people called it. There a few ignorant prospectors poked and scrabbled in the unproductive streams directly across from the settlement at Canyon of Gold, but most of the island was covered with virgin forest. Kevin pulled the boat above the high tide mark, set out walking, and within half an hour had killed a small blacktailed deer. He dragged it to the boat and went back into the forest to the north. Before the day was over he had four deer on the beach. He lashed them together, stuck pieces of driftwood through the crooks and angles and between the lashings, and floated them across the channel behind the small boat.

It was simple to sell them: he didn't even bother skinning, just poured the entrails on the beach, quartered the carcasses, then started a fire and roasted a haunch. Soon the aroma of cooking meat had wafted up the canyon a mile and emissaries were showing up from a dozen claims to trade golden flakes for meat. The miners were too busy working gravel to eat properly and certainly weren't going to take the time to hunt. That night he sold fifteen quarters of deer meat. He ate the other one all by himself. In the pocket of his coat was a small pouch with almost two ounces of gold in it. A good day at the mines, he reckoned.

His business prospered. Demand was constant and growing, the supply seemed endless and the profit was right. The only brake on his business was the effort required to stalk the game and deliver it. He solved that by hiring four Indians who showed up looking for work. One of the Indians, a man named Albert Blake, became his good friend and his field supervisor. Several times Kevin visited Albert's village on remote Admiralty Island and eventually, contrary to the wishes of other Indians, Albert sold him a little parcel of isolated land in a cloudy but magnificent bay, land on which Kevin hoped to someday build a small hunting lodge. Admiralty Island was a two-day trip by boat from Canyon of Gold and its sheltered, unpeopled bays were a nice change from the hustle of life in the settlement. Kevin came back from his occasional solitary visits there with a glint in his eye.

Soon another down-on-his-luck miner started selling meat, which put pressure on the supply and on the price, and Kevin Aspin's hunters had to range further afield. He hired a couple more Indians for use as mules and kept Albert and his hunters out in a series of remote camps. Soon the upstart competitor ran out of local deer and went north to Skagway to marry a woman who owned a restaurant.

Kevin then added fish to his store but he couldn't find much of a market for it until he built a smoker and turned out sweet smoked salmon. Three more Indians got in on that. He was making good money when the increasingly chilly nights told him he'd soon have to come up with a winter scheme or take a vacation. When terminal dust powdered the tops of the mountains he weighed his gold, said to hell with winter in Alaska, and caught a boat to Mexico for a long holiday.

While he was in Sacramento enjoying his transit he met, sampled, and bought a half-caste Chinese whore with the most perfect skin he'd ever seen. Her name was Lo An, which he pronounced, "Lou Ann," and she was his in every sense of the word.

The madam hadn't wanted to sell her. "You have no idea how that Lo An brings in customers," she'd told him over tea. "She has regulars coming all the way from Stockton and sometimes even a gentleman from San Francisco asks for her."

Kevin Aspin could tell the madam was no lady. "Well, Ma'am, I can understand her value..." And indeed he could. Lo An had inherited the body of a voluptuous Caucasian ancestor and the skin of a Mandarin's courtesan. She was perfect, and though he eventually paid too much in gold for her he solaced himself with the thought of the warmth she'd add to his bed in Alaska.

There was no question of abandoning Alaska – there was just too much money to be made there by a man with imagination and the courage to capitalize it. In fact by that time he'd already put in motion his next scheme.

The placer deposits in the Canyon of Gold were quickly playing out but that didn't mean the mining was finished. Placer gold is merely the alluvial evidence of a mother lode higher up the watershed, and every miner knew that. Soon the mountain slopes and canyon walls themselves were searched, exploratory tunnels were dug, shafts were sunk. The trees in the immediate area disappeared and reappeared as wood smoke and tunnel bracing. Shortly, of course, the vein was found and men began serious tunneling into the steep slopes, hoping to cross it beneath their own claims. It was hard work, tunneling, and frantic, because if a miner wasn't on the vein he didn't earn anything but pain and poverty for his efforts. Gradually, over the months, business corporations formed among the miners to consolidate efforts and share out the costs and profits. Outside companies from Seattle and San Jose came in, buying up claims, buying out partners and small outfits, buying each other. Then those corporations began expanding their mines and men in shafts weren't working for their own profit any more, they were working for wages.

Kevin saw it coming and set out to provide men who were willing to work in bad conditions for next to nothing. He arranged with a dealer in Los Angeles to have a hundred coolies shipped from Shanghai to Canyon of Gold, to be delivered live and able to stand.

****

The coolies had arrived. Kevin Aspin couldn't contain his excitement. He whirled like a dervish in the snow, ear flaps on his cap, arms and coat hem all standing out like wings. He hopped over in front of Lo An and did a little jig, then pulled his gloves off and separated the scarves that hid all her face except her magnificent Oriental eyes. He leaned close and peered at her, a grin on his face. "Ah, my Lovely, we did it, eh?" He put a finger in through the folds of her scarves and laid it against her cheek. "Eh?"

She didn't say anything.

A rowboat chartered by Kevin Aspin carried the coolies ashore in groups of ten, the boat making slow headway through chunks of ice clogging the edges of the narrow channel. The first group came ashore clumsily, several of the men slipping at their first contact with snow. They were all inadequately dressed for the winter and Kevin cursed himself for overlooking that in the contract fee – it would have been so much cheaper to clothe them in China. If he didn't take immediate steps some of them were going to die of exposure. They were wet, falling in the icy water, splashing ashore, shivering convulsively, hugging themselves. He reached back and dragged Lo An to his side, not turning his eyes from the coolies making their way out of the rowboat, afraid one might drown on him. "Lou Ann, tell them to get up here quickly, up here away from the water, and tell them all to bunch up real tight, right here." He raced a few steps and made a mark in the snow with his fur boot. "Tell them now, Lou Ann."

Lo An started in Mandarin, which only some would understand, then she switched to Cantonese, then she gave the same commands in Fukienese. She spoke right through the scarves wrapped around her head and for a few moments the shivering men stared open-mouthed at her, then, too cold to rejoice at having found another Chinese ashore, a few moved to obey her, then others. She commanded them, "Quickly. Put that wet one in the middle. Close in, close in. Squeeze together." She herded them with her voice and soon they were all shaking in violent unison, a vibrating huddle beginning already to ice on the outside edges. Some of them were bound to die.

Another group of coolies was climbing over the ship's side into the rowboat and Kevin raised on his toes and threw his arms in exasperation when he saw one of them fall overboard. *"Fools,"* he yelled. "Fish him out, you fools!" He was going to lose some of these men unless he did something immediately. He thought a moment, then spun Lo An around and told her, "Keep them coming, Lou Ann. Keep them as warm as you can. Huddle them up, make them dance, show them your tits, but for God's sake, keep them warm. I'll be right back." Without waiting for acknowledgement he wheeled and raced off down the beach toward the houses, his flaps all flying and flapping vigorously and whipping him to greater speed.

Before the next load of men had completely disembarked he was on his way back, dragging a heavy bundle through the snow. When he got to the shivering mass of men he turned to the bundle and Lo An recognized it: deer pelts, untanned deer skins he'd started saving from his hunting operation when he realized they were potentially profitable. They were frozen hard into flat, hairy boards. He ripped the top few off the stack and flung them at the freezing coolies, yelling, "Lou Ann, tell them to wrap up in these. These'll keep them warm. And tell those four coming up from the boat to follow me, we'll go get some more."

"But they're frozen stiff, Kai Win." Astonishment pitched her voice.

"Never mind, I say. The run will warm them up. Now tell them!"

"No, Kai Win, I mean the *skins* are frozen stiff."

"Hell's bells, Lou Ann, those skins will thaw out fast. Tell them to put the flesh side in and that'll make them thaw faster and then they can turn them over and wrap up good. Now tell them, Lou Ann!" He pushed her toward the men, yelling, "Come on, you pig-tailed coolies, *let's go!*" He gestured wildly at the last four men just arrived from the boat, grabbed them by sleeves and arms and pulled them, made them understand, then started running off, turned, gestured again, finally got them moving toward the shed where the deer hides were stored.

When they got back and distributed the skins they'd brought, Kevin realized it wasn't enough. He wailed in exasperation, tossing his head, holding the flaps on his cap out at right angles. "Oh stupid, stupid, stupid," he moaned.

Lo An took his arm and caught his attention. "Kai Win, why not move the men all to the shed instead of moving the skins here?" Her face, uncovered now, showed no guile, only curiosity, and Kevin gaped at her for a moment, closed his mouth with a snap, then clamped both his hands on her bundled shoulders. "Lou Ann, you're a genius. Why in hell didn't I think of that?"

Soon they'd herded the coolies already ashore to the shed and others were coming from the boat landing, shivering, sliding in the snow, silent in their misery, absolutely docile. Kevin waved them in as they arrived, touching them as they stumbled through the small door into the low-ceilinged log shack. The place was soon crowded with men and fogged with their breath and the temperature had risen several degrees.

By midday they were all ashore, all huddled together in the shed. Kevin stood at the door regarding them, thankful he hadn't lost any in the operation. There were eighty-nine. Nine of his hundred, the captain would later tell him, had died of *natural causes* at sea, one had been stabbed to death by an unknown assailant, and one had succumbed after a vicious beating delivered by a seaman who, as punishment, had been put ashore that morning without his wages.

Altogether, Kevin was pleased. He had a good profit in this shed, not even counting the deer skins. "I'm going down and settle up with the skipper," he told Lo An. "You stay here. I'll be back in about an hour. You can open up that back hole over there if it gets too stuffy in here, but don't let any of them go wandering around, hear? And don't let them start any fires. When I get back we'll take care of them."

She nodded gravely. "Yes, Kai Win." In a moment he was gone from sight. She stood in the door of the shed, turned to look once more, making sure he was gone, and then barked for attention. The small amount of talk ceased. The coolies all looked at her small figure standing in the door. She'd opened her coat and they could see she was dressed in trousers of heavy wool and a warm sweater. She surveyed them, then spoke bitingly. "Men. Ha! You call yourselves men. Look at you!" She paused, all eyes on her. "Well, look at you!" Her arm swept up and around to encompass them all.

The closest ones crouched back as if she'd struck them. Eyes began to shift, then a few heads turned and soon they were all looking around at each other. One man had actually managed to put on a deer skin, hairy side in, had his arms and legs stuck through slashes so he looked as if *he* had been skinned. Dried bloody veins and small pieces of pale flesh clung to the hide. Another man pointed at him and chuckled, then laughed. Another caught it and joined in. Then a coolie with a skin draped over his shoulders put his arms up, fingers spread like antlers, and pretended to gore the man next to him. More laughter. Before long laughter and loud talk filled the shed as men recognized shipboard companions and found common dialects.

Lo An stood in the door watching for a few minutes, then commanded them to silence. She spoke in one dialect, then switched to another, then continued in another and soon there were men throughout the shed muttering simultaneous translations so that any dialect she spoke was heard and understood by all. "You men have come to a terrible place. You've suffered to arrive here, but hear me as if the words were dripping from your grandmother's lips: there's more suffering ahead of you. *Listen to me!* I'll tell you what you need to know to survive. Listen carefully, remember, and remind each other. Are you listening?"

She let her gaze wander. They were listening. Outside, the sound of stevedores unloading another ship cut through the cold air. Machinery clanks and the sound of a small locomotive somewhere up on the mountain made a background noise like the comfortable blanket of cricket-chirping in warm places. The men had heated the shed with their own escaping warmth.

"First, never forget you are people of the Middle Kingdom. It doesn't matter if you're a Chinese coolie, or a Chinese miner, or a Chinese cook, or a Chinese slave or a rich Chinese with gold rings in your ears – it doesn't even matter if you're a stinking, swollen Chinese corpse – as long as you remember you're Chinese, you'll win in the end. Because you are members of *families.*"

She lowered her voice and they leaned forward to hear. "If you ever forget your heritage, your ancestors, your family, you'll lose everything.

"Second, Chinese men, and don't forget this either: never underestimate these barbarians. There are more of them than you'll ever see. They're powerful. And they're clever. But they're greedy. We smile to hide our embarrassments, they smile to conceal their designs. Don't be fooled by their cleverness. Bow if they demand it – you lose nothing. But remember greed blinds men, so as you bow, milk the riches from these blind men as a man milks the pleasure from his groin. But beware of their cleverness or they'll catch you…" She went on, telling them how to live in this place to which their joss had brought them, encouraging them, giving them not just knowledge, but strength.

"And finally, remember *this*," she said. " The one who saved you from the cold today and gave you survival lessons is the Chinese whore Lo An, and when she *or her descendents* call on you to repay your debt, do it with thankfulness."

She spent long minutes looking around in the gloom at the men crouched and sprawled, or standing, or squatting on piles of frozen skins, looking each of the eighty-nine men in the eyes, sealing them to their debt. Then she turned and stepped out into the frozen air, closing her coat and scarves around herself.

There wasn't a sound from within the shed.

Kevin Aspin returned, bounding up the beach, rubbing his hands together and looking altogether boyish despite his twenty-five years. "Well, my dear Lou Ann, we're fixed with the skipper; they're all ours, and a pretty penny too. Let's get them up the canyon."

******

In the shed Hong Deng Wei stood still, stunned. While the woman spoke, her arms akimbo, her coat open, he'd stared at her with total absorption. Her forehead was high, her face oval. A strong jaw line emphasized the bones of her cheeks. The crimson lips of her small mouth worked like spells to draw him in. He'd seldom noticed a woman for the shape of her body – in his experience they were sexless in baggy clothes, the same in their nakedness – but this whore, this woman he wanted, was a woman whose presence alone could suck the agonies from a man. When she left the shed Deng Wei felt as if she'd taken his breath with her. He had no idea whether he'd ever see her again.

****

It snowed. The sun was long down.

The coolies followed Kevin Aspin and Lo An from the shed, past the little round hill and into the canyon mouth, then up along the frozen stream, following a snowy path, climbing gradually. After an hour-long brisk walk the path steepened, leading up and over the lip of a rocky bowl near the head of the canyon. The men were all tired when they reached the floor of the bowl and Kevin pushed them hard to keep them warm. Another ten minutes and they were standing on a rough stone sidewalk in front of a plank building. Kevin said, "Tell them not to move from here, Lou Ann."

She turned to face them as they clustered in front of the building. "Don't worry, Chinamen. They'll feed you here." She turned back to Kevin, nodded, and together they disappeared into the building.

Outside in the dark, in the falling snow, the men huddled together and tried to keep from freezing, their efforts aided by the thought of food and by the raw hides they clutched around their shoulders. The snow clung to the fleshy surfaces of the skins.

Shortly Kevin and the Chinese whore reappeared with another man, a great, bearded, bear-like barbarian made even more to resemble that beast by the bearskin coat he wore. It was massive, the long hairs hanging like a pelt of his own to the ground. His red beard and uncovered hair blended into the bear fur so there was no line of difference. When he first stepped through the door of the building behind Lo An, the light from the room making him only a silhouette, the coolies gasped. Several were about to run. Then an outside light was turned on and in its glow they could see the mine overseer for what he was. The coolies settled and the three people on the porch surveyed them in the pool of yellow light. The men were pitiful. They crowded together, some with their arms around each other, shaking uncontrollably now that the warmth generated by their climb up the canyon had fled. Some wore woven fiber hats that had survived the ocean trip, a few had cloth caps of one sort or another – mostly small black skullcaps – but the majority were bareheaded. The snow settled over them. Beneath the deer skins – which alone kept them from perishing – they wore light cotton pajama-like clothes. Some had quilted jackets but most didn't. On their feet they wore black felt slippers that didn't cover their bare ankles. Long queues hung down every back. Many of the men moaned with their pains.

The bear man said something to Lo An, then began to speak to them in the gibberish the barbarians called a language. She translated into Cantonese and, as before, others repeated the gist of it in other dialects so everyone understood what was said. All their eyes were fixed on the woman. "Chinamen. The red-haired bear is as powerful as a warlord from the mountains beyond the great Yellow River. He's welcoming you into his care. He tells me to say he's glad to see you, and that's true, because he'll profit greatly at your expense. He says if you work until the sweat blinds you and the flesh falls off your limbs you'll be happy here and well cared for, and someday you'll receive a small payment for your labors. He says you'll have a warm place to sleep and enough food to eat.

"He says if you don't obey or if you're lazy you'll be punished. Bear Man wants you to tell him if you're not satisfied with your condition, though I advise you to be cautious about that. You'll begin work in the morning. He says you'll work thirty days and then have one day of no work. That's true; it's their foolish custom.

"He says you can ask him any question now."

The men stood silently. A small wind had picked up and the snow moved with purpose, reaching beneath flaps and into holes to strike the cold deeper. It wasn't a time for questioning, but for finding a place to survive. Lo An turned to the overseer and said something in the gibberish. He nodded and replied. She turned to face them again and said, "Now you'll be taken to your living place, and he says he wishes you all well. I think in his own way he means it, despite his hideous appearance and customs. Remember what I told you earlier in the house of the deer skins."

Bear Man bellowed and an assistant came out of the building, shrugging into a pea coat. He listened to instructions, then clumped in heavy boots down the wooden porch steps, pushed his way along in front of the coolies – holding his nose with his gloved hand – and stomped off down the snowy, crushed stone path.

Lo An said, "Follow him."

They turned as one and shuffled, stumbling in frozen, stiff-kneed pain through the snow.

The building to which they were taken was another plank-built affair with a snow-covered tin roof. It was snuggled against a granite cliff next to other buildings, all of which looked the same. The man in the boots shoved open the single door at one end of the building and disappeared through it. A moment later a coal oil lamp had been lit, and tentatively the men went in. The man who'd guided them walked out the door, pushed it closed, and they were alone.

Hong Deng Wei was near the lamp and he turned full circle, looking at this place to which the river and his long travels had brought him. It was a building that would easily provide sleeping space for them all, being absolutely empty except for the men themselves and the single oil lamp sitting in a pool of frozen light on the crushed rock floor. Slowly it dawned on him this was his home for the immediate future, but it wasn't an easy thought. He had no knowledge of luxury and his wants were simple but even to him this was harsh. And still he hadn't eaten.

As if his thought had brought the realty, the door opened and several barbarians came in carrying large galvanized tubs. The coolies crowded around the fragrant steam. The men who'd brought the food looked curiously at them, then went out and returned with other things. One of the tubs was full of boiled red beans which soaked the building in a delicious aroma. In another was a watery soup with pieces of dried fish floating in it. Several of the men cried out and would have dipped with their hands if the barbarians hadn't reappeared with a box full of bowls and big tin spoons. Another box held loaves of bread.

It was a delicious meal even without rice or noodles, and there was enough. They squatted on the cold floor eating, and conversations began, the men grouping themselves by language.

After they'd eaten and stacked their bowls and spoons in the tubs, a few men lay down to sleep, curling up as well as they could in their deer robes, which were beginning to shed hair. One man opened the door, poked his head outside, looked around, then stepped out into the snow to relieve himself. Others followed. Lights glowed from several buildings and the noise of barbarians talking and laughing poked through the falling snow.

The next morning Hong Deng Wei, exhausted after a long shivery night pressed against others on the rugged floor, was assigned to a group of outside coolies. They were given the task of keeping the narrow ore-cart tracks along the steep canyon walls clear and maintained: rock slides and washouts were common, and dangerous. He and the other men were given blankets which they slit and wore as ponchos, and rubber gum boots which came almost to their knees and which they wore over their wet felt slippers. Deng Wei's boots fit poorly and made him stumble if he hurried.

The deer skins rotted quickly, shedding clumps of sticky hair over everything and stinking until the men were sickened, so one by one at first and then en masse they were thrown into the snow where they were soon covered and forgotten.

The bear man came into their building one night shortly after their arrival and stood looking at them as they lay in groups together, trying to stay warm enough to sleep. He hugged his hairy coat to himself after a moment to keep the cold of the building from stealing his own warmth, then turned and went back outside, closing the door behind him. The door fit poorly and he muscled it closed, the sound of its scraping and the thud of his shoulder against it awakening even those who'd managed to fall asleep.

An hour later several barbarians came in with armloads of more blankets, which they dumped on the floor. Before they were out the door the lamp flickered and died, out of oil. One of the barbarians said something and they all groped their way out. Soon they were back. One of them carried another lamp which he placed on the floor next to the empty one. He put a can next to it, and a sack of lucifers.

The next evening when the coolies came into their building after work they found a stove had been set in the center of the building, its stack disappearing through the roof. A pile of wood was jumbled against a wall, a small hatchet waiting in a chunk of spruce.

Gradually the men's comforts accumulated. They weren't fed in their building any more but went to another one for their morning and evening meals. If they ate anything during the workday it was something they'd saved from breakfast, or from the night before. The food was dull but hot and plentiful, which in itself was luxury to most of them.

They weren't systematically abused but their lives were grim. They trudged to their labors after a quick breakfast in the cold dark morning, shuffled back to their mess hall in the black evenings. Most of them, slaving in the tunnels, never saw the light, much less the feeble sun which once in a while leaked through the clouds.

When they weren't working they were left to themselves. They didn't mix at all with the other workers. At the beginning there were Caucasians doing some of the same work but shortly those men had elevated themselves so the most menial of the jobs were done by the Chinese. Nevertheless, Hong Deng Wei's life seemed relatively bright as spring approached. At least he'd survived the winter. He thought he could survive another.

While the coolies were eating their supper one night Bear Man came in accompanied by Lo An. He had exchanged his huge coat for a cloth one and seemed less ferocious. He stood next to the big wood stove in the center of the room where they ate and when the coolies were silent he spoke and Lo An translated. "Bear Man says he's pleased with the work you've done for him. He says you haven't complained and there hasn't been any trouble. He says he's happy he paid the money to have you brought here to dig the gold, and because you've been good he wants to reward you. He's set aside some of the gold for you. He's taken most of that back to pay for the food you eat, and now he's going to give you what's left, for your own. It's your payment for working."

There was a general stirring among them and Bear man smiled happily at the obvious reference to his good nature.

"The gold he's showing you has to be divided equally among you. I'll help you do that. Each of you will get enough to buy a suit of barbarian clothes or two blankets, or something of equal worth."

Bear Man held a small pouch above his head so they could all see it. Looking very pleased with himself, he handed it to Lo An. Then he smiled in several directions and left.

Lo An spoke again to the men sitting on benches at the long, rough tables. "If any of you wants to save his share rather than spend it, tell me and I'll arrange it. Also it's possible to have your share sent to your family in the Middle Kingdom, if they can be found and if that's your wish."

Almost to a man that was their wish.

38

Hong Deng Wei, however, used the opportunity as an excuse to speak to the woman, so his share was saved for him. As a result when she next saw him, after the avalanche, she remembered his face and his name.

4

The frozen torrent came down a steep chute – a gully that had avalanched the spring before and the spring before that and forever before that. As the weather warmed, men stopped and looked up before they stepped onto that part of the path wandering through the boulders and trash left from the previous year's avalanche. All winter the snow had accumulated and clutched at the faces of the gully but as the warming weather changed the interface between ice and snow and rock the bonding was loosened. Eventually it would let go.

Kevin Aspin was deep in thought as he and Lo An walked up the canyon toward the mine. She stopped briefly in front of him to consider the gully but he was close behind and pushed her, urging her. "Come on, Lou Ann, I've got to close that deal this morning."

She stole another glance up toward the mountain's shoulder, then stepped out again. They were halfway through the dangerous area, perhaps a bit more, when a rumbling in the ground penetrated the soles of their feet. They both looked up at once, knowing they were caught. Kevin screamed, *"Run!"*

They ran.

Lo An was very quick and was soon yards ahead of Kevin, who suffered the effects of good living. They hadn't far to go… The avalanche would stay within well defined bounds… Five feet one way or the other…

All over the settlement, from the deep tunnels in the upper canyon bowl to the workings and houses at the mouth of the canyon and across the channel on Deer Island, the sound of the avalanche stopped men in their work. Its heavy booming lasted half a minute, emphasizing the silence of a warming spring day. Because the almost perpetual clouds had lifted and the sky was beginning to clear, workers at the mines on the face of the mountain could look down the canyon and see the rising fog of snow thrown up by the sliding debris in the gully. As the avalanche crashed down the fog boiled up, shutting out all but the strongest light, and then fell on the settlement like ash from a volcano.

****

A gang of outside coolies was working on the ore-cart rail that followed a contour along the side of the mountain. They were a quarter of a mile up the canyon from the avalanche and because they could hear it and feel it they knew what was coming, but not where. Then, *"There!"* one of them shouted. His cry brought all eyes to the fog of swirling snow which hid the avalanche as it roared down the almost vertical gully.

Another man saw the two running figures on the path below and yelled, pointing. The figures were unmistakably those of Kai Win and Lo An. As the coolies on the track watched in stupefaction, the snow cloud reached the two running people and enveloped them.

Hong Deng Wei was the first to break from the spell, throwing down his shovel, starting, then reaching down again to retrieve it, shouting, "Come on, bring your tools. Quickly!" If he'd been more experienced he wouldn't have bothered, but the other men were shaken from their own thoughts and began to follow, picking up speed as they focused on the task, running and slipping down the tracks. Deng Wei stumbled, his oversized gum boots sloshing on his feet.

When Deng Wei reached the place where the tracks had crossed the avalanche gully on a short trestle he stopped momentarily. The tracks and the trestle were all gone. He turned, bounded down through the winter-bare bushes and saplings until he was at the footpath on the narrow floor of the canyon. He followed the footpath through more bushes, other men racing behind him, and ran head-on into a wall. It hadn't been there before. It was taller than a man, twice as tall, hard and compacted and dirty, stones ground together in the snow, boulders the size of the ore-carts, all tumbled together, settling. And somewhere in that solid freezing mass, the Chinese whore and the man, Kai Win.

Deng Wei would have despaired, thrown down his shovel, wept at the memory of the woman but just then there were shouts from the other side – barbarians – and Deng Wei looked up toward the source of the slide, then forgot hopelessness and threw himself at the wall of snow, digging frantically. Other men came up behind him, joined in.

A voice yelled from above. *'Hey! You coolies!* Get up here. Come on, up here!" An excited barbarian in his shirts sleeves was above them on the densely packed snow and though Deng Wei couldn't understand what he was yelling, his motions were clear. Deng Wei scrambled up the wall of debris, yelling for the others to follow.

The barbarians were standing around, looking, unsure. One of them, a bald little man with red braces holding up his trousers, came over and shook the arm of one of the coolies, gesticulating, shouting something at him. The coolie was confused, and bowed, and the man began to shake him again, but Deng Wei had reached him by then and with frantic gestures made the man understand that Kai Win and Lo An had been caught. He flapped his hands out like Kevin Aspin's ear flaps. He held his fists to his chest. "Yes,

Lo An also..." Then he threw his hands toward the ground, tumbled them in the air, and still shouting in Chinese, pointed to the edge of the path below them.

The bald man in the red braces understood him and took charge, organizing search teams, sending one group down along the edge of the snow, others to spread out and move down the face. Some of the men carried sticks they poked into soft places between rocks and clumps of ice, probing. Others lifted what they could, trying to see down into the snow for a piece of cloth, a hand. Others had tools – shovels and bars and picks – and they dug carefully at random, all odds against them.

Then a cry lifted from one of the Chinese down along the bush line, forty feet below the path. Men looked up, rushed to the spot, leaped to join others. A piece of red cloth – Lo An! She couldn't be alive. Frantically men scrambled to remove the snow. They used their bare hands, scooping it out, pulling out little rocks and chunks of ice.

"There!"

An elbow. Another. Her head, cradled in her arms, blood on her forehead and chin, a sharp stone cutting into her cheek.

"Get the snow away from her face."

"Let her breathe!"

Men were on their knees, digging the snow from around her.

"She's alive. Careful there!"

Then a shout from another man, ten feet away and on top of the slide. "Here's the other one!"

****

When Kevin Aspin regained consciousness, lying wrapped in blanket ponchos on the trail, the first face he saw was Hong Deng Wei's.

Kevin opened his eyes, blinked, moved one hand feebly, opened his eyes again and focused on the man who happened to be standing there in his line of sight, among all of them peering down at him. His hand reached up and someone took it, tried to put his arm back down under the blanket, but Kevin shook the man's grip off weakly and reached again, his lips trying to form words. He caught the leg of Deng Wei's trousers, pulled him until Deng Wei, embarrassed, was on his knees beside him. Kevin's hand groped up, clutched Deng Wei's tunic, dragged him down close. He got his arm around his neck and kissed his face.

With both victims saved this scene was the perfect cap and men laughed, clapped Deng Wei on the back, shook hands with each other, stood talking and looking up at the now bare gully. Beyond, a clear blue sky silhouetted the brilliant mountain peaks.

****

The next day while Deng Wei was at work with the rest of his gang shoveling a path through the slide so the trestle and track could be rebuilt, Kevin Aspin arrived on the scene. He had no major injuries. He was considerably bruised and he felt like all his bones had bent to the breaking point, but there he was, up and about. He stood looking at the slide for a few minutes, then limped over to where the coolies were working under the supervision of a white crew boss who was directing half a dozen of them to lever a big boulder down the slope. Kevin studied the men, who ignored him, until he saw Deng Wei. He moved closer until he was almost in the arc of Deng Wei's swinging pickax, confirming his recognition, then he picked his way over to the crew boss. "What's the name of that Chinaman over there? The one with the pick." He pointed.

"Mister Aspin, that's a good question, I suppose, but I don't even begin to know that Chinaman's name. They's just Chinamen

44

to me; when I needs one I holler and they all look up, then I points to the one I wants. Don't need no names that way. 'Sides, you know what they say 'bout them all lookin' alike."

"Yes, yes, I know. But I also know they do have names, and I need to know that one's name."

"Why's that? He steal something?"

Kevin shook his head. "No, on the contrary. Well, I'm going to talk to him anyway." He walked back to where Deng Wei was working. "Hey," he said. All the coolies in that immediate area stopped work and looked up at him. Kevin smiled, glancing over at the crew chief, who laughed at the confirmation of his system, then he pointed at Deng Wei. "You. What you name?"

Deng Wei bowed.

Kevin pointed at himself and said, "Kai Win," the name Lo An called him. Then he pointed at Deng Wei and asked, "What you?"

The Chinaman bowed again, then replied, "Hong Deng Wei."

Kevin repeated it. "Hongdong-way?" The Chinaman bowed again, still holding his pickax. 'Hongdong?" Another bow. "Well, Hongdong, that's a hell of a name but as far as I'm concerned you could call yourself Mary, Queen of Scots. You saved my life yesterday, and Lou Ann's too, and I'm obliged to you." He stuck out his hand. He hadn't decided yet to go beyond that, kept his face to himself.

****

Deng Wei recognized the barbarian gesture. He bowed again, then seeing the hand still thrust out at him, and after looking around at the other coolies, who were all staring, he tentatively took it.

Kai Win pumped his arm up and down a couple of times as if to make water flow from Deng Wei's mouth. Deng Wei couldn't get his hand back and was being pulled off balance in the snow. He prevented himself from falling by thrusting the pickax head down onto the snow like a cane, then he tugged, tried again to get his hand back. Still Kai Win held it with a grip that surprised Deng Wei. Finally, feeling he had no choice, he began to pump back and as they stood there shaking their arms up and down, Deng Wei at last smiled, unable any longer to contain his embarrassment. The barbarian's face cracked into a huge answering grin.

That night at supper Bear Man caught Deng Wei's shoulder as he passed. Lo An was with him. She had a bandage covering her cheek, another on her forehead. Deng Wei bowed, his supper bowl in his hands. Lo An told him, "Bear Man says that from now on you work for Kai Win, the man who gave you the deer skin."

"Yes, Lo An. The barbarian who was saved yesterday when the snow caught him. And you." Because of her beauty and her authority he was shy and kept his eyes averted. "Am I going to be punished?"

"No, you're being rewarded. The man believes in his heart you saved us both from the snow, all by yourself. Others have told him the truth, that you only helped, but still he thinks he owes our lives to you. He wants to be kind to you because of that feeling. To reward you. It's his way. And he says he likes your smile."

Deng Wei looked at her curiously. Was this true? Or was she playing with him for her own womanly reasons? He looked in her eyes and she looked back directly until he dropped his own and bowed again. "What am I supposed to do, Lo An?"

"In the morning after your meal gather what you own and come to the house where Kai Win lives. It's the one behind the log house of the deer skins. Come and stand there and wait, and someone will tell you what to do."

"Yes, Lo An."

46

"And Hong Deng Wei, I also thank you, and wish you to tell the others who helped find us that I'm grateful." With that the woman turned and walked out with Bear Man.

****

Hong Deng Wei went to work for Kevin Aspin as a general handyman, doing errands, caulking Kevin's small sailboat, fixing the stairs leading up from the beach area to Kevin's house, running from one part of the mine community to another, his queue flying and his missions urgent. As he worked, he smiled, but not from embarrassment now; he just couldn't keep his face quiet. His work for Kai Win was an opportunity to be near Lo An.

Kevin soon saw that Deng Wei was quiet and competent and that his adaptability and willingness to tackle any job were useful, especially at the cost of his keep. Kevin was altogether pleased with the arrangement.

Lo An was annoyed at first. She thought it'd be a bore and a nuisance to have the coolie around, but she changed her mind. The Chinese men of the encampment left her alone because of her status as a speaker of the foreign devils' language and because of her position of power next to and beneath the barbarian Kai Win. But as Deng Wei worked she recognized a depth of purpose in his approach to life and in the way he did his daily chores. That intrigued her and in the soils of that recognition grew the strange roots of mystery. She could see him hiding the stolen glances of the enamored, but he was respectful, and careful to control his staring, and she went from pique to amusement, to curiosity. Over the months of the summer she got to know a few things about him. Not that they sat in deep conversation, but she remembered short comments from a piece here, a short exchange there as he worked at one task or another. She formed an image of the hamlet at the junction of the swirling rivers where he'd lived, and she filled the corners of her imagination with pictures of him riding logs down the rivers, and she learned respect for him. Even once in a while the sight of his strong neck against a load excited her and if other things were right and if she allowed herself, she lubricated, and secretly thanked him for the feeling.

Lo An was Chinese because she'd suckled as a Chinese and she knew the virtues of the Chinese, though in her young life she'd seldom had the opportunity to choose the virtuous path. Her white father had squirted no genes that drew her toward the pale arms of White America. If a man were to ask her, with hope of fondling her fantasies as well as her luscious flesh, he would best be Chinese. Bear Man might throw her down if Kai Win were to say he could, but that would be outside of her, even as his shaft pushed, burning through the barrier of her dry lips.

Deng Wei, however, might find a slippery welcome.

****

The community grew considerably that summer with the opening of a major tunnel through the mountain from the channel side which would eventually join others coming from the canyon side. Still the miners followed the richness of the vein, still the mountain took in men and gave out its tons of ore. More coolies arrived in two shipments – neither of them Kevin Aspin's – so that by the arrival of the next snows on the mountain there were almost two hundred Chinese. Too many. The white population had grown to just over five hundred.

Tragedy struck early, though it wasn't recognized until the hunger started.

Canyon of Gold was an isolated community. There were no roads – indeed no place for a road to go. Everything came by sea, much of it in sailboats bringing small consignments from Seattle or Vancouver or Sitka. Most of what the community needed was brought in on small steamships. There were few luxuries: the cost of freight was high and there were too many essentials.

When the first blizzard roared down from the ice fields above, a full two months before any major winter weather was expected, the men dug themselves out and pushed on with their work, certain the snow would melt, Indian summer would appear, and life would continue normally. Steamships would arrive bringing the supplies needed to get the community through the winter. There were two company stores which distributed food against credit or gold dust, and several private vendors who would also lay in supplies for the winter.

It didn't happen. Another blizzard followed immediately, piling up snow to the depth of a man's waist. That was followed by a cold spell, with the temperatures falling to well below zero. When the temperature began to rise the barometer dipped and then plunged. One steamship with a heavy consignment of food – tinned goods and kegs of salt pork – turned back to Seattle when the barometer dove beyond the captain's red line. The seas were treacherous at best and deadly when furious.

A smaller steamship was caught in the week-long storm that followed the plunging barometer, was lashed by vicious seas even among the islands of the Inland Passage, and was thrown aground on jagged rocks when it tried to retreat to the south. Its crew of six was lost, as was the entire cargo. A huddled group of Indians shivering in a hunting camp watched it happen, eventually reported its loss. There was nothing else they could do.

In Canyon of Gold where men depended on the arrival of a number of ships still scheduled, there were stirrings of concern. True, it was only early October, and the previous year ships had arrived during good spells all winter – the coolie ship had come in late January – but everyone knew if ships didn't start getting through there could be long hungry times.

Ships tried, but none made it.

One intrepid skipper out of Bremerton did force his way up to a river estuary sixteen miles south of town. There was a single little cove offering limited shelter there and he anchored, swinging heavily, the weather still ugly and bitterly cold, the seas beyond his tenuous shelter heavy and rising. He put two men ashore with instructions to snowshoe through the forest up the coast to Canyon of Gold and return with porters. He couldn't endanger his ship by going further but he could offload his cargo there and the townsmen could carry it back to the settlement. He was on the wrong side of the river but they'd have to work that out; he had problems of his own.

His cargo consisted of a ton of canned milk, two tons of flour, nine hundred pounds of salt in fifty pound sacks, a considerable amount of red beans in one hundred pound sacks, and odds and ends including one hundred pounds of ground black pepper.

When an exhausted column of men – mostly Chinese – arrived on the snowy banks of the river two days later the little freighter was gone but on the far shore, across the estuary, they could see a tiny pile of supplies, licked by the tide. After considerable effort and the near-drowning of four men, scouts managed to get across on a log raft. The other men stood watching, sheltering as they could from the cold, crouched around fires at the edge of the beach. They knew from the size of the pile on the far shore there wasn't much – the tide had washed most of it away – but at this desperate point everything counted. They watched anxiously as the scouts made the far shore, secured their flimsy raft, and moved to the stack of goods.

The cry came back feebly across the icy water, snatched by the growing wind. "Pepperrr... Nothing but black pepperrr..."

There was no civil government in the settlement. The town was on federal territorial land and a federal magistrate spent the summers in a small office near the beach. That was the only tie with outside civil organization. There were two major mining companies developing the vein and they cooperated closely in all things. That cooperation and the rule of well-known mining law settled most disputes among the whites. Overseers settled coolie problems on the spot. The growth of the settlement, except for the companies' building developments at the mine facilities, had been haphazard. There were no horses, no wagons in the area. All goods were carried from the boat landing by long-queued coolies to the rail track which circuited the mines.

The bitter winter swooped down from the Arctic two months early and stayed, its claws sunk deep into the tiny, abandoned community. By December every miner was hungry, scores were clinically famished. By Christmas Eve four men had been found in their lonesome shacks, log-hard and ice-rimed. Patrols were established to visit other isolated dwellings but they were largely defeated by weakness and weather. Rumored deaths went unconfirmed. In the unrelenting frost of endless night hushed men discussed the afterlife, and listed morbid choices. Some said frozen meat shouldn't be wasted. "It is a gift from a merciful god." Some agreed. Finally, on New Year's Day, a desperation meeting was called. Few men had the strength to attend but virtually all heard the consensus and if any disputed the decision that was taken there, they had no strength to oppose it. In the long run few people outside the community would ever really know about it; even fewer would ever care, though the warrant condemned men to death: they were only coolies.

5

Kai Win struggled up the stairs, pushed open the door, shoved it shut, panted, croaked for Lo An and Deng Wei. He found them wrapped in the heat of the stove in the kitchen, the only livable room in the house. When he'd warmed his breath and could talk he blurted, "There's trouble. Bad trouble. Some of the miners have got together. They say..." His hands went to the sides of his head as if the pain of what he'd heard had settled there. "They say the coolies have to get out of town. Right now! All of them!" He collapsed into a chair, his head in his hands, the snow on his boots and legs beading, dripping to the floor. Lo An and Deng Wei stood looking at him, silent, uncomprehending but worried over his agitation. The spruce in the stove spit knots and crackled. Kai Win looked up at Lo An and said, "Don't you understand? They're going to drive all of you out of town into that... that *hell* out there, so they don't have to waste food on you!"

Lo An could understand his words and could feel the depth of his despair but confusion stunted her reaction.

"It's murder! Nobody can live out there," Kai Win declared. "We've got to think of something. Those animals are crazy with hunger and they're afraid, and they've gone to get their guns. They're going to hunt you like rats." He held out his hands to Lo An and she stepped closer. She took his hands in hers and looked over at Deng Wei, who could only know something was terribly wrong. Quickly she explained to him, though she hardly understood.

When she finished, Deng Wei gathered himself and marched from the room. In a moment he was back. He held Kai Win's revolver. He thrust it toward the seated man.

"Hongdong, what…"

Lo An listened to Deng Wei, then explained. "He thinks you'll protect us. He says we're of your house and it's your duty to protect us, as we'd protect you. It's Chinese thinking, Kai Win."

"Well, goddammit, this isn't China," Kai Win snapped at her. "I'm trying to tell you…" He pulled his hands from hers, stood shakily, paced the room. "I can't shoot… That's crazy. No, think… could I hide you here?" He threw his glance around at the pitiful hiding places offered by the frozen corners of the small house. "No, if they found you they might shoot you on the spot. Where could we… Wait, I've got an idea." He pressed his temples with his bony, frost-reddened fists, still pacing, trying to form a plan.

Lo An and Deng Wei couldn't help him: it wasn't ever up to them to decide their own fates. Deng Wei lit another lamp, refilled another from the almost-empty kerosene can. Lo An added a hemlock chunk to the stove and poured hot water into their mugs.

Finally Kai Win looked as if he'd decided something. He made them sit at the rough table. "Lou Ann. Hongdong." He regarded each of them. "You both have to get out. Tonight. Those miners will start up at the mines in the canyon but soon they'll be all over town looking for coolies and whatever food they can find. Here's what we'll do…"

When Kai Win paused, Lo An translated. "He says we have to leave, that we have to hide. He says we have to pack what we can carry, quickly. We can take the food that's left here. He says we should go north along the coast to the small cove shaped like a crab, the one where the Indians who used to hunt for him have their camp. Do you know it?"

Deng Wei's face wrinkled in thought. Lo An knew he'd been to the crab-shaped cove with Kai Win by boat, if not through the forest. He'd probably be able to recognize it. It'd take them several days to get there on foot. He answered. "Yes, I can find it. But what if the Indians aren't there?"

Lo An turned to Kai Win. "He can find it but he's worried. What if the Indians aren't there?"

"Yeah, Hongdong, they might not be there, unless they got caught by the weather. But there's no place else, dammit. There's shelter there. And there're probably some deer around. You might have a chance there." Kai Win turned his haggard face to Lo An, took one of her hands, put his other hand on Deng Wei's arm. "I'm sorry. We're friends. Lou Ann, you're still my beautiful Chinese whore and I haven't wanted another woman since I saw you. And Hongdong, you saved my life. Both our lives. I didn't want this to happen to you."

Lo An repeated his words for Deng Wei, softly, her eyes stinging.

"You have to go," Kai Win continued, "together. It's the only way. If you wait those... those barbarians..." he shared a slight, wry smile with Lo An, "they'll force you out with nothing but the clothes on your backs." A gust of frozen wind gushed out of the canyon, flung itself like a curse at the snow-buried community. Smoke squished from the top of the stove. "Hurry now..."

They rushed around the chilled house collecting things they could use. Canvas backpacks. Blankets. An extra-heavy coat made of sheepskin. An ax. Lo An packed some small pots and pans into a galvanized tin bucket. Deng Wei scooped up several boxes of friction matches and wrapped them in a square of cloth. If those ever got wet... He helped Kai Win roll a large piece of canvas into a long roll. It might shelter them.

There wasn't much food – some tins of milk, some dried salmon, a cloth bag with red beans, another with several pounds of flour. Some rock salt and a paper sack full of sugar, and they were finished. Then Kai Win remembered a sack of venison jerky hanging in the shed where the deer skins had been. As he was outside getting that Deng Wei and Lo An quickly packed everything into the two backpacks. She couldn't even lift hers. Deng Wei quickly repacked, putting the heavier things in his, the blankets and the lighter foods in hers. He held the bundle of matches, deciding, then pushed it into her pack. He lashed the heavy canvas roll into a horseshoe around his own pack.

The sack of meat Kai Win found was larger than he'd remembered. "I'm glad it was forgotten until now. You'll need it, my friends."

Deng Wei and Lo An spoke rapidly together, then she told Kai Win, "Hong Deng Wei says we have enough, and I agree. You should keep the meat."

"No, no. Those bastards up the canyon will have to share out what's left with me." He couldn't really know that. This whole thing was crazy. "You'll need this and more to make it until spring. Oh, stupid... I almost wasn't thinking. Here..." He held the revolver out toward Deng Wei, who drew back from it. Kevin shook it, said, "Take the damn thing, Hongdong. Here, let me show you..." In a quick lesson he showed Deng Wei how to load it, how to cock it. Then he emptied the cylinders and, standing behind Deng Wei, guiding his arms, showed him how to hold it with both hands and sight it. He rummaged through a canvas sack hanging near the door, found two boxes of ammunition, thrust them into the pocket of the sheepskin coat. "I wish I could find my old rifle, but never mind. You can kill deer with that pistol but wait until they're very close, got it? And be careful, Hongdong, it's easy to shoot yourself with a pistol."

Lo An repeated what he'd said and Deng Wei nodded, shoved the revolver into the coat's other pocket.

"And don't lose that, Hongdong. It might mean you eat or don't eat." Kai Win patted the pocket, buttoned the flap down. Deng Wei understood and buttoned the flap down over the pocket with the ammunition in it.

"Anything else? Can you think of anything else, Lou Ann? Oh…" He raced out to the shed again, returned, clumped the snow off his boots, handed Deng Wei a small bundle wrapped in oilskin. "This is fish line and hooks. Use anything for bait. And don't wait until the ice is gone before you try fishing, hear?"

Lo An said, "Thank you, Kai Win. You're a good man. But how long do you think we'll have to stay away? You can't mean until the ice is gone."

Once again Kai Win put his hands on them. "I wish it didn't have to be at all. This is criminal, what they're doing, and they'll pay, don't you worry. You can't treat people like this, not even coolies. But yes, stay until spring if you can." Lo An moved to object but he silenced her with shakes of his head. He held both her hands clasped in one of his and gripped Deng Wei by the coat sleeve. It was warm enough by the popping stove, but beyond a slight radius the house was frozen. "Stay until you're positive ships have come in with more food. Don't worry, the Indians'll take care of you. And if the situation changes, if it's OK to come back earlier, I'll come fetch you." From his shirt pocket he took a piece of paper with writing on it. "There's one more thing. Just in case anything should happen to me this winter, and you make it back, this is my will. Lou Ann, I'm leaving everything I own here in your name. If you come back and I'm dead, take this paper to the government man down in the house by the beach. Show it to him. Tell him what happened, what we did, what I said. He'll know how to protect you. And you take care of Hongdong, OK?"

Tears coursed from Lo An's eyes. She been purchased outright by this man for his use, and he had used her. But he'd been kind. For all his bluster and in spite of his nervous and sometimes narrow ways he was a nice man and she'd gotten used to being used by him; she didn't mind it anymore. He'd taken good care of her, and since the avalanche he'd taken care of Deng Wei. "Yes, Kai Win," was all she could say now. She tucked the folded paper beneath her clothes.

As they stood in the doorway ready to leave, the lamp out and the house dark so they wouldn't be seen, Deng Wei turned to Kai Win. He put out his right hand, fingers stiff, thumb rigid, and said in the pieces of English he'd learned, "Than-ka-yu, Kai Win. We go now. We come back one time. Me Hong. Deng. Wei."

Kai Win took Deng Wei's outstretched hand, clasped it. "Yes, Hongdong, you come back one time." His voice was thick.

Deng Wei held the white man's hands, emphasized each word with a shake of their grip, repeated, "Me. Hong. Deng. Wei."

"Yes. You Hong. Deng. Wei." There was a bright glistening in Kai Win's eyes. "Go on now. To the beach first, then up the coast. Hurry."

They were gone forever in the dark.

****

Deng Wei hurried through the snow, sliding, helping Lo An, stumbling in the darkness. A few scattered lights glowed through frosted windows but the settlement was essentially dark. Ten minutes after abandoning Kai Win's house they reached Canyon Creek just above its junction with the channel. Deng Wei stopped at the bank of the frozen stream. Lo An was already breathing heavily, grabbing his pack and his clothes to make sure she didn't lose contact. It was only a week beyond the longest night of the Alaska winter. The cold clutched at their bodies.

The sound of crackers – two quick gunshots – echoed down from the canyon, followed by the faint chime of mobbed men yelling. They were coming. Deng Wei spurred himself, waded through the snow, reaching behind himself every few steps to drag Lo An. They crawled and fell, stumbling, tripped by hidden logs and boulders beneath the snow, slapped by overhanging branches, defending their faces as well as they could in the darkness from the snags that reached out and clawed at them. They left a trail anybody could follow.

Once he stopped and pulled the scarf away from his ears. "Quiet, woman. Let me listen." She was gasping, already worn out. He turned his ear for sounds of pursuit or danger, heard none and continued on. She shifted the weight of her pack and shoved herself away from the sapling she'd leaned against for support. They came suddenly out of the trees and found instant relief in the firmer footing on the pebbly beach, but felt also the heavier cold of the open night. Turning right, they headed north.

Deng Wei moved confidently along the frozen beach. Except for scattered chunks of ice shoved up by the tides it was an easy avenue of travel. The narrow channel waters were frozen between Deer Island and the mainland shore but the tide broke and jumbled the ice, making travel out on the channel itself impossible. Above the tide line, however, not quite into the heavy evergreen trees, they could walk. Occasionally a fallen tree or a boulder or a large hunk of driftwood blocked the way, but they were able to get around those.

"Deng Wei. Deng Wei, stop. I have to rest." Lo An had fallen behind. He stopped and she stumbled up to him. "I'm so tired, Deng Wei, and this pack..." He stepped behind her and lifted the pack, easing the pressure from her shoulders. Did it feel lighter than it had at Kai Win's house? He decided not. They stood that way a minute while she caught her breath. "Can't we stop here and spend the night, wait until light, then move on? Why do we have to go so far in the dark, and so fast?" The light she craved would be little more than slightly faded darkness for a few hours. The tide groaned and crunched the ice in the channel. Behind them

58

the town lay around bends and beyond forest, its chilling sounds unheard, its few feeble lamps hidden. They wouldn't be able to detect pursuers until they were too close to avoid. Deng Wei could feel Lo An's condensed breath in the air when she turned her head to speak to him, but he couldn't see much more than the darker black of the forest against the snow and ice around them. Heavy clouds blocked any heavenly light. "What if someone's following us?"

"Who would follow us, Deng Wei? All the savages want is the food we would have eaten, and we have that with us. They don't know that. Who'll chase us? Please, let's rest."

"No. Others will come this way. The savages will drive them out of the canyon and they can go only two ways when they reach the channel." He leaned into her, talking in a low voice. "Many of them will be forced in this direction. And if they see us they'll want to stay with us. There are so many of them. Can we feed them all?"

Lo An was quiet, thinking. Then she answered. "No. You're right, Deng Wei. They're Chinese and we'd try to save them if we could, but we can't. We have to protect ourselves. Go on, Deng Wei, I'll try to keep up."

"In a moment," he answered. He jerked the flap of his coat pocket loose, took the revolver out, fumbled a box of shells from the other one. His hands were cold and his fingers wouldn't obey and in the dark he dropped a palmful of bullets into the snow. Lo An groped for them while he poked cartridges into the cylinder of the weapon. She could only find two of the half dozen he'd dropped. He took them from her, put them back in his pocket, loose, shoved the handgun back into the other pocket, then started walking again.

They moved on through the night. Deng Wei was a seasoned traveler in all weather but Lo An wasn't. Both of them were weakened by hunger. They stopped often to rest, easing their loads, shifting straps, rearranging their clothing. But if they stopped for long the cold reached to their souls and they were forced to flee it.

Just as the dark was thinning – it was actually mid-morning – they came to a river covered with ice and snow. They had to decide: should they make a camp while they could see, then get some rest? Or should they go on in the light while they could cover more ground, try to make it across the river? "This is a strong river. It comes from a glacier," Deng Wei announced. "Kai Win told me. I know where we are. We're a long way from the settlement. We'll cross while we can see, then make a camp and rest one night. I don't think the others will come as quickly as we have. They don't know about the deer hunters' camp so they don't have a reason to come this far."

"Will the ice hold us?"

Deng Wei didn't know. "Yes, it will." He led her out onto the river.

They crossed, then followed the beach northward. Now they could see obstacles and avoid them instead of falling over them. They'd left Deer Island and its channel far behind and the open water along this stretch of the mainland had washed the snow off the beach. Within an hour they'd covered another mile but then Lo An couldn't go any further even though, from the frozen river, Deng Wei had carried her pack as well as his own, wearing it backwards, hanging on his chest. She carried the tin bucket with the sack of deer jerky in it. Every time Lo An fell the sack of precious meat tumbled out. She'd grope in the snow for it, put it back in the bucket, struggle on.

They found a small stream running under a thick cover of snow and he said, "We'll stop here." He led her up the sloping beach to the tree line. He dumped both packs beneath a towering hemlock's branches, pulled her over, sat her down. "Don't move. I'll come right back."

In spite of her exhaustion, in spite of their plight and the horror of the night just past, she laughed. It was a feeble sound – almost a croak – but he smiled in response and asked, "What's funny?"

"You're funny. Telling me not to move. I've stopped moving, you can be certain." She shivered, pulled her clothes tighter. "Now go find me a soft bed with a thick quilt or I'll go to sleep right here and freeze to death." It wasn't a frivolous threat.

They made camp under a huge hemlock that had blown over in a storm. With a small amount of ax work he was able to cut an entrance through the branches and clear an area under the huge slanting trunk; there was only a fine dusting of snow there. He arranged the cut branches on the ground to make a mattress where the thick bole of the tree was only three feet above them, unrolled their canvas over the mat of branches, then spread their four blankets on that. He folded the excess canvas back over the blankets like a big envelope flap.

"While I'm starting a fire," he told her, "you take off your wet outer clothes and hang them there, and there." He pointed out branch stumps to her. "They'll dry in the smoke. Put on the sheepskin coat or get in the bed if you're cold." Lo An was collapsed on boughs left over from the bed, obviously worn out. The low sun glowed weakly through the cloud cover. It gave no warmth. Deng Wei noticed she hadn't moved. He stopped gathering wood and looked at her. "What's the matter?"

"Nothing."

"Then why don't you do it?"

"I will. I was just watching you work. You know what to do. You can live out here."

"Yes, I can live out here, and I will. And so will you if you do as you're told."

"Do you hate me because I'm worthless?"

He looked at her and his face verified the truth. "No, Lo An. You're not worthless, and I couldn't hate you, ever."

They spent the rest of that day and the long night there. Deng Wei kept a small fire going until the afternoon turned fully dark, then he let it die out so its light wouldn't attract other refugees. During the day they heated water and Deng Wei made pungent tea for them from spruce needles. They boiled a couple of the beans and a small piece of jerky. The thin soup tasted bland and turpentiny, more like the tea they'd made in the same pot, and they argued. She wanted to add a pinch of salt, he thought it needed a touch of sugar. They ate it as it was, sipping it from a shared enamel cup, eating the slivers of meat and the few beans with crooked little chopsticks Deng Wei whittled.

Just before it got dark Deng Wei went down to the edge of the tree line at the beach and looked back in the direction they'd come. The waves thumped into the pebbles – it had been another day of seas too rough for ships to bring food to Canyon of Gold.

Back in their shelter Lo An was already in bed, sound asleep. When he crawled in he discovered she'd put the big sheepskin coat down where he'd lie beside her. He slipped beneath the blankets, arranged himself on the softness of the sheepskin-covered boughs, and with the warmth of her body against him, fell instantly asleep, the lump of the revolver in its pocket unnoticed.

They trudged north for three more days with less urgency now that they'd put so much distance between themselves and the town. They talked again, one morning, about the probability of other Chinese getting that far north. Deng Wei thought some might, Lo An thought they wouldn't. "I think as soon as possible they'd turn around and go back in the other direction. They know there's civilization to the south someplace."

Deng Wei had a vague idea of the coastal geography and said, "It's impossible. Too far. And the pepper river would stop them. It doesn't ice over. By now they'll be desperate, and dangerous."

"But why would any of them come in this direction?"

Deng Wei pondered while he sipped spruce tea. "Maybe they'll follow our tracks."

"Maybe, but I don't think so." She looked at him and he could see the dependence. "What will happen if they do come? If they are desperate and dangerous, like you say?"

"I don't know, Lo An."

****

There was an Indian at the hunting camp at the crab-shaped cove. He was stretched below a snow-covered mound of rocks gathered from the beach and piled to keep the animals from his body. Lo An made out the words on the simple wooden slab stuck into the stones at one end of the grave. "Albert Blake."

Probably after the first blizzard – the one that sealed off the settlement – the Indians who hunted there had gotten a decent day and had taken their boats back to their village on Admiralty Island. They wouldn't come again until March or early April when the first black bears started grazing on the beaches of the mainland. There weren't any black bears on Admiralty Island because the huge, black-bear-eating coastal grizzlies lived there. For the Indians spring black bear was lean and stringy meat but it was a welcome change from a winter diet of very lean, very stringy deer jerky and dried fish.

Lo An was bitterly disappointed. "Kai Win said they'd be here," she pouted.

"He said they might be here."

"Maybe they're someplace else, a nearby camp. On the other side there?" She pointed to the far side of the sheltered little cove. The day was grey again, but not as cold. The sky hung close, pressing down on the tops of the trees and hiding the horizon. A bald eagle shrieked from his perch in a tree and small long-legged birds sprinted mindlessly at the edge of the frozen cove.

"No, this is their camp. But that's all right, Lo An," Deng Wei answered, looking around. "This is a good place. We can live here. We don't need them. The ice on this cove is thick enough to hold us, so we can cut holes and fish. There's everything we need here. Shelter, water, firewood. We'll find enough food. We have our blankets. We can talk together, keep each other from being lonely."

She looked up, her lower lip pouted. "And you'll want to use my body, I suppose." She tilted her chin defiantly, petulant, and waited for his answer as if she knew what he'd say.

He didn't know what to say. Some nights when they slept together in the blankets he thought about sex with her. One morning he'd awakened and found himself pressed in the warmth against her back, hard, throbbing, his arm thrown over her and his hand cupped against her skinny breast. Yes, he'd wanted her then, but he'd moved away and she hadn't awakened. Now he didn't know how to answer her question. He thought, then spoke as honestly as he could. "Yes, I'd like that. I think you're beautiful, and wonderful, and I've wanted you since the day of the deer skins." He couldn't look at her any more, dropped his eyes. "Many times."

"Many times?" Her tone was half mocking.

He straightened and faced her again, looking down at her as she sat on the canvas. "Yes, Lo An, many times. But I don't want you now, and I'll only want you again when you've stopped being a Chinese whore and have become a Chinese woman again." He strode off, ax in hand.

She sat with her mouth hanging open.

The hunting camp needed serious improvements before it'd be suitable as a wintering place but the beginnings were there, and that gave them hope they might survive. A low-ceilinged cave, a shallow dugout, had been cut by the Indians into the face of a slope on one of the arms that formed the cove. It provided the basics of a shelter. Deng Wei and Lo An worked together hauling branches, finding rocks, stacking them until they had a thick windbreak. Then they built an awning in front of the cave and stacked more rocks, cementing them with clay from the back of the cave to make low walls, which they topped with branches. Deng Wei built a stone fireplace with a high, angled reflector of more stones, and when even a small fire was lit it shot enough heat under the awning to warm the entire shelter. As they worked, Deng Wei stopped often to listen, to peer through the trees.

After they'd been in the camp about a week, working hard during the short daylight hours, sitting wrapped in blankets before a small, hidden fire after dark, Lo An announced, "I want a bath." The evening air was warm enough so that tea left standing in their drinking cup for several minutes hadn't yet frozen, though it soon would.

Deng Wei just grunted.

She persisted, punching him in the ribs, almost knocking him over. "I'm serious, Deng Wei, I want a bath."

"So take one, woman! There's the sea! Use our fishing hole. Don't drown." He pointed toward the ice in the cove.

She coyed, looking at him from the sides of her beautiful eyes. "No. I mean a real bath, with clean, fresh, hot water." She stood up, threw the blanket from her shoulders back onto the bed they'd made in the cave. "Help me?" It was a plea and he turned his face to her. "Please?" she said.

He rolled his head, tossed his own blanket onto the bed and with a resigned, husbandly tone said, "OK, I'll help you. What do I do?"

She hopped up and down, clapping her hands. "Oh, thank you." She turned one way, the other, organizing the possibilities. "We'll use the bucket. We'll use our cup to fill the bucket from the little stream, and we'll put it next to the fire and make it hot and then we'll strip down and wash."

"I thought *you* were going to take a bath. Now I hear *we* are going to strip down and wash. Do *I* have to take a bath?"

"That's for you to decide, Deng Wei."

"We'll freeze."

"We'll do it quickly."

And they did. Very quickly. He raced back and forth between the bucket and the hole they'd broken in the ice over the stream, and from the wood pile to the fire. While the water was heating, steaming in the chill air as soon as it was even slightly warm, he brought more wood and piled it close to use when it was his turn. All his energies were directed toward his tasks and he forgot completely about the forest at their backs.

The fire leaped, throwing heat from the reflector stones until he worried the entire hill would melt. When the first bucket of water was hot she changed their plan. "We'll do it together. It'll be faster that way. There's enough water in that bucket for us both. Get the cup and the bowl. We can dip with them. And take the bucket off the fire before the water's too hot. And put some more wood on the fire to keep us warm. And don't drip where we're going to stand…"

He didn't move.

"Well," she urged, "will you please hurry?"

He shook his head ruefully but carried out her instructions and when he'd done everything, muttering to himself, and looked up, she stood naked. He straightened and stared. She was as beautiful as he'd imagined but the winter had made her gaunt. Her skin was goose dimply and her brown nipples stood out from her thin breasts like thumbs in the cold. She shivered in spite of the radiated heat from the fire but she remained still, her arms at her side so he could look at her.

Finally she couldn't stand the chill any longer. "Enough, you outlaw. Hand me the bowl, and if you want some of this water you'd better hurry and strip down."

They both shivered while they washed, then they dried each other with one of the blankets, careful not to drip on their bough bed. She got in first, and when he'd quickly put another log on the fire and had thrown off the wet blanket, he crawled in with her, his teeth chattering.

She chided him. "Don't mess up the blankets so much. Oh, don't let so much cold air in. You coolie, your queue's soaking wet, oh…" She reached out with both arms under the blankets and pulled him to her and stopped talking, her teeth chattering.

He rolled her over, hugged her bare back to him, wrapped his arms and legs around her and held her until first she, then he stopped shivering. They lay quietly for a few minutes.

"Deng Wei?" Her voice was small. "Am I a Chinese woman now?"

His cheeks pulled his lips into a smile she couldn't see. He teased her, moving his hand over her face, her breast. He felt her nipple between his thumb and fingers, ran his hand down her flat belly, felt her bony flank. Finally he nuzzled his nose behind her ear and said, "I'll have to wait until daylight to know whether you're Chinese. But even in the dark I can tell you're a woman."

She turned to him.

6

The winter slashed like a vengeful sword through the fjords, churning the open seas, slicing men's lungs. Ships were driven onto rocks and lost trying to get to Sitka. A warehouse caught fire in Petersburg and the whole town might have burned if the wind hadn't steadied. There was an earthquake at sea and a huge wave took out much of the coast to the north, in Prince William Sound. In the narrow coastal channels south of Canyon of Gold the surface of the waters broke and heaved with every new storm. There was no relief.

Deng Wei and Lo An heard only a few of the Chinese who'd been driven from the mines. One group of three struggled along the beach on the other side of their cove, seen only briefly. They were obviously trying to make it north to Skagway. It was a long way. They were poorly dressed for the weather, carried almost nothing, and Deng Wei wondered how they'd survived. Lo An didn't see them and he didn't tell her about them. They heard another group in the frozen forest, calling pitifully to each other. Lo An and Deng Wei looked at each other. He shook his head. They sat quietly by the coals of the fire, the revolver loose in Deng Wei's lap. The voices were gone quickly and not heard again.

The two of them lived in adequate circumstances, not always comfortable, but surviving. Deng Wei killed deer which provided not only meat but hides, which he cured with sea salt and brains and urine, then softened with a rubbing stone. The pelts made their bed warmer. From the exposed shores beyond their protected and iced-over cove they took seaweed and kelp that collected on the beach. When the tides were low they found shellfish and octopus. They caught an occasional fish. Spruce tea was their steady drink.

They spent the short daylight hours of the deep winter foraging for food, collecting firewood and improving their camp. In the evenings they sat in front of a small fire talking or just staring at the flames. When they'd crawled into their bed, they made love.

One day it just became spring. The heavy, depressive clouds were gone, washed into the north Pacific. The dawn was clear. The sun shined brightly for the first time since they'd been in the camp. It was magic, and every creature and plant rejoiced. Even the ice in the cove creaked and groaned.

They emptied their shelter of everything, dragging blankets and canvas, and pelts, and extra clothing, and even the branches of their bed and the top layer of dirt on the floor out into the sunlight. By midday it was even warm enough to strip themselves, and they did, two children in a sandbox. They bathed, then washed their clothes. They spent an hour just combing each other's long hair.

And they talked.

"Deng Wei, do you think we can go back to Canyon of Gold now?" The pregnant question had to be asked someday.

He was suddenly quiet, subdued.

"Deng Wei?"

"Do you want to rush back to that place, Lo An?" It was the first time they'd talked about the settlement, or about their lives there, or about the possibility of returning. They'd shunned the subject during the winter, as if speaking about it would have deepened the cold. "Do you want to go back, thinking we can just start again where we were before?"

"I... I hadn't thought very much about it. I don't know what I think."

"Well, I know what *I* think, Lo An." He was sitting on a chunk of log, had been sharpening the ax with a stone from the beach. Now he held his hands still, straightened his back so his long queue fell straight. "Can you really imagine going back there: the white man's coolie and the white man's whore again. Can you forget so easily? You want to start again like it was all just a bad dream? Look at us here..." He swept his arm around, then brought the stone in his hand back behind his ear and threw it toward the beach. There was challenge in the light of his eye and determination in the set of his head. "We're more than just alive, Lo An. We're *living!* And we're *free.* We don't have to bow to any warlord, white or Mandarin. We had nothing but we found everything. And we cared for each other."

She dropped her eyes and studied her hands in her lap. The sun sparkled through a tree and danced on her hair, dappling the dark cotton pants she wore. She was naked above them, her skin glowing in the sunshine. He knew he'd never seen such a beautiful woman.

"And our lovemaking? If we go back to Canyon of Gold do I have to ask Kai Win before I touch you? Do you crave his hairy hands again?"

She raised her head sharply.

"Well, do you? Is that what you want?"

She looked at him steadily, calming herself, then stood up in the sunshine. He almost cried at the sight of her, felt the swell of want pushing past the intensity of the questions they were struggling to answer.

"Deng Wei, I'll tell you honestly. I don't know what I want because I don't know what the choices are. We can't live here in this hole in the ground for the rest of our lives... Or maybe *you* can? I can't. I wasn't born in the wilderness like you." She paused,

70

looking down. "And I haven't felt the memory of Kai Win's hands…" She hugged her arms around herself and whirled in exasperation. "Oh, Deng Wei, I am happy with you." When she turned the sound of the shifting gravel beneath her feet was like music. He didn't say anything, sensing there was more. The ice shifted in the cove, melting. "I will stay with you if you want me, Deng Wei. I'll be your woman and you'll be my man, if you want." She looked at him and resolution was clear in her face and in her voice. "But not here. We can't be as we were before, it's true. But maybe we could find a way to live, to support ourselves, without having to be a coolie, or a whore. We have to go back and see. We can talk to Kai Win, see what things are like."

He knew it was necessary. "All right. We'll see."

They approached the settlement in the middle of March, though they had no calendar to verify the day. They were driven by a restlessness to see the face of fate, and the continuing mild weather seduced them. When Deng Wei recognized they were close to where the trees were cut back from the settlement he halted and they put their packs down. Although they carried most of their few belongings they'd left small things to provide a reason for their return to the cove. Their camp had been closed up, not abandoned. They could return to it. They had no idea what they faced in Canyon of Gold. "We're close, Lo An. Soon someone will see us. Are you sure you want to go on?"

"I think we have to. Do you?"

He'd wavered often. "Maybe not. What we may have owed Kai Win is paid. What Kai Win owed to us is paid. We've said we won't be their slaves again. Are you so sure they won't force us?"

"Yes, Deng Wei, I'm sure." There was no way she could be so certain. She didn't know any more than he did. "We'll just look, see what's happened to the others, explain to Kai Win about us. He saved us once. He won't harm us now."

"All right, but I wish I had your certainty." His mournful face drew her and she put her arms around him and pressed her face against his chest. His arms went around her and they held each other tightly, standing in the shaded forest. Then he sighed. They stood apart, shouldered their packs and went to see, hardly able to face each other.

The settlement hadn't changed as far as they could see. They looked first from the edge of the forest, then worked their way through the stumps and slag where trees had been cut for the mines, finally exposing themselves completely. It was midday. A high overcast dulled the sun. From the canyon came the distant noise of the stamp mill. Smoke climbed from chimneys.

"Look." Lo An pointed. In the channel a steamship swung gently at its anchor. Long boats full of men and supplies were ferrying back and forth through scattered chunks of rotten ice. Even from a distance of half a mile Deng Wei could see the workers were coolies. He and Lo An exchanged a glance. The presence of other Chinese in the settlement confused him. Were things just as they'd been? They'd only know by plunging on. "Come on," he said, stepping from behind the pile of brush that concealed them. "We'll go to Kai Win's house. He'll let us in."

Kevin Aspin's house looked the same, and there were footprints in the muddy path. They stood in front of the closed door. So far they'd seen nobody close enough to talk with. The people were all at their work. Lo An stepped up to the door, knocked twice on the boards and jumped back, startled, as the door was immediately jerked open from inside. It was dark in the house and they couldn't see who was there but they didn't have to wait long to find out.

A woman thrust herself through the door into the daylight. She was wearing Kai Win's clothes and her face was so much like his that for a moment Deng Wei was confused, knew Lo An must be also. It wasn't Kai Win, but who... The woman screeched, raised her finger and pointed it at Lo An. Her fingernails were long and broken and there was thick black dirt caked under them. "I know who *you* are," she shrilled. She advanced a step as Deng Wei and Lo An drew back, frightened of her madness. "You're that Chinese trollop everybody talked about. And *you,*" the grimy finger swung like a pistol barrel to Deng Wei, "you're Hongdong."

The hand fell back to her side and for a moment there was a flash of sanity in her eyes, then it was gone. She pursed her lips, purring to herself, shaking her head slowly from side to side. One hand went into her stringy hair, twirled strands around a finger. The focus left her eyes, then burned back. "Well, he's dead," she said. "He's dead and buried and you can't hurt him any more." Her arm fell and she found a wistful, curious look, put it on her face. Hair fell across her eyes and she brushed it away, distracted. "My brother Kevin's gone to his Maker, Lord be praised and have mercy on his soul, and the Lord God sent him straight to hell..." She trailed off into a secret world.

Deng Wei glanced at Lo An. He was about to ask her what was going on, what the hag was saying, when she started again, shaking her finger at Lo An and shrieking, "It's because of *you* and the *likes* of you that he's burning in the fires of damnation." She screamed the last words. She raised both her arms to the sky and then slowly lowered her right one, extended straight, rigid, the finger a lance pointed at Lo An's breast. "Out, Jezebel, out of my sight or I'll smite you with the righteousness of the Saved Ones of the Lord!" She whirled, ducked back into the house, reappeared with a broken-stock old rifle that even Deng Wei recognized as useless. The trigger was broken off, the hammer rusted to the receiver. Sawdust clogged the barrel. The witch in Kevin's clothes waved it at them and screeched, "Be *gone*, I say!"

Lo An started to say something but the woman shrieked again and advanced on her, the rifle held up as a club. Deng Wei stepped in front of her, shielding her, taking the woman's feeble blow on the shoulder, then he caught the rifle before she could lift it again and pulled it out of her hands. He threw it into the mud. The woman seemed to collapse inside Kai Win's clothes. Without moving, his feet spread in the mud and his body between her and Lo An, Deng Wei asked, "Is Kai Win dead?"

"Yes," Lo An answered from behind him in a tired voice, "at least this one says so. His sister, she says."

"Then come on, there's nothing for us here." He turned his back to the woman. Lo An started to protest, tried to say something around him to the woman, but Deng Wei put his hands on her, turned her around, pushed her toward the forest.

When they got to the trees they stopped, their energy sapped. Lo An leaned against a tree trunk, crying into her arm. Deng Wei just stood, looking back at the town. Finally she stopped, and sitting together on a fallen log they talked about what to do. She told him what the woman had said, and they sat thinking.

"Did she say how he died?"

"No."

"Do you believe he's dead?"

"Yes. No. Oh, Deng Wei, I don't know. She's crazy. But she's in his house. Even in his clothes. And there's no mistake, she has to be his sister, she looked so much like him. But she's so ugly…"

"Then there's only one more thing we have to do before we can leave. That paper Kai Win gave you. We have to know what to do about that, then we can decide where to go."

"Yes, I forgot about that. We'll see the government man, like Kai Win told us. He'll tell us why the crazy woman's in Kai Win's house."

The building they went to had a small sign lettered on a board, stuck like a grave marker in the yard. They went to the door and Lo An stepped forward and knocked.

"Come in, come in," the government man told them when he opened the door. He brushed a long-haired cat off one chair, took a thick book off another. He seemed to know right away who they were. Deng Wei could have been just another coolie in any of a thousand work camps from San Diego to Nome, but Lo An was memorable.

They sat in straight chairs in a small room with a cluttered desk, a wooden filing cabinet, a clothes tree. The magistrate was a middle-aged white man with sparse hair parted down the middle, greased and combed back on each side. His nose had at one time been broken and then pushed far to one side. Deng Wei couldn't take his eyes off it even when Lo An produced the paper and handed it over.

The magistrate studied the single page a moment, holding a thick round lens in front of one eye. Then he leaned back in his swivel chair and said, "Yes, Lo An, I know for a fact this paper was written and signed by Kevin Aspin. Just like it says, he wanted you to have everything he left, including that house his sister's in." He reached up with one hand and scratched the middle of his face where his nose should have been and Deng Wei was fascinated, trying to imagine where he felt the itch.

The magistrate looked again at the paper, then put it with the clutter on his desk and said, "Problem is, Lo An, it just ain't going to happen that way, no matter what he wanted. His sister showed up, as you probably found out." He waited for her to acknowledge the meeting, then went on.

Deng Wei sat silently, understanding nothing. Lo An would tell him. In the meantime he watched the nose, wondering how the man could breathe through it.

"She came in on the first ship that got through this spring, about a month ago. She was one of the *rescuers* sent by some mission. Town didn't need rescuing so much as it needed the food. They wasted space on the rescuers that could have gone to bacon and beans, ask me, for Christ's sake. People living on snowballs and pepper all winter… But that's aside the point. I'm here now and I'll tell you, I'm well aware what went on up here this winter. A Federal Marshal's just come in on that ship you saw unloading and there's going to be a report filed, I can tell you. Mighty unsavory thing, all right." He put his arms up, locked his fingers behind his head, leaned back until Deng Wei could look right up the nose. Lo An sat with her pack held in front of her knees, hands on top of it, watching him.

"Now I'll tell you, Lo An and, uh… Hongdong, right? I'll tell you what you might salvage out of this mess. Your friend Kevin Aspin went and got himself killed…"

"Killed?" Lo An said, her hand covering her mouth.

"Apparently so, Lo An. That's one of the things the Marshal's going to investigate, you can be sure. As far as we know somebody bashed his head, left him stretched on his bunk. 'Course he was froze before someone found him. Nobody knows who did it. There was bad times up here this winter…" He shook his head in sympathy with the sufferers.

Deng Wei prompted Lo An and she told him quickly about Kevin's murder.

The magistrate waited until she'd finished, then went on. "Anyway, for the here and now, Kevin Aspin went and left you a will you can't hope to get anything out of. Not with the dead man's only living relative sitting in his house, and her not too stable it would seem, and you being… Well, not a chance. But there is this…" He snapped forward, swiveled the chair, pulled a squeaking drawer out of the cabinet.

Deng Wei asked Lo An with a knitted face what was going on but she waved him off.

The magistrate turned, waving a piece of paper like he was airing it out. His other hand held a small pouch. He set that on the desk. "Before he died Kevin Aspin signed this over to you. It's dated and signed before he died, naturally," he smiled to himself at his little joke, "and so it's not covered in any will. It's incontestable. It's yours. Yours and Hongdong's." He held it out to Lo An and she took it.

Deng Wei knew Lo An could read a few simple words, but he could see this paper was entirely covered with scratching. He watched her shift her eyes back to the official, who said, "Of course, of course." The magistrate reached for the paper. He held it in one hand, the lens in the other, read it to himself, then he handed it back to her. "It's a deed, Lo An, a simple deed, and it's made out to you and Hongdong. It's for a small piece of land Kevin Aspin bought off an Indian, all legal like, name of, uh, let me see… ah, Albert Blake. It's over on Admiralty Island in a place called Cloud Bay, and it's yours. He told me about it once. Said it was a special little place. His word, I remember, 'special.' Now what do you think about that?"

It took a moment for the facts to settle in Lo An's mind, then she said, "Thank you. Please, may we talk, Deng Wei and I?"

"Sure, Lo An, talk away."

They sat in the magistrate's office speaking Chinese, back and forth. Spoken Chinese often sounds like an argument, even when it's not. The magistrate couldn't know who was arguing for what, but finally Deng Wei appeared to win something.

They were arguing, and Deng Wei did win. He told her, "Woman, there's nothing in this town for us. There's nothing for us anywhere except in that place on that piece of paper. This man says land is ours. Land! A place he says no person can take from us. By the rivers that flow through your body, woman, what more can you want?"

"OK, but where is that land? In the wilderness? Who knows if we can live there? Maybe it's a desert."

"It's not a desert. Kai Win chose it himself. He said it was special. And of course we can live there. Look what we've just lived through with almost nothing." Deng Wei was leaning forward so far on the chair in pursuit of his intensity he almost fell off. He caught himself by shifting to a hunched, standing position, raising his glance for a moment from Lo An's eyes. The white man was caught in his peripheral vision. Deng Wei turned to look at him and the nose grabbed his attention for a second. He lost his train of thought, sat back down, finally found the path of his thoughts again. "And what is a wilderness? Was this town civilized when the barbarians decided we weren't fit to share their food? Ha!" He almost spat on the magistrate's floor, caught himself. "Now I'll tell you, woman. You're as close to me as the blood in my kidneys. I don't know what my life would be like without you beside me, but I know what it's like to be a coolie in the white man's mine, and I won't do that. No more. I'll go to this place Kai Win gave us, even from his grave. I'll go there and make a home and then it won't be a wilderness any more."

Lo An sat quietly through the last part of their conversation, listening to him. Then she sighed, said, "And I'll go with you. You're right. And I... I didn't ever think I'd ever find a man like you."

There were some quiet moments punctuated only by the sounds of the ship unloading in the channel, an occasional shout, the noise of chugging machinery. Finally the magistrate cleared his throat and addressed Lo An. "Have you decided something?" he asked.

"Yes, we've decided to go to this place and live there," she answered. "Is there a house, do you know?"

"Not to my knowledge, Lo An, but there's bound to be lots of timber. Do you have any supplies?"

"No," she said, and smiled toward Deng Wei. "But this man's able to make supplies from nothing. We'll be fine." She meant it. "Is there a way we can go there?"

"Well, as a matter of fact this ship that's unloading now is going over to Sitka when she's empty. She'll pass right by the north end of Admiralty Island. That's the island where Cloud Bay is. Maybe the skipper would drop you off at the Indian village and you could walk in from there. Of course you'd have to pay passage, but…" He reached for the little deer skin pouch sitting on the desk, untied the mouth and poured half a dozen knuckle-sized nuggets of gold into the palm of his hand. He looked at them a moment, then extended them to Lo An. "Kevin left these for you. I don't know where he got them. They're what we call stranger-nuggets, not local gold. California maybe. Maybe Mexican. Quite a few people tried to make him tell where they came from, but as far as I know he never would. But never mind, they're still good as gold." He smiled again at his own wit and the nose slid toward his ear.

Fifteen minutes later Deng Wei and Lo An walked out of the magistrate's office. They were richer, and poorer by the cost of a small administrative fee, and husband and wife. Five days later they looked into a cove near the head of Cloud Bay at land that belonged to them. It was wilderness but they could make their home there – would make a home there, would raise their family there, perhaps begin a dynasty. Deng Wei and Lo An were both prepared to suffer and work hard. They knew about life and its struggles. And they'd heard from others about some of the monsters that would come to Cloud Bay.

7

At six years of age Tom Archer was grimy as a miner, scrawny, nearly dumb. He didn't begin to understand real human life, hadn't yet been exposed to any. His intellect was famished and his emotional core as hollow as the rotted foundation stumps of the Archer shack. He craved the sensation of a soft human touch but he didn't really know that because he'd never felt one, had never even seen one, and like a thin dusty puppy he edged close to the source of violence to solicit blows and kicks when the agonies of loneliness overwhelmed his spirit: abuse was attention, cruelty affection. He didn't even know he was lonely, couldn't know the paradox because he'd never experienced friendship. Tom Archer's childhood did nothing to prepare him for life, it only tenderized him for what was to come. The field was plowed for the planting of madness.

"Git in here and wash yourself," his mother commanded one morning. It was unusual but he did it anyway because she said to do it. "Put these clothes on. You're going to school." There'd been no anticipation; this was the first he'd heard about it. He didn't know what *school* meant and he didn't ask.

The walk down the dirt street to the schoolhouse was a journey across fabulous continents. He'd never before been out of the yard. He was forbidden to approach the gate; caught once with his hand on its latch when he was about four, he'd been beaten senseless by his enraged mother. Only the poverty of her strength kept him from permanent injury. That night after the mine shift he was hauled whimpering from his box in the alcove and mauled by his father, then again by his mother, then by both in impassioned concert. The cracked pelvis and torn ligaments he earned that night for his disobedience at the gate hurt him every day for the rest of his life and crabbed the quality of his walk.

He hadn't touched the gate again nor imagined life beyond the fence.

Now, as he scuttled down the road in his mother's dust the houses he'd seen before from behind the pickets of his yard suddenly took on different dimensions, with corners and windows and doorways in walls he hadn't known existed. The moon had another side. The schoolhouse, two stories high, was a palace. He'd never known a happier day.

After they'd sat awhile in the hallway the principal came out and said, "He'll have to wait 'til next year, Miz Archer. He may be six but his birthday's on the wrong side of the cutoff date." His mother said nothing, stood, walked out of the building. Tom followed. She took him back to the house, made him take off his shiny clothes and returned him, dazed, to exile in the yard. The experience taught him the length of a year, one day at a time. It was a lesson he was doomed to learn again, in a different kind of prison.

****

A Mexican came to Outcrop once. He stepped off the northbound bus on a dead morning. The sun had come up dirty and weak, would soon disappear after a short winter shift. The bus discharged the man and then farted pale blue fumes and clattered off. Three townsmen sat on a splintery bench near the garage, chewing, chafing their hands at a small coal glow in a frozen rut at their feet. They watched the Mexican turn one way, the other.

Tom Archer was walking up the road, a bucksaw in his hand; he'd seen a forked limb he wanted, would build an easel from it. He passed the Mexican, stopped when the man said, "Hola…" Tom turned to him. He'd never talked to a stranger: the road and all the people it carried traveled *through* Outcrop. "Yeah?" he answered. Beyond the Mexican he could see the three miners watching, spitting.

"Is one mine here?"

"Nothin' else."

The man nodded, as if he knew it, as if he knew about the world. "Is jobs? Is work?"

Tom didn't have to think. "No. Ain't none." He glanced toward the three men, back at the Mexican. "You shouldn't have stopped here, Mister. Th'ain't no work here. Nothin' for you. You better move on out." He tossed his jaw northward.

The Mexican hung his head, then picked it up, swiveled it slowly past the shantied rows of clapboard buildings, toward the three men on the bench. No humanity obscured the situation. A hostile breeze shoved bitter air down his neck, past his worn collar. He shrugged himself tighter into his poor coat, nodded at Tom. "Si. I know. But maybe…"

Tom glanced again at the three men. Two of them were standing, humping their shoulders, stamping worn leather against the hard earth. "Listen, Mister, I'm tellin' you, you'd better head on out'a here." He pointed in the direction the bus had taken. The road disappeared beyond tumbledown shacks, turning up around the grimy, flat-lighted hill that covered the coal vein. "You better walk right on out that'a way. Th'ain't nothin' for you here, and maybe you'll get hurt if you don't leave. Unerstan'? Go on now, git." He tossed the man's attention north with his free hand. "Go on, git."

82

The Mexican delayed, his desperation an anchor. A scuffle behind made him turn. One of the men there was busting a chunk of hard mud from a rut, kicking it with his heel. Another had a short stick held like a tool in his hand, was shambling forward. The stranger threw a quick plea toward Tom as if the two of them had had a real conversation, as if their brief eye contact made them brothers or at least accomplices, but Tom wouldn't meet his look again, was already backing away. The Mexican put his feet in motion, slowly at first, then he saw the third man rise heavily off the bench and he began scurrying off behind the stink of the bus.

Tom watched him for a second – later he'd sketch the man's aquiline face from memory – then glanced toward the settling miners, then continued up the road. The fact he'd saved a man's health, probably his life, didn't touch his sensibilities or bolster his conscience. In fourteen years of life he'd only seen three people who weren't white skinned and one of those was a bruised black corpse. "Ain't no place for 'em here," people always said, and Tom knew it was true.

****

Tom Archer's life in Outcrop slogged past with single, synonymous purpose: to stay out of the mine, to remain in school. Nobody pushed him one way or the other except his parents. There wasn't a shortage of workers to feed into the maw in the hill so no pressure from the Company compelled him to take up the burden of his heritage until he was ready. He knew he could go there any time, could draw small pay, could hack the soft black rock from the outcrop until he died, but he refused. His parents hawked the thick spit of rebuke at him but he'd learned to ignore them, as they had ignored him until his appetite demanded a full share of their food. The simple, twisted codes that ruled their lives forced them to give him shelter but they fed him niggardly and poisoned his share of their lives with resentment. "You're trash, boy…"

School was his only haven against them and that sucking black hole in the hill and Tom was smart enough to know it. He wouldn't quit it until they kicked him out. He knew there was a law on his side and he hunkered in the shelter of the school like a trapped miner in a bolt-hole.

He was seventeen before a person who desired him arrived in his life. He'd never had the opportunity to learn the difference between lust and longing so he wasn't prepared for the onslaught of desire.

He'd had a girlfriend for a while. He and the girl had kissed with the outsides of their lips and he'd fondled her breasts behind the machine shop and she made him cum once, rubbing him through his pants, but then she told him one of her girlfriends said if she got any jisim on her it'd make her pregnant. After that she wouldn't let him touch her, and shortly after that Mr. Banning arrived.

Paul Banning was hired at midyear to teach Tom and the six other students of Outcrop's upper school. His subjects were arithmetic, geography, grammar, art and history.

Tom couldn't figure, and couldn't envision other lands, couldn't focus on the rules of speech or the ancient failings of long-dead men, but he knew his drawings were good and he knew they impressed Mr. Banning. All his pictures were bundles of broad charcoal strokes – like stick scratches in the dirt: broken-down fences, crushers and sorters, rotting automobiles and machinery, tailings. Grim, helmeted faces rising from the shafts, adumbral, all lines and shadows. Pinched women with haunted faces.

"Tom, there's an art festival in Tacoma next weekend. Would you like to go?" It was a spring day. "You can take twenty drawings, and they'll go up on the wall of the gallery, and it's a good chance for you. What do you say?" Mr. Banning fancied

84

himself an athlete and he punched Tom in the biceps, a playing field gesture that said, "Come on, guy, you can do it."

"Aw, Mr. Banning, I don't know." He wanted to rub the bone of his arm, but wouldn't.

"Well what do you know then? You want to live forever in this nowhere hole?" It was rumored Mr. Banning hadn't ended up in their town solely because he imagined it a nice place to live but Tom didn't understand the gist of the rumors so he ignored them. Now he hung his head and scuffed his foot and sucked the side of his cheek. The largest parts of him were his elbows and his hands. The rest of him was slight. There'd never been such a thing as seconds on the Archer table. "You planning to live behind the stove in that shack the rest of your life? Going down the mine pretty soon?"

Tom scratched at the precocious stubble in the dimple on his bony chin. If he'd ever drawn himself, a self-portrait – he never did – he'd have noticed something called aestheticism in the planes of his face. His brow was a little heavy but he knew he wasn't a stupid boy. The desert days of his childhood had been watered by the wonders of school. He'd learned to talk and to read, and to draw on real paper, and the magic of all that had stripped away some of the sullen overburden on his personality. Yet still, behind the black penetrating eyes there was caution, a picket fence of memories that held him back and made him only suspicious instead of curious. If he wasn't whole it wasn't his fault. He'd never, not even for a second, felt the warm breath of real human love and in consequence he was doomed to the emptiness of a life spent for its own sake. He had no defense now against the whimsical urgings of others, and so would have none later against the hot compelling drives of his own madness.

Mr. Banning pushed him. "You think you're going to have the time and the energy to draw once you start working in that mine like everybody else? You see many miners rushing home at night so they can paint pictures or write books or things like that?" He knuckled Tom's arm. "I thought you told me you wanted to work for a publishing house in the city, draw pictures for books. What happened to that, huh?"

Tom knew he could do it. "Yes sir, that's what I want to do, Mr. Banning. I been through every book in the li-bary, looking at pictures. I kin do that. I kin draw pictures good as that. Easy."

Mr. Banning encouraged him. "But," Tom heard him say, "you've got to become known to get a job like that. You've got to show people you can draw. This exhibit's just a one-day thing but lots of people will see it. Would it help if I talked to your parents?"

Tom looked at Mr. Banning with eyes that could have attracted any of the few girls in school except that they took light in, didn't let any back out. "That don't matter. How much it gonna' cost?"

"It won't cost you anything, Tom. The school art fund will pay for our bus tickets, and we can both stay at my brother's place. He and his wife want us to. We'll get back late Sunday night. Well, what do you say? You got twenty drawings?" He must have known Tom did.

******

They met Saturday morning in front of Harper's Garage, where the bus stopped. Tom had twenty of his favorite pictures in an old cardboard suitcase he'd found one day on the street and fixed up. He had a change of clothes in a small cloth sack. On his head was a flat workman's cap. It was a warm, early April day. Mr. Banning showed up in a tie, a dusty carpetbag in his hand, adventure in his smile.

When they got off the bus in Tacoma – whirling sounds and sights – they made their way through working pedestrians to a general dry goods store and post office branch where Mr. Banning said there'd be a telephone. "I'll tell my brother we're in town and on our way, Tom. You hang out here. I'll be right back." He went into the store.

Tom stood with their luggage on the narrow walk. It was almost noon and his stomach rumbled. He could hardly ever get enough in his belly these days. He wondered what they'd eat at Mr. Banning's brother's house. He'd never been a guest at someone's house. All around him pedestrian traffic bumped and elbowed, vehicles honked in the street, horses clip-clopped, people talked. It was all new and grand and he felt a warm rush of affection for Mr. Banning, who'd made this possible. It wasn't a known feeling and the heat of it flushed his face.

"Tom, I got bad news for us but we'll survive it. Seems we can't stay where we planned. The nephew's got measles and the house is quarantined. We'll have to stay in a hotel. Come on, grab your stuff." Mr. Banning picked up his carpetbag and headed off, leaving Tom no chance to reply. He led him down one street after another, onto a trolley, off again and down several more streets, around corners. The town really wasn't much, but Tom looked at everything. Three times Mr. Banning had to come back and take him by the elbow. "Come on, Tom. I'm starved. We'll get where we're going and then eat and then look around. Lots of time for that. Keep up now."

When they arrived at the Seaview Hotel Mr. Banning stopped. Tom was looking around and ran into him. "Sorry," he said, having banged his suitcase into the back of the teacher's leg.

"Wow, Tom, you're dangerous. I'd better not let you out of my sight if you're going to be so goggle-eyed."

"Well, I never been here before, that's all. Is this where we're staying?" He looked up at the brick and board front of the four-story hotel.

"Yeah. It's not very luxurious but it hasn't got any bedbugs. I know this neighborhood. It's not too bad. We can get whatever we want around here." There was a glint in his voice.

Tom hung his head. "Well, I'll tell you, Mr. Banning. I weren't figuring on having to come up with no money for no hotel, what with your brother's place and all… How much it gonna cost to stay here?"

"Tom, don't worry about it. It's my fault we got stuck like this. I'm sure as hell not going to sleep in the street and I can afford a room in a hotel for one night so there's no sense you sleeping in the street either. Now come on. And try not to beat me to death with that suitcase of yours." He laughed. "When you get your pictures up on that wall tomorrow people will probably roll all over themselves to give you money for them so don't worry about a thing."

"You really think that'll happen?"

"Sure it will, Tom. If not tomorrow, then another day. Come on, let's get checked in."

Their room was on the third floor, which was higher above the ground than Tom had ever been. He entered hesitantly behind Mr. Banning, his eyes moving constantly.

There were two iron beds with lumpy mattresses and thin comforters. Mr. Banning pointed. "You take that one, Tom." He threw his own carpetbag and cap on the one nearest the window and sat, hallo-ing when the bed squeaked under his weight. "I hope your squeaking doesn't keep me awake all night," he said, laughing and loosening his tie. There was a porcelain spittoon peeking from under the bed. He leaned over to look at it, scrunched his face in disgust, edged it carefully under the bed and out of sight with his heel.

A window with musty grey lace curtains framed a view of bricks – the side of the building across the alley. Tom put his cloth sack and suitcase down at the foot of his bed, then stood in front of the window, pulled the curtain aside, craned his head around, looking. The grimy window was swollen shut. There wasn't any sea view. He turned back, surveyed the room. Against the wall between the heads of the beds a ceramic lamp with a yellowed shade brooded in the center of a discolored doily. One leg of the small disreputable lamp table was splinted with rusty wire and the whole thing leaned against the wall like a wounded soldier. A green metal-shaded bulb glowered from the middle of the ceiling. Beneath the window a peeling radiator squatted, dissolute and wrinkled. There was a faded picture of a pasture on the wall opposite the beds and beneath it a cracked marble-top stand with an enamel basin and an open pitcher. A moth fluttered in circles on the dusty surface of the water. A single striped towel hung on a brass hook screwed into the wooden side of the stand and a tall mirror, brown around its unframed edges, pressed tiredly against the wall.

"There's a bath and a toilet down the hall," Mr. Banning said, pointing in the direction where it'd be. "Don't get lost."

Tom turned. "Aw, I won't, Mr. Banning. If it's anything like our closet at home I kin find it by the smell. And your squeaking'll get me back."

At that Mr. Banning threw himself back, moving his hips roughly up and down, jerking his fist in the air and wringing great metallic shrieks from the bed. They both laughed. "There sure won't be any secrets in here tonight," he said.

"Heck," Tom replied, his eyes on the wide floorboards, "a person like *you* wouldn't have no secrets like that, anyway."

"Don't be too sure of it, Tom." Mr. Banning sat up, swung his feet to the floor between the beds and dragged his small carpetbag next to his hip. He opened it, rummaged for a moment, brought out a large silver flask with a dark leather cover. "Ah…" he exclaimed, partly in anticipation of the contents, perhaps, but as much to get Tom's attention. He unscrewed the lid and raised it to his lips, poured a good slug down his throat. "Here," he said, holding the opened flask toward Tom, who sat on the other bed facing him, "have a belt. It'll fortify you for what's to come and for the world at large. "But first…" He withdrew his offer, put the flask to his own lips again. "Now," he said with a gasp, "your turn. I had to make double-sure it wasn't poison." He giggled, gave a slight shudder. "It *is*. Go ahead." He shook the flask slightly at Tom.

"Aw gee, Mr. Banning, I don't know…"

"I'll tell you what," the teacher thumped the flask on Tom's knee and a small squirt of whisky jumped out and landed on his hand. "Why don't you call me Paul while we're here, long as we're roommates for the weekend. Hell, when you're a famous book illustrator I want to tell folks I knew you back when, on a first-name basis. Tell them you and I used to tear the town up together before you got rich and famous. Go ahead, have a slug." He proffered the flask again. "I won't tell folks you took it if you don't tell them I offered it."

"Heck, Mr. Banning…"

"Paul…"

Tom hesitated, then took the flask Paul Banning still pressed to his knee. "Well… Paul… I guess I might as well." He saluted with the flask and raised it to his lips for a tentative swig, then a heavier one.

Paul gave Tom's knee a light slap. "Good man. Let the party begin," he said, taking the flask and raising it to his own lips again. "OK, now we've worked up an appetite, what say we wash some of that road dust off and get something to eat. I'm about half hungry. You?"

"Oh, heck yeah. My big gut's like to eat my little one."

There was a small restaurant just next door. It was mid-afternoon and they were the only customers. Paul ordered pea soup and a sandwich, Tom ate a piece of meat loaf and a potato and a salad, exclaiming over the fresh greens.

When they'd finished and Paul had paid he said, "Let's walk it off a little, and then I fancy another snort and a short nap, get me ready for the *night time.*"

"What's the *night time?*" Tom asked.

"The *night* time. You know, darkness, city comes to life, music and gaiety and those sorts of things. You know?"

"Well, not exactly,: Tom replied. He didn't know at all. "Ain't much of that in Outcrop, if you'll recollect."

"*Isn't* much of that. But we're going to make up for it tonight. What say, you game to paint the town a little?"

Tom walked beside his teacher, trying to concentrate on the assaulting sights and sounds and listen to Paul at the same time. They were walking down a wooden sidewalk along shop fronts, stepping down to cross dirt alleys at the end of each block, dodging aside to let other people pass, stopping to look in windows. It wasn't a crowded street but to Tom it was the rest of the world. He tried to focus on what Paul was telling him but it was difficult. "Sure," he answered, "whatever you say, Mr. ... uh, Paul."

They made a circuit of several blocks around their hotel, then climbed to their room again. Paul joked with the clerk at the desk as they went up. "If any messages come from Paris for me, tell them to call back tomorrow." He laughed, taking Tom by the arm and heading for the stairs. The desk man watched them go, shook his head.

"Well, I'm for a couple hours of shut-eye, Thomas," Paul said, sitting on the edge of his bed and pulling his shoes off. He flopped back, then sat up again and flipped the end of the thin comforter so it covered his stockinged feet, then lay back down. "This pillow feels like it's stuffed with broken bricks, but never mind. We can rest up some, then head out and see what's what in this metropolis."

"Sounds good to me," Tom said, taking his cue from Paul. He stretched out but couldn't fall asleep right away, even after Paul had. When he finally did his sleep was filled with the noise and rush of crowds.

****

A blaring auto horn woke them. Paul looked at the watch he wore strapped to his wrist in the style that had become popular during the recent war. "Five-fifteen," he said, stretching, kicking the comforter off his feet. "We 'bout slept the night away, Tom." He swung around, facing the window, his back to Tom, his feet on the floor. He rubbed his face, lifted his arm to smell his pit. "Whew. I don't know how I've stood myself so long." He turned to look over his shoulder at Tom, who was still supine on the bed. "I'm going to see how well that bath down the hall works. If it'll work for me it'll work for anybody. Then, watch out Tacoma-town, 'cause here we come." He swung his legs around and over the bed, reached down and pulled the flask out of his bag. "But first…" He swished a mouthful of the whisky in his cheeks, gargled, choked noisily and almost lost it. "Ahhh," he said at last, "feels so good to have clean teeth again. Want a slug?"

Tom waved him off, declining. "No thanks. But after I get clean, I might."

When both of them had bathed, which turned out to be easy, with a separate spigot for hot water coming from a boiler in the basement, they sat again on their beds, facing each other. "Well, what do you fancy first? Some chow?" Paul asked.

"Sure. We gonna eat at the same place again?"

"Naw, let's broaden our horizons. There's a couple places I know not far from here. We can walk. How's this sound? We get some groceries in our bellies, then poke around a couple of spots I know, see what's going on. I ought to be able to find us a bit of music and some company, even." He winked lasciviously. "Who knows what the night will bring, eh?"

92

Tom quizzed his expression, tilting his head, then the implications of what Paul was saying dawned on him and he smiled, showing crooked yellow teeth. "Yeah," he answered, "who knows?"

Paul said, "In the morning…" he gave an exaggerated wink, "if there *is* a morning tomorrow…" he screwed his face into a satyric mask and moved his fist up and down vigorously against the top of his thigh, eliciting a suddenly knowing look from Tom, "we'll go to the bookstore where the exhibit is. We'll have to be there bright and early but tonight we might as well shoot up the town. What do you say?"

"I say why not?" Tom answered, completely willing to follow Paul's lead.

"Good boy," Paul said, reaching for his carpetbag on the end of the bed and dragging it to him. He unbuttoned the flap and reached in without looking, his hand going directly to a small leather pouch. He pushed the carpetbag back and opened the pouch with his forefingers and thumbs. The bag seemed to open almost of its own volition as soon as the draw-cord was loosened. From it he produced a small wooden pipe and a flat Prince Albert tobacco can. He put them both carefully on the bed beside him and smoothed the leather pouch on his lap, like a napkin at a fancy restaurant.

Tom sat watching quietly.

Paul looked up once from his tasks and grinned, saying nothing. Shifting himself on one hip so he could get his fingers into the tight front pocket of his trousers, he produced a small flat penknife. Then he picked up the Prince Albert can and flipped open the hinged lid with his thumbs. He looked inside and smelled the contents and smiled as if a tiny person stood inside smiling back at him. Then into his palm he spilled a small brownish-black chunk.

"What's that?" Tom asked, leaning forward, looking.

"That's wacky-backy, my son, and it'll make Tacoma look like Venice and the least of them all the fairest, believe me." He looked up from his work. "Want to try some?"

"Oh, I don't know, Mr. Banning…" He shook his head hesitantly to one side, the newly unfolding wonders of the world flying quickly in his face.

"Paul."

Tom jabbed the air with his fist, having forgotten again to respect their new relationship. "Oh, yeah, I'm sorry."

"Well, you want some? It'll do you a world of good, for sure."

"Oh, I don't know… I never been a smoker…"

Paul chuckled. "That's OK. You don't smoke this stuff, Tom, you just take a good puff and hold it in your lungs for awhile." He cut a curly sliver off the chunk and pushed it off the knife blade into the bowl of the pipe with his thumbnail. He put the chunk and penknife down on the doily by his elbow and struck a big wooden match against the steel bedpost. The match strobed in the dimly lit room and the sulphur stung Tom's nostrils. It was dark outside, the single window like a black, quartered painting on the wall. Paul held the match close against the bowl of the pipe until the flame reached his finger, sucking, greedy, his eyes nearly closed.

Tom watched, fascinated. After a few moments Paul breathed out and looked lovingly at the pipe in his hand. There was a strong acrid fragrance in the room now and Tom liked it. "Maybe I will try a couple of puffs of that, if you don't mind. I might as well, huh?"

Paul looked at him, then slowly reached for his penknife. "Yes, you might as well."

Paul helped him, cutting a piece of the hash into the pipe, holding a match to the glowing little chunk in the bowl while Tom inhaled, coughed, inhaled again. Their knees touched between the beds as they leaned toward each other in the smoking ritual. "I don't know what it's supposed to do," Tom said after he'd gotten the last of the smoke from the pipe, "but it sure does taste good, don't it?"

"You bet."

"Maybe I should try some more, do you think?"

"Well, actually," Paul said, smiling benignly while he replaced his paraphernalia in the leather pouch, "you probably had enough there for a healthy two-hundred pound Turk. This is pretty good stuff, straight from Asmara, and you don't want to go overboard. At least not right yet." He gave Tom a significant look, studying him. "I'll tell you what. Let's go find something to eat and get our evening rolling." He giggled.

"Oh, I don't think I could eat a thing," Tom said, and he laughed, fascinated at the way his tongue touched the back of his teeth when he said *thing*. He said it again. *Thing*. He laughed again, slapping his knee.

Paul was smiling clear across the width of his face. "Don't you worry a bit about that, my boy. In a couple minutes you'll be hungry enough to eat a frozen dog."

That was enormously funny and they laughed, Tom too loudly, Paul with little chuckling sounds, almost under his breath. His friendly eyes watched Tom closely.

****

They made it out onto the street after about an hour, both of them stoned but mobile. An ignorant observer would have noticed their artificial hilarity, their sudden seriousness, their missed steps, and would have looked twice, figuring they'd been tippling before supper. They had a meal, which seemed to take forever to come from the kitchen, in a small café down the street from the hotel. They both ate ravenously: fried chicken, potatoes mashed with the skins still on, carrots cut into thick disks, and at Paul's insistence, several cups of black coffee. "It wouldn't do for you to fall asleep too early tonight, Thomas my boy, believe me," he said.

When they finished their meal they walked through poor, poorly-lit streets but Tom didn't notice the general air of disrepute through which they moved. He was wholly animated now, pointing out the sights to Paul as they walked. There weren't many other people on the street but to Tom it was a bustling metropolis. And being stoned amplified every sound and image. They clumped down a street lined with pool halls and rough-looking people, passing unmolested, everybody looking down-headed at everybody else, all knowing in this part of town you minded your own business, kept your hands on your wallet, and found your pleasure only after you'd paid for it.

"Are you excited about the show tomorrow?" Paul asked as they strolled down the broken, crusted sidewalk. There was a nervous corner in his voice.

"Yeah, sure," Tom answered, giggling uncontrollably.

"Did you ever draw a woman?" The question slid out like a mugger from an alley.

"Sure, lots of 'em."

"No, I mean a real woman. All of her."

"Oh," Tom replied, stepping off the sidewalk into the street and looking at Paul. "You mean with no clothes on her?"

Paul sniggered, covered his mouth with his hand. "Yeah."

"No," tom answered, his eyes shining now, "never did."

"Bet you never even seen one. *Saw* one."

Tom drew his heavy eyebrows together as if he'd have to stop and think whether he'd ever seen a naked woman, and then grinned. "Nope. Never did."

"Well, would you like to? Draw one, I mean."

"Sure. Why not?"

"Come on, then."

They marched off, suddenly straight, each of them on a common but separate mission. Tom's trust was complete.

Paul guided them to a Chinese restaurant, small but not crowded. The hazy single room was stuffy with the smells of ancient grease and Oriental herbs. They sat in rickety chairs at a back corner table. A battle-worn rat trap lurked in armed certainty at the angle of floor and walls, its pan baited with a piece of slimy pork. The waiter was a middle-aged Chinese man with a large goiter under his chin.

"Bring us two cups of tea," Paul told him briskly. "And tell Anthony to come here." The man grunted and walked away, then reappeared with two chipped porcelain glasses of indeterminate color and a stained pot with dirty steam oozing from its spout.

Paul poured jasmine-flavored liquid into both glasses and pushed one toward Tom, who sat watching the other occupants of the room in fascination. He'd never been this close to Chinese before, though he'd seen several on the street outside, in passing. In Outcrop they weren't allowed. Same with Nigras and Jews and red Indians and Mexicans.

Before they finished their first glass of tea a slight Chinese boy with very distinctive Oriental eyes pushed through the greasy beaded curtain that served as a kitchen door. He came over to their table. He looked once at Tom then stood smiling in front of Paul.

"This is Anthony," Paul said to Tom, and then he stood up next to the Chinese boy and turned so their conversation would be private. Tom couldn't hear what they were saying but at one point he saw Paul take some money out of his pocket and hand it to Anthony, who nodded, smiling, and left, having said little. He looked at Tom as he went back toward the kitchen curtain, a lingering, measuring look. He smiled about secret knowledge, perhaps other things as well.

"OK, it's all set up," Paul said. "We've got about an hour so we'll finish our tea and then head back for the room and see what happens." He picked up his tea glass and held it out toward Tom, a toasting motion. "And I'm ready for another touch of the wacky-backy."

Tom was a willing participant in the whole evening, had already decided Paul was his big brother, worthy of respect. And Paul was a likeable guy. He'd always gone out of his way to talk to Tom, to exclaim over his drawings. Those, Tom knew, were worth exclaiming over. He knew he was good at drawing.

He had actually drawn a naked woman once, from a picture postcard one of the other kids owned. The boy's uncle had brought it back from France, after the war. Tom had rented the postcard for one night from the kid and had sat in his alcove staring at it for an hour before he'd put it away in a school book. Then he'd drawn it from memory, a woman's bare back, thick at the waist, the backs of her arms white and smooth, the tip of one breast peeking out. When he finished he compared his drawing with the postcard and felt the flush of satisfaction, knowing he had talent in his hands and in his eyes and in his memory, for seeing things. Later that night, the quiet of the shack broken only by the crackling of cooling coal in the stove and the heavy breathing of his sleeping parents, he felt another kind of satisfaction, the gush at his groin.

As he and Paul walked back to their hotel the remembrance of that postcard and the anticipation of what might happen this night flushed his face and thickened the bulge at his crotch, and he felt again a hot, brotherly affection that included Paul but somehow reached even beyond, was more encompassing. It was a feeling that included excitement, that challenged the tight confines of convention.

Tom washed his face in the basin while Paul loaded his pipe.

"Here," Paul grunted through clenched lips, smoky breath captured deep in his lungs. He held the pipe out toward Tom.

This time they reloaded it twice and when they'd finished Tom's head reeled. He loved it: the smell, the taste, the sensation of flying in his mind. He loved the feelings of warmth it gave him for his friend. He almost wanted to cry with it.

"You better get your drawing stuff ready." Paul was leaning back against the head rail of his bed. He'd kicked his shoes off and was rubbing the sole of one foot up and down against the blanket.

Tom struggled to concentrate. Finally he remembered Paul had spoken and said, "I didn't bring much. Just a pencil and a small pad." *Pad* sound funny in his ears and he giggled.

"Well, everything you got, you better get ready." Paul drew his knees up and stretched, then threw his arms and legs out like an upended tortoise, shaking them and laughing, "because you're gonna need everything you got in that pencil of yours tonight, for sure."

They were both laughing when a knuckle sounded on their door. "I'll get it," Paul said, swinging his stockinged feet toward the floor. Tom sat expectantly on the edge of his bed.

Anthony stood at the door.

"Come in, come in," Paul said effusively, with the overstated gestures of a butler at a ritzy club. Anthony took two steps into the room, looked around, then turned and said something in Chinese toward the door. At his command a Chinese girl in a quilted coat stepped into the room. Below the hem of the coat Tom, who watched her intently, could see a plain brown dress.

In English Anthony said, "This Gloria. She my numba-one sister." He turned to Tom, then to Paul, and swept his arm toward the girl.

Tom stood unsteadily as she walked through the doorway. Gloria was the most beautiful creature he'd ever seen. Her hair was a shining fall reaching almost to her hips. Dark heavy waves. With an artist's eye he admired the smooth lines of her round face, the small mouth, the curve of her chin. It hadn't yet occurred to him to wonder about the rest of her. She kept her head down slightly, her eyes coy, averted, angled toward Anthony as if watching for instructions.

Tom was hooked.

Paul watched Tom assess the girl, his own eyes moving from Tom to Gloria, to Anthony, watching them all. He was grinning. "OK, everybody," he said, closing the door, locking it and crossing in front of Anthony and Gloria to reach for his carpetbag, "let the party begin." He produced the silver flask with the dark leather cover, unscrewing its top and holding it like an offering toward the sky. "But first, a touch of a toast..." He waved the flask to encompass them all. "To the artist and his subject." He bowed dramatically toward Tom and Gloria and then helped himself to a good slug from the flask. "Ahhh," he said, holding it out toward Tom, "and don't worry about draining it, there's more where that came from."

Tom was already flying from the hash but wanted to refuse nothing his friend was promoting this night. He knew he was in good hands. He helped himself to the whisky, then, gasping at its harshness, passed the flask to Anthony, who helped himself and passed it on to Gloria. Tom was surprised at that but Gloria tilted the flask as eagerly as the rest of them.

"All right," Paul said enthusiastically, thickness like tar in his voice. He gestured toward Gloria, moved over next to her, put his hands out above her shoulders to take her coat. "Gloria, you're the beautiful flar... *flower* with us terr-ble thorns tonight. We better get you comf-tible... *comfortable*... and let the party begin, right?"

****

When Tom Archer woke up he was lying on his bed. His head was spinning and the tastes on his tongue were thick and bitter. The bulb in the ceiling and the small lamp on the stand between the beds were out but there was light coming through the shade drawn over the window. Anthony was lying next to him, awake. He was looking at Tom and his Oriental face was burned forever onto the screen of Tom's memory. It was the kind of look Tom knew he'd worn himself years before when he'd caught a cat squatting, wetting the fine dirt of his playground under the porch. He knew the look and the carnal feel of it, knew what it meant. As he watched Anthony now he could remember the same leer on his own face as he proved his place in creation by squeezing the life from the small thing in his hands. It was the ancient, sordid mask of secret, shared knowledge and it said, "Now you belong to me…"

No!

He heard a sound and turned toward the other bed, his brain loose in his skull, grating. Gloria was on her back, her head turned toward him, her eyes on him. The expression on her face was the one captured on the pad on the floor. Paul was kneeling above her. She never looked away from Tom and the expression on her face never changed.

"*No!*" He tried to cry again but it was only a sound in his whirling head. Then the Chinese boy's hands were there and they were suddenly alone in the world and Tom's voice and his denial and his struggle were all no more than a consenting moan.

****

For days Tom suffered the physical effects of his debauchery. His whole lower back hurt as if he'd poisoned his kidneys, or been punched. His tongue felt swollen and his nasal passages and lungs burned. In the back of his throat he could taste the bile of vomited whisky and on his memory forever was a coppery taste and every breath carried the smell of the smoke, and of other things.

There'd been no art show but Tom barely knew that, lost it in the storms of his mind. He didn't hold that against Banning. He didn't think about Banning at all. He tried to think about Gloria, wanted to desperately, but he couldn't. Even when he looked at the sketch he'd made of her and felt himself thickening, it was the Chinese boy, Anthony…

No!

But still the images and the memories came back to him in the darkness of his nights and tricked his body and it responded until his father heard his noise and yelled through the thin wall, "You lay still, you trash. And quit poundin' yourself."

Days shuffled past like drunks. He went to school but barely knew it, was jostled in the hall by strangers he'd known before, spoke, when forced, from a daze. His mind was a dark spinning pool, turning back and back again into itself, same-faced images floating up from black nowhere like wispy, half-seen ghouls in dreams, compelling, crooning and calling, tearing at him, too horrible to confront but irresistible. In the private places where he sought refuge they hounded him like the soldiers of an evil curse, overwhelming his feeble resistance, driving him into hot, flashing, gushing relief that left him shuddering, a slave to his weakness. With shamed groans and shudders he shook them from his consciousness, squeezed his eyes shut against them and willed them to leave him alone but they wouldn't. Like the sins of fathers.

Their faces were one, always the same, contorted, lustful, heaved back in neck-stretched ecstasy, lips parted, glistening with the sweat and the juices and he knew the face was a mirror and he threw his head aside and denied it all, "No!" And the faces, all the faces, the one single face, was Chinese. In the dark sexual fog of Tom Archer's confusion bitterness became a bridge over the awesome morass of his guilt, and on the other side he saw the refuge of hate, and when he got there he wrapped himself in the protective cloak of bigotry, a shroud he'd wear through all the miseries of his life and finally to Cloud Bay.

8

The waters had been their deepest blue, the Southeast Alaska sky bright to its most spectacular depths when Lo An and Hong Deng Wei stepped off the steamship at Wrengoon, the Indian village on Admiralty Island. Then in two days of hard bargaining they'd traded much of their gold for a rowing and sailing skiff with two good oars, a so-so spare oar, a mast and a small patched sail, another ax, a small drift net for fishing, some used cooking utensils, a Swedish saw with two extra blades, varied lengths of rope, a large sack of rough salt and enough preserved foodstuffs to keep them going for a couple of weeks. Deng Wei had wanted to buy a rifle but none of the Indians had a decent one to sell for what he wanted to pay. The pistol would have to do. One of the Indians had bullets that fit, and Deng Wei haggled with him until a price was settled. The Indians were surprised at Deng Wei's bargaining skill: they wanted all the gold he had, but were disappointed in that, and he kept some in the little deer pouch, never actually showing them how much he had left, though they tried to see. He wondered if they were acquisitive over gold. Who wouldn't be?

While they were in the village the Indians clustered, curious but showing something besides, as well. They weren't openly hostile but there was an undercurrent of resentment Lo An could feel. Deng Wei admitted that he noticed it too. A white person might not have registered the subtle nuances but Chinese and

Indians aren't different in many ways and the newly married couple sensed some opposition to their settling on the island, even though the small parcel of land in the bay down the coast was grudgingly but officially recognized as theirs. Nothing was overt, however – they eventually learned nothing is *ever* overt among Indians – and they managed to acquire what they needed to survive. Whatever qualms the Indians apparently had about their presence was reduced by the color of the gold nuggets in Deng Wei's outstretched palm, though not without some serious counsel among the Indians, none of which Deng Wei or Lo An could understand.

Their first sight of their own land, in a small cove, was a quieting, long-lived moment. They sat in reverent silence in the skiff, allowing the tide to push them toward a small pebble beach cut by a stream running from the forest. They could see good timber, a profusion of blueberry bushes. The land that formed the cove was flat enough to build on yet high enough above the beach so storms wouldn't wash them away. There was a heavily pocked tidal mud flat where the collective suck of breath from huge colonies of clams and cockles bubbled like foam. Behind their land and around them on the other side of the bay mountains rose protectively. It was all astoundingly beautiful.

"Oh, Deng Wei," Lo An said, astonished at their fortune, "it *is* special, just as Kai Win said."

Their small boat bobbed, nudged against the beach, grounded, and the Hongs were home.

Life wasn't easy at first. They had no shelter. Unlike the crab-shaped cove where they'd wintered, here there weren't even the leavings of an old hunting camp. They spent the first night sleeping under the boat, which they dragged up into a small clearing Deng Wei cut next to the stream. Propped against a tree stump, the hull at least separated them from the open sky. The sun set late, rose early.

The next day while Lo An was crouched over the stream getting water and Deng Wei was trying to fire a patch of thorny nettles to expand their clearing they were frightened into the realization that their lives were shallow vessels, easily spilled.

She looked up and her breath clogged in her chest. A thin, shaggy brown bear stood on the beach watching Deng Wei. Drool spilled from its lower jaw. Lo An screamed and threw the pot of water.

Deng Wei spun and saw the creature. It had come up on them by accident in its browsing along the coast, from upwind, unaware. Lo An's scream surprised the animal and it brought its massive head up abruptly and fixed its eyes on her. Then Deng Wei shouted and waved a fiery branch. There was no fear in the beast and neither the shouting nor the small flame in Deng Wei's hand could have stopped its charge, but after a small moment the bear turned and trotted off, hackles raised, looking back over its shoulder at them. Where the beach ended, about forty yards away, it planted both front feet like a bull confronting the picador and pivoted to face them, its lips laid back. Then it snorted, spun again, and trotted into the bushes.

Deng Wei shouted and waved his smoking branch, then turned and ran to Lo An, who collapsed to her knees and held her face in her hands. He knelt in front of her. "It's gone. It didn't mean us any harm. Come on, sit with me under the boat. I'll hold you. It's safe now." He led her to their makeshift shelter where he held her, rocking her, talking gently and crooning her to calmness. When the fear was gone she told him she was carrying their baby.

That night they slept on the water, bobbing uncomfortably, anchored to a big rock Deng Wei carried out in the boat and levered overboard. But they felt safer than they had ashore. They continued to sleep in the boat at night until, five days later, he'd finished building a small, rough but solid cabin out of unbarked logs. It had no floor, no windows, only a small, low door they had to crawl through, but when they dragged the boat over it for a roof, and had that lashed tightly in place, they felt secure.

When winter arrived the Hongs were in basically sound circumstance. They'd worked from dawn to dusk and beyond, all summer, even when the sun was below the horizon for only a few hours. Knowing what the winter was like, they ignored their fatigue. They were happy to be working with each other in their own place. In all their lives neither had ever hoped so much as to be the owner of land.

Deng Wei killed eleven deer before the snows came, and Lo An cured the pelts to use as insulation on the walls of the cabin, and on their hemlock pole bed, which occupied most of the hut's space. He added another room, a larger one, and cut the door bigger so they could enter without crawling. He cut two small windows – too small for a bear to crawl through – covering the holes with stretched canvas which let in some light. They made a stove of rocks and muddy clay in one corner which kept the place warm and allowed them to cook inside. The roof was made of poles with thick curving pieces of hemlock bark laid over them, interlocked like Chinese tiles.

In the late summer the salmon ran past their cove into a wide stream at the very head of the bay, a couple of miles away. They rowed there, discovered the fish clogging the stream, and in three days and nights of hard work caught several hundred.

There were coastal grizzly bears – Kodiaks, white people called them – sometimes as many as twenty of them fishing in the same stream. The bears and the two humans were all nervous about fishing together but Deng Wei made his stand, building bonfires at the stream's edge and in several places around, and firing the pistol twice into the air. He yelled and beat pots and pans together, generally making the place as inhospitable as he could. When he desisted the bears seemed relieved and left the noisy creatures to their spot and they all fished in peaceful if suspicious coexistence. If any bears came too near Deng Wei beat with the pistol against a pot – which was soon ruined, much to Lo An's displeasure – and the bears would turn away from the noise to seek a quieter place. When exhaustion overcame Lo An and her husband they napped uncomfortably but secure in the bobbing skiff, their catch tied up in the drift net and flapping in the water.

When they thought they had enough fish they rowed home again and Deng Wei was up for four nervous days and nights keeping smoky alder fires under racks he fashioned to dry the fish. Lo An did what she could to help, and worked at getting the cabin chinked with clay mixed with the stringy dried bark he stripped off his smoke wood.

They picked bucketsful of blueberries when those ripened and dried them on their big piece of stretched-out canvas. When rain fell, as it often did, they rushed to roll up the canvas and drag it into the house. They took several varieties of kelp and seaweed from the bay, cut it up, dried it, hung it in the cabin from the roof poles. The Indians had told them about rose hips, and they were able to find them in profusion not far from the cabin. They picked them and spread them out also on the canvas to dry, eventually storing them in a bag made from the sail.

All in all, when that first gentle snow started, they felt as if they'd done what they could to be ready and though their labors would continue well into the winter in spite of the snow, they had two of the major necessities – shelter and a stock of preserved food – taken care of.

After the last deer was cut into strips and dried Deng Wei devoted the rest of the rapidly shortening days to increasing their stock of firewood. Shortly after their arrival he'd killed six big spruce trees by cutting them deeply all around their trunks, but leaving them standing. Now he felled three of them with the ax, and with the saw he'd bought from the Indians he cut them, stacking great heaps of wood against the back wall of the cabin.

Lo An asked him, "Why are you stacking the wood there?"

"So it'll be close at hand when we want it."

"I mean why only on *that* side of the house? Why don't you stack it all around? Wouldn't it help keep the cold out?"

He thought for a minute, then said, "Well, I don't know, but it might. I'll do it." Soon they were living inside a big wood stack.

****

During the darkest part of that winter there'd been pain, and fear, then a baby's cries from the center of the wood stack. A branch of the Family Hong was established in Cloud Bay. They named the newcomer Hong Kai Win. Deng Wei was proud, and he spent hours when he should have been working just looking at the perfectly formed little boy. He fingered the amulet around his own neck, remembering the old grandmother who'd given it to him, but he tried to forget what she'd seen when she studied his wrinkles.

9

In mid-May, on a Tuesday morning, Tom didn't show up for school. On his way home that night Banning stopped by Archers' shack.

"Naw, he ain't sick," Mrs. Archer said from the rotting stoop where she stood looking down at him. "Ain't here no more. Left last night. Said he's going someplace else. Didn't catch the name. Said he's sick of this place. Said maybe he'd join up in the army or somethin'. No loss, particular. All he done was make pictures anyway." She turned to go back into the house. "Left something, said to give it to you." She was back in a moment with Tom's cardboard suitcase. "Might as well you have it. Ain't nothing but pictures nohow."

Banning took the suitcase from her, said thanks to her retreating back and went to his room in Mrs. Gage's boarding house. He put the suitcase on his bed and opened it. It was full of portraits Tom had drawn, maybe all of them. Paul leafed through them, shaking his head, looking.

Every one had been ruined, slashed through the eyes with a knife.

****

"Young man, you look to be of uncommon-good common sense." The sergeant's chevrons were the brightest light in the small office that served as a military recruiting center in Tacoma. "The Army can use a man like you," he told Tom. "Now, how old are you?" He glanced up from the form in front of him on the scarred desk.

"Eighteen," the boy said.

The sergeant spelled aloud as he wrote into the record. "Have you got a birth certificate or something else to prove your birthday?" he asked.

Tom shook his head. "Nope, got nothing like that."

"Well, you look like a truthful young fellow. I guess we can waive that requirement in your case." He asked a couple other questions, made some more entries on the form, then stood up and looked Tom over carefully, turning him, feeling the flesh of his arms and legs. Nothing was made of wood. "Open your mouth," he instructed. Tom opened his mouth and the sergeant peered in, then grunted in satisfaction, sat back down at the desk, signed his name with a flourish and spun the paper so it faced Tom. "Sign right there, Mr. Archer." He pointed to a line at the bottom.

It was the first time in Tom's life he'd been called *Mr. Archer.* He signed.

The sergeant slid the paper into a folder and tucked it into a deep drawer and then stood up behind the desk. He said to Tom, "Raise your right hand…" When Tom had sworn his allegiance to his country and his body to the U.S. Army, the sergeant shook his hand, then handed him bus fare to Seattle, where he'd start his training. He walked Tom to the door. "You're an upstanding young man and the United States Army is going to be mighty glad to have a soldier of your quality, Son," he said, cementing the recruitment

110

as much as he could. "I'll count on you not to disappoint me," he said, shaking Tom's hand again and looking him in the eye.

"I won't Sergeant. Sir." It was the first time in a long time Tom had looked anybody in the eye.

The next morning he caught his bus headed toward the Army Training Center Depot near Seattle. He settled back in the seat, scratched at his crotch for a moment, crossed his legs and put his head back. He felt purged, satisfied, more relaxed than he'd felt in a long time. He didn't feel as guilty as he had since that night… He blocked the images with a blank screen. Now he knew what he had to do to keep the images away. He wondered briefly how often he'd have the urges. No way of telling.

As the outskirts of Tacoma faded toward the outskirts of Seattle, he fell asleep.

Late that afternoon a young Oriental male was found stuffed in a battered galvanized iron garbage can in a deep alley in Tacoma. He'd been stabbed to death with a pointed object about the size of a chopstick or a wooden pencil. He'd been slashed deeply across the face at the eye line. His penis had been hacked off flush with the body with a small sharp instrument, like a penknife. The amputated organ wasn't found with the rest of the body. The assistant coroner who did the autopsy found a deposit of semen on the mutilated face of the deceased and declared it a case of sexually-aberrant homicide. The Tacoma cops knew the kid as a local hustler, pimp and prostitute and didn't sympathize much, and the case folder went into a drawer. Years later when the precinct station burned the file perished.

****

While the bored Tacoma police watched an ambulance crew lift the carcass of a wasted, unwanted Chinese youth onto a stretcher for transport to the morgue, a white woman in a good

111

hospital thirteen blocks north shrieked a final short effort and a head burst from between her legs. She grunted, again, sucked breath in tiny gasps, and at the urging of her doctor, bore down one final time. The tiny living creature she and her husband had made on purpose squirted from her birth canal. That night while her husband held her hand they named the boy William, after his grandfather. "William Hood." she mouthed for the twentieth time, "I like it. It's vigorous and straightforward, just like him." She looked at the sleeping William Hood, then up at her man. "And just like you, my husband, he's going to make me very proud."

William Hood's parents were consistent, firm and loving, and the child – who would be their only one, they'd decided – responded like an oak sapling in a sunny glade. When he was four and they all moved to Virginia he was already able to understand his father's esoteric explanation of the move. "We're going to get back more than we're going to give up, William." In fact that's what transpired, proving again young William's faith in his parents and sealing the lesson forever into his psyche. He'd need that outlook often during the adventures of his life and would harbor no regrets, in spite of the affair there, when a decision based on that perspective led him to Cloud Bay.

****

Over the years, occasionally, visitors stopped in Cloud Bay. Indians on hunting trips from the village came by sometimes and though Deng Wei had never learned more than a few words of English, he did learn some Tlingit. Sometimes a big commercial fishing boat would pull into their cove to ride out a spell of bad weather, and Deng Wei would make Lo An stay in the cabin until it had left. Once, when the boy Kai Win was old enough to know the love of land, a party of drunken foreign devils arrived in a fancy yacht. For three days they filled the air with the sound of gunfire,

112

the beaches with the skinned carcasses of brown bears, and the surface of the water with bloody duck feathers. Kai Win wanted to paddle out at night and sink their yacht, but was forbidden, and soon enough the cove was quiet again.

Then one drizzling summer afternoon a large powerboat chugged around the point of the bay, headed into the cove and dropped a polished anchor. There was an air of different business about its decks and there was a proposal carried in the leather briefcase of the bespectacled Chinese who was rowed ashore in the powerboat's jolly. He stepped gingerly ashore, keeping his leather shoes out of the salt water. He clutched his briefcase to his chest with one hand and held an umbrella with the other. When he bowed his glasses slipped forward on his nose, almost falling off, and in his effort to get them pushed back up he knocked his hat askew.

Kai Win stood in awe, completely entertained. Aside from his parents, he'd never seen another Chinese.

The crewman who'd rowed the Chinese man ashore, a young foreign devil with a thin black beard and long hair, said, "I'll take 'er back out, Mr. Yang. You just holler when you want me to come fetch you," and he wheeled the jolly boat around expertly and rowed back out into the cove. The three Hongs noticed the *"Mister* Yang." Obviously this was an important man, no coolie.

When initial introductions had been made Deng Wei invited the well-dressed man into their house where he was shown a seat at the table. Deng Wei, his cheeks creased with curiosity, sat across from him. Lo An, beautiful, distracted the visitor to the point of embarrassment and served spruce tea.

"Mister Hong," the stranger began, "I am an associate with the firm of Wang Associates in Seattle. The firm represents numerous interests in… Mister Hong?" It had become apparent that the man to whom he was speaking didn't understand a word so he switched back to Mandarin, in which they'd greeted each other. "Our company has a client which operates several businesses associated with the catching, processing and export of fish and fish products and it's in this regard that I'm here today."

Deng Wei looked up at Lo An, who shrugged. Her arms were crossed below her full breasts. "Who knows?" her look said.

"It has come to our attention that you own this property here and that you are firmly established on the land. I can certainly see that's true. You have quite a nice place here." He looked around as if he could see an infant city, stopped the sweep of his eyes when they came to rest just above Lo An's wrists, then caught himself and continued. "We – my firm, that is, on behalf of this client – would like to purchase this property from you, at a very fair price, of course. I have papers here with me..." He started to reach for his briefcase but Lo An stopped him with a hand on his shoulder. "Mr. Yang, we appreciate your long journey to visit us and you're welcome to stay as long as you like, but there will be no more talk about selling this property."

"But my company..."

"*None*, Mr. Yang. It is not for sale, period, at any price, to anybody. Now," she removed her hand from his shoulder and he watched it go as if it were taking his heat, "what other things do you have in your briefcase to talk to us about?"

"Ahem," he started, then started again, "Yes. Well of course I understand. Such a beautiful place... What my company would like to do in lieu of a purchase is to contract with you for certain services. Services and the use of certain facilities to be constructed." He looked at Deng Wei hopefully.

Deng Wei smiled enigmatically and drank from his tea glass, then said, "You could be, perhaps, more specific?"

"Yes, of course. My firm would like to build here – to have you build here if you care to contract for the construction and operation thereof – a small processing plant for the salt preservation of herring and herring roe, which as you must know

114

run in profusion in this bay, and which attract large markets in the Orient."

"I see, Mr. Yang." Deng Wei looked up at Lo An, standing behind their visitor, and saw tears gush into her eyes. Not anguish or sadness, happiness. To their visitor he said, "Perhaps you'd like to stay with us for supper and we can talk some more." Then he raised his voice, almost clapped his hands as if servants were waiting behind curtains, "Would someone please prepare a nice supper for our guest while he and I go outside under the awning to talk? I think fat wild duck would be a nice dish to start with." He pushed up from the table. "Come, Mr. Yang, we have chairs outside on the porch where we can look at the bay."

Lo An sent Kai Win to the meathouse for a smoked mallard.

Mr. Yang didn't know it but his offer was timely. The Hongs needed clothes. Ammunition cost money. And flour, fish nets and kerosene, tools. Pots and pans wear out. Deng Wei had sold smoked salmon to the occasional tourist through the cove and had guided some bear hunters once, but there wasn't any economic vitality in that sort of occasional enterprise. He and Lo An had had many conversations, had tried to think of ways money could be generated without going away from their land. Now this.

After supper, when Mr. Yang had been ferried back out to spend the night on the big motorboat, the Hongs sat at the table and discussed the offer, trying to see it as their fortune, struggling to project how it would change their lives. As he lay in bed that night, his thigh pressed against his wife's, Deng Wei thought of his village by the rivers, and of his journeys, and he fingered the amulet around his neck. He had the wife the crone had seen, and the son, and now the fortune.

The next morning Mr. Yang was summoned and before he left that afternoon they'd reached agreement on all points. The saltery in Cloud Bay was established, the continuity of life in the cove assured, as much as such things can be in such places.

10

Tom Archer survived basic training. That's all any of them did though some claimed to have loved the experience. Most of those were liars. Tom had his share of conflicts with the system and with some of his fellow trainees but he responded to the discipline positively and focused himself on being a good soldier. Like the other recruits he was always famished but slowly he got into physical shape, putting on weight, thickening in the legs and arms. He was proud to see the sergeant who'd recruited him standing next to the reviewing stand when his class passed in review during the graduation ceremony, which was brief and followed immediately by reassignment. 22-K Company, their guidon proclaimed in snapping grey and yellow: the eleventh graduating class of 1922.

With the rest of his class Private Archer crowded the bulletin board where their orders were posted. There was shoving and noise, men yelling out their assignments to friends, whooping at favored destinations, anguished over others. But Tom was indifferent. He was going to remain in Washington State, assigned to one of the companies providing training support, but he was beyond Outcrop and that had been his singular goal.

He never went to town with the others on pass, preferring instead to hang out around the barracks and draw. He was a model, dull soldier who did what he was told. He didn't drink to excess or fight, didn't complain. The other soldiers avoided him for the most part, his dour, solitary countenance an impressive obstacle to friendship. His character was as barren as the dusty yard where it had formed.

In 1923 he shipped out to the Philippines with several other men from Washington State. His ship made a stop at Pearl Harbor where the men were all granted a forty-eight hour pass, then it steamed for Manila. The country's forces were nowhere in action but in the Philippines, which had earlier been chosen as the single long-term American fortress in the Pacific, there was activity that resembled military motion. There were always bandits in the hills to provide patrolling and bivouacking experience, and there were constant mapping missions.

On a hot Sunday morning Private Archer was sitting on an old Spanish stone bench near the barracks, drawing. Lazy. Sketching one quick scene, then flipping the page of his pad and doing another. Scenery, never people.

"That's pretty good, Private."

Tom looked up lazily at the speaker who'd approached across the grass from behind. A small ugly dog strained against a leash looped over the man's wrist. As Tom recognized the officer, a captain, he started to rise, flipping the pad closed and prepared to pay his respects.

The officer waved him down. "Relax, Private. Keep working. No need to move too fast on a day as hot as this one." He pointed to the pad which was now closed in Tom's hand. "I only caught a glance but it looked like a pretty good rendering," he said, nodding toward the distant hill that Tom had just captured in charcoal. "Mind if I look again?"

"No sir," Tom answered, standing in spite of the officer's relaxation of protocol and flipping through the pad.

"That's the one," the captain said, reaching out with a well-manicured hand to the one he liked. With just a few strokes Tom had caught the essence of the high ground to their front. The captain admired the drawing, holding one edge of the pad and glancing to the hills, then back again, comparing. "Very good indeed." He looked at Tom then, jerking the straining dog back from where it struggled to raise a leg on the stone bench. "What's your duty here, Private?"

"Ordnance Depot, sir, Thirty-First Infantry Regiment," Tom responded, stiffening.

"I see. What's your name?"

"Private Thomas Archer, sir."

"OK. Good easy name to remember. Private Archer." He waved one hand airily. "Stand easy, Archer, stand easy."

Tom un-tensed his shoulders but maintained a relatively stiff military pose approximating attention. Even at his best he wasn't the Grand Duke of military bearing. He was short beside most of the other soldiers, like a carbine in a rifle stack, and he tended to stoop a little to his left side so when he walked he reached out further with his right foot than with his left, giving his gait a crabbing, sideways quality. When he was marching, of course, he straightened up and stepped out smartly to the cadence but it wasn't natural to him.

The captain said, "Thanks, Private Archer. I'll leave you alone and you can go back to your work. You got a good talent and you ought to be using it."

Tom had heard it before from others, well meaning, genuine. Each time though, it was Paul Banning's voice bringing images like foggy scenes beyond dirty windows. The light vanished in Tom's dark eyes. "Yes sir," he responded, saluting.

The officer returned his salute casually, then walked on down the cobblestone path, dragging the dog at the end of the leash.

Tuesday afternoon Tom's boss, Corporal Steinmetz, called him down off a ladder propped against a stack of baled uniform material. The smell of wool, of which most of their uniforms were made, was heavy in the steamy heat of the warehouse. "Report to Headquarters building, Archer," Steinmetz told him. "And don't even ask, 'cause I haven't got the foggiest idea what it's about."

"I didn't do nothing'," Tom groused.

"Maybe that's what the brass wants to talk to you about, Archer." He laughed and took the inventory clipboard from Tom's hands. "Maybe they're going to make you a general. Who knows? Go on, and don't fool around on the way back, Private, we got work to do." He had a big smile on his face: it was a recognized fact they had very little to do. The ancient commander of the Thirty-First, who'd fought the Sioux on the Great Plains of North America in his time, was not a martinet. "See a Captain Morris," the corporal said as Tom moved off.

In the headquarters building he reported to a clerk who told him to wait and pointed to a hard, polished wooden bench. Tom sat and waited, standing respectfully each time a sergeant or officer passed in front of him. After an hour the clerk took him down a wide hallway and into another waiting room. He sat for another hour on another hard bench, mentally drawing the desks and chairs and the lines of the windows and trying to guess what he'd done to deserve this misfortune. In the caste system he was stranded among the princes.

A door opened and a big sergeant pointed at Tom's chest with a forefinger the size of a steamed German sausage, beckoned him toward the door. "Archer?" he asked.

Tom nodded. "Yes, Sergeant."

"Knock on that door," he put one heavy hand on Tom's shoulder and propelled him toward a closed door on the other side of the small office, "and report to Captain Morris when he says, 'Enter'."

Tom did that.

"I understand you're an artist, Private Archer," Captain Morris said. He was stiff-backed, balding, probably close to forty-five, maybe older. He had heavy brown nicotine stains on his fingers and on the right side of his graying mustache.

Tom stiffened his own stance. "Yes, sir, I draw some." He didn't want to commit himself to swimming in these deep waters until he'd counted the sharks.

"Well, let's just see how much of an artist you are, Private." Captain Morris stood, pulling a pad of lined paper and a brown pencil from a drawer in the desk. "Come with me," he ordered, and led Tom out through the successive anterooms and arched hallways of the old building. Soon they were standing on the walk in front, heat waves prickling up their wool-clad legs and reaching for their armpits. "Come on," he said to Tom, stepping off smartly toward the corner of the building, "we'll get out of this heat and find you something to draw."

Tom hurried to catch up, watching the officer's feet and skipping to get into step with him.

"I do a little field sketching myself," Captain Morris said with pride, one warrior to another, as they stepped out.

"Yes, sir," Tom answered noncommittally.

They left the stifling heat of the cobbled squares and streets behind as they rounded the corner of the building. A manicured blue-green lawn half the size of a Washington farm stretched before them, sets of bleachers and droopy awnings waiting patiently on its perimeter for the weekend polo matches. Beyond a distant hedgerow of trees hills climbed each other, curved lines building higher and higher through the haze toward the white-hot sky. Captain Morris pointed toward a ridge line running down from one of the closer mountains and said, "I want you to give me a good rendering of that ridge line, Private. Look at it with a military eye, if you can, and don't spare the detail. Know what I mean?" He peered at Tom.

"Yes sir," Tom replied, looking off at the objective. "You want just that ridge, sir?"

Captain Morris nodded, smiled. "Yes, just that ridge." He chuckled. Drawing *just that ridge,* which shimmered in the heat and presented a number of perspective difficulties, would be a good task for a trained engineering artist. "I'll give you about half an hour, then you come in and show me what you've got. I think that one ridge will keep you plenty busy."

Tom knocked on the captain's door twenty minutes later. He saluted the desk. The captain asked, "What's the matter? Light's wrong? Pencil's too hard? You need more elevation? What?"

"No sir, none of them. I'm done." Tom extended the lined paper pad and the pencil with his left hand, taking a brisk step toward the desk as he did so.

The captain snorted. "I want a good drawing, Archer, your best effort."

"Yes sir," Tom said, still holding out the pad of paper.

The captain looked warily at him, then took the pad and pencil. He looked down at the pad, turned it to orient it, and actually swallowed hard. He looked up at Tom, who'd stepped back and now stood at attention, his eyes somewhere on the wall behind the captain's desk, and then looked back at the pad. "Humph," he grunted. "Pretty good, Private, pretty good indeed." He ripped the paper with the sketch off the pad and strode around from behind his desk. "But we'd better take it outside and have a look at the terrain itself, don't you think? Make sure we're talking about the same ridge before we judge it."

"Yes sir," Tom replied, turning to follow, skipping once again to pick up the captain's step, one pace behind and to his left.

Captain Morris was rightfully impressed. There wasn't any question. Tom had drawn the correct ridge and had captured the lay of the land so perfectly the trees might have been all stripped away so he could see the earth itself, its folds, the angles of its stream beds. "This is very good, Private Archer, very good indeed," the captain allowed, looking back and forth from the paper to the ridge line. Then he turned away, striding back toward the front of the building. "Come with me, Private Archer," he ordered over his shoulder. Tom followed, skipping once.

After another hour in yet another anteroom Tom was ushered into a colonel's office. He'd never spoken to an officer higher than a captain before. Fortunately for Tom's nerves the colonel was a grandfatherly sort, a genial man with a potbelly and hair just longer than regulation. "Private Archer, we need a man with your talent in the headquarters cartography section." He looked expectantly at Tom, who stood rigidly, the prescribed two steps in front of the colonel's desk.

"Yes sir."

"Well, would you do a good job for us?"

Tom had no doubts about what to say. This was the Army and certain answers were expected. "Yes sir, my best, sir."

"I believe you would," the colonel told him, nodding his head as if at a nephew's intention to seek entrance to Harvard. "All right, you go out and report to the sergeant at the desk in the front office there," he waved toward the other side of his office door, "and he'll get you organized. Glad to have you, my boy. Dismissed."

"Yes sir," Tom said, saluting. He did an about face and marched out the door. In the outer office the sergeant already had Private Archer's new orders written up. When the sergeant finished telling him where to report the next morning to take up his new duties Tom said to him, "Right, Sergeant. And, uh… can I ask a question?"

"Speak."

"What's *cartoon graffee?*"

Tom Archer's future in the U.S. Army was assured with the assignment, as much as such things can be.

****

William Hood's future wasn't ever assured – neither of his iconoclastic parents tried to establish a test-free environment for the boy – but his days were surrounded with learning and his nights with warmth and stuffed bears. He excelled in most of his school studies, especially those requiring the energies of a right-sided brain. He favored the individual sports: tennis, skiing, riding. His parents were smart enough to let him develop his own interests, and he did. He lost his virginity at fifteen, the tip of his right little finger in the car door at fourteen, and his innocence about horses at thirteen, when one of them scraped him intentionally from the saddle against a tree. The subsequent fall into a drainage ditch and the resultant broken thigh cured him of his youthful passion for hairy beasts and established a pocket of fear that he carried for the rest of his life. As soon as he was mobile again, on crutches, he threw away every stuffed bear in his room, even his favorite, a cuddly grizzly with a stubby tail and a broad face. "I'm too old for them," he claimed.

****

For nine years Tom Archer worked in the cartography section of the Headquarters of the U.S. Army in the Philippines. After he'd been at it a couple of years, and in view of his excellent work and increasing responsibilities, he was promoted to corporal. He still didn't drink to excess, nor fight. While he lived in the Philippines Tom was never a tourist. The stunted curiosity in his character, un-nurtured, stillborn in the dust of a yard with picketed horizons, generated no interest in foreign sights. He could have been stationed in Greenland for all he really cared. He was never seen to abuse nor heard to denigrate the local people, but he learned nothing of any of their languages, not even *Hello* or *Thank you,* and cared nothing for them either. He really didn't even notice them except when they obscured something he was drawing, and then he waved his arm, shooing them, like scattering the droves of evening mosquitoes.

He spent his off-duty time lounging around the barracks or sitting in an out-of-the-way open-air café he'd chosen as a haunt, in old cotton uniform pants and a collarless shirt, glancing without true interest through ancient newspapers and curled-page magazines, sketching, or just sitting in the sunshine, his face turned up to catch the rays.

Because of his artwork he was rather a local celebrity. The colonel's wife asked him to do some special Christmas drawings one year, for cards, and the NCO Players theater group prevailed upon him to design some sets and backdrops for a play they were doing. When asked, he declined to do portraits. Finally he quit saying, "...I can, but just don't," and said instead that he'd never learned how to do people, just couldn't get the hang of it.

He spent many of his workdays in a brightly lit office hunched over a drawing table putting contour lines and terrain features on maps, but he also spent time in the field with mapping and survey parties. While the surveyors made their measurements Tom sketched the terrain reliefs and relationships, sometimes working from a perch high in a jungle tree where he'd been hoisted for the view he needed. He enjoyed the field missions, especially the ones to Bataan during which he was seconded to the Philippine Scout Brigade and worked directly for a zealous young Brigadier General named Douglas MacArthur.

But generally he didn't seem to care for much of anything at all. He had no close friends, never got mail, wrote no letters, never applied for leave to go anywhere. He was socially ignored by the rest of the NCO's and left to his own quiet, simple pursuits.

In 1933 he was reassigned to duty at the Presidio of San Francisco. He was ready to leave the Philippines. Not that he longed to be elsewhere, but just because it was time for a change. Like breathing in and breathing out. He had deep brown skin, and wrinkles around his eyes now, at the age of twenty-nine. He'd never written to nor heard from his parents, didn't even know if they were alive, didn't care. He knew nobody in San Francisco, nor anywhere else in the States. Not even any names.

Except Paul Banning's... and Gloria's, and Anthony's... *Stop!* They have to be blocked!

****

The day after Corporal Archer's ship steamed for the United States, returning him to his own country for the first time in almost a decade, his worldly belongs in a standard-issue footlocker and one duffle bag, the body of a young male prostitute was found in an empty shipping crate in an alley in the wharf area of Manila. The corpse had scores of puncture wounds and a deep slash through both eyes and the ridge of its nose. Its penis had been cut off and removed from the scene and there was a deposit of dried, flaky semen on its mutilated face.

It was obviously a sex crime, one of many, many in Manila, and the victim had owed the investigating detective a small sum of money which was now well beyond collection, so the police weren't inspired in their investigation. Within four hours of its discovery the crime was forgotten by all except the boy's pimp, who now had one less income. Within six hours even that situation had been rectified. Chinese boys were plentiful.

****

The quality of Corporal Archer's work at the Presidio of San Francisco brought him recognition. His experience, especially his field time, made his judgment calls good and he was respected among the other map makers. Their job was to collect, collate and correct, as much as possible, the U.S. Army's collection of all maps of land west of the Mississippi River. After he'd been at the Presidio about two years he was put in charge of a small new office focused specifically on the islands and territories of the Pacific, and the Orient. There were few military planners who didn't recognize the nature of the growing peril in the Pacific. The three technicians under Tom's direction in the new section gathered every map or maritime chart available from wherever they could be found. They sent letters to travelogue writers and steamship companies, made long distance telephone calls and pored over old collections in libraries and archives. The National Geographic society and one of the Methodist missionary groups were among their best sources.

Tom's boss, a lanky thirty-five year old lieutenant with striking blue eyes and bad breath, stopped by Tom's desk one afternoon. It was a warm day for the Bay area, with the summer of 1937 just beginning. "Corporal," the lieutenant said, scratching at his left armpit, a contented grimace on his face, "I need you to dig up the best we've got on these island paradises." He handed Tom a handwritten list. "The top brass someplace needs it all right away, of course."

Tom looked at the list. "The Marshalls, especially Jaluit and Kwajalein," the list said, "Truk, Yap, Saipan, the Lae area of New Guinea." He looked up at the lieutenant. "Too bad you can't just ask the squints for this," he said.

"You mean the Japs?"

"Squints, Japs, all the same to me, Lieutenant. But they're the ones with the good maps of these places. What's up?"

"Ours is not to know, Corporal... Dig up whatever you've got, anyway, and get it over to me as soon as you can."

"Big mystery, huh?"

"Seems to be. One thing I can tell you though..." He reached down and pulled a piece of scrap paper out of a wastebasket, smoothed it on the surface of Tom's table, wrote briefly on it, then shoved the piece of crinkled paper toward him. "If you see any geographical or topography stuff coming across your desk with any of these names on it, zero in."

Tom looked at the piece of paper as the lieutenant left. Written in clear print was, "AE, F. Noonan, Gold Star, Chaumont, Henderson, Blackhawk." None of it made sense and he looked up but the lieutenant was gone. He took the piece of paper to the door and said to the backs of the three men working over their tables in the map room, "Any you guys recognize any these names…" and he read them off. One of the men, his uniform shirt wet with sweat, said without looking up from his work, "I don't know about most of them other names, Corporal, but AE means Amelia Earhart, or ain't you been reading the papers? Noonan's her navigator. They're flyin' around the world in a souped-up Electra, in case you hadn't heard."

When he took the maps to the lieutenant later that day, Tom asked him, "What's Amelia Earhart got to do with us, Lieutenant?"

The lieutenant answered, "As far as anybody knows, and I mean officially: nothing. But if she should just happen to fly that fast, high-flying Electra close to one of those Jap-held blank spots on your map, and just happened to stop by here when she gets back, and happened to show you a couple of sketches she made or photos she took along the way, it'd be right nice, wouldn't it? Especially if they showed airfields and trench lines and machine gun emplacements with rising sun flags on them. Get it?"

"Got it, Lieutenant. How about them other names, Blackhawk…"

"…Chaumont, Gold Star and Henderson?"

"Yes sir."

"Those are U.S. ships in the Pacific now. I don't know much, but what I hear leads me to think they're trying to find out what the

Japs are doing out in all those islands. We know they've got to be building up but they won't let anybody take a look, naturally."

Tom's eyes shadowed and he said, "Yeah, little yellow bastards probably getting ready to pounce us."

"Well, I don't know anything about that," the lieutenant replied, "but I know this whole section hasn't got any maps worth dog poop. Hell, we're still using Captain Cook's." He waved the skinny roll of maps and charts Tom had brought in to him. "Just keep your eyes peeled. You see a short-haired gal with freckles and pants walk through here, grab her quick and get her to look at your maps. She's due back in a couple weeks."

"Right, Lieutenant," Tom said, and went back to his own section.

On the first day of July there wasn't a lot of news in the paper Tom picked up on his way to work. The President's son, Franklin Roosevelt, Jr., had just gotten married. Big deal. Joe DiMaggio lost a game for the Yankees but knocked one over the wall doing it, his seventeenth of the season. But later in the day the radio reported news which was almost immediately on the street in special editions of every newspaper: "Earhart Disappears!"

"Shit," Tom said, "there go my map corrections. Goddam squints." Although he'd made a prophetic guess – perhaps – about her fate it was the Japanese, not the Chinese who may have captured and killed her, but Tom Archer made no distinction among Orientals.

Two days after the loss of Amelia Earhart and Fred Noonan the seven enlisted men in the Presidio map-confirmation office were separated and told by an official in civilian clothes to be quiet about what they might have heard concerning certain events in the Pacific relating to Amelia Earhart. Then they were all shipped to other installations. Tom was reassigned to the U.S. Army's Second Infantry Division at Fort Sam Houston, Texas. He was given a travel voucher for a train leaving the following morning. That was good. It would give him a chance to purge himself again. Better to do it now than later…

****

As Tom was presenting his orders to the First Sergeant of his new Headquarters Company at Fort Sam two policemen back in San Francisco were looking at a body found under a pile of cardboard and old newspapers in an alley behind a warehouse in San Francisco. The corpse was identified as that of a seventeen year old male prostitute with a long string of arrests. He'd died of wounds received from a round pointed instrument which pierced many of his internal organs including his spleen, liver and heart. There was dried semen on his face and on his slashed eyelids. His penis had been cut off with ragged short strokes of a sharp knife. An intensive search of the alley failed to find the missing organ and the body was buried in the Chinese section of a county graveyard without it. The thin case file eventually joined others in a four-drawer file cabinet in the precinct station. The hand-printed label on the drawer into which the file went said, "Open – No Arrest/Sex Related."

****

Tom's previous record of assignments and the favorable evaluations of his job performance in his file led to a series of interviews with more high-ranking noncommissioned officers and officers than Tom had ever talked to before. "You're going to the Division G-2 staff, Corporal. The Division Intelligence Officer wants you," the Headquarters Company First Sergeant told him.

"Thank you, First Sergeant," Tom replied. It didn't really make much difference to him, though.

"Oh, you got no cause to thank me, Corporal. We got us a new Brigadier General here who's going to make you want to go to momma, unless you're actually as good with maps as the record says you are. Joseph Stillwell by name, and tough on goof-offs by reputation." He looked thoughtfully at Tom, who stood on the public side of a small railing in the company headquarters which fenced off the First Sergeant's desk and the door to the Company Commander's office. "You're not a goof-off, are you, Corporal?"

"No, First Sergeant, not a bit."

"Good," the First Sergeant said, suddenly smiling and taking a set of sergeant's chevrons out of the *IN* basket on his desk, "because this outfit's got no use for goof-off sergeants." He held the chevrons out to Tom. "Congratulations, Sergeant Archer. Go ahead and take 'em but don't wear 'em 'til the Old Man gets a chance to hand you your promotion orders in front of the men. Your new pay starts today." He held up his hand palm out. "And don't thank me, the promotion comes with the assignment, and believe me, you'll earn 'em in the days to come, if you haven't already."

****

One night, late, Tom was putting work away, getting ready to walk out of the office, headed back to his room in the barracks, when out of the hallway and into the map room strode The General like a scrawny rooster looking for a fight in the gander's pen. "Where'd everybody go?" he questioned, moving between the desks and drawing boards, pulling open desk drawers, moving acetate sheets and looking at the maps below.

Tom stood at rigid attention near the door, cap in his hand.

"Well?" The General demanded, looking up briefly and fixing Tom with a fighting look. "You the only one works here?" Every utterance was an invitation to combat. Tom started to answer in the negative but The General gave him no chance. "Never mind, I

130

know you're not. What's your name, Sergeant?" He was still digging in drawers, looking for nothing in particular but into everything.

"Sergeant Thomas Archer, sir."

The General straightened up. He removed the wire spectacles he was wearing and put them in his shirt pocket, buttoning it, looking closely at Tom. "Oh yes. I heard about you: Sergeant Sketch. Here…" He ripped a piece of paper off a map-sized sheet on a drafting table and thrust it at Tom, taking him by the elbow and leading him to one of the high slanting tables. He took Tom's uniform cap out of his hand and put it on a desk and reached for a pencil from a cup, thrusting it at him hilt first. "Draw," he ordered, sitting on a tall stool and turning his face to give Tom a three-quarter view.

"Oh, but I don't do portraits, General," Tom said, putting the pencil down.

"You do now, Sergeant." General Stillwell got off his stool, reached over, picked up the pencil and put it back in Tom's hand. Tom was too stunned by the whole encounter to remember his usual arguments. "Please," The General said then. He looked Tom in the eye.

When they parted thirty minutes later, The General helping Tom lock the office doors behind them, The General had a small piece of map-drafting paper rolled into a smooth cylinder and tucked into the crown of his cap where it wouldn't be crushed. It was the first portrait Tom had done since Tacoma.

The General not only showed the portrait to his wife but had it framed, then showed up with it in hand one morning, much to the surprise of the others in the office, and made Tom sign it. "Write, 'to my favorite General,' if you would, Sergeant, and sign clearly so people can read your name, OK?"

Tom looked at The General and down at the sketch. For a moment he was too overwhelmed to move or speak. He was into his third decade of life and in all those years he'd never once been appreciated honestly, as a human being. His parents had only kept him from freezing and starving and were glad when he left. He'd known no women capable of honesty with a man. His few acquaintances were soldiers, their own lives to live in their own ways. Now here was this tough little fighting man with stars on his collar telling him he wanted to be Tom's favorite general. To The General it was a simple request of a man whose talent he appreciated, a man he respected. To Tom it was an act of love.

Tom signed, The General thanked him and shook his hand and left about his business, and Tom never heard the end of it from the other NCO's. From that day forward Tom said he didn't do portraits because he had an exclusive portrait arrangement with General Joseph Stillwell himself, "...the only real general in the whole damn U.S. Army."

As autumn set in Stillwell set a frantic pace. He'd been given command of the aggressor forces for the massive U.S. Army field maneuvers to be held that winter. During the maneuvers, which involved over seventy thousand troops and ranged from Texas to Missouri to Georgia, The General was everywhere. And every time he ran into Sergeant sketch he'd shake his hand. Tom Archer would have followed Joe Stillwell to hell, or even to China.

****

In Cloud Bay Hong Kai Win followed Deng Wei everywhere. To some extent devotion propelled him in the footsteps of his father, but it was usually necessity that pointed his steps: most trips anywhere out of the cove were in pursuit of resources that would feed or clothe or warm the residents of the cove. And there was safety in numbers. Occasionally there were other men there: visitors sometimes, workers during the season when the herring spawned in the bay. But all Kai Win's interests tied him closely to his father. From him he learned the lessons of the forests, and of the bay, and of life itself.

11

During the summer of 1940 General Stillwell was reassigned to command the Seventh Infantry Division based at Camp Ord, California, on the Monterey Peninsula. When he went he took many of his favorite staff with him, including Sergeant Sketch. One of Tom's first assignments was to draw the artwork for the sign painters who would make the new signs when Camp Ord was re-designated as Fort Ord. His mind was clear and he felt relaxed, so he did a good job and The General was pleased.

At Fort Ord General Stillwell was a dervish, driving his officers and NCO's to the farthest edges of their capabilities, or driving them to other assignments. Some hated him and couldn't wait to get to sane assignments elsewhere, but others saw him working eighteen hours a day and followed doggedly. The General was everywhere, watching tents being erected, crouched in sandbagged holes with training sergeants demonstrating the use of grenades, lying on his side in the dust of a firing range to coach a city boy through his first use of a rifle.

Tom worked in the Training Aids Department of a school The General set up for training company officers coming to active duty from the Reserves, and from the National Guards. The work wasn't exactly what Tom liked to do but because he was serving his favorite general he was more than willing to give it his best. His best was very good and his work both as a conceptual artist and as a section supervisor was lauded. He lashed the men under him if they produced anything imperfect and drove them to do it over, again and again, until he was satisfied.

****

William Hood joined the U.S. Army the day Congress declared war against Germany. Pearl Harbor was several days old by then but it took him that long to get permission from his father, who relented only after William promised to apply for OCS. His subsequent commissioning and assignment to a unit that would eventually land in Normandy placed him in circumstances far different from Tom Archer's, so the two men, the middle-aged sergeant and the young lieutenant, never met during the four years the conflict lasted. Even had they crossed paths, their subsequent meeting in Cloud Bay would have probably turned out no different, for both of them were set in their character by then.

****

In the Pacific the war was going as the Japanese wished. After their initial successes they tightened their hold on the theater by landing at Rabaul and then they cut into the American supply route to Australia with a landing in the Solomon Islands. The Japanese soldiers were *not military* in their approach to war, according to one British observer. They used bicycles, for instance, and they refused to come down the roads where the British had built slitted bunkers to oppose their advance to Singapore, instead sneaking through the jungle like wild animals to take the bunkers from the rear. *Entirely ungentlemanly,* an officer declared. Singapore was due to fall and the Japanese knew it and The General knew it and everybody of the slightest military discernment except the British knew it. Burma would also fall unless something extraordinary could be done. India might follow.

Chiang Kai Shek's brother-in-law, T.V. Soong, was the Chinese Foreign Minister, and spent much of the war in America. His mission in the United States, and that of his sister, Madam Chiang Kai Shek, was to arrange as much U.S. aid for Generalissimo Chiang as possible. Soong was *devious and slippery,* according to The General and he was therefore very effective among American politicians, who doted on him and crowded to get their pictures taken with him.

America's popular opinion of China, her form of government, her democratic ideal, her effectiveness against the Japanese enemy and her potential force for good in the world following the war were all fictionalized by a stupid, enamored press. The truth was far, far away and admitted by few. Among those few, because of his earlier assignments in China, was Tom Archer's General, who spoke fluent Mandarin, liked the Chinese people, deplored their suffering, and absolutely, correctly, mistrusted their leaders.

Chiang Kai Shek's Burma strategy was to build a road from Ledo, Assam, India, to tie in with the Burma Road on the Chinese side at Lungling. With such a road, he and his supporters contended, the massive Chinese armies would have access to the great valleys of Burma where the Japanese already threatened, and could stem the flow. It would take a great, great deal of American aid to the Generalissimo to accomplish a victory in the area, of course. Of course.

President Roosevelt and his military chief George Marshall needed to take control of the rapidly deteriorating situation in south Asia. That meant having their own man in command on the scene. Tom's General was given his third star and in spite of his hope that he'd be appointed to lead Operation GYMNAST, a proposed but often-postponed Allied attack at Casablanca, he was appointed to command the China mission. His orders designated him as "Commanding General of the U.S. Army in the China/Burma/India Theater of War and Chief of Staff to the Supreme Commander of the China Theater," who was none other than Chiang Kai Shek.

The entire "U.S. Army in the China/Burma/India Theater" amounted to the thirty-five officers and five enlisted men who landed with General Stillwell in New Delhi. Later they'd be joined by four hundred other officers and NCO's who would have the task of training the Chinese army. Sergeant Tom Archer was among them.

The Japanese were quickly eating Burma, moving up toward Mandalay, up the Irrawaddy and the Sittang River valleys which form the heartland of Burma, from their beachheads at Moulmein. Other Japanese columns were approaching overland through the Southern Shan States from Indo-China, which the French had handed them without so much as a fist fight. When Mandalay, the hub of rail, river and road transportation fell, Burma would belong to Emperor Hirohito's Greater East Asia Co-Prosperity Sphere. India would be next. A linkup between Japanese and Nazi forces at the Suez Canal would likely follow that.

Slowing their advance, but not stopping it, were several brigades of Indians and Burmese. Chiang Kai Shek was carefully keeping his hoards, in their American-supplied uniforms, hidden in the mountains to the east where they and their American equipment were safe. He knew he'd need his fattened divisions to fight Mao Tse Tung after the Americans beat the Japanese.

Into this mess came Galloping Joe Stillwell, as he'd become known at Fort Ord, and with him, still willing to follow him to China, Sergeant Tom Archer. Both were due for a change of name.

****

Tom was standing on a stony river bank, a feeder into the Sittang River near Pyinmana, a hundred miles south of Mandalay. He had a carbine in his left hand and held a pair of field glasses to his eyes with his other. He was dressed in dirty fatigues. Torn leggings crimped his trousers and covered the tops of his short boots in a hopeless effort to keep the bugs and leeches from his legs. A canvas hat with a floppy wide brim kept his face in shadow. His right forearm had a huge festering jungle sore on it, oozing pus and refusing to heal. His lip was split: he'd walked into a tree branch. He hadn't had his boots off in three days and had no time to wonder what his feet must look like. The day before he'd narrowly escaped a strafing run by a Japanese fighter plane and, leaping for cover, had banged his left knee against a rock. It still hurt and he limped slightly. All in all he was in the same kind of shape as the others, even better than some.

Before him the brown river waters shallowed, riffling over stones, sweeping in urgent little currents past him. A big white bird with long legs saw him come hesitantly from the bushes on the riverbank and took to noisy, frantic flight down-river. Tom could see no other life. In a semicircle of protection behind him a bodyguard of Chinese troops from the Fifty-Fifth Division of General Chen Li Wu watched for Japs.

His job was to reconnoiter a crossing spot over the river. When he'd confirmed its location well enough to find it again in the dark he'd rejoin the bodyguard troops and then they'd work their way carefully through the underbrush and fallow gardens along the river and back to where Vinegar Joe Stillwell, as he was now known, had his headquarters. The Japanese commander in the area had put a price on General Stillwell's head, and not wishing that it be collected, The General's staff kept track — as much as they could under the circumstances — of possible routes by which the headquarters could be moved quickly to safer places. The number of safer places was rapidly diminishing.

Tom stepped carefully from the sloping bank into the knee-deep water. He crouched, the carbine held ready in front of him. There were Japanese patrols everywhere.

As he began to test the footing of the ford there was a sudden outbreak of firing behind him and he whirled in the river and dove for the bushes on the bank. His finger on the carbine's trigger, expecting at any moment to see Japs, he waited, but after the first short volley of shots echoed off across the broad valley there was only silence and the sighing swirl of the river behind him.

He cautiously raised his head. One of the Chinese soldiers standing watch must have seen something and fired. Tom got slowly to his knees, peering through the light brush, trying to decide exactly where the firing had come from. He couldn't see any of the Chinese troops but that was correct because he'd concealed them carefully.

He stood, crouched low, the carbine forward, and made his way quietly toward the fallen tree where the Chinese lieutenant in charge of the bodyguard was supposed to be waiting for him. Whistling softly as agreed, he waited for the recognition signal. All was quiet. He advanced a few more paces, whistled lightly again. Nothing.

The lieutenant was gone.

Tom dropped to the soft earth next to the tree trunk, wincing at the pain in his knee, and looked carefully around, moving his head slowly, trying to see through the underbrush, wishing he could see through the tree trunks themselves. A bird fluttered in a burst of leafy noise and Tom's heart kept cadence. Sweat dripped into one eye and he was afraid to make the motion it would require to wipe the sting away. A mosquito feasted unbothered on his wrist and a leech swelled itself behind Tom's ear. Could the lieutenant be out checking the position of his men? Tom mentally shook his head. "Not likely," he mused wryly. He'd gotten along with the squints because that served The General, but he had no illusions about their value in combat.

He crouched, his eyes moving constantly, his ears straining through the tiny noises of the jungle to the sounds that mattered, to the sounds of other men creeping, or breathing, or not breathing. His legs didn't want to obey but he had to know. Slowly, trying to move without motion, he picked his way to the patch of brush where the next man should have been. Gone. And the next. They were *all* gone. The smell of his sweat changed. It was acid now, bursting in tiny explosions through the cells of his skin, coating his body in the cold film of his fear. Like others in this campaign he'd seen the rotted, mutilated carcasses of British soldiers tied to trees, their eyes out, their entrails spilled by bayonets, stinking, black with insects. His chest was tight with the pounding pressure of his blood as he slunk back toward the river, all his senses raging. Flies gathered at his mouth, sucking at the vileness of his breath.

What was his best chance to get back? The headquarters was about a mile away. The day was only half gone. Should he move during daylight while he could see or should he wait for night? He knew the way, he could find it at night, but he didn't want to bump into a Jap patrol in the dark. And if he waited before trying to make his way back there was a good chance the headquarters wouldn't even be there anymore. The Japs were pressing hard. "Those fucking squint bodyguards must have spotted a Jap patrol...the whole bunch of them tooken off for the hills..." They were probably already back in their holes near the headquarters telling The General Sergeant Archer was dead and they'd been lucky to escape with their lives.

The General would know better, though. How soon would they send a patrol out for him? Should he lay dog someplace nearby and wait to be rescued? The choices were excruciating. Tom was hungry and his tongue was swollen in his throat. The water bottle hanging on a strap over his shoulder was empty. "God damn squints," he swore silently. This should have been a cakewalk, but now…

There was movement to his front. He shrank slowly back to the earth.

More sounds of movement, to his rear now, between him and the river. "Chinese squints or Jap squints?" he asked himself, turning his head slowly. Definitely men moving stealthily through the underbrush. "Japs," he decided, and pressed himself into the ground. Ten minutes. That's how long he'd wait after they passed. Then he'd make his way slowly toward the headquarters before another Jap patrol came by. He couldn't take the chance of waiting for nightfall.

When the ten minutes had passed with no further sound he raised his head slowly, then moved carefully to his knees, looking intently in the direction the Japs had gone.

He got to his feet then, hunched, was just ready to sneak off toward safety when the *WHAK!* of a bullet slammed past his head close enough to knock him back on his heels. He stumbled, almost fell, wanted to hit the dirt but knew he'd been seen so he had to move and he started to throw himself into a run forward when the next shot exploded into the tree trunk next to him. He turned wildly to see where the shots were coming from.

Six Jap soldiers were standing among the small trees to his left, not twenty yards away. All of them had their rifles pointed at him. Every rifle had a long, dirty bayonet beside the bore. The soldiers were dressed in earth-colored gym shorts and singlets. Small-brimmed baseball caps on their heads gave them the ludicrous appearance of a sandlot baseball team but there was nothing silly about the weapons they pointed or the lethal looks on their faces.

Tom raised both his hands, letting the carbine fall to the ground.

They closed on him quickly, their rifles held casually once his hands were in the air. He knew a quick death was his best hope now and he cursed himself for putting his hands up, for dropping the carbine. He willed himself to attack them, to end it cleanly with bullets. But he couldn't.

"Ingrish?" one of the soldiers said to him, pushing him in the chest with his hand so Tom stumbled backward, away from the carbine on the ground.

He didn't know whether to respond or not. Would they kill him more swiftly if he said he was English? They were used to killing Englishmen by now.

The soldier pushed him again. "Ingrish?" he repeated.

Tom stumbled back a step with the shove and decided to try to live. "American," he said. He lowered one hand to tap himself on the side of the chest and said it again, "American..." A blinding flash of pain exploded in his left arm and he nearly passed out. The soldier questioning him had swung the butt of his rifle up and smashed it into Tom's elbow. Tom gave his voice to the pain and grimaced and bent over, squeezing the fiery elbow in his other hand and pressing it to his side, trying to ease the burning, trying not to pass out, to keep his feet, stumbling where he stood.

The soldier prodded him with his bayonet, got the long blade in against Tom's side under the sore elbow and raised it, forcing it up, pushing Tom's arms up again, then separating them. The Jap was smiling. The pain swirled through Tom's arm and up to the ends of his fingers like hot electricity and he thought there was no way he could avoid hugging it to himself again but the bayonet prodded him, poked him in the arm and drew blood that trickled down and into his armpit. He knew if he put his arms down again he'd feel the bayonet in his guts.

He wanted that. But he couldn't face it. He grimaced, his arm throbbing and waves of nausea and blackness washing over him, but he managed to keep his hands high.

The soldiers had dispersed and were watching the bushes beyond the small perimeter they'd formed. One of them said something to the soldier with the bayonet at Tom's chest and the man replied in a few short syllables, then prodded Tom with the bayonet, cutting his shirt and slicing the skin below, turning him, prodding him in the kidneys and buttocks, making him stumble forward.

They took him west, poking him with their bayonets whenever he stumbled or lowered his hands, until they reached a small collection of huts near the railroad tracks running north to Pyinmana, Pyawbwe, and on to Mandalay. Tom knew exactly where they were. Two days earlier it'd taken him only fifteen minutes on foot to get from The General's headquarters to these very huts.

He was left standing in front of one of the little buildings, a bayonet still pointed at his bleeding back, while the soldier who'd hit him on the elbow went inside. Except for his guard, the other soldiers wandered off without another look at him, moving toward other Japs gathered in small relaxed groups around the area. Tom noticed they appeared tired, but sounder than the soldiers opposing them. They *all* looked as if they felt better than Tom did at that moment.

The soldier came out of the dark interior of the hut with another soldier in long pants. That one came up to Tom and looked at him, studying his face. He was the same height as Tom, but heaver. Tom had been eating poorly for weeks.

Long Pants reached out and groped at Tom's chest, found the small chain with his dog tags on it and with a jerk, ripped it from Tom's neck. He gave Tom a look of contempt, turned and went back into the hut. Tom continued to stand in the sun, blood running from a dozen bayonet cuts, his elbow throbbing, his knee burning, his tongue a gag in his throat. The leech behind his ear finished gorging on what was left of Tom's strength and fell off. In seconds the flies found the new wound and were feasting.

As the swoons that come before a faint began to roll up behind Tom's eyes, Long Pants came out again and barked at the soldier guarding him. Tom's head jerked up. The guard raised his bayonet and poked him in the back with it, forcing him forward into the building. After his hours in the powerful sun the relative dark of the hut was blinding and he stumbled at the threshold, then against a chair he couldn't see. The guard was close behind him with the bayonet, pushing him when he faltered, poking and jabbing with the sharp point. Tom wanted to wheel on him and take his rifle, beat him with it and stab him over and over again, slash his eyes until it was finished but the man was cautious, wary, jabbing, jabbing, driving Tom forward. Finally Tom's eyes adjusted and a small table in front of him materialized from the gloom. Long Pants was sitting on the far side smoking a cigarette. Tom could smell the cheap mixture of tobacco and hemp straw.

The bayonet forced Tom into the chair facing the table.

"Merica!" Long Pants said with a sharp nod, throwing the word toward the ground. Tom's dog tags lay like thin slices of his life on the table in front of him. "Yes, American."

"Sa-jet."

"Yes. American sergeant."

Long Pants said something to the guard, who raised his bayonet and poked Tom in the triceps above his throbbing elbow. Tom jumped in the seat but the blade of the long knife came down on top of his shoulder, holding him in the chair.

"Ye-sa you say."

Tom looked intently at Long Pants, who continued to smoke his cigarette, one eye closed against a pungent wisp. "Merica Sa-jet."

144

"Yes. *Sir.* American Sergeant," Tom answered grudgingly.

"No Stee-wir."

Tom was shocked, didn't know how to respond but when he saw Long Pant's eyes move toward the soldier with the bayonet, he blurted out, "No. No, *sir!* Not Stillwell! American Sergeant. Thomas Archer."

Long Pants ground out his cigarette on top of the table and stood. Tom would have stood as well but the bayonet blade on his shoulder pressed him down again. Long Pants walked around the table and stood at Tom's side, then hauled his hand back and delivered a slap across his face with such force Tom was hurled to the floor. Looking down at the cringing American in the dirt of the floor, Long Pants said something to the guard, then said, "Stee-wir," again, nodding to himself, and went out through the door.

Tom was prodded to his feet and taken back outside where his guard called another soldier from a group lounging in the shade at the side of the hut. They pulled the laces from his boots, slashing off his leggings with a sharp, wicked clasp knife, and then shoved him up face-first against a small tree and lashed his wrists tightly together on the far side of it with the laces. Then they pushed him to his knees and walked off, talking casually, their prisoner forgotten.

Their neglect was torture. The wounds they'd opened in his arms and back and buttocks had stopped bleeding but the tree rising between his arms crawled with a thick column of voracious black ants and within minutes they found all the clots on his body and were busy ripping off bloody chunks to carry home to their queen. Tom squirmed and rubbed himself against the tree, tried to use his one good knee to crush them where they crawled beneath his shirt, chewed them, spit them out, butted hundreds to pulp against the tree with his forehead and face, but it was all useless. After half an hour he thought his body would explode. He knew they had crawled into his ears and were eating his brain. He threw back his head and tried to scream, praying one of the soldiers would come over and finish him with a bullet or a bayonet. Even a long filthy blade in his guts would be better... The scream ripped from his chest and up like a rusted rasp through his dry throat and then burst past the split of his swollen lips in a moan, rose to a wail, then finally cracked into a piercing agonized howl.

Some of the soldiers sitting nearby looked over at the source of the noise, the hairy dishonored white monkey writhing against the torment of the ants. One of them said something and they all laughed and then another of them picked up a sharp rock the size of a golf ball and threw it at the prisoner. It thudded into his ribs. Another stone, bigger, thrown like a pitched ball, hit him in the left ear, splitting the skin and cartilage and rocking him back against his bond. A third one hit him on the thumb, tearing open the knuckle and starting a fresh eating spot for the ants and the biting flies.

Tom fainted.

Water splashing into his face brought him to consciousness again. It was dusk. His hands had been untied and he'd been moved away from the ant tree. He was sitting, propped against the outside wall of the building where Long Pants had sat. A small British truck stood in the clearing in front of him.

12

Another pan of water was thrown in Tom's face and he shook his head, gasping, licking the water from his lips, stretching his tongue, reaching for the moisture. He realized his hands were untied and wiped his face with stiff, painful movements, licking water off his swollen palms, trying to lubricate his throat so he could swallow. His eyes were puffed and his vision was blurry but he could see the shape and markings of the British truck in front of him and a wave of relief rushed through him.

When he wiped his eyes and blinked, looked again, he saw the Japanese officer standing in front of the truck, watching him. "Sa-jet A-cha," the officer intoned, like a prosecutor with an accusation. Tom tried to focus. His head was pounding. Dizzy. Pain everywhere burning through his body. Slipping away into darkness again. He heard the man say something and felt someone at his side. He forced open his eyes, bracing himself for the stab of a bayonet.

One of the soldiers was squatting beside him, a water bottle in his hand. He was holding it toward Tom's lips. The man poured tepid water into Tom's mouth, paused while he choked part of it down, poured some more. It burned going through Tom's closed throat and when it spilled over his chin and ran down his chest it burned where the bayonets had opened his skin and the ants had eaten. A flame was consuming his body.

Long Pants said something to the soldier and the man moved away, wiping the mouth of the bottle with his palm as if the white monkey-man might have left disease on it. "Sa-jet A-cha," the officer said again. He stood, feet planted, fists on his hips, accusing Tom. He wore a complete uniform now and had a canvas belt around his waist from which dangled a huge revolver on a short string tied to the trigger guard. No holster.

Idly, hilariously, Tom wondered how the man avoided shooting himself in the balls with an arrangement like that. His mind smiled for a brief moment but his swollen face didn't.

A soldier was summoned who dragged him to his feet. At first he leaned against the flimsy wall of the hut for support, Long Pants patiently watching his struggle, then gradually, rubbing his throbbing elbow, pushing against the wall with swollen hands, finally standing on his feet unsupported, he faced the Japanese officer. Tom could see other soldiers around, carrying rifles, eating rice from shallow pans or from the palms of their hands, or just lounging. In their campaigns they'd all seen many white prisoners awaiting death and just one more held no interest for them.

Finally Tom looked the officer in the face, gathered a small amount of spit in his mouth, and said, "Yeah, you squint-eyed Jap, I'm Sergeant Thomas Archer, United States Army. And you're a pile of yellow shit." He spit the wad. They might as well kill him here and now.

The officer said something to the soldier who'd put Tom on his feet and a second later everything went black.

Several times during the night Tom was jolted into semi-consciousness as the captured truck carried him along a rough road through the jungle. Then he awoke with the sensation of falling and couldn't separate the worlds of dream and reality. For just an instant he knew he was conscious and knew he was floating in air and he was starting to wonder how that could be when he hit the ground. Two soldiers had thrown him like a sack of rice from the back of the truck.

When he next regained consciousness it was full daylight. He was in another thatched hut, dumped on the floor in one of the corners. He was alone. Slowly he tried to bring his senses to bear on his condition. He was still alive and though he hurt all over none of his wounds would kill him, though infection might. He moved his eyes around the hut and even that hurt him, but he could see, and that was something. Japs liked to blind the prisoners they were going to use for bayonet practice. Slowly he flexed his fingers, moved his wrists and ankles, gradually worked motion into his limbs.

A soldier in a small-brimmed baseball cap poked his head through the open doorway, saw Tom's open eyes, and withdrew. He came back in a few minutes and put a leaf with a small mound of rice on it, and a small bowl of water, on the floor by the doorway.

"Well," Tom thought, "they're not going to cut my head off right away… wouldn't waste the rice…" He couldn't feel his hunger, but he needed the water desperately so he pulled himself toward it, drank it greedily, not even looking out the doorway at the Jap in the baseball cap. He didn't bother with the rice until he could stand without holding on to the thatch of the wall. When he had massaged his arms, being gentle with his swollen elbow, and had gently flexed his wrists and knees, he stooped and picked the ball of rice off the leaf, looked at it, and raised it toward his mouth. His glance went out the doorway and he saw the soldier watching him. He turned away from the man and moved so the wall was between them before he ate the rice. He hadn't felt hungry but when the last kernel of rice was gone he licked his filthy fingers and would have licked the leaf sitting on the dirt floor, but he wouldn't do that in front of a Japanese.

****

The *kempei-tai* officer in charge of Tom's interrogation was straightforward about his fate. "You were captured because your Chinese *allies* deserted you. I have spoken to the patrol leader who took you prisoner and I know what happened."

Tom knew also, and wouldn't have argued the point. He remained silent.

The secret police officer said, "When you have answered all my questions your head will be cut off with a sword and your corpse will be left in the jungle for the insects and animals to eat. Your head will be put on a sharp pole and left alongside the road as a warning to others of your race to leave Asia to Asians."

Tom's head drooped, his death now verbalized, now that much more certain, but still impossible to understand.

"However," the Jap said, and Tom's head came up, against his will, "if you do *not* answer my questions quickly, forthrightly, completely and truthfully, you will suffer horribly. After you have suffered, then you will answer my questions, and *then* your head will be struck off. Do you understand?"

Tom had no illusions, but he also knew he had no control. Although he could only hope for a fast death as a reward for his cooperation, he also knew they might well torture him just for sport after he cooperated. His best hope was to goad them into killing him outright, or leave him alone long enough to let him figure out how to kill himself. "You speak pretty good English for the afterbirth of a squint-eyed Jap whore," he said, looking the other man in the eyes. They were alone under a canvas fly strung between trees. Tom was too weak to escape or to injure the other man, and they both knew it. He couldn't see a guard standing behind him but he hoped one was there, holding a pistol to the back of his head at that moment, waiting for the nod from the kempei-tai officer. Tom longed for the oblivion.

150

"So," the officer said, "you find your tongue. Yes, Sergeant Archer, I speak pretty good English. Probably better than you, even. I have no trouble saying L's, and you will note I have no buck teeth."

"Fuck you."

"Good," the Jap officer replied. "I am glad you've decided to cooperate. Now please confirm for me that you are assigned to the Headquarters of General Stillwater, and state your duties in that headquarters."

Tom's surprise showed on his face, in the slight widening of his eyes. He was too battered, too exhausted to play subtle games with this man. If he gave him what he wanted, what did anybody have to lose? Shit, they knew everything anyway. Probably knew exactly where The General was at that very moment, what he was doing. If he didn't say something they were going to hurt him and even though he'd faint they'd bring him around. They probably knew how to keep him conscious while they worked on him. It was better to give them useless information and opt for the quick execution. But he didn't have to be nice about it. "You got that right, Tojo-shit. I'm his right hand man. I shine his shoes and hand him his coffee in the morning."

It was the other man's turn to look surprised. "Is that true?" he asked, leaning forward.

"Yeah, shit-for-brains, that's true. I'm his personal valet."

"Ah!" The officer sat back. "I see you are trying to insult me. Let me advise you, Sergeant Archer...." he brought his hands together in his lap. He was sitting in an upright wicker chair. His prisoner was sitting in the dirt in front of him. Flies buzzed in a hoard at Tom's split ear and at the leech bite behind it and he raised his hand constantly, shooing, rubbing them away. Other flies crowded head down, eating at his other wounds. His shirt was in tatters. "...that I am not an uncivilized man. I come from an honorable family, I have an excellent education in the classics, both

Eastern and Occidental, and I have no desire to bring you personal agony. I have a task to perform, however, and if it is necessary for me to order your torture to gain your cooperation, I will accept that duty as one of the requirements of war, and shall do so unhesitatingly. If you continue to insult me I will order your torture just to get even. Do I make myself clear?"

Tom considered another insult, but faced an adversary who threatened him not lustfully, but out of a demand for respect. Tom could understand that and responded to it. "Yeah, I got it."

The officer wasn't satisfied and said so. "I am a major in the service of my country and you are a sergeant in the service of yours. I expect you to say *Sir* when you speak to me. Is that understood?"

"OK, Major, you made your point," Tom replied.

"I am glad. Now, what was your position on General Stillwell's headquarters staff?"

"I'm a cook."

"And how many officers' meals did you prepare each day?"

"I worked in the enlisted mess."

"And how many *enlisted* meals did you prepare each day?"

"Three. Breakfast, dinner and supper."

"Sergeant Archer," the major said, taking a deep breath, "I feel you are not being forthright to me. Nor respectful. Let's try once more, which will exhaust my patience. How many enlisted meals did you prepare each day?"

Tom thought. Maybe he could carry on with the cook charade a while longer, but this Jap was cagy and probably already knew he was lying. He didn't expect to live much beyond the end of this interrogation, but he didn't want to be tortured either. "I wasn't a cook, Major," he said, rubbing his sore elbow and looking at the officer sitting in the chair. "I was a truck driver."

"I see. Is that, now, the truth?"

"Yeah. Yeah, *sir*. I was a truck driver."

"All right, I believe you, though I find it strange that you should have been advanced to the rank of sergeant and yet still be driving trucks." He paused, letting that thought settle on Tom, and raised his eyes toward the canvas fly above them. Tom sat quite still on the ground, wanting to stretch his sore muscles but allowing himself only the luxury of brushing the flies from his bloody ear. "Tell me, Sergeant truck-driver Archer, did you ever see General Stillwell in person?"

Tom was shocked again at the question. Why General Stillwell? Every Allied soldier in the Irrawaddy Valley had seen The General in person, most had probably talked to him, almost all had had their ass chewed at one time or another by him, or knew of someone who had. The General was everywhere, into everything. Surely this Jap knew The General's reputation. "Yes. Sir," he said. A lie wouldn't work.

"Recently?"

Tom almost chuckled. "Not since yesterday, Major."

"Yes, I see," the major said. "Very humorous, Sergeant. Shall we say you saw him within the past several days?"

What was the Jap trying to get out of him? Was he trying to figure out if The General was still in the area? Hell, their planes flew over the headquarters twice a day dropping bombs and strafing, and The General rarely missed the opportunity to stand alongside Major Frank Merrill and fire at the bastards with his pistol while the Major blazed away with a Bren gun. The pilots certainly must have reported the precise location of the headquarters after every run, even though they couldn't seem to hit it. Tom decided for simplicity. "Yes, sir."

"Good, Sergeant." The kempei-tai major stood up and yelled a short string of instructions to someone out of Tom's sight. Tom braced himself for a bayonet thrust or for the sound a sword swishing through the air, the last sound he would hear before the blade reached his neck. But a soldier appeared at his side and took him by the elbow, started to drag him to his feet but it was Tom's sore elbow he'd gripped and Tom yelled in sudden sharp pain and anger, pushed himself away from the man, hugged his arm to his stomach, struggled to his feet before the man could touch him again. The major was walking toward a small folding table which had been set in the sunlight that filtered through the trees. One soldier carried the major's chair while the other pushed Tom toward the table.

"Sit, Sergeant," the major ordered.

Tom sat in the chair. One of the soldiers scooted the camp table closer to him. On the table was a piece of paper and a small artist brush, like the Japs used for their writing. The major stood on the other side of the table and said to him, "Now you will draw a picture of the face of General Stillwell."

"What?" Tom spouted, incredulous. Did the major *know*?

"You heard me, Sergeant. You have seen him recently, and so you will now draw an accurate representation of him. His face. If he has a beard, you will draw that also. Begin."

Tom almost laughed. These stupid fuckers had a price on The General's head but they didn't even know what he *looked like!* Hell, they might already be paying for every white head brought in on a stick, and with all the Brits around there was sure as hell no shortage of heads, and somebody must be looking pretty stupid by now. Fucking amazing... He knew he'd have to give them something but they might as well work for it. "OK, Major, I can do that, but not with this stupid thing." He picked up the brush and tossed it into the dirt at the feet of the soldier who'd brought the table. "You can't draw with a brush. Give me a pencil and I'll give you your picture, all right."

"A pencil," the major said, sighing. "You try me, Sergeant Archer, but I appreciate your willingness to cooperate, and we will search for a pencil."

154

"Something to drink, too," Tom said, pushing his advantage and brushing at the flies feasting at his ear.

The major looked harshly at him, then gave instructions to the soldier.

It took them over two hours to find a pencil, which added two long hours to Tom Archer's life. While they searched, canvassing each other and every possible place they might have a pencil, Tom relaxed for the first time since they'd captured him. His wounds still hurt but except for the throbbing at his elbow and the confounded flies at his burning ear, he wasn't too bad off. He knew when he finished this last portrait they'd kill him. They'd only kept him alive for this one thing. There was no way they could know he was the personal portrait-sketcher of General Stillwell but perhaps in Japan everybody learned to paint pictures in school. With little brushes. He was more tired than he'd ever been in his life, exhausted by mental and physical anguish and abuse, and that weariness lulled him, making it easier for him to accept his imminent death. He guessed having his head cut off with a sword would be pretty quick. Messy, but then he wouldn't care about that, would he? He smiled at that.

Had he wasted his life? Maybe, maybe part of it, he thought. But not since he'd met The General. He didn't even think much about his life before that. He'd done things in those years that weren't so good, he knew, but in light of what was going on in the world these days, and right here in this jungle clearing, what he'd done hadn't been much of a big deal. He wished now he'd done more of it. God damn squints, sure enough. The death of him.

The major himself finally found a pencil in the obvious place, the glove box of the British truck. He slapped it angrily onto the paper on the table in front of Tom and said, "Enough delay. Draw!"

Tom picked up the pencil. The lead had broken off when the major slammed it down. He held it up. The major, impatient now, snatched it out of his hand and handed it to a soldier, snapping at him in Japanese. The man hurried away with the pencil, then was back with the tip carefully hewn to a needle-sharp point. The major laid it carefully on the paper. "Draw now, Sergeant." His voice was flat, full of death.

Tom picked up the pencil, blunted the point a bit by drawing concentric circles on the table top, then, turning the paper to an angle that suited him, he began to sketch from memory.

He worked for an hour, twice as long as necessary, drawing slowly, getting every shade and stroke correct. There was no eraser on the pencil but he didn't need one anyway. Every line, every shadow went in perfectly.

The major stood watching, his eyes never leaving the portrait as it developed.

Finally Tom couldn't refine it any more When the major looked away he quickly drew an American flag in the background. He laid the pencil down next to the paper, sat back against his wounds in the chair, looked up and around at the major and at the clearing in which he sat, took a deep breath and said, "There you go, Major. Now let's get things over with."

The major picked up the piece of paper, turned it in his hands, studied the likeness on it. "This is very good, Sergeant. I didn't know you were actually an artist."

"Yeah, well, I don't usually do portraits, see…"

"Yes," the major acknowledged, 'but this is excellent, regardless. A piece of art, I'd say. Only one thing worries me about it."

"What's that, Major?"

"How do I know this is a likeness of General Stillwell?"

Tom put back his head and snorted, a painful, short laugh. The flies buzzed off his ear, then settled back quickly and he swatted carefully at them, picked off and squeezed several that wouldn't fly. "You don't, I guess, Major. You're just going to have to take my word for it though, aren't you? Shit, the word of a man on his deathbed's supposed to be pretty good, ain't it?"

The major studied the drawing again, then rolled it into a cylinder. He looked at Tom, who still sat in the chair. "That's correct, Sergeant, but I think in this case, at least until this has reached higher headquarters and been confirmed, that you should consider yourself off your deathbed and in a temporary condition of expectancy."

Tom was shocked at the reprieve and after a moment he smiled, but said nothing. The major continued, "But I would not like to think about how you will suffer if this is an incorrect rendering, Sergeant."

"I guess you better get it to the post office then, Major. We're all on pins and needles 'til the word comes back, ain't we."

The major nodded slowly several times in thought, unrolled the drawing and looked at it again, re-rolled it, and then, turning, walking away, said something to the soldier standing guard behind Tom.

****

After two days in the jungle camp, during which he was left alone with his wounds and his flies, Sergeant Archer was sent to higher headquarters in the Salween River port city of Moulmein, where the Japs had come ashore in Burma. The picture he'd drawn was wrapped in rice paper and tied with a piece of string. His captors kept his hands tied in front of him, and fed him a small ball of sticky rice and a bowl of water at dawn and again at dusk each day. Except for an occasional kick or shove he wasn't abused further.

He went through several layers of the Japanese military bureaucracy, expecting each day to be executed. He continued to lose weight and his belly cramped so badly he could hardly stand.

At the second layer of headquarters above the jungle clearing he was separated from the drawing, which he last saw being carried into a building that looked like a bank in Moulmein. He was taken to the rail station where he was herded into a storage room with several other prisoners, all British.

The wounds on his back had filled with maggots while he'd been held in solitary confinement in the jungle and were crawling with the writhing little larvae when he reached the storeroom-cell. They probably saved his life, eating at the dead flesh and infection in the wounds, keeping them clean. When he got to the rail station the other prisoners scraped the maggots out and washed the wounds. All the men suffered from hunger but they were able to puncture a small water pipe which passed along the wall of the storeroom on its way elsewhere in the train station, and survived on the little spray it provided.

When he'd been three days in the storeroom one of the British prisoners died and the others, after hearing about Tom's suspended death sentence, supported his switch of identity with the dead David Lawrence. 'Tom Archer's' body was dragged by the heels from the storeroom and consigned to a common, lime-white trench of a grave. The new David Lawrence didn't actually heal, but he didn't die right away, either.

A week later the prisoners were thrown into the stinking hold of a converted Japanese fishing boat and taken to Changi Prison on the eastern end of Singapore Island. Tom had successfully cheated the kempei-tai major of the good English and classical education and during his years of captivity and suffering he drew frequent, private solace at the thought of the major's fate when his superiors finally identified the portrait of a lightly bearded, crew-cut Eleanor Roosevelt.

13

The only commodity that had no value in Changi, the most notorious of all the hideous Japanese prison camps, was someone else's life. In Changi a man died many small deaths every day, over and over again until finally he stopped breathing and began to putrefy not just in specific areas of his body, but all over. Only then, as the deceased owner of a few small treasures, did he become important and even while his starved and festered body was being dragged to the pits his poor possessions were being scattered among others according to his *will* or, more often, according to the will of the strongest of his camp-mates.

In the fetid barbed wire enclosures of Changi, where clouds of swamp-born mosquitoes sucked a billion lives from the naked, louse-infested men, everything but the lives of others had value.

Though there were civilians among them, mostly they were soldiers: seventy thousand fighting-fit Brits, Aussies and New Zealanders had been betrayed by their leaders and many of them were subsequently herded into Changi when Percival gave Singapore to Yamashita. As did they all, Tom tried to forestall the final death. He stole, and scavenged, and he pounded three gold-filled teeth from the corpse of an Australian corporal before the others could get to it. He joined in the rat-raising schemes that flourished, scrounging for carrion to feed his own flea-bitten stock which gnawed constantly at the dirt walls of the trenches beneath the hut, where they were bred and fattened. When he could find nothing else he fed the snarling creatures to each other. He sold their carcasses to a soldier who wholesaled them out as food, and their skins to another who made little bear-shaped souvenirs for sale to the guards.

And, temporarily ignoring the old fragmented images of Gloria and Anthony and Paul Banning, Tom Archer returned to portraits. The guards prized his work and sat stiffly while he captured their heroic faces on rice paper, and watched proudly when the artist signed his name, "David Lawrence, Changi, Shonan." Shonan was the Jap's new name for Singapore – *Bright South*. And in the strokes of a lock of hair or camouflaged within the charcoaled folds of a uniform tunic, or hidden in the lines of a shadow beneath a chin, in every portrait, he wrote, "Fuck Tojo." The guards, unknowing, loved his work and sent it to families in all parts of their homeland, where the pictures were proudly displayed.

Tom soon had to devote all his time to his portrait studio, and sold his rat ranch. He went into business with a crippled Australian who fashioned frames for Tom's portraits from carved bone. Tom never once wondered where the Aussie got the bones. Their business flourished. Tom Archer was surviving.

During his second year as a prisoner a small tough clique of British soldiers advised him they wanted his studio space – a tiny patch of dry dirt next to the main gate – for one of their own business schemes. When he refused to deal they accused him of collaboration. The charge was a complete fabrication but for Tom it was an indefensible indictment because it carried the possibility of truth. The artist spent his days in close private proximity with the Japs so he had the opportunity to pass on camp secrets. That opportunity alone, though common to many of the men in the camp, was agar for the germ of the lie and Tom, without the slightest hearing, was soon isolated.

160

But still he wouldn't give up his space, which he'd purchased at great expense on the open camp market, and the clique couldn't force him off because of his clientele. So during a monsoon storm one night four hired thugs pinned him on his pallet and broke the fingers of his right hand, one by one, bending them back, popping them out at the knuckles. A rag stuffed in his mouth muffled first his protestations of innocence, then his screams.

It never occurred to Tom Archer, ever again, to draw.

****

William Hood discovered his own drawing talents during the course of his artillery work; his inclinations and aptitude both pointed more toward the engineered than the freely associated line. While Oriental circumstances were ending Tom Archer's association with rendered lines, William Hood was just finding his. His acceptance to engineering school in Virginia arrived on the day Nagasaki died.

****

Tom Archer was a translucent, fragile shell, one among many. The Allied doctors who stumbled disbelieving from one corpse-like inmate to another were certain he'd die within a day from scurvy. He didn't. Malaria wracked him so viciously he convulsed off the stretcher as they carried him from the camp. There were four teeth left in his head, all loose. His gums were so inflamed he couldn't bear the weight of fluid against them, and he was fed through a tube in his arm. His eyesight was permanently damaged and his left ear, its drum perforated by the rock blow at the ant tree, was almost deaf. He weighed seventy-six pounds.

After four days in a makeshift trauma-stabilization tent on Serangoon road, where he received vitamins and glucose in an

161

effort to build his strength enough for the journey home, he was moved to an American hospital ship at anchor in the harbor near Sentosa Island. On the hospital ship the medics coaxed a tapeworm six and a half feet long from his bowels. Thirty-two days later the ship steamed under the Golden Gate Bridge carrying Tom Archer, still in critical condition, about three hundred other ex-prisoners from various Japanese POW cages, and the refrigerated corpses of fifty-four other Americans who didn't make it all the way home.

As the shadow of the bridge raced from stem to stern Tom was sleeping far below decks, his eyes bandaged and a drip in his arm, and in the city above the bay merchants were stocking turkeys for Thanksgiving, 1945. When he was admitted to the hospital on the outskirts of San Francisco the nurse wrote *forty-one* in the age block of his admittance form, but he looked seventy. It was the end of March before he was released. He'd regained much of his weight. His elbow, smashed by the Jap soldier when he was captured, still hurt him but an operation had helped, and he could use the arm. They'd saved three of his teeth and had fitted him with dentures but his gums still hurt him much of the time and he didn't wear the new teeth except to eat. Arthritis had settled around the broken joints in his right hand and though he could move the fingers enough to pull the triggers of a shotgun, as he'd later demonstrate, the hand had essentially become his holding hand. He became more dexterous with his left.

The medical staff was glad to see him leave. He made them feel afraid, though they didn't know why.

Not robust, but minimally capable, Tom purged himself two weeks after he left the hospital, then roamed south toward warmer weather until summer came, spending most of his time drowsing in a backwater cantina in Ensenada, then he wandered north again, shiftless, staying in cheap hotels, waiting patiently in dirty bus stations for a connection, conversing only enough to meet his needs. He was almost ugly now, and repellent, and sensed it but

162

didn't care. He was alive, and the pressures in his brain which drove him to purge himself were ageing, and those images that tried to float up were of a thing that had happened so long ago, and it didn't seem to matter so much any more. He'd get by, as long as the squints kept their distance.

He was hunched over a bar in Seaside, California, near Fort Ord, when a man on his right asked, "Ain't you Sergeant Sketch?"

Tom hadn't heard the name for years. He turned his head slowly and recognized the speaker, a sergeant he'd known when he'd worked for The General. "Coon-ass. You ain't killed yet, huh?"

"Not likely. Passin' through?" Sergeant Luthier was from south of Baton Rouge, and he and Tom had gotten along in the old days.

Tom raised his head at the bartender and waggled with his finger for a couple of beers. "Yeah, just passin' through, Coon-ass. Seems that's all I do these days. You still in?"

"Naw," Coon-ass said. "Got out soon's the outfit got back. Didn't seem to be much to stay in for, anymore. Everything's changed. It ain't the Old Army anymore, Sketch."

"I suppose not." Tom nodded thanks when the bartender brought their drinks and looked sideways without much interest at his old acquaintance. "You makin' a livin' these days?"

Coon-ass brightened. He straightened up on the bar stool, arranged his beer in the center of the paper coaster, and looking at Tom in the mirror behind the bar, said, "Yeah. Yeah, Sketch, I'm makin' a good livin', and enjoying it too."

Tom thought Coon-ass was just being over-reactive about a job he probably didn't like, and he didn't expect to hear any more about it but the man went on, turning the sweaty beer bottle on the coaster with both hands. "I got a helluva' good job down in Monterey, at Cannery Row. Supervise a shift in one of the fish canneries, and doin' good, too. Make a good buck," he nodded his head once vigorously, affirming the truth of what he said or congratulating himself, "and it ain't all that different from what I was doing. Hell, supervisin's supervisin'. Puttin' treads on tanks or fish in cans, still takes someone watching and making sure it gets done right. The manager's kind of strange but he's OK, leaves you alone." He finished with a high sound, as if he knew he was doing a good job and wasn't shy to brag in front of an old acquaintance. "How 'bout you, Sketch? What you got goin' for yourself?"

Tom drew his lips to one side, rocked his head a little, looked down at his beer, pushed his stiff forefinger around in the puddle the cold bottle had made on the bar. He shrugged, would have been willing to tell if he'd had anything to tell. "Just pokin' around, Coon-ass." He looked up and caught Coon-ass watching him in the mirror, held his eyes a moment, then went back to his puddle. "Got busted up some overseas, ain't been out of the wards too long. I got enough to get by for awhile."

"That all you aimin' to do? Get by?"

The question was friendly, not a challenge. These days men as used up as Tom Archer didn't need to prove what they could do by picking up challenges in barrooms. The tiredness oozed out all over him. He and Coon-ass had been OK together. Not bosom-buddies or anything like that, but they'd got along all right, had done each other favors from time to time, had tipped a beer or two together. Tom gave a little snort, like the question had brought something to mind. "I'll tell you, Coon-ass, I been *not* getting by for so long now, feels good just to do *that.*"

Coon-ass looked sympathetic. "Where'd they get you, Sketch?"

"All over. 'Bout rubbed me out. Spent a couple years at Changi. Just got back. Been recuperatin', you could say." He paused, not finished, and Coon-ass thought he was going to tell what had happened but then Tom just said, "Fuckin' squints."

164

Coon-ass had to know the end of a conversation when he heard one. He climbed down off his bar stool, reached into his jeans pocket for money. Tom put his hand up. "My treat, Coon-ass. I remember right, you got the last one."

"Yeah, but we was both drawing cash pay then. I still am." Coon-ass withdrew a wad of bills from his front pocket, threw one on the bar. "Gonna' be around for a couple of days, maybe I'll see you again." He put his hand out and Tom twirled on his bar stool to take it in his own. "Good to see you again, Sketch. I'm glad you made it OK. Hang in, yeah?"

"Yeah, Coon-ass, hangin' in. See you 'round."

****

The two men met again the next night, sitting in the same places. When they'd talked about nothing and drank a couple of beers apiece, Tom said, "Tell me 'bout your work, Coon-ass. Is it any good?"

Coon-ass smiled broadly at himself in the mirror and said, "Oh hell yes, Sketch. It's a good-kept secret, working cannery..."

By the time both of them were moderately drunk on beer, Tom had agreed to go to the cannery office with Coon-ass next morning to fill in a work application. "Shit," he said, his voice thick and beginning to slur, "I guess I got to do something, make a livin'. Can't just keep on killin' squints."

To Coon-ass his comment was obviously a statement about the war being over. "You mean Japs."

"Yeah, them too," Tom said.

Tom Archer started work two days later on Cannery Row in a factory owned by Whittaker Fisheries, a big outfit headquartered in Seattle.

****

Thap thap.

The manager said, "I got lots'a Indians. It's chiefs're hard to come by, doncha' see?" *Thap.* He didn't wait to see if Tom could see, went on without pausing. While he talked he flipped through a receipt book with the hairiest hands Tom had ever seen, turning the flimsy pages and stamping each page with a small rubber stamp.

Tom watched. *Thap thap* – the hands looked like two litters of furry animals snuffling and leaping at the book. He tried to pay attention to what the man was saying but between trying to hear beyond the noises of the factory and through the distractions of the man himself, it was hard to concentrate.

"Cannin's simple and anybody can do it. Least the individual parts. Them people down there," – *thap thap thap* – a mother and five of her furry offspring leaped from the desk top toward the processing floor below the loft office where Tom and the manager sat and then back at the receipt book without missing a beat, "are good people, good workers, but they're not *versa-tile,* and they're transient. They get doin' one job, forkin' or cleanin' or workin' a topper, and then that's all they want to do, even though every other job – *thap thap* – is just as simple. Not versa-tile, doncha see?"

Tom reached up and scratched the lower half of his split ear, and the manager seemed to take it as a sign that Tom did see.

"Lots of 'em just work here long enough to find a fishin' boat needs a hand then they're tossin' their rubber on the floor and wantin' their time. More money in crew shares, doncha see?" *Thap.*

The sounds of machinery and people working in a loud place came up through the floorboards. A foghorn sounded out in the bay and a dazzlingly clean gull tried to settle itself against the too-narrow ledge outside the window, squawking, banging its elbows against the thin panes of the window as it fought for purchase with its feet. It gave up as soon as the two men looked at it, squirted a

166

grey and white stream of wet excrement onto the ledge, and dropped off into flight.

"What I need is supervisors – *thap* – who can keep all the various little pieces movin' together. Versa-tile, doncha see? No time for delays in this business. Things can't stack up. Raw fish don't wait. If it ain't in a can, cooked, topped, cooled, labeled, and sittin' in a case on a pallet, it ain't done. I need a guy can keep people workin'. *Thap*. Coon-ass says you can. Says you're versa-tile. True?" *Thap*.

Tom sat a little straighter in the caned straight chair in front of the manager's desk. He wanted the job now that he'd seen the place. Coon-ass had given him a good recommendation, and the thought of having regular work again made him feel better than he'd felt for a very, very long time. "Yes sir, I can do that. I don't know nothin' about cannin' fish, though, I'll tell you right up front…"

Thap thap. "Coon-ass already told me that."

"…But I pick up quick, and I made Tech Sergeant, so I think I can do a good job soon as I learn how to fit a fish in a can, that is." At his own small joke, he smiled honestly. He didn't very often get real pleasure.

"OK Sarge. I'm gonna give you three days on the floor at each station from pier-side where they unload the boats and pump ice to the bays where the finished product goes into the trucks. Then you'll spend a couple days with me seein' the paperwork." *Thap*. The furry animals on the ends of the manager's arms finished with the receipt book and one litter nosed it aside, the mother following closely, while the other family dragged the rubber stamp into a top drawer. Both mothers and their litters then curled up together on the desk, snuggling into a big fur ball, sleeping. A wonderful calm seemed to settle in the room.

"Like I said, the individual tasks, nothin' to 'em. It's keepin' everything movin' smooth from one task to another, never mind workers quittin' and machines breakin' down and cans not comin' in on time, doncha see, and every other damn thing that can go wrong. You won't have any trouble. Keep your eyes open, plan ahead, stay versa-tile, and watch how every job ties in to the ones before and the ones after." He swiveled in his chair and pulled the bottom drawer of a wooden filing cabinet open, rummaged for a paper, pulled it out, shoved the drawer closed with his foot, and spun back around. The little black animals were awake and working again, nosing the paper across the top of the desk to Tom. "Here's an employment form. Fill it out and sign it and we'll get to work. You got a pair of rubber boots?"

****

Tom did a good job for Whittaker, and was glad to have the job. Times weren't all that good, and he wasn't all that employable. He'd received a huge amount of money in back pay from the Army, but it wouldn't have lasted forever. It sat in a bank in San Francisco. He worked as a dockside floor supervisor for a year and a half, then spent two years on the machine side and then, when a shift supervisor moved on, he took that job. He was a quiet man, though he raised his voice when he had to. Nobody seemed to like him much – he was on the sullen side of moody most of the time – but he kept the ice and the fish, the water and the cans and lids, the machines and labels and cases and pallets all moving, and that's what mattered to the man up in the loft office.

His stooped, shoulder-forward walk stopped just short of giving him the look of a cripple. He carried his left arm carefully, and the knuckled fingers of his right hand were stiff and useful mostly for poking things or grasping full-sized objects. His left ear, split into a top and a bottom about halfway along its curve, was one of his parts the workers tried not to look at when they talked to him. People tended to try to look at his eyes, at first, but the black depths confused them and usually when they spoke to him they focused on a point just above the meeting of his bushy, graying eyebrows. He wore his dentures all the time now but it would have taken a smile to show them off and he hardly ever did that. He never talked about his war days but everybody who worked for him knew he'd been in the Pacific someplace, that he'd been a POW of the Japanese, because Coon-ass had spread the word early.

When he wasn't working Tom wandered without goal around Monterey and Pacific Grove, or if the Peninsula was fogged in or rainy on his day off and he wanted sunshine he'd catch a bus and head up into Carmel Valley or over to Salinas. He didn't know anybody in either place but he didn't go looking for company anyway. He'd spend the day walking around looking at the farmers and their town, or find a bridge over the Carmel River and sit tossing gravel into the water, dangling his feet, the warm sun on his back. Practically every American in the country was waiting to buy a new car, or had bought one, but Tom didn't, and didn't care. The lie he'd told the Japanese major in the Burmese jungle about being a truck driver was ironic: he'd never learned to drive. And now he never would.

He appeared to have no friends, though he and Coon-ass did get together once in a while for a beer. They'd get a little drunk, sit through long silences, swirling their bottles on the bar top, then head off to their respective homes. Tom had a week-to-week arrangement in a cheap hotel in Pacific Grove, Coon-ass had a Mexican wife and he lived with her and a couple of her kids in Monterey.

Almost all the cannery workers were Anglos and Mexicans but once in a while the manager would hire a Chinese if he came recommended. Tom knew he had to get along, just as he'd had to when he worked for The General, but he didn't like it, and if the man didn't do everything right the first time, Tom was on him.

Tom's prejudice normally hid below thick layers of dourness but when it shoved its ugly head through and focused, it was repulsive, and other workers would turn away from the wretched Chinese worker, even the ones who'd worked in the strawberries down toward San Diego or in the vegetable fields of Central Valley where bigotry thrived as a separate crop. Most of them had faced the attitude before and turned their shoulders to it, closed in protectively on the victim, but when Tom struck the venom he spit carried the stench of distilled evil, and the others moved away.

At the end of his shift one day the manager called him into his office. "Sarge," he said, "I want you to move along."

Tom was sitting in the same caned chair he'd sat in on the day he was hired. He'd been tired a lot lately, for no reason, and the day before he'd poisoned the atmosphere on the floor below with a particularly cruel, malevolent vilification of one of the Chinese workers who was generally well regarded by the others on the floor. There had been grumbling, and shoddy work and waste during the rest of the shift, and workers gathered in sullen groups turned their backs when Tom walked by.

"You done good work here, Sarge, but lately you been actin' like you need a change, so I'm movin' you along, doncha see? Summer's coming. Good time for movin' on."

Tom said nothing. It'd been pretty good at the cannery but his feelings had been wildly erratic lately, with mood sinkings that left a nameless swelling wrath just waiting to explode out of him. He'd thought yesterday about actually killing the squint who'd messed up the conveyor, about following him to wherever he lived and...

"...And because a' that," the manager was saying, "I'm gonna give you a good recommendation to the comp'ny, see if I can't get you on up north if you want. I figure you just need a change, doncha see?"

170

Tom nodded dully, his mind swimming in mud. Maybe he just needed a vacation but in the dark caves of his mind where the monster lived, he...

"Well, Sarge, you want, or not? I'll call 'em now, you want."

"Oh yeah, that'd be good," Tom answered listlessly, giving himself to the confusion, taking his life to the next step, and to the end of it.

"You'll like it up there," the manager said as one of the furry litters jumped off the desk and landed on the phone. "Lots'a scenery, easy work, good pay. Good place to rest up, doncha see?"

14

Looking for an old Army buddy, William Hood stumbled into the middle of a blooming tragedy in a corridor of a veterans hospital in Arlington.

A burly red-faced man in hospital-green pajamas was backed up against an elevator door. Assorted people in white and green uniforms were pressed against the walls or cringed on the floor when William pushed through the swinging doors into the middle of things. The red-faced man had a .45 pistol in his hand, held it expertly, moved its hollow snout to cover everyone in turn. He had his bare foot on the neck of a prone MP. Another military policeman stood against the wall, his own pistol in the holster at his belt, his hands demonstratively far from it, high in the air.

The .45 swung to cover William when he came unannounced and unaware through the door at the end of the corridor, and though there was a harried look in the man's eyes he wasn't panicked. If there was madness, William missed it in his rush to get his own hands into the air, palms out. The man had for his own reasons knocked the MP to the floor and had gotten the drop on the other one, and now had the whole corridor at bay. He didn't say a word, just kept his foot on the prone man's neck, covered all moves with the .45, and punched the elevator call button repeatedly.

At that point a young nurse with a steady look and a trim physique came through the same door William had just used. The .45 swung her way and she saw it clearly, but instead of stopping she walked directly toward the man, not even glancing at the pistol or at the cowering figures or at the MP on the floor. She looked the man squarely in the eyes and advanced without slowing her pace until she stood directly in front of him. The barrel of the cannon in his hand held steady six inches in front of her throat.

Without changing her face or shifting her eyes from his, she held one hand up and in a quiet voice said, "Give me the *fucking* pistol, Sergeant Berkel, and get your *fucking* foot off that man's neck, and haul you ass directly back into your bed and take the *fucking* medicine I've put on your table for you. Do it now." A sharp collective intake of breath disturbed the otherwise quiet hallway during a pause of six, maybe seven seconds. The red-faced man's eyes wavered, darting to the MP with his hands stretched toward the ceiling. "Do it now, Sergeant. I'll take care of these people."

After a further pause the man slowly lowered his pistol until it pointed first at the nurse's sternum, than at her groin, finally at the MP under his foot. Then he stepped off and began to shamble down the hall. Those against the wall shrank back even further, clutching themselves or those next to them.

"Sergeant!" the woman ordered, her voice only part of an octave higher than normal. "The pistol, Sergeant."

He looked back at her over his shoulder with eyes now turned docile, then bent and put the pistol on the floor, straightened, looked once more at her, and pushed through the doors toward his room.

William found out who she was, courted her quickly and fervently, and before the end of that year they were married.

About a year later, happy to have dodged the call-up of forces to deal with the affair in Korea, in a wildcatting response to an ad he saw in the November, 1950 issue of an engineering trade journal, he sent off his resume and a letter to an outfit with a Seattle address. Putting in sewers for a Virginia construction company hadn't fulfilled him. In the first mail delivery of the new year he was offered the job he'd applied for in Alaska.

Sitting in the small kitchen of their rented apartment, drinking a beer and waiting for Bonnie to get home from the hospital where she worked, he re-read the letter from Ian Morgan, manager of the Whittaker Fisheries cannery in Cloud Bay, on Admiralty Island. William hadn't been to Admiralty but when he'd taken the tour ship from Seattle to Skagway – a two week trip during his senior summer at college – he'd read the tourist brochures and learned a little about the area. He'd liked what he'd seen on the trip and wanted to go back.

The cannery was apparently situated in one of the coves of a long twisty bay that reached in among the mountains of Admiralty Island. Captain James Cook had circumnavigated the island, creeping into its folds and bays and carefully recording everything, as was his custom. His maps show a large island some five hundred miles north of Vancouver, sheltered among others which together with a thin strip of mountainous mainland form the Southeast Alaska coast. High, wild, wintry ranges and ice fields isolate the coastal strip of Alaskan islands and fjords from the rest of the continent. There isn't any road access into the area, not even into Juneau, the capital of Alaska.

Just over one hundred miles long and a third as wide, Admiralty Island is a dark brooding hump of forest rising steeply from the surrounding sheltered waters to jagged peaks and flowered alpine meadows. The Indian village, Wrengoon, is nestled next to the rich waters on a small peninsula twenty miles up the coast from the mouth of Cloud Bay. Some three hundred stalwart Tlingits there lived well on fish, and berries, and deer, and checks from their sons in the Alaska National Guard. William remembered one piece of remarkable lore about Admiralty: the density of brown bears on the island was one adult per square mile.

The Whittaker Cloud Bay cannery, built in 1936, had been boarded up and posted against trespassers – *No Jap Rats!* said the sign – since the beginning of the Second World War and now, Ian Morgan's letter explained, the facilities were going to be reopened and his application as waterworks engineer had been accepted. In the letter Morgan said William's hydro-engineering degree had gotten him the job, and that he should be in Juneau on the 12th of April to begin work. A cadre would go to the cannery on the 15th to put it in shape to operate. William knew virtually nothing about the process of canning fish but he was educated enough to know it must require huge amounts of fresh water, which explained the hiring of an engineer who could theoretically make deserts bloom.

Bonnie walked in the door and when she'd changed out of her whites and joined him at the table, a beer in her hand, he said, "Sugar, how does Alaska sound?"

She stared for a full five seconds, then closed her mouth and swished her short dark hair back and forth. "Ohhhhhh no, you're not sucking me into anything stupid. What exactly do you mean…" she gave herself a dullards voice, sticking her chin out and weaving it in the air, mocking him, "…How does *Alaaaaska* sound?" Her voice went normal again but was more suspicious than usual. "You mean as a place to store *Eskimos,* or as a market for *gas* heaters, or what? Are you trying to tell me something I'm supposed to *know* about? Something to do with Alaska? What the hell is *Alaska?*"

"Sugar, hold on." He reached across the corner of the table and retrieved her hands from her hair. "Be calm. I haven't accepted anything, I just wanted to see what you'd think…"

"William Hood, you're lying to your beloved wife and that's *serious.* You've *done* something and I want revenge as soon as I finish this beer. Tell me the truth *immediately."*

She listened in silence while he explained how he'd seen the ad, and on a whim had applied, "...just to see what'd happen, and that's the truth, Bonnie, and that's why I didn't even remember to mention it to you."

She sat in silence, sipping her beer straight from the bottle, watching him. He had a clean-cut look and she called him *Campus Willie* sometimes.

"It's nothing I can't back out of. Really. And I don't even know for sure that I want it. I just sent in the application to see what'd happen." He had stood and was pacing while he talked. He stopped and leaned back against the counter, thumbs hooked in the pockets of his jeans, and looked down at her. "Well, what do you think?"

She was calm now. "I think you're going to get the back of your lap all wet from that drain board. Come sit down and let me ask you questions."

Before they realized it the sun was down and it was dark, and he got up to turn on the light. They'd decided to do it, but she made a stipulation. "They've got to put me on the payroll too, otherwise I won't go. I don't care how much they pay me but I'm not going to the north pole without having something useful and routine to do. I don't care what it is – stuff fish in cans or whatever they do, run the local kindergarten, be your assistant valve turner – but whatever it is, they've got to hire me too, Willie."

William called Seattle, talked directly to Ian Morgan, explained the situation and waited impatiently with Bonnie, eating popcorn in front of the stove until Ian called back delighted to put Bonnie on as the medical resident for the cannery. She'd take a cut in salary but that didn't matter to them, and it was settled.

Three months later William was in Juneau. Bonnie was to follow in two weeks when the cannery would begin work.

****

William loved the bay as soon as he saw it from the bridge of the sixty-five foot boat carrying the men and a stock of provisions and the equipment Ian Morgan had calculated would be needed to get the factory working again. William had personally inventoried the various plumbing parts and pieces now stowed in the hold, pipe and joints and valves and pump parts, things he supposed would be needed. He'd argued for an initial quick recon over to the island to see what state of repair things were in, but Ian had nixed that. "Joe Badhand told me on the phone from Wrengoon things don't look too bad. He's an Indian, a friend of mine, went around to the factory and had a look for me during the winter. No, we'll just go ahead and take what we think we might need to get the place running, then some. You've seen the blueprints and the waterworks drawings, so you ought to be able to guess what's most likely to have froze and burst or rusted out and need replacement. Use your best judgment."

William had done that, and now what seemed like a lot of plumbing material was stashed below decks. He'd commented twice about the cost and the second time Ian Morgan had scoffed. "Only a few things a cannery's got to have to operate. Cans, of course," he'd chuckled, "and fish to put in them. And water. But then without the cans we could salt or smoke a catch and still come out OK. Without the fish we could lay off most of the hands, send them to town and go dormant until things picked up. But without a flow of constant water we're one hundred percent shut down."

The cruise down Cloud Bay – protected from the North Pacific weather by its twisting course as it reached deep into the island – was much more pleasant than the first fifteen hours of the trip from Juneau had been. Besides William and Ian there were two other cannery employees aboard, and the skipper of the boat, Milton Trent, and his single crewman, who had the helm. None had gotten throw up seasick but the choppy seas had left several of them – Ian Morgan the worst among those – with queasy guts and pale skin. Ian had a nervous look in his eye when finally they turned into the calmer waters of the long bay but soon he was feeling fine, pointing out landmarks as they passed. Lost Jimmy's cove, named for an Indian who'd lived there. Needle Point, the West Fork, Dead Bear Beach, and the entrance to Chinaman's Cove.

By the time they rounded the last of five points of land, following the bay's thickest arm ten miles back into the mass of the island, the water was ceramic and the weathered cannery buildings, when they finally came into sight, looked like distant, mirrored cathedrals cuddled against the skirt of the mountain on a small level space just above high water. A wooden pier faced the bay along the entire front of the main factory, like a long front porch built out over the water. The forest crowded against one end of the pier and rose quickly from close behind the small collection of buildings. Other than the cannery itself and a small settlement in Chinaman's Cove, the bay was completely unpopulated.

William and Ian leaned on the railing at the bow and watched the cannery draw closer. Tom Archer stood next to them. As they chugged past steep beaches of pebble and dark stone they saw blacktailed Sitka deer stepping delicately along the water's edge, stopping to watch the boat pass, unafraid. On two strips of beach stood brown bears, massive, alert, their winter coats shedding in ugly clumps. One raised its flat-faced head from the offal it had found, glanced at them, and returned to its feed. The other didn't bother looking their way as it ambled along the shoreline but through Milt's field glasses William saw its ears come alert.

The air against their skin was damp, unwarmed by the dull, mid-afternoon sun. All three men were in wools and jackets of various styles. Ian had an old crushed-crown, floppy-brimmed Stetson pulled low over his slightly fleshy, florid face. Damp ringlets, not Irish but almost, leaked out from under it. William wore a yellow slicker.

Ian pointed to a big red buoy floating about fifty yards in front of the cannery pier and said, "We'll tie up to that Norwegian tonight. We can take the skiff in and look the place over, talk to Joe Badhand for a while, kind of get a feel for what's got to be done, but we might as well stay aboard tonight. Joe can come out and have supper with us."

There was a trace of something linear visible at times along the heavily forested face of the mountain behind the cannery, coming down at a very slight angle from the left, sloping into the area of the buildings. It might have been a narrow-gauge rail track if someone had reported finding gold in the mountain and this had been mining country. It was straight and its slope constant and it bridged the gullies instead of following the contours, so it wasn't a road. William Hood pointed to it. "That your flume?"

"Yep, that's it," Ian said. "It picks up water out of a ravine about four miles that-a-way," he pointed back along the mountainside toward Chinaman's Cove, "and drops it about six hundred feet in a gentle slope all the way, supplying all we use. It's really just a long covered wooden trough on pilings and trestles, but it works good if it's kept repaired. Good water too, out of a ravine above Chinaman's Cove, right from the snowfields."

After they'd tied up to the big fishing buoy and the boat's engine had been shut down the men unlashed an aluminum skiff sitting bottom up on the stern deck. They got it into the bay without shipping too much water, then got the outboard clamped onto its stern. A red gas can and a fuel line followed, and Milton Trent's crewman plugged it all together, pumped the bulb to start the fuel flow, and pulled the outboard's starting rope. The motor started right up, loud in the quiet of the bay. An eagle, its white head turned sideways to watch them, left its roost and flapped past on its way to a quieter spot. The clouds seemed to have lowered, as had the temperature.

On the cannery pier a black-haired man in a plaid wool shirt had appeared and was now squatting next to a large bollard, watching the boat. Milton saw him and waved, then nudged Ian Morgan and pointed. Ian looked up at the man on shore, snapped his fingers in annoyed remembrance and disappeared below. He reappeared after a moment with what looked like a bottle in a brown paper sack. "Sour mash," he said to Milton, joining the other men in the skiff. He caught the skiff's painter which Milton tossed him and said, "You sure you don't want to come ashore?"

"Naw, you guys go ahead. I'll start some biscuits."

Ian pushed them off and they putt-putted toward the shore. The tide was in but the pier fronting the factory building was still about eight or ten feet above the water level, and William remarked on that as they approached. "Yeah, the spring tides are in now," Ian told him, "but she'll go two or three feet higher yet in the fall. On top of that they got to allow for storms and such, all of which makes for a mighty high pier. You got to be careful of the tides around here. This bay's got about twenty foot of tide. Up north there's places got more'n thirty feet. It'll steal your crab pot if you don't leave enough slack in the buoy rope, and it'll swipe your boat off the beach and leave you stranded if you don't tie her up good, and high, I'll tell you." William saw Tom Archer listening closely.

The skiff started to pull in at one of several steel ladders hanging along the face of the pier. The pilings marched back into darkness underneath the factory building, a bizarre orchard rising from the water. It looked cold and uninviting under there and Ian started to warn the other men in the boat to be careful of the ladder, then changed his mind and yelled up to the silent man squatting above, watching them. "Too many rungs for an old man with a bottle of hooch in one hand, Joe. We'll put her on the beach."

180

Joe Badhand nodded his head in acknowledgement and stood as the skiff altered course, paralleling the rows of pilings, heading toward a small gravel beach forty yards to the left. He joined them as the bow of the boat came ashore. "Don't get your feet wet, Ian, I'll bring her up," he said. The men in the skiff kept their seats as Joe waded half a foot into the water in rubber gum boots and pulled the bow of the skiff up onto the black pebbles. When almost a third of the boat was on dry land the men got out over the bow, their feet dry. Tom Archer took the bow painter up above the beach to tie it off while Ian greeted Joe Badhand, handing him the paper sack and clapping him on the shoulder. "Good to see you, Joe. How was your winter?"

William saw that Ian really was glad to see the Indian, that the two men were friends. When Ian introduced him William felt the strength in Joe's right hand and saw the mutilation of the left one, an old wound, mostly gnarled scar tissue that disappeared up into his shirt sleeve. As the four men moved toward the main factory building William studied the Indian.

Joe Badhand was short and stocky and moved with a slight limp and a rolling gait William had seen in other Indians. It was almost a sailor's walk, or the swinging step of a man wearing snowshoes. His features were strongly Asian, his skin a dark brown. Smallpox scars marked both cheeks and his forehead. His eyes were jet black under fine eyebrows and when he looked, he concentrated. His English was correct, but stated haltingly, as if he were composing his words as he spoke them, or translating them from Tlingit between his brain and his mouth. William liked him.

As they clumped along the boardwalk paralleling the short beach where they'd come ashore, their heads ducked against the mist and a light drizzle, they passed a row of small two-room and three-room bungalows that would serve as quarters for some of the supervisory staff and for the married couples among the crew who'd work the cannery. A fork in the boardwalk just before it reached the main factory building led to storage sheds, tool houses, generator shacks and other small separate buildings squatting in a tight row close behind the factory itself, which loomed over them.

The main building's rusted tin roof, pitched steeply toward the bay, dripped noisily from the channels of its corrugations into gutters two and a half stories above the pier. The upper walls were the same wrinkled rusted tin as the roof, and long Rawlins-red streamers stained the once-green walls below. A full row of twelve-pane windows facing the bay gave the place an eastern seacoast look, as if cold Newfoundlanders who craved the morning sun had built their hopes into it. There was a door on the end of the building and a stout wooden stairway with three square landings climbing the wall to another door above.

To their right the pressing darkness was punctured only by the lonely, misted ports of Milton Trent's boat out at the buoy.

On the small landing at the top of the stairs the men brushed rain from their shoulders and went through the door into the end of the main building. Joe turned on a hanging bulb. They were in a big loft with thick glass windows overlooking the main floor of the cannery, furnished with a fine old desk, sturdy oak chairs, clothes trees, wooden filing cabinets, a dusty, ancient typewriter. The rain was heavy now, pounding on the roof. Joe Badhand went to a junction box to throw a lever and lights came on all over the cavernous building. The sound of a generator picking up revs whined through the drumming above their heads.

Ian took William by the arm and led him to a set of the big windows, pushed one open and leaned – a proud proprietor – on the wide sill. Below were various arrangements of galvanized tin tables with rolled edges forming big shallow sinks. Drains led from the centers and from corners. Connecting chutes and conveyors linked the sinks into a big shiny maze.

Beyond were more conveyor belts leading to a confusion of factory machines – canners and cookers and toppers and labelers.

At the far end were scattered piles of open-ended cans and lids in boxes, and against the farthest wall great stacks of wooden pallets. Narrow gutters crisscrossed the cement floor. Directly above the working area was a system of pipes feeding central manifolds over each sink-table, and from each of the manifolds a dozen rubber hoses drooped almost to the sinks. Big showerhead nozzles with deadman valve handles hung like squashed, worm-holed fruit on the ends of the hoses.

Ian pointed down to the flat sinks. "That's where we make our profit, William. We get a dozen fish people around those gut-tables, each one working like a Ford factory worker during pink slip times, and we're making money."

He pointed to the manifolds. "That's the paycheck end of your job, those hoses. If there are fish on the boats there's got to be water in those *mannies*. Later on you can go over the whole thing and figure it out but what it comes down to is, we've got to have water by the ton. Water to clean fish, which is messy at best. Water to keep the drains and tables flushed, water for cleaning the equipment, the trays, the decks, everything. God, we'd have fish guts and scales two feet thick on every thing and every one, without water.

"We've got to have water to run the camp – showers, cooking, laundry. And we've got to have all that much water again for the beast next door." He rolled his hand to indicate something beyond the far wall.

"The beast?"

"The ice machine, my engineer friend. And you'll know why we call that system the beast the first time it goes down on us during a run of boats. Each fishing boat that comes in here, whether she's full of cod and snapper and halibut – long-lined fish caught on the seabed with hooks – or salmon caught in seiners and drift nets, has got to have fresh ice before she heads back out. *Tons* of it. Without ice the boats can't keep a catch fresh, so they're shut down. If we don't have ice here for 'em they've got to run all the way to Juneau, or across to Sitka, and either way they can't afford to fish these grounds and bring their catches here if we've got no ice."

Ian thumbed back over his shoulder toward a locked cabinet. "We've got a two way radio, and though most of these fishermen still don't have 'em, those who do always give us a call before they come in. They call for one reason, and it's not to see if we're buying fish – we're always buying fish – they want to confirm that the beast is working and they'll be able to fill their holds with ice."

William nodded, beginning to appreciate his own importance in the scheme of things. "What'd they do before ice machines?" he asked.

"Mostly they used glacier ice. The boats would have to spend one in every five days not fishing, but chipping icebergs in front of one of the glaciers. Sometimes there'd be a place they could buy glacier or river ice somebody else had chopped for them and stored in sawdust, but it's not near as good. Glacier ice is dirty, leaves a lot of mud and stuff on the fish, and doesn't prevent spoilage as long as fresh, clean, crushed ice. Same with snow – it'll work in a pinch to get a boat through a day of bad weather stuck behind an island somewhere, but there's no real substitute for what we sell them." Ian chuckled. "This place's been closed up for a while and those fishermen are going to be glad to see us here this year." He straightened, holding his lower back for a moment while he looked fondly down at the cannery floor, then he pushed up the sleeve of his jacket, glanced at the watch on his wrist, looked around at the others and announced, "We'd better get back to the boat. Milton said he'd have biscuits on the table about now."

Ian turned to William as they started toward the door. "I'd suggest you start tomorrow at every water outlet and trace the pipes backwards until you know where everything is and where everything comes from. When you're ready to walk the flume let me know and I'll have somebody go with you. Which reminds me. Don't leave the cannery by yourself. And when we get back to the boat I'll give you a shotgun. We got bears here that love engineers like fat ladies love stickybuns."

****

Later that night after a supper of soda-biscuits, corned beef and canned hominy – a *delight*, Milton called it, though nobody else did – the topic of bears came up again. William brought up the subject by reminding Ian of his shotgun comment. They were alone in the pilot house. Milton Trent was out on deck, fiddling with something under a spotlight, a fine mist glistening on his yellow slicker. Everyone else had turned in. Joe had declined the invitation of supper on the boat and had stayed ashore, sleeping in one of the small bungalows Ian had designated. He'd get a small salary during the season, for which he'd help out around the place as needed. Ian had been going over some lists he'd spread out on the chart table. He gathered them up and regarded William over the half-glasses he used for reading. William was reminded of a police sergeant he'd once known in New York. "Yeah. Bears," Ian responded. "They got more damn brownies on this one island than anyplace else I know of. I don't know much about them myself and don't care to – they haven't yet wandered into the cannery building itself – but I do know they've got to be figured into things. First rule is, try not to get into thick brush if you've got to be in the woods for something. There's blueberry patches in there you can't get through or see through, but a brownie might be laid up in there and you disturb him… You just want to avoid the damn things.

"Used to be, in the very old days, we killed every one we saw, but I guess times change and we don't do that anymore. Matter of fact you've got to have an expensive permit to shoot one now." Ian picked up a glass from the table beside him, regarded it, then tipped

185

the contents into his mouth. He held up a pint bottle of apricot brandy. William declined. Ian poured an inch into the glass then continued talking, his ample butt centered on a four-legged stool. "You see that bad hand on Joe?"

William nodded.

"Well, that's a lucky man. Get him to tell you how it happened someday, or I could tell you, I get the time. Most times when one of these coastal brown bears gets that close to somebody there's a death in the family. In the morning I'll give you a short pump shotgun to carry, and you want to hope you never have to use it. Carry it plumb full of the slugs I'll give you and if you can't get up a tree fast enough, and I mean far up a tree, then you might as well blast away, though you'll be lucky if you do any good and you can probably kiss your ass goodbye.

"If you shoot, try to do it from a prone position. Don't bother letting him get in until you can smell him, just start blastin' away. Try to get slugs in up under his chin, which would be your best head-on shot, I'm told. It'd be nice if you could bust both his front shoulders, but take what you can get. 'Course this is all theory to me, though I do know several men who've been mauled and lived to tell it, like Joe, and knew a couple others who didn't. Milt's lost a couple of friends also, boat skippers or crew who got careless ashore."

Ian tossed back his brandy and stood up, patting his belly. "There's not much I can really tell you beyond that. They swim, they climb spruce trees until they run out of big branches – about twelve feet at most – they're smart and unpredictable and they aren't afraid of a thing. If you surprise one, figure he's a bully and try for a tree as quick as you can, got it?"

William nodded again, wanting to ask questions but not knowing what to ask. He was fascinated at the understanding that he was working in a place where grizzly bears were a daily factor. He remembered clearly throwing all his own stuffed bears into a box for transfer to the trash, an event sponsored by the pain in his leg and a kernel of fear that made him eye all large creatures with reserve. The last time he'd carried a weapon for his health had been in the hedgerows of France.

"Like I said, though, best advice is to avoid them, and good night, Engineer."

"Good night, Ian." He filed the conversation where he could find it in his memory.

15

The poured lead sky was still leaking mist when the new day arrived damp and cold, the darkness diminishing grudgingly. Milton Trent's boat floated in its own perfect reflection. A flight of ducks skimmed in over the peninsula that jutted to the north of the cannery, saw movement on the deck of the boat, and wheeled away looking for a better place. On shore there was a fat column of smoke over the mess building.

It was still early morning when the men loaded into the skiff and headed ashore. The tide was coming in. When it reached its flood Milton Trent and his crewman would bring the boat to the pier and start lifting supplies ashore with the cannery's air tugger.

All morning William and Tom Archer went over the working parts of the cannery. Tom started out looking like a man who'd hunted bedbugs in his mattress all night but as the morning progressed he loosened up a bit. At one point they were joined at one of the canning machines by Johnson, the other member of the startup crew and one of Tom's mechanics for the season. Johnson had worked in Cloud Bay before the war. The two men drew aside and had a short conversation with some clenched fists and angry words William couldn't hear, Johnson pointing off toward Chinaman's Cove, and later William heard Tom muttering, "…Goddam squints…" He didn't know what that meant and didn't ask. As far as William could tell, the skinny, unhealthy-

188

looking Johnson was upset over something broken or missing. Johnson went off muttering to himself and wiping his hands on the seat of his dirty trousers.

The whole group of them gathered for lunch in the mess hall where Joe Badhand had fired one wood stove to heat coffee and tins of food he'd opened. It was an uninspired meal but nobody seemed to care, each person caught up now in the process of getting the cannery and all its parts operable before the season started. They all sat at one end of a long table, closest to the stove, comfortable in the heat it was putting out. There were several conversations going on, each man talking about what he'd found during his particular inspections, comparing items from little notebooks hauled from inside pockets, pencils or pens occasionally out to jot a remembrance.

Tom Archer leaned toward Ian. William could hear his words. "Johnson says there's two hydraulic ball valves gone off that lid crimper down there. An' he told me there's a bunch of thievin' Chinese around here." It was easy to see how any discussion with Tom Archer could become an argument. William forked a Vienna sausage through a puddle of ketchup on his plate and into his mouth, then looked over at Ian's reaction.

Ian had heard, all right, but appeared unintimidated by the belligerence in the statement. He stuffed a ship's cracker into his mouth, poured coffee in after it, shifted his eyes to Tom Archer, and when he'd swallowed he told him plainly, "Look in the shop, Tom. There's spares. Anybody else notice things gone?" Ian looked around at the others, who were shaking their heads. "Well if you do, let me know." He looked at Tom. "And there's no evidence those Chinese are thieves."

Tom Archer started to say something but changed his mind at Ian Morgan's look.

"Anyway, make sure everything we need's on line." Ian proceeded then to outline the procedures they'd follow during the next ten days, glancing at a clipboard, turning papers up, moving plates and cups and rolling out some blueprints at one point. Each man there was responsible for certain areas, and Ian had a sensible plan for checking various components of the plant individually, then progressively wedding systems together until he was sure everything would operate as it should when the work crews arrived. Ian would coordinate everything from his office in the loft. Tom Archer was in charge of the production line machinery and the beast.

The pinch-faced mechanic, Johnson, was responsible for all the support machinery – the generators, the compressed air system that ran the tuggers on the pier, the conveyors, and the two small forklifts that moved pallets. Also he'd help resolve any mechanical problems that came up. He wiped his hands continually on whatever he could find, as if the grease in his life would never go away. It filled the prints of his out-sized hands like ink at a police booking desk.

William, the only college-trained man in the crew, was responsible for water from its source to the outlet where it flushed into the bay, used and full of fish offal, down among the pilings where the local crabs waited eagerly for it. Although the plumbing was only plumbing, and everything was straightforward, it was not foolproof. An avalanche or a rock slide could take out the flume, a fallen tree could divert the flow in the source ravine, a critical pump in the labyrinth behind the generator house could fail, and any of these things could happen just after the cannery had bought twenty tons of fish, with other boats inbound to unload and replenish their ice. If that ever happened William would earn his money, diverting flows, tapping the various reservoirs and leading men to fix, bypass or rebuild the failure spot. It was a job that required training, imagination, and an appreciation for the importance of water.

That evening after a long day of following lead pipes through crawl spaces and behind machinery, tracing flows and discovering junctures and valves that had been added or changed since the plans had been drawn, William was enjoying the luxury of a hot shower. Tom Archer came into the shower room. He peeled off the slightly tattered bathrobe he was wearing and hung it on a peg, then stepped under a showerhead and turned on the steaming spray.

When William got the soap out of his eyes and saw Tom he immediately noticed the scars all over the man's back, on his buttocks and his upper arms. Tom turned his head and saw William's look. "Burma. And Changi," he said, toweling himself off. "Goddam squints near rubbed me out."

William looked hard at Tom's face, at the hate behind the words, and glanced again at the mass of scars. Archer's skin was almost grey in shade, except his hands, which were a darkened brown. His hair was thin, cut short. But his most distinctive feature, not considering the scars hidden under his clothes or the split ear, or the almost-crippled way he moved, was his perpetual scowl, as if his face had been set for a scene in a stage play that went on forever. Wrinkles and lines that might have been the work of a makeup artist fixed the look, and William wondered whether the personality was cause or effect of the countenance. A little of both, he supposed. He wondered how deep the scowl went and decided few people probably knew. The obstacles to intimacy were just too severe to overcome.

Later, at supper – meals were obviously going to be the time for coordination – Ian Morgan went over each man's findings, making an occasional note in the small black loose-leaf notebook he carried, making suggestions, asking questions. William's respect for the man and his style, his sense of what he was doing and how it should be done, continued to grow. Ian listened when a man spoke and when there was a problem he seemed to remove the subject of blame and focus on the solution, as when Johnson, the greasy mechanic, pointed out that caulking he needed had been forgotten. It could have been anybody's fault.

Ian listened, nodded, made a note, then said, "Work around it as much as you can, Johnson, and in the morning check with Milton Trent on the boat – he might have some in his engine room. There might also be some over with that stuff in the pump room. If you don't do any good, let me know and we'll think of something else." Johnson, who'd looked defensive when he brought the issue up, nodded as if the problem had been solved. Ian was that kind of a superintendent. "Anything else missing besides those two valves on the topper?" he asked.

Tom looked up, then put his head back down and continued eating. William noticed, and wondered why Archer was so upset by the small loss of two valves. Anything could have happened to them. The last crew, the crew that had shut down the operation years ago and left the place dormant, could have removed them in spite of their requirement to leave the place fully operational. Some boat skipper, or bear hunters even, could have come in and removed them. But it was apparent Tom Archer didn't think so... "William," Ian Morgan interrupted the engineer's thought. "Are you ready to walk that flume? It might be your biggest headache and we might have to get a crew in to fix it, if there's much down. I don't want to wait too long."

"Yeah, I think I've got most of this stuff in the factory figured out. We look to be in pretty good shape here, far as I can tell. I just need to replace some split valves that didn't get fully drained, and that reservoir tank has some rot that needs patching. What kind of shape you expect that flume to be in?"

Ian was chewing a big greasy hunk of canned ham. He finished chewing, wiped his chin with a small hand towel, then waved his fork in Joe's direction. Joe was stirring pudding in a big enamel saucepan on the stove. It was warm in the mess hall from the fire they'd kept in one big cook stove, and the men had taken off wool shirts and opened union suit tops – all except Tom Archer, who seemed not to notice the warmth. William saw a big drop of sweat fall from Joe's forearm into the pudding, and decided not to eat any. "Joe claims she's in pretty good shape, right, Joe?" Ian said.

Joe raised his chin in affirmation, and in the fullest monologue William had yet heard from the Indian, said, "The flume is in adequate shape considering its disuse for so long. I have walked its course three times this past winter, the last time just a week before your arrival. There are two places where complete rebuilds are required because of fallen trees, and a number of other places where trestle timbers or flume planking needs to be replaced, but I believe you will find no other major rebuilding necessary."

During this speech, which left William with his lower jaw hanging open, his fork suspended, Joe had shoved the saucepan over onto the cool side of the stove and had stood quietly, stirring spoon in his right hand, his gnarled left fist hanging next to the stove. Only when he was finished, as if he'd just completed a memorized stanza in front of his school class, did he look away from Ian. As he turned back to retrieve his pudding he glanced down and saw his left shirt cuff smoldering. *"God, damn,"* he muttered, making two complete words of it, and raising his left arm away from the stove. He beat at the cuff with the big metal stirring spoon in his right hand, ignoring the bright red skin and scar tissue on his left hand. Everyone else in the room must have felt his own left hand burning, but obviously Joe didn't. A collective sigh of relief went through the room when Joe thrust his hand and forearm under a faucet and a gush of water spilled over them. Joe cursed again, the same muttered oath, inspected the charred spot on the cuff of his blue wool shirt, and looked at Ian to see if there were any more questions about the flume.

Nobody said a word and later, with coffee, William joined the rest of the men – excepting Tom Archer – in praising the pudding.

****

They were sleeping ashore now in several of the small bungalows above the beach, Ian and William each taking a room in one, Tom Archer and Johnson bunking up in another bungalow. Joe Badhand was staying in one on the end of the row closest to the factory building.

Ian and William were sitting in the diminutive living room facing the wood stove, Ian on a dilapidated settee, William in a broken-legged overstuffed chair. A piece of firewood jammed under a corner kept the chair from listing. Ian had broken out his apparently bottomless bottle of apricot brandy and William, a book unopened on his lap, had begun to wonder if he might not even learn to like the stuff before the season was over. Outside it was cold, dark, and quiet, as if the whole warm world were contained in the flower-walled, low-ceilinged living room with the two men. Ian poured, then set the open bottle on the upended chunk of spruce log serving for a coffee table, and spoke. "You're probably curious about Joe." It was a statement.

"Yeah, as a matter of fact, I am. That was quite a speech he delivered tonight and it'd be tough to follow that finale." William took a sip of the brandy, made an apricot flavored belch, and patted his belly. "And good pudding, too. Tell me about him."

"Well, I'll tell you what I know, which is quite a bit, I guess. Over the years I've known him – since we first opened this cannery, in fact – I guess I've heard most of the details…"

****

Joe Arnold had been born in a bobbing fishing skiff about a mile offshore from Wrengoon, with no ill effects to mother, baby, or the day's catch of salmon.

194

That had been the year the white men started their big war with the other white men, the one that had something to do with making the world safe for democracy. The war had had no discernible effect on life in Wrengoon except that the postmaster, a young white man with a fat wife, had gone off and had been replaced a month later with a cross-eyed white woman who thumbtacked posters on the wall: a white, pointing grandfather in a high hat saying, "I want you!" For years Joe and the other kids of the village thought the poster was a picture of the white man's God, Jesus Christ, whose name was heard so often in so many different circumstances and who, it was said, wanted men's souls. It never occurred to them to wonder about connections between the U. S. Post Office and heaven. The postal system was as much a mystery as everything else the white people did, or anything attributed to their Postal God, Jesus Christ.

Almost a thousand people lived in Wrengoon then, most of them in crowded shacks made from rough-milled spruce, some in half-dugouts with sod roofs, others in substantial log cabins. A family's wealth or energies weren't reckoned by an examination of their living quarters, which were always dark, smoky and dirty, but by comparing their fishing skiffs.

In that regard Joe came from one of the wealthier families. His family of two living uncles and fourteen male cousins had a total among them of three skiffs, and if the family shared several log and plank cabins in sad need of repair, nobody noticed because each of their skiffs – long, well built, beautifully painted – more than established their place in the village. When there was a subject for serious discussion in the village – and there always was – then the Arnold family was represented and respectfully heard.

An elderly aunt was the head of the family and though she was too fat and sick to attend most of the discussions in the community house, young Joe often heard men and women talking to her as she reclined on her pallet in the darkness, asking her opinion, telling her the facts, sharing the gossip. The discussions at the community house continued day and night, summer and winter, people wandering in, sitting on the floor to listen, speaking in turn or saying nothing, falling asleep, nursing babies, wandering out again. Only during the salmon runs did the consultations lag when every villager, able-bodied or not, helped in some way to catch or preserve the winter's food staple. Even then there were always two or three people in the community house keeping the lamp lit, the discussion alive. They talked about each other, and about the fishing and the hunting, shared gossip brought from Juneau or Sitka, or wondered about the Chinese people who lived in the cove twenty miles down the coast, in the bay.

It was a good way for a boy to grow – or a girl. There were games to be played, chores to be done, places to explore. And always there was the anticipation that an uncle would allow a small worthless boy to accompany him in a skiff on a hunting trip.

Smallpox struck the village when Joe was an older child with five small black hairs just sprouting on the bone below his belly. The sickness took one in three villagers, driving the rest to the woods in fear. Joe had sickened, forgotten for days in a smoky dugout, his fever raging, his eyes running, his skin pustulated. But he had survived.

Two years of bare existence in an isolated fishing camp had followed before those left in his immediate family decided it was safe to return to the village. When they returned they found the village changed, but the consultation in the village community house continued. It never occurred to wonder whether there had been a time when there was nothing being decided by the consensus of the village. Some things are constant, and older than the forest.

Joe's first rifle, a .30-40 Krag with a tightly wired split at the small of the stock, was given to him by his older brother. At first he had only four rounds of ammunition for it and he didn't consider wasting any of them in practice. He'd dry-fired it a thousand times though, and he kept the four rounds oiled and polished and clean in a leather pouch he'd made. The deer which provided the skin from which the white pouch came had been killed with a club after coming to investigate a wounded fawn's cry – a call Joe made by blowing on a leaf held in his mouth.

There wasn't anything unusual about Joe's life until the first summer he came back from boarding school in Sitka. He did his share of work, got his share of fish and girls and scrapes. He and his playmates were almost never disciplined and seemed no worse for the lack, and they had no word in their vocabulary for shame. They spoke of trouble, and of pain, and of missing some departed friend or relative whom everybody knew but nobody named, and they talked of the things around them, but not of shame. Joe hadn't learned about that until he'd gone to the boarding school and seen it among the Christians, though he still didn't have any himself.

The few boys and girls who stayed in school went away after the eighth grade, which they completed in their village school. High school was serious though, and not to be trusted to provincial administrators or teachers. As did thousands of his peers from villages from all over Alaska, Joe packed his few clothes and the four rifle rounds in their small pouch and, taking the fortnightly boat with the others from his village, he went off to the nearest government school for village Indians.

Three weeks into his first summer home he was caught by the brown bear.

****

Joe had gone out with Billy John, who was the son of one of the village storekeepers and whose uncle and namesake was a well respected Indian statesman living in Juneau. The two boys had taken their rifles and a skiff with a motor and had gone deep into

197

the bay country behind the village. There were hunting camps and fishing camps all over the area, most of which had been used longer than anyone could recall, and the two boys beached their boat at one of those which they'd used the summer before.

A pole lean-to with a corrugated tin roof kept the rain off, and there were two dead hemlocks that would provide firewood for years. The camp had a small freshwater stream and enough exposure so the wind would keep the evening mosquitoes down, if not the daytime flies.

Billy John killed a small buck the afternoon of the first day, and because the boys were hungry for meat they brought the whole carcass back to camp in the skiff and tied it high in a small spruce tree with most of the lower branches lobbed off. Joe later would wonder if the year at school, being away from this place and his own family, had dulled his feelings for who he was and what he should do or not do, because both boys knew better than to hang meat near their camp.

The grizzly arrived during the night, just before the sun set, drawn by the smell of the cooking meat and charred scraps the boys tossed in the coals. It just appeared there on the beach before them, the breeze in its nose. It hadn't made a sound except for the shifting scrape of pebbles beneath its pads, but the noise of the flying bugs and the crackling cooling of the dying fire had more than covered that.

The two youths were lying back in the lean-to, each with a tin can of coffee. Billy John had a pipe lit. Joe was telling him about a girl he'd had at school. They were laughing when the terrible, pungent stink of bear overwhelmed them.

Joe felt his nostrils dilate and his testicles suck up into his body. He sat up abruptly, jarring the roof of the shelter, one hand throwing the tin can aside, the other reaching for his Krag.

But he knew he and Billy John were dead. They'd probably foolishly killed themselves by asking this bear to come to them.

The beast filled the world on all fours, facing them just beyond the embers of their fire. It blocked out sights of the bay, the mountains beyond. It replaced the greenness of life with the brown evil sight of no-more-living. Great streams of saliva drooled from its jaws as the aroma of the boys' meat rumbled in its belly and focused its wants.

Joe's scream brought the beast's ears forward and made it hump up its shoulders. Simple hunger had drawn it to this place and without confrontation it would have eaten and slept and eaten again, eventually wandering off leaving nothing but piles of dung and smashed places in the blueberry bushes. Now there was a challenge. It would eliminate that and then it would feed and sleep. It threw its weight forward in two swift hopping motions, stiff legged, like a cat pouncing, and with one blurring sweep of an arm it tumbled the shelter into a pile of bent tin and tangled poles.

As the lean-to crashed under the bear's weighted fury, one of its uprights smashed into the side of Billy John's head, knocking him flat, unconscious and bleeding from his ear. The lean-to roof collapsed on top of him.

The bear made a move back, away from the noise of the tin, took another hop, was trying to focus its eyes on something worthy, and saw Joe rolling away from the tangle. The sound coming from its throat changed, rose in pitch and anticipation, and the bear took a step forward, shifting its weight to pounce on Joe but its left front paw came down on the hot coals of the fire and it jerked back, whirling, slavering and issuing its own scream, suddenly mad to slaughter. A hind foot landed in the same coals and the beast was crazed, spinning, slashing the air. Its burned feet upset its balance and it rolled once, smashing across what was left of the woodpile, raging at its hurt. The boys were forgotten in its fury, the meat was forgotten, everything in the universe was dead to the killing animal.

In those moments Joe found himself several yards away from the bear and began to wonder if he might escape. The rifle crossed his mind but he discarded the thought, edged away, staying on the ground, trying to be like the ferns and bushes that littered the forest floor, trying for as much distance as possible before the animal's fury turned again to him. He had only seconds to withdraw from the circle of total destruction the bear would leave, but if he could get beyond that line he had the slimmest of chances.

He slithered away – another yard, another – trying to move without moving, his face cast down to hide but his eyes locked on the blur of terror. His nose prickled with the stench of the bear and with the bile of his own last fear. Another yard. His scurrying body came up against the sloping lower branches of a big spruce tree. If he could only get beneath them, hide.

He willed himself to look away, to see a hole in the thick branches but he couldn't tear his eyes from the bear. The creature had overcome the shock of its burned pads and was ravaging the lean-to, throwing sheets of tin and shaking poles in its mouth like a dog with a rat. Joe could visualize his own body held in those jaws, his chest and back punctured by those huge fangs, his face and belly clawed to shreds by the raking paws. He pushed against the barrier of the foliage which opposed and taunted him, the springy branches of the spruce tree. Finally, in a surge of fear and desperation he was through the outer branches but he had to rise up to break through and when he did he knew the beast had seen him.

He screamed his mortal terror and threw himself through the spiky branches, lunging for the bole of the tree, hurling himself toward his only salvation. Old jagged branches punctured his face and scratched his eyes, another stump of branch, a deadly spike, caught his ear and ripped it, another snagged his shirt but they were nothing compared to the hurtling mass behind him. Through his own ear-pounding terror he could hear the bear's roar as it focused its attack, gathered itself, charged over the intervening yards. It should have had him there, ended it then, but as it clattered across the wreckage of the lean-to a jagged sheet of tin caught it in the soft junction of a hind leg at its groin, slowed it, pained it, opened a wound, maddened it more.

Joe clawed his way up through the branches, trying to swing around the rough trunk of the tree, up and over the sagging branches of the big evergreen, briefly out of sight, momentarily in its greenness. The tough bark peeled the skin from his face and hands and forearms, the palms of his hands were ripped and punctured by stubby branches against the trunk. He felt one stab through his pants and poke deeply into his thigh but he kept moving, scrambling for height.

Behind him, too close, the furious grizzly thrust his head into the lower branches of the tree. Joe hoped for one flashing instant the branches would be too thick, would defeat the bear and make it possible for him to get beyond the animal's persistence, but the monster came clawing through the needles and small outer branches like they were blades of grass and suddenly it was within the sanctum. The boy screamed again and threw himself higher and the bear, scant feet below, looked up, seeing its prey. With a snort that sprayed Joe with stinking snot and foam the creature focused its piggy bloodshot eyes into Joe's, shaping his nightmares forever, then it started up after him, trying to climb the branches. Though it snapped the dead limbs off the trunk like dry kindling, the living branches were resilient and they opposed its strength, bent against its fury, pushed back with power of their own, combined against its rush. The maddened bear couldn't climb. It howled its rage at the figure above and lunged up, reaching with outstretched claws. Two long, shiny black scimitars cut through the rubber of Joe's boot and raked across the top of his foot, slicing through bones and ripping nerves and when the boy felt the fire he screamed again and the pain loosened his grasping holds on the branches and he reached down instinctively toward the agony and again the bear heaved itself up through the intervening thicket of branches, slashing in a small arc, and Joe's left hand and arm up to the gristle of his elbow were shredded. His final scream was lost in the maelstrom of the bear's own howls as its overpowering weight dragged it back toward the ground.

It crashed down, rolling onto its back, trying to gain its feet, but was bowled by the thick springy branches. The shock of being out of the tree came suddenly to the bear and it shook its head, confused. Clouds of night flies swarmed at its face, drawn by the heat of its raging, by the stench of blood, by the foamy saliva and snot that covered the bear's muzzle and ran from its jaws. Its tongue and gums bled from the wounds the branches and spikes had caused, its nose was torn and both eyes were bloodshot with the pressure of its fury. It roared, shaking its head and humping its back, looking around, turning, looking. It saw the tumbled mess of the lean-to, the tendrils of smoke from the scattered coals. Then its eyes caught the movement of an oilcloth raincoat Billy John had earlier hung on a branch.

The bear pushed its chin to the ground, humping its back, issued a low-throated growl, half reared up and clawed the air, threw its head around, then moved sideways, crabbing toward the raincoat, leading with its shoulder, head low to the ground, puffing breath disturbing clouds of needles and forest floor trash. When it was close, it sprang, sweeping the raincoat into its arms, hugging the cloth against its chest, ripping with its teeth, tearing at it with jaws and claws and when the raincoat was tatters on the disturbed earth it pounced on it with all four feet, jumped on it again, spinning, still raging.

The creature stopped then, huffing from exertion. It looked around at the destruction, sniffing, turning to peer at one thing, then something else. Finally it looked down at the bits of yellow cloth on the ground. It sniffed at them. Then it squatted and urinated on what was left of the raincoat. A satisfied groan came from its chest. It was done.

The animal moved off down the beach, the meat, the burnt pads all forgotten, the anger all purged.

Billy John twitched once under the junk that had been the lean-to, then was still again. Beneath the spruce tree the dry needles and the flies sucked up the blood that dripped from above.

It was full dark when Joe completed the process of falling from the tree. He didn't know for certain the bear was gone but it didn't matter, he couldn't stay in the tree any longer. It was the consuming and growing pain that drove him to loosen his body and fall from one branch to another until finally he lay on the ground where the trunk joined the earth. If the bear was still there waiting, or sleeping, it would finish killing him.

He shuddered, cold, sick, his whole body shaking from the wet night and the shock. He had no idea what he'd find beyond the sheltering, spiny branches. He'd been able to spare no thought for his friend Billy John. A light rain fell. There was almost no light. Slowly, as quietly as possible, Joe dragged himself out from under the tree. There was only his pain and the strange silence of the rain and the terrible stench of the bear. Red agony coursed through him from all his parts, beyond source, all of life.

As he neared the broken pile that had been the lean-to his weight came onto a piece of bent tin and it screeched against another and he shuddered back, waiting, eyes wide to see the final darkness of the bear descending on him. It didn't come. After a few moments he moved again, pulling himself with one arm, dragging his body. Mosquitoes drawn by the blood clogged his ears and his nostrils and died in his eyes. His hand touched something yielding. Wool. Wet. Cold. It was Billy John, his leg. Joe shook the leg feebly. There was no response. Joe wanted to sob but couldn't. He patted Billy John's leg, then dragged himself toward the beach.

He managed to cut the bow painter, pull himself into the skiff. The boat's stern bobbed, afloat, but the bow was aground and though he tried, he didn't have the small strength required to budge it off the beach. The tide would have to lift it.

****

Late the next afternoon a group of women picking sticks and seaweed out of a fishing net strung from a rocky point saw the skiff drift by, heading slowly for the saltwater tide-river that flowed past Wrengoon. One of them called to a boy on the rocks toward the village and soon two men were motoring out to retrieve the drifter. They knew whose skiff it was.

It took Joe the rest of the summer and more to recover from his wounds. The village nurse cleaned and stitched them, dusting sulfa powders liberally as she did so. Joe was in very poor shape for several weeks and if the nurse had had her way he'd have been sent to the hospital in Juneau. He refused to go though, knowing the white doctors would cut something off, either his hand or his arm or his ear or his foot. Over the months his foot healed well, his hand healed poorly, and the nurse did a fair job of stitching his ear, which hardly ever showed through his hair anyway.

Six men in two skiffs went to get Billy John's body. They expected to find only parts but in fact he was whole, cold, stiff, the only mark on him a bloody gash along one side of his head. They wrapped him in a tarpaulin and tied it with rope, and after they collected what they could find of the two boys' equipment, including their rifles, they left the camp as they'd found it, torn, shattered, still stinking. Three of the men motored back to the village in one skiff with Billy John's body stretched stiffly across the thwarts. Three rode in the other boat with the deer Billy John had shot. It was a good contribution to the feast at the boy's funeral.

16

It had gotten colder while Ian told William about Joe Badhand, He stood, stretched, moved his arms and flexed his legs to get the stiffness out. The pint bottle of apricot brandy on the stump table was three-fourths gone, and it was time for bed. "You saw tonight there's not much nerve left in that one hand of Joe's but it doesn't seem to slow him down much, and you'll only notice him limp once in awhile when you see him on a stretch of level ground. Still, he was lucky. We should all be so lucky. And with that nice thought," Ian said, headed toward his room, "I'm going to bed. If you put a chunk in that Airtight stove and close it up we'll still have some heat in the morning." With a raised-hand wave of goodnight he pushed through the curtain and soon William heard the creak of the bed and shortly after that the snores of a sound sleeper. William finished the sweet fruit brandy in his glass and went to bed.

Sometime during the night a shape crossed the beach below the small houses near the cannery, but it was a silent passing and disturbed no one.

By the next morning the gossamer rain had stopped and the clouds were lifting, breaking, until finally thick bright beams poked through everywhere. William was awed by his first really clear view of the bay. The water shimmered with frostings of tiny whitecaps lifted from the wave tops by snowfield breezes. Directly across from the cannery cove rose a trio of mountains, one behind the other, each capped with dazzle, sparkling above the tree line. Shoulders of dark green forest sloped down to either side, one ridge running out toward the mouth of the bay and forming the opposite shore, the other dipping to the salmon creek valley and then rising to the system of mountains behind the cannery. William stood on the boardwalk in front of the house, contemplating the view, bundled in jacket and gloves against the chill of the breeze. A bald eagle soared above him, high enough to be a speck. William envied its view.

Ian Morgan came out of the house and joined him on the boardwalk. "Now that's a sight," he said with reverence as they looked at the bay. The two men stood for a moment, each making his own silent medicine in his own way, then they turned together and went to the mess hall beyond the factory building.

Joe Badhand had biscuits and coffee made. He stood aside while the others fried eggs and slabs of canned ham to their own liking. Tom Archer came in and sat scrunched over a mug of coffee, still trying to wake up. A cut on his chin claimed he'd shaved but his cheeks and jaw were as dark as ever. Conversation was sparse as each man got his own motors started.

As food warmed up Ian began getting the day organized. Tom Archer and Johnson, who hadn't shown up yet, were scheduled to get the conveyors all lubricated, and then they'd try to start a couple of the machines on the exit side of the canning complex. Ian planned to spend his day working on the ice maker.

William was looking forward to this spectacular clear day. He was going to inspect the flume, starting at the big wooden reservoir tank and walking the length of it through the forest until, four miles to the north and six hundred feet higher, it reached the chilly waters of the ravine. Joe Badhand would walk with him. They'd packed a lunch of biscuits and ham, and William filled a thermos with coffee to take along. He was just screwing the thermos top down when the mess hall door slammed open and Johnson came in, agitated, an ever-present greasy rag bunched in one hand.

Ian Morgan looked up from his plate at the mechanic striding toward him and over a mouthful of scrambled eggs muttered, "Oh boy, here we go." Before Johnson could speak Ian was wiping his lips and paying attention. "What've you got, Johnson?"

"Boss, it's them Chinamen again. They've gone too far this time and I think we ought to do something, take the boat around and…"

"Hold on, Johnson. Joe! Joe, give the man some coffee, will you please? Now pull up here, Johnson, and sit down, right here." Ian pushed out a chair next to himself and guided the man into it, his hand on his arm. Johnson sat. Ian hadn't gotten up, but he'd succeeded in getting the angry mechanic on an eyeball-to-eyeball level, the first step in calming him down.

Joe put a steaming mug of coffee on the table, watching with apparent indifference as Johnson carefully put his greasy rag beside his cup. Ian slid a can of milk over with the back of one hand. "Now, what's the trouble?" he asked.

"Well, Mr. Morgan, Tom told you about them valves missing on the topper…"

"Yeah. Did you find spares?"

"No sir. Not only that but somebody's been into the main generator room and there's enough parts gone to build half a dozen generators from scratch. This cannery ain't going to can many fish on that two-fifty KW we got going for house lights now, and I'll tell you, there's enough gone from the big generator that I'm going to need a parts manual just to write out a list." He paused, calmer now, and cupped the steaming mug in his stained hands. "I'll tell you something else. This time we got *proof* it was them damned Chinese. Take a look at this…" He put his mug aside and unrolled his dirty rag on the table in front of him, standing, pushing his chair back with the backs of his legs, carefully pulling the wrinkles out of the center of the rag. Joe Badhand and the other men crowded around to see his evidence, but there wasn't anything to see, just a large, dirty, greasy cotton rag.

Ian spoke. "Look at what, Johnson?"

Johnson pointed to a few shiny specks in the center of the rag along a dark crease. "Those," he said. "Know what those are, Mr. Morgan?" He looked up, triumphant, and Tom Archer, seeing, nodded, agreeing. "Them's fish scales, Mr. Morgan," Johnson declared. "*Herring* fish scales. And there's just one place in this whole area where people got herring scales on their boots and on their clothes and in their filthy hair, and that's over to that Chinese saltery. *That's* who's got them parts, and there's the proof." He pointed significantly to the shiny specks, which William could barely see in the grease and general dirt of the rag, then he finished like a district attorney telling how he'd seen the dripping knife himself. "I wiped 'em off the floor right next to that piece of shit we got for a generator now."

****

Ian had resisted coming to any hasty conclusions when Tom Archer had prejudicially blamed the Chinese at the saltery for scrounging from the cannery. Now the accusation was repeated, the loss much more significant. The evidence – a few herring scales found on the floor – was just so ludicrous and flimsy... But maybe the Chinese in the cove *had* come over and lifted a few things from the cannery. Ian didn't know, and he didn't know how to find out without making an outright accusation, and he certainly couldn't do that on the basis of a few fish scales. If Johnson hadn't exaggerated, the generator they needed to run the machines and the pumps was out of action. He'd have to have parts flown out by floatplane.

He didn't want to believe it had been the Hongs. He *didn't* believe it. He knew them, though not well. Thievery was against their nature, so far as he knew, and although they did have a generator over at the saltery he didn't have any idea whether it was compatible with the one that had been stripped. Any fishing boat could have come by and its crew could have done the robbing. Halibut fishermen used herring for bait and could have tracked in those scales. Hell, those scales could be years old.

On the other hand, the Chinese *were* nearby, and they certainly could have come around the point in a skiff or walked through the forest along the flume. But instead of speaking any of these thoughts which raced through his mind as Johnson carefully bunched up his rag, Ian made up his mind to be a force for reason. It was possible that real trouble would flare between the two camps; racial disorder was the order of the day across America. "Johnson," he said, "I want you to make me that list, first thing, so I can order the replacement parts we need, and I want you to go over every other machine you're in charge of and make sure nothing *else* is missing. Got that?"

Johnson nodded his head seriously.

"And as far as who took those parts, maybe you're right, maybe is was our friends around the point, but I can't put the blame on them just because they work around herring. So you just forget about who did it and concentrate on getting the situation fixed. If there's flying weather I'll have those parts out from Juneau tomorrow or the next day. Clear?"

"Yes sir, I can do that, but…"

"No buts, Johnson. I'll take care of worrying about who robbed this place, you worry about my goddam machines." Ian said the last part emphatically and Johnson had to quit, knuckled by Ian's force of authority. Johnson held his mug up in a mock salute and said, "You're the boss," but when he looked over at Tom

Archer it was obvious he didn't think the matter was settled. He was right.

****

The long wooden box that brought water to the cannery was quite a marvel. Its construction had been started in 1934 and it was completed and ready for use when the cannery itself was built in 1936. A sawmill from Port Angeles, Washington, had been erected on a barge that was then hauled by a tugboat up the Inside Passage and anchored in Cloud Bay. It produced all the lumber needed for the construction of the cannery and all its out-buildings, pier and boardwalks, and for the flume. The flume had been engineered by a man who'd worked in gold mining and who knew how to move large quantities of water from one place to another. Spruce logs had become planks which had dried in covered stacks for a year. The long, one-and-a-half-inch-thick planks selected for use in the flume were angle-planed on their edges. Then the planks were carried up along the mountain's slopes where they were carefully fitted together into a four-mile-long box, bound with external roundabout wooden braces every yard so the planed boards fit tightly, and so the inside was smooth, with no internal projections to cause cavitations or trap debris.

At the lower end of the flume a twenty-five foot round wooden storage tank served as a reservoir. Water flowed continuously through the flume if a gate at the upper end was open, a steady flow that overflowed the reservoir. The excess water poured over the lip and ended up in the bay among the pilings of the pier.

The flume's water source in the ravine below the snowfields was as certain as the mountains themselves. In the summer, during use, the upper gate was opened, diverting some of the rushing stream through a grate and into the flume, which leaked thoroughly for the first couple of days but gradually swelled until hardly any water was lost over the entire four miles of its journey. It was simple and effective. In winter snow covered the long box, sheltering it.

Joe went first, leading William up muddy steps chopped out of the base of the mountain behind the cannery until they were almost level with the roof of the factory building. There they picked up the flume at its lower end, ducking under where it crossed a low spot on trestles, then balancing on a plank laid from the steep hillside to the top of the flume itself. At this point the box stood out about seven feet from the ground, which rose steeply through the trees. The flume was a solid walkway just over three feet wide and almost level. As the two men walked they adjusted their individual paces between the roundabout external two-by-twos which clamped the flume boards together, like gandy dancers walking railroad ties.

Both men were armed, Joe with a short-barrel .44-40 slung over his shoulder on a homemade rope sling, and William with the 12-gauge pump Remington Ian had provided him. It too had a short barrel. It would pivot quickly onto a target. Its magazine was loaded with heavy slugs that would punch great, shocking, bone-breaking holes through flesh. As soon as they were on the flume, with the cannery still within talking distance, Joe levered a big round into the chamber of his rifle and set the safety. He didn't tell William to follow suit but William also pumped a shell into the chamber of his weapon. As a studied afterthought William pulled another shell out of his jacket pocket and brought the magazine to full again. He had four rounds now. He slung the shotgun with its leather sling and started after Joe. Within a few minutes he'd forgotten the gun and was concentrating on his inspection of the flume.

****

Half a mile ahead of the two men a cinnamon sow, about six hundred pounds of coastal grizzly bear, felt the vibrations of other beings on the flume beneath its feet. It stopped and looked over its shoulder, then stepped off the flume onto a patch of snow and ambled down the slope of the mountain, through the trees and bushes, toward the beach, looking for something with the taste of salt.

****

The two men never saw the bear because it was long gone by the time they reached that spot but as they passed the place where it had crossed the flume Joe Badhand pointed to the fresh pad marks in the snow, gave William a meaningful look, and walked on.

At the top end of the flume, where it would pick up the ravine water, Joe and William sat and ate their lunch. It was still a beautiful day, with puffy white clouds just beginning to form around the tops of the mountains. The two men were relatively low on their own mountainside but from their perch they had a clear view over the tops of the trees below them and across the bay. The air was almost warm and both men had their jackets off and their shirts open.

The flume where they sat jutted into space over a very steep gully in the mountain's face, a ravine, really, coming down in a straight – almost vertical – course from above and behind them. The ravine passed under the end of the flume's catchment box and cut through the forest below, eventually leveling out on an old alluvial bench just above the beach. That bench, Joe told William, was one of the best deer hunting spots in the bay. The ravine wasn't an avalanche chute because of the convex shape of the mountain above it, where snow was blown by the wind instead of

212

being compacted. Its sharp, water-cleaned sides were an interesting geological window into the mountain's bedrock through the thin mantle of the forest humus. William could see clear evidence of a major inclusion and the glints of quartz.

There was a steady rush of icy white water down the ravine now – almost a waterfall – but as the season advanced and the weather warmed, more snow above would melt and the rushing stream would become a torrent, reaching the lip of the catchment box and, when the gate was open, filling the flume. In full roar the spot would be too loud for sanity. Now it was just pleasant.

Below them about thirty yards, just visible inside the trees on the opposite side of the ravine, was a well beaten path. William pointed to it. "Where's it go?"

"To the saltery in Chinaman's Cove. Just out of sight below us in the forest is a catchment for a pipe that goes to the saltery, which is over there on the shore." He pointed down to their right front near the alluvial bench he'd described. "Their pipe drops much more steeply than our flume, then becomes level when it gets lower down. The path parallels the pipe part of the way, then continues on past the saltery and down the bay through the forest."

"It looks like it continues on over this way." William pointed to where the faint trail did appear to cross the ravine and angle up toward the flume.

Joe chewed a mouthful of biscuit and wiped crumbs from his lips with his gnarled hand. "Yes. There used to be some traffic between the cannery and the saltery, but no more. Also, that is the path a person would take through the forest to get to my village. It is a long walk, but to follow the beach is much farther."

"You said there used to be traffic, but no more. You mean because the cannery's been closed?" William hadn't heard Joe speak a single negative word since he'd met him. He glanced at the Indian now as they ate. He'd learned Joe was generally a quiet man, speaking when he was spoken to, looking his listener in the eyes, then speaking shyly once he'd established that contact. William had been puzzled by Joe's syntax at first but then he realized it fit with his education and his village background, where Tlingit was spoken. Now William could see the man silently considering the question he'd been asked, framing an answer, perhaps searching for a positive approach to something inherently negative.

Finally Joe answered. "Until it closed, when the war started, the cannery operated every summer because fishing was good here. People came from Juneau and Sitka and Seattle to work in the cannery, as they do now. The land over there," Joe nudged his chin in the direction of the bench, "was acquired by the Hongs early in the century." He frowned, thoughtful, then went on. "In 1936 the cannery was built and there was traffic between the two places. Mostly by skiff, but sometimes by the path too. The old man, Hong Deng Wei, was younger then and he and his wife, Lo An, built the saltery shortly before the World War One because it was a way for them to make cash money. The herring come into this bay very strongly, even now. They would not only catch the herring, which they salted and shipped to the Orient, but they would collect the eggs of the herring also. There has always been a very strong price for herring roe in Asia. There was an agreement they had with some Chinese company. The family of Deng Wei and Lo An grew into three generations but has never become very large. They have a fine son, Kai Win, and he has a wife, Gwen, and there's a grandson, Tako. People would visit."

A sadness drifted into Joe's voice and he paused, looked directly at William's face. "The Japanese attacked Pearl Harbor in the winter, while the cannery was closed. However, as soon as the weather was calm in the spring a government boat from Juneau came to Chinaman's Cove and the Hongs were taken to the government office in the town and asked many questions about themselves and their relationships. It was a troublesome time for them because the old Hongs had no papers. They were forced to hire an immigration lawyer, and finally it was resolved so they could remain, but it was expensive for them and left some bitterness."

A light breeze had begun to flow with the water down the ravine and it carried a chill with it from the high country, still buried in its snows. Where they sat, just barely up the side of the mountain, it was spring but the breeze and inactivity had cooled the men. Scattered clouds pursued their own shadows across the bay. Joe buttoned his shirt and William shrugged into his jacket.

Joe seemed again to be pondering his next comments. "It was a very difficult time for people of Asian descent because of what the Japanese were doing," he finally said.

"But the Hongs are *Chinese*, not Japanese."

"Yes, of course. And the Chinese themselves were at desperate war with the Japanese, who had invaded their country, and there was hate and bitterness between them. But as I said, it was a very hard time for all persons who appeared Asian, because many people did not see differences."

William thought, "That's stupid," and almost said it, but when he looked at Joe and saw the humanity there he realized the man already had his own very clear understanding of the stupidity of those events, and instead of speaking he shook his head and was quiet.

Joe allowed the silence to sit a few moments, then stood, preparing to start the return walk. He slung his rifle and said, "The Hongs are a family that is very old, and I think they have learned patience, even more patience than Indians, perhaps." He smiled a wry, enigmatic look, and William was intrigued. There was a mysterious wistfulness in Joe's eyes and a story left untold in his comment. William thought about trying to draw it out but the moment passed. "Yes, my friend, I'll bet that's God's own truth," he said. Then they turned and under thickening skies made their way back along the flume toward the cannery.

****

The men had the cannery ready to open on schedule. It was a near thing with the big generator because some of the parts had to be flown in to Juneau from Seattle, but when Milton Trent finally got them out to the bay, along with other stores from town, Tom Archer and Johnson got the machine running without any further problems.

The camp cook, Jim Bell – Jimbelly – arrived on the same boat with the generator parts. He looked like a pear with legs. Ian had arranged for him to come before the rest of the crew because it'd take him a couple of days to get his stores arranged and to get the kitchen and mess hall ready to feed the crews that would soon follow. Ian and the others, superbly tired of their own halfhearted culinary efforts, were glad to see him. Jimbelly was a bit of a fairy and very fussy about his kitchen but he was an excellent cook, a good organizer and sometimes good company. He seemed to actually like Tom Archer.

The cannery crew arrived about midday three days later and after they'd all come ashore, climbing the steel ladder from the deck of Milton's boat to the pier, a net was lowered onto the deck of the boat. Their luggage was piled in it and lifted with the air tugger crane and then swung onto the pier. There was a lot of milling around and chatter as the crew – men and women and a couple of children – found their possessions, looked the place over and began to drift toward their quarters. When his boat was unloaded Milton swung her away from the pier and headed back to Juneau to get another load of supplies they'd need.

There were two married couples besides William and Bonnie. Each couple would live in one of the small houses. The four single women would also take houses, doubling up. The unmarried men would stay in the bunkhouse beyond the showers and washroom.

216

Over the next weeks the cannery shifted into its working schedule, with the creaking of the fishing boats against the pilings and the brazen, squawking sea gulls fighting over every scrap, the quick puffing of the air tugger, the soft clatter of crushed ice rushing through the chutes into the boats' holds, and the *chunk-chunk-chunk* of the lifting conveyors carrying fish. Laughter was a common sound.

****

Bonnie Hood fell in love with the place as quickly as her husband had. She was completely happy. Her duties were light – to keep the small clinic in shape, to take care of any injuries or illnesses any of the workers might suffer, and to make sure sanitation was maintained – and she felt carefree. She liked the simple, rugged cannery workers and the wolfish fishing crews who adopted her as their sweetheart on sight. She was pretty, with her dark flouncy hair and her girlish face. But more than her physical features and her shapely body, difficult to conceal even beneath jeans and a wool shirt, there was a boldness about her, a willingness to lock eyes with the scruffiest of the fishermen as if to say, "And don't I *know* you would, buddy, but take a good look 'cause that's all you're going to get…"

Only with Milton Trent was she different, almost coy. Milton was on contract for the season and he sortied every week, bringing perishables and mail and machine parts, taking a worker into town for one reason or another, and bringing loads of diesel in fifty-five gallon drums for the generators and other machines.

William asked her about it one night as they lay under the covers, almost asleep. "You got eyes for that boat captain?"

She rolled toward him sleepily and snuggled. "Sure."

"You wench. Aren't you even going to ask *which* boat captain, or you got eyes for *all* of 'em?" He tickled her and she jumped, wiggled away, then snuggled back into him, her bottom pressed into his lap. She took his arm and wrapped it around her, moving it so her breast rested in his hand, holding herself against him. "If you're jealous of Milt Trent," she said in a drowsy, eyes-closed voice, "you don't have to be, lover. He's cute and if I didn't adore you to pieces he might have a chance to get what you've got," she wiggled herself against him, "but don't worry, OK? Besides, I'd get seasick doing it in a hammock all the time."

"You fool, he's got a regular bunk aboard that boat, not a hammock."

"See? Shows what I know. Now be a good boy and help me go to sleep." She turned and though it was pitch dark they could feel each others gaze. She told him, "I only sleep with you, Campus Willie..." and started to say something else but his hands changed her words to moans.

****

The summer swished past, the long hours of sunshine distracting the humans in the bay from the pages of the calendar on the mess hall wall which Jimbelly ripped off one by one, yet swiftly.

There were a slack couple of days with only a few boats unloading their catches, so Ian kept a small skeleton crew in the factory and let the rest of the workers off to do their own things. It was a bright warm day which itself was a good reason for a holiday, considering the almost constant rain. Some of the people had laundry and bedding hanging in the sunlight, others sat in the sun, lazy, soaking up the warmth and slapping flies.

William, Joe and Bonnie took one of the cannery's two sixteen foot skiffs out into the bay where they wouldn't have to fight the summer insects so much. The day was too nice to spend cooped up behind screen doors. There were fewer deerflies out on the water but the horseflies still managed to find them so they

218

watched each other's blind places as they talked. Joe had stuffed kinnikinick into an old pipe and was trying to keep it lit without much success. It was just as well, thought William – the few puffs Joe managed to unleash on them smelled like burning seaweed mixed with old tire rubber. Finally Joe gave up and put the pipe in a pocket, still full.

William knew Bonnie liked the old Indian. "Funny," he thought, looking at his wife and Joe, "it must be his limp and his ruined hand and the wrinkled, serious look in his face that makes him the *old* Indian – he isn't really that old..." He'd told her some of what he knew about Joe and she'd been fascinated and had gone out of her way to spend time with him. Once when William stopped at the dispensary room for a quick kiss and a secret feel he'd found them together, sitting close. He'd had his sleeve pushed up and his arm extended across the corner of the table which served Bonnie for a desk. She'd had her chair pulled up so their knees were almost touching and when William first saw them he thought she was drawing blood – it was that intimate kind of closeness. Then he saw she was looking closely at his wounds, holding his gnarled hand in hers and studying it like she could fix it, make it work right again. Joe was sitting calmly, just looking at her, letting her look, and it was obvious he was smitten. It was a condition William shared with him. William had smiled to himself and pushed through the screen door, breaking the spell.

In the skiff, Bonnie lay back against a roll of canvas they'd brought along for comfort and said to Joe, "Do you ever go over to visit the Hongs in Chinaman's Cove?"

William slapped futilely at a big horsefly on his knee.

Joe was silent, thoughtful for a full minute – a habit with which they'd finally relaxed – and then spoke in his almost pontifical voice, using the language carefully. "Sometimes, yes. They are unusual. I think Chinese people do not often separate themselves from society as these have done."

"Do they visit in your village?" Bonnie asked.

Again Joe waited, thinking before he answered. "Yes, they have, but not often." He pondered as if he could tell them something more, and William was reminded of their discussion up on the flume when he thought the Indian could have said more than he had. Then Joe said, "Perhaps not everyone in the village is pleased that they live on our island."

"But why?" Bonnie asked.

Joe reflected, absently rubbing the back of his hand against his trousers leg. William could see that a horsefly had taken a huge chunk of skin off Joe's hand and had raised a knot half an inch high – a bite that would have hurt like hell on his own hand. Apparently only the slightest irritation passed the mangled nerves of Joe's hand. "Well," he eventually answered, "perhaps some of the people are just of the old ways. The land of this island is all we have. It was against the will of the people when the land in the cove was sold, many years ago. The old people still remember that. Maybe they hope someday the Chinese will leave."

17

Ian Morgan awoke with a headache, the throb behind his eyes pulling his hands to his head in a reflexive effort to distract the nerves, without effect. His morning was started poorly and he didn't have enough energy to stop the sorry-for-himself feelings. He rubbed his temples and supposed he'd have to go to the optometrist and have his prescription changed again after the season was over. "Age…" he thought.

He sat for a while in the cold living room of his bungalow in flannel pajamas and a heavy bathrobe, trying to get himself together to start his day. As the summer waned the nights sent down a chill from the high peaks and the bay gave it up slowly in the mornings. He put three small chunks of dry hemlock in among the coals in the stove, opened the vents, heard the wood catch immediately. Then he sat and waited for the room to warm up, listening to the rain and the sound of the stovepipe creaking and the pounding in his own head until the pot on the stove was steaming from the spout and around the enameled lid, then he poured hot water over instant coffee powder in his ceramic mug. "Amazing," he said, contemplating the thin foamy whirlpool that resulted. "Another advancement for civilization."

His mood reflected the weather. The noise of thunderous rain on the tin roof had awakened him, grumbling and hurting, from a frenzied dream about his father. "Strange," he thought. He didn't remember ever before dreaming about his long-dead father. The engendered melancholies suited the gloom of the morning.

There were resolute foot-stomps on the front stoop. "Jesus," he muttered, putting the steaming mug of ersatz coffee down, tightening the belt of his robe around his portliness. The door to their shared bungalow opened on a dripping William Hood standing apologetically on the covered porch, his soggy Stetson in both hands. Water was streaming off William's raincoat sleeve into the hat and onto the porch. The rain was dark, the heavy beat of its fall staccato against the bass rumbling of thunder.

"I'm really sorry to bother you before breakfast, Ian," William yelled, "but we've got a problem I'm about to go fix. I thought you should know about it early, just in case it turns out to be something major and I need more manpower."

"What have you got, William?" A gust darted in under the porch eaves and carried a spray into the room. "Oh, come on in, come in." He stood back, motioning William in. "Don't worry about the water."

William waved the invitation off with the Stetson, flipping water across Ian's slippered feet and onto the floor. Ian was stoic, and William didn't notice what he'd done, wrapped up in what he had to tell. An electric bolt somewhere among the mountains of cloud flashed light, strobing. "Thanks, Ian, but I think I'll move right along." He shouted over the noise of the morning. Behind him the waters of the bay leaped, escaping, crashing against the wind in angry spray and colliding with the driven rain in great mists of confusion. "And actually that's just what I am worried about – water. The flume's dry as a lead pencil this morning – not a drop coming through. Joe and I are about to follow it up, see what's wrong."

"You say it's absolutely dry, not even a small stream?"

"Right. I think if something clogged her we'd still get at least a small flow, but this is no flow. Zip. I figure either the bottom fell

222

out at some point along the line, or the whole thing's washed out someplace. Or I suppose there's the off chance somebody closed the gate up at the catchment box, but I don't know who'd do that, or what for. Probably something with the flume."

"Well, I'd agree with you. You want to take a bunch of guys up with you now?"

"No, I think Joe and I'll just take a quick trip up, see what's wrong, then we'll know exactly what it's going to take to fix it." He looked down at his hat, noticed the puddle in it, and poured it onto the porch. Then he put the Stetson back on his head, settling it, pulled the collar of his slicker up, shrugging into what would have to pass for comfort this morning. "Oh, one more thing. Tom Archer's all fired up to go with us. He's got this hair up his butt there's sabotage involved. Says the Chinese are trying to drive us out. He wanted to go with Joe and me. I couldn't think of any reason to tell him no."

"Damn it, I can! You and Joe go take care of the flume. Tell Tom to stop over and see me, if you would. There's something I need to talk to him about anyway."

"OK, I'll tell him. Talk to you later."

"And let me know what you find, soon as you get back. Whatever the problem is, it's first priority. You guys be careful up in the woods. Those boards'll be slippery."

William acknowledged with a tilt of his head, stepped off the porch and back into the rain. He raised his hand and said something but the noise on the roof blocked it. Ian turned back into the house, sniffling and deciding he had a cold coming on. It was going to be a lousy day. He resolved to get some aspirin from Bonnie.

A few minutes later there were more footsteps on the porch, a rustling of heavy rain gear, a knock.

"Come in!"

The door opened to admit a dripping Tom Archer.

"Morning, Tom. Thanks for coming by. I haven't got up and moving yet. Want some of this lousy instant coffee?"

Tom stood, water pooling on the floor. "No thanks, Mr. Morgan. I was going to walk up the flume with the engineer. Guess he's told you the water's off."

"Yeah, he told me. Matter of fact there's something else I want you to get on instead, and this is the perfect time to do it."

Tom bent his head to one side, wondering, frowning like a grave digger seeing a big rock.

"Get hold of Johnson and get him to help you. You two get that compressor coil replaced on the ice machine while we're shut down. We haven't got any boats scheduled in today, though now I've said that, we'll get fifteen, at least if the weather breaks. Let me know when the beast is back on line."

Tom wasn't happy and the cloud of his scowl darkened. He spoke and his petulance was a closed blade, a heavy switchblade knife in a trembling fist. "Johnson kin handle that by hisself. Them other guys might need another shotgun."

"What the hell for, Tom? They're just walking the flume, not sneaking around the forest stealing grizzly cubs."

"Yeah, I know. But there's something fishy going on around here. Maybe you don't notice 'cause you've got paperwork and such to do, but there's too many little things 'round here don't make no sense and I, for one, think we ought to be takin' a look at it."

"No pun intended, I'm positive, but what fishy things are you talking about, Tom?" Ian resolved himself to settle this matter with the factory floor supervisor, who was, aside from this… this *fanaticism* about the Chinese, a valuable employee. "Here, take off that slicker, sit down here, have some of this blasted powdered coffee – help me get rid of it – and tell me what's on your mind. God knows I'm not getting anything else done today, might as well get to the bottom of this…"

Tom reacted, backed up again, started a new puddle on the floor. "Well, you kin laugh if you want..." He stopped undressing with his slicker half off, his elbows back and his neck thrown forward.

"I'm not laughing, Tom. Far from it. *You* think there's something going on around here, and *I* damn well want to hear about it." Ian held his hand to his forehead, pinched the bridge of his nose. "Now sit down here and quit dripping on my floor and let's hear it."

Tom hung his oilskin slicker on a rusted nail next to the door above floor boards warped over the years by the dripping of countless other raincoats. He sat in the broken-legged chair across from Ian and leaned forward like that'd help him get into the story quicker. "Somebody's sabotaging us in little ways on purpose, Mr. Morgan, and I think it's them squints over to the saltery what's doing it."

Ian sighed, unable any more to avoid this issue that Tom had been raising at every opportunity. He took a large blue bandanna from his bathrobe pocket and, turning his head, nodding for Tom to forgive him, blew his nose forcefully, then he turned back and said, "All right, Tom, let's hear this theory of yours."

Tom spoke his convictions, his deep eyes glinting with zealous prosecution. "It's lots of little things unless I'm right about the flume, but that ain't little. You remember we had them valves missing, right?"

"Right, and you blamed the Chinese. But that was a wild guess."

"Yeah, but then Johnson found them herring scales in the generator room. And you know what it took to put that generator back together again."

Ian's patience was at full choke. "And have you turned up anything else, anything else at all to make *me* believe, as you obviously do, that those Chinese people over there are trying to harass us? Because that's all it amounts to even if it *is* happening on purpose. Nothing's occurred that's in any way a big deal except the generator, and *that* could have been done by the crew of any passing boat."

"But most likely it weren't. I'll tell you, I got me a natural dislike for squints…"

"You talking about Chinese?"

"Yeah. Chinamen, Japs, slopes, they's all squints to me and you kin call me prejudice if you want and never mind, but I'll tell you I got good reasons for feeling the way I do. Soon's I got to Juneau and heard there was this bunch of squints out here to that so-called saltery I done some pokin' around. Talked to other people in town. There's people ain't so dumb, you know. People who know what's goin' on…"

"People like you?"

"Yeah. People like me. All kind of people. Everywhere. Other guys what've been overseas and seen what them people live like, how they treat people. You know that ain't even their land over there." He shrugged in the general direction of the saltery. "Shit, they ain't even Americans."

"What do you mean it isn't their land? They've been there for fifty years, for crying out loud."

"Yeah, may be. But what I hear, they stole it from them Indians, and that's all them Clink-it Indians *got,* is their land."

Ian Morgan sat holding his cup in his hands, wishing it were hot. Wishing it were real coffee. Wishing he were sitting on the deck of his Lake Union houseboat…

"And I'll tell you something else, Mr. Morgan. I seen 'em work. Chinamen, as you call 'em. Shit, I ought to know." He stopped and the fervid look on his face changed to placid and it looked for a moment as if he might relent. It was a thoughtful expression, and on another man would precede a concession. But it passed swiftly across Tom's eyes, taking any thought of

226

compromise with it, and the hardness came back. "Mr. Morgan, Chinese ain't like us. None of them squints is. Look at 'em, for Christ's sake, millions of 'em starving to death. And it's a good God damn thing or they'd be all over the place. Like deerflies." A realization showed. "Shit, they *are* all over the place. Even *here*, for God's sake, in fuckin' Alaska. In this bay. The end of the earth, and there's fuckin' *squints* in it…"

"Tom…"

Tom Archer wasn't finished. He leaned forward. "Mr. Morgan, in this world there's a place for everybody, and I believe that. This is *our* place, and their place is on the other side of that ocean." His arm stuck out. "But they ain't satisfied. There's too many of 'em." Tom studied Ian's face, puzzlement showing in the frown lines of his own. "Maybe you don't care, but I do."

"All right, Tom, I've heard you, now what's the point?"

"The point is them people have got a foothold over here now but that ain't good enough for 'em. They's gonna keep pushin' and pushin' and gettin' a little bit here and a little bit there until they's all over the place. 'Til there ain't nobody but them. They just keep pushin' us, pickin' here and pickin' there until we're picked to pieces and get tired of it and move out. That's what's happening. Can't you see that?"

Ian just sat in his frayed, padded armchair holding his cold coffee mug in both hands, sniffing, wishing his head wouldn't pound, wishing he were someplace else… Finally he said, "Tom, I believe that's about the biggest load of horse crap I've ever heard."

"Hey…"

"No, I'm going to finish this, Tom. You've had your say, now I'm going to have mine and here it is in a couple of words, Tom: lay off." Ian put the mug down and drew his robe tighter around himself, sighed, not wanting a battle this morning but needing to control this affair. "Tom, you're a good supervisor and I'm glad to have you working for me but you've got to get off this Chinese thing. Listen," he evened out his voice, building a bridge with it. "We're just here for a little while longer. The season's going to be over soon enough and then we'll all go elsewhere, so just leave it alone, can't you? Let it be."

Tom started to open his mouth.

"Tom, I *mean* it." Ian looked at him hard. "Maybe everything you say is true, but I don't give a damn. The season's been going along fine. The summer's going to be over soon. All I want to do is finish out this season in peace and go on to the next thing. Nobody's going to shut us down, and if somebody *is* fooling around, sooner or later we'll catch them at it and that'll be that. But until then, leave it alone, understand?"

Tom had no choices. "Yeah, I hear what you say, but I think you're wrong. And I'll do it 'cause you're the boss, but I'll tell you, I'm going to keep my eyes open and if I catch one of them…"

"Tom, don't even tell me. If you catch somebody sabotaging something around here, I'll personally help you kick 'em blind before I call the Troopers. In the meantime I don't want to hear another word about the Chinese. Stick to business, Tom."

Tom glowered. He stood, put his slicker on without another word, put his hat on his head. Then, with his hand on the door knob, he said, "I heard you, Mr. Morgan. I'm goin' to work on that ice machine." He closed the door behind him and Ian sat for a few minutes, sighing, sniffling, blowing into his blue bandanna, looking at the still puddle of water on the wide floorboards next to the door, listening to the rain and the empty echoes of his conversation with Tom Archer. Then he got up and began his day. Surprisingly, by the time he got himself out the door his headache had vanished.

******

About mid-morning, as Ian was working on paperwork in his loft office in the main factory building, William came dripping in.

He shook his hat, stripped off his slicker and hung it on the clothes tree, wiped water off his face with the sleeve of his shirt. "Well, we'll be back in the water business shortly. We found a couple boards rotted out of the bottom about a mile up. I've already lined up a crew to go up after lunch to fix it. No big deal. One of them will just have to walk up to the ravine and put in the gate – water was running a full head until it got to that big hole, then there was one hell of a gusher. We cut a new stream bed down through the woods that somebody will wonder about some day. Probably figure it for a prospector sluicing off the topsoil…"

"I'm glad that's all it was," Ian said, putting his pencil down. "Good work. By the way… Any evidence – and I mean *any* evidence – it was caused by some person or persons? As opposed to being an Act of God?"

"Tom Archer again?"

"Yup."

"Sorry to squash the latest sabotage theory, but unless they used ancient Oriental magic to cause rot in a couple of those boards…"

"All right. I had to ask, I suppose."

18

It was a Sunday afternoon. There weren't any boats due in and Ian had given almost everybody a day off again. It was good timing – the week before had been hectic, with lots of boats in, and with Whittaker's mother-ship arriving from Seattle to carry away the stocks they'd canned so far. It was one of those rare beautifully clear days in Southeast Alaska and there was a weekend air about the place, which normally operated without regard to the days of the week.

Tom and Jimbelly had taken a couple of shotguns and were motoring clear across the bay in one of the cannery's two skiffs to shoot some ducks in a small lagoon around one of the points. It was too early for the duck season to be open but the scruples of both men stopped well short of the game laws. In fact if they didn't even see a duck it wouldn't matter that much – they had a quart of the raw grain whisky Tom Archer drank occasionally, and a cardboard box full of snacks Jimbelly had stowed. Earlier they had mentioned to Joe Badhand that they wanted to shoot some ducks and Joe had told them about the lagoon where they were now headed, had pointed it out to Tom on the chart. Joe had declined an invitation to go with them, claiming he had someplace else to go, and had taken his own skiff and headed out from the cannery while Tom and Jimbelly were getting their stuff ready.

As Tom and Jimbelly boated around the point of land across the bay, out of sight of the cannery and almost opposite from the cove where the saltery lay, Tom said, "Jimbelly, we want to cut the motor and coast up to them rocks there." He pointed to the left of a very narrow channel of water running into the bay from a flat area of forested land at the foot of the ridge. "That channel goes back in about forty or fifty yards and then it opens up into a big lagoon. If there's any ducks that's where they'll be, back in there. I've scoped the whole thing off the chart. We can't miss. We get up on the shore there," he pointed, "and hunker down so we can get a good shot over that there channel, then give a yell and them ducks'll start wingin' out of that lagoon, right down that cut channel makes through them trees. I hope you're a better shot than you are a cook."

"You don't worry 'bout my shootin' none, Archer. I've busted more ducks than you'll ever know. Now pass that quart over here before you suck it dry." Jimbelly shut off the outboard motor while a thick band of heavy trees still screened them from the lagoon and they drifted ashore well to the left of the channel. It was a steep shore covered with big, sharp boulders.

"Shhh. You gotta' be quiet," Tom whispered. If they hear us before we get to the channel they'll all get out fast, before we get a shot."

"Shhh yourself, Bigfoot. Tie that bow line off and let's get to it." Jimbelly tucked at a fleeing shirt tail. He did it by feel, having long ago lost sight of his belt. He scratched under one edge of his watch cap. His hands, like most cooks', were clean, the fingernails trim and glossy. He found the itchy place on his scalp, gouged at it, then squared the watch cap on his head, examined the attacking fingernail for prisoners, found none, and wiped the weapon against the side of his pants leg.

The two men worked their way along the shore from where the boat was tied to where they could see the tide running in the channel, which was a narrow drain for the lagoon, and then they cut into the forest and sneaked up onto the edge of the channel. They were both carrying a good portion of the quart of whisky internally but neither was stumbling or noisy and they had a good chance to get into position unheard.

When they arrived at the edge of the trees and bushes and were ready, Tom yelled, "Hey, ducks," loudly, once, and raised his shotgun, ready to fire. They heard water being beaten within the lagoon and then a fast whirring of wings.

Boom, boom! Boom! Boom! Tom and Jimbelly both let go with two barrels each and were breaking their guns, empty cartridges popping from smoking breeches, reloading with number fours before the three ducks they'd shot hit the water. More ducks followed. The shotguns blasted again. More ducks fell, some splashing into the channel, others onto one of the banks. Another reload.

One more duck, a teal, tried the gauntlet above the channel, cutting to sea through the gap in the forest, racing at fantastic speed. Jimbelly was standing ten feet from Tom. He started to say, "He's mine…" when Tom fired. The teal flew right into Tom's pattern and pitched to the ground twenty feet beyond, a flutter of feathers drifting down behind him. Tom reloaded and both men stood waiting, ready, but there were no more ducks. Finally they lowered their pieces, broke them, replaced the shells in their pockets. Neither was thinking beyond ducks.

"It's duck for supper, Jimbelly, and I take back what I said about your shootin'. Now if you kin cook ducks as well as you knock 'em down we ought to have a feed tonight."

"Like I told you, I been a duck fan a long time. Let's round 'em up. There's a couple fell in the water and some more on the other side. Why don't you get the skiff and bring it around, get those floating into the bay. I'll get these on this side and then we can pull the boat up on the other side and get those. I think I saw at least two go down over there. Here's that teal you got." He held up a small bundle of feathers. "He weighs about twice what he did when he headed down this way, I'll tell you. Watch your teeth on this one, he's full of shot."

Tom made a sound that passed for his laugh and said, "Full of shot... Wish I'd said that, Jimbelly. *You're* full of shot. Full of shit, too. OK, I'll get the skiff." Tom started off through the trees toward the rocky shoreline.

Jimbelly began looking for the other birds that had gone down on their side of the channel. He was just reaching for a fat mallard hen in the grass when Tom's voice came at him, fully alarmed, frantic. *"Jim! Jim Bell! Help! Quick!"*

****

Tom's yell came from beyond the screen of trees where they'd landed the boat. Jim's immediate thought was, *bear!* He dropped the two ducks he'd retrieved, turned and started toward the sound of Tom's yell, reaching in his pocket for the heavy slugs for the shotgun. He burst out of the trees ready to shoot a brownie off Tom but Tom was standing on the rocks, pointing out into the bay. About twenty yards offshore and moving swiftly on the outgoing tide was their skiff, its motor locked in the up position, its manila painter angled into the water off the bow.

"Oh, shit," said Jimbelly, dismayed at the lost boat but relieved not to be confronting a charging brown bear. "I thought you tied that good, you ninny."

Tom rounded on him. "I *did* tie it good, you sonofabitch."

"Well, what's it doing out there, then? Way to go, Tom. *Now* what the hell we gonna' do?"

"Don't give me none of your shit, Bell. I tell you I tied it good. Right here to this big rock. What do you think, I never tied up a skiff before? I tell you I tied it good!"

"Well, it's sure as hell gone. Can you swim it?"

"Swim it? You're outta' your mind. *You* swim it!"

"The hell, you say."

"Well, fuck."

"Yeah. Hey! The bottle's in that boat, too!"

"Goddam *double* fuck." Tom plopped down on a rock, watched the boat drift further out, glanced up to see how much daylight was left, looked at his watch, then looked at the boat again. "Is there any chance that skiff'll come close to that point down there? Maybe we can snag it." He pointed half a mile down the shore to where the land jutted out, cliffy big rocks, some sticking up offshore.

"Maybe," Jimbelly answered, "but how we going to get down there in time? Have to either swim this channel or walk all the way around this lagoon and either way, no way. We're stuck, Tom. What time is it, oh great boatman?"

"I told you, I tied that boat *good*. It's four o'clock. About five hours of daylight left. Well, shit." He stood up on the rock, looked around. "We might as well start planning on spending the night. We don't' get back by morning, Morgan'll send somebody over in the other skiff to get us. God damn, I *know* I tied that skiff."

The two men retreated up the beach to where the forest began and picked a place to camp for the night finally, after arguing the merits of several places. They were starting to gather firewood when they heard a motor. Tom cocked his head. "Listen…"

"Yeah, I hear it. Come on!"

They both picked their way carefully out onto the rocks along the shore, looking to see where the motorboat sound was coming from. They could hear it more plainly now, far away or around a bend, but close enough to retrieve their own skiff for them.

"There!" Jimbelly pointed deeper into the bay, in the opposite direction their skiff was drifting. Coming around a far point of land about three-quarters of a mile away was a skiff, its bow making the wave of a light boat moving quickly, one man at the motor in the stern. Jimbelly and Tom both began to wave and shout. The boat continued on.

"Fire a round, quick!" Tom said.

"*You* fire a round – I'm loaded with my only two bear slugs.'

"Oh hell!" Tom quickly found a shell, loaded his gun, raised it to his shoulder and fired. The deep boom of the report went rolling across the bay, echoing off the mountain behind them. The motorboat continued on. "He's headed over to the saltery. Hell, Jim, that must be one of them squints." The motorboat was too far away for them to clearly see the man aboard. "I'm gonna fire one more – he must'a seen us."

"Yeah, maybe he seen us, but so what? He don't know we want him to turn over here. Unless he sees our skiff out there…"

"Ah, hell, even then he probably won't turn. He's in too big a fuckin' hurry to get home and eat some fish heads or seaweed or something, screw some of them squint women they got over there." Tom forgot about shooting another round, headed back up the rocks to where the trees began. "Waste of time," he said.

"Talk about a waste – there goes our good duck dinner, too." Jimbelly pointed to the channel. Several dead ducks and one wounded one, clumps of bloody feathers, were drifting slowly out into the bay, following after the skiff which was now a good hundred yards down the coast, forty or fifty yards offshore. "At least we got them two that fell on this side. That teal you got and one mallard. Maybe there's another one too. I haven't looked yet. Come on."

The two men made a rough camp just inside the trees. They didn't have any tools or shelter so getting comfortable was just a matter of picking the most sheltering tree and gathering as much loose dry firewood as they could find. It was still a fine afternoon, with a clear sky now easing toward violet as the sun began to disappear beyond the mountains. They were lucky it wasn't raining, but that couldn't hold for long. With or without rain it would be a long night unless someone did happen to come rescue them, and there was slight chance of that until morning.

Sitting under the branches of their chosen tree roasting little pieces of the ducks Jimbelly had skinned and gutted, Tom reiterated, "I did tie that skiff, Jimbelly, and I tied it good. Used a round turn and two half hitches. I've been over it again and again in my mind, even went down and looked at that rock – there ain't no way that rope came off by itself. Know what I mean?"

Jimbelly licked grease off one of his pudgy fingers. "Sure I do. You think that Chinaman in the skiff snuck down the shore while we was shooting those ducks and untied that skiff, pushed it off, then scooted back to his own boat around the bend and took off, right?"

"Just exactly right, Jimbelly."

"OK, but why? Why would somebody – even a Chinaman – do that?"

"You ever heard of *H and I?*"

"Sure, *harassment and interdiction*. It means to cause trouble for the enemy, make him nervous, keep him off guard with un-regular artillery fire. But shit, there ain't no war on here." He pointed. "Turn that piece of duck over before it burns. It don't make any sense, unless you've done something to them and one of them's gettin' even. Hell, I sure as hell ain't done nothin to 'em, not even after the bastards took and stole my crab pot that time. Hell," Jimbelly muttered, half to himself, "I *know* the tide didn't get it…"

"Maybe so, Jimbelly, but I'll tell you one thing. They sure as hell done something to me now, and if there weren't no war in this fucking bay before, there sure as hell is *now*. They'll find out they messed with the wrong person…"

Their night was miserable and on the edge of being dangerous. Aside from taunting pneumonia, they'd put their camp just within the fringe of trees above the high water line, the main

236

avenue the bears used in their travels through that area. They didn't collect enough firewood to sustain even a small flicker all night, much less enough to build a bonfire which might have attracted an early rescue, so shortly after two in the morning their fire died for want of nourishment. A heavy drizzle soddened the ashes.

They sat shoulder to shoulder with their backs against the rough bark of a hemlock tree, their shotguns across their knees. They shivered, cursed, dozed, and through the night Tom Archer plotted one, then another retribution against the people at the saltery.

On their return to the cannery next morning they had to bear a lot of good-natured ribbing about the tide and its voraciousness with skiffs, until their ill humor dampened even the most vicious kidders. A couple of men set off in the other motorboat to look for the runaway and found it washed up on a rocky point about five miles down the bay.

Ian Morgan asked them what had happened as they ate a huge breakfast in the overheated kitchen. Jimbelly started to say something about their conclusion but Tom quickly interjected. "The damn thing just got away. You know how it happens. I thought I tied her off good but the rope musta' just slipped off." He put a forkful of canned bacon into his mouth, said over it, "But I sure learned my lesson, you kin be sure of that."

****

At the saltery the law was being laid down, again. The grandson of Deng Wei and Lo An was the defendant. Deng Wei put his hand down sharply on the table beside his favorite chair in the main room of their house. "I will not say it again." He spoke sharply in Mandarin, but not loudly. He was the patriarch in every respect and his voice needed no volume to carry its authority. "Tai Co, the son of my son Kai Win, may *not* take the motorboat to the cannery to pay attention to the young foreign girl. Nor may he row, *nor* may he walk the beach or the path beside the water pipe, nor fly over the trees like a bird to get there. For the last time, and hear me well, all of you. The members of this family and all who find shelter on this honorable property will not traffic with the barbarians. Their ways are not ours. They are only temporary intruders here. We are the permanent residents. There is no good that can come of such traffic, only bad, and I forbid it. Now speak no more of this matter." He looked around the room at the members of his family assembled to hear him.

Lo An stood with a long set of cooking sticks in her hand. She was grey, and wrinkled around her eyes and mouth but still a remarkably beautiful old woman. Their daughter-in-law, Gwen Do, wouldn't meet the eyes of her son, Tai Co, who looked around the room defiantly for support but found none.

Five people lived at the saltery year-round. In the summertime during the herring runs and during the frantic two weeks of prime season when they collected and salted as much roe as possible several other Chinese came from Juneau to help out. The herring season was over now and those workers had gone back to town.

Deng Wei, a coolie who'd wrapped himself in a raw deer skin to keep from freezing to death and Lo An, the woman who'd been driven from Canyon of Gold with him, had made a good home in Cloud Bay. Kai Win, named for Kevin Aspin, had been born that first winter in their original small log cabin in the middle of the wood pile. Lo An had had two other children. Both had died, one at birth, the other after only a few months. Both tiny graves behind the main house were still tended regularly.

Kai Win had grown to be a fine, handsome man. He loved his parents for the life they'd given him and respected them not only because he was taught to do so, but because he knew what they'd lived through to bring him to life. He had no other home but the saltery, had little knowledge of the outside world, but had learned to read and had educated himself during long winters in the bay when the kitchen stove was the center of all activity. He'd been to the Indian village with his father and had several times in his life been to Juneau, but he'd never been beyond and had no desire to leave Cloud Bay, his home. He'd found a wife, Gwen Do, on one of his trips to Juneau and they had a son, Tai Co, but they called him Tako, Little Octopus. As a small child Tako had been into everything, his grabby little hands going eight directions at once. Tako had recently reached the age of adolescent glandular activity.

Tako had been sent to stay with other Hongs in Juneau when he was eight so he could learn English and attend public school. It hadn't been a good experience for any of them but in the intervening years since, he'd forgotten the harassment he'd suffered over his poor English and his Chinese ways and now remembered only the excitements and the liberties taken by his classmates as they began their own rebellions. His Grandmother Lo An had continued his education – over Deng Wei's objection – by having a teacher come from the Indian village and live with them during the darkest winter months to tutor him in English and arithmetic. The Indian teacher, an English-speaking, gnomish woman who'd never found a husband, was happy for the work and Tako became proficient enough so that all of them except Deng Wei, who refused to speak it, could carry on conversations in the foreign devils' tongue.

Tako was driven, beyond sense or thought, to further the acquaintance he'd managed to make with one of the older female children at the cannery, but his grandfather had realized why the boy was going over there so often and had put his hand down. Tako still burned on the fiery edge of rebellion, his infatuation driving him to outright disobedience. He was busily putting things into one of the two skiffs tied up to the spindly pier which reached over the mud flats of Chinaman's Cove to where the low tide retreated. Kai Win came out of their house and saw him carrying the outboard motor fuel can from the gas barrel on the edge of the woods. "Hold on there, Tako," his father said to him. "Where're you going so fast?"

Tako stopped dead in his tracks but didn't set the red fuel can down, hoping he'd be allowed to proceed with little delay. He was a boy with a mission. "Oh. Father. I'm going to take the skiff down to the grass fields at the head of the bay. Last year I watched to see where the Canada geese were feeding. This year I'm going to make some blinds so that later, when they come again, I'll be ready for them."

His father's eyes sparkled at him. "Admirable, my young goose hunter. And who's going with you, may I inquire?"

"Uh, well, actually nobody, Father."

"Well then, this is your lucky day. I'd love to go with you."

The youth threw his head up, a wild look on his open face. "Oh, no. I mean… Haven't you got *important* things to do? Other than making duck blinds?"

"Goose blinds, you mean." His father looked penetratingly at him. "And how could anything be more important than that? You finish getting the boat ready, I'll get my gun. We'll take that yellow retriever…"

In a few minutes they were skimming down the bay, Tako running the outboard on the stern, Kai Win sitting on the mid-boat thwart with the dog's head in his lap. As they passed in front of the cannery, half a mile offshore, the boat swerved from side to side as Tako forgot his steering and craned his neck to see if the girl was waiting on their secret beach.

"Most likely there aren't any submarines in Cloud Bay, so you don't need to zigzag," Kai win told him.

The boat straightened out and the boy sat back down, resigned to his shattered day. They got two ducks though, and on the way home his father seemed not to notice when their course took them close to the cannery shore. Tako hoped he'd get another chance to see the girl. No, more than that, he was determined. At any cost.

****

Bonnie Hood was alone in a small dinghy, bobbing on the calm shaded water among the pilings underneath the pier, a crab net below her on the muddy bottom, when the Chinese man and boy motored by in their skiff about two hundred yards in front of her. She was sitting quietly, splicing a new bridle onto the rope of another crab net. Two sets of rubber-booted feet clumped on the planking over her head. She shrank back as first one, then another pair of feet and legs flopped over the edge of the pier.

One of the men above her hawked and spit heavily, the glob landing not three feet out from her little dinghy. The men were apparently watching the motorboat with the Chinese in it, unaware of her presence. She was smiling, just about to surprise the hell out of them by grabbing their legs, when one of them began to speak and she recognized who they were. Muffled sounds of machinery worked their way out of the factory and an occasional voice rose as somebody spoke loudly to someone else beyond a sink. Water trickled into the bay from a small drain pipe near her, and the bay in front of her livened the air with its own noises – a bald eagle screeching from a tree top, the hum of insects, the lapping of water – all background for the steady putt-putt of the passing motorboat. But still she could hear Tom Archer's voice clearly, without mistake, and once he began to speak she was embarrassed to let them find her eavesdropping on a private conversation – immediately obvious as a *very* private conversation.

"I'm gonna make them squints pay for what they done to us, Jimbelly. We coulda' got mauled by brownies over there that night, you know. That bastard squint who untied our skiff didn't even *think* of that."

"What've you got in mind, Tom? You gonna sneak over and untie all their skiffs?"

The motorboat carrying the man and the boy had drawn almost abreast of the cannery now and the man in it waved. Bonnie hoped they wouldn't turn in to visit and give her away. If she waved back, or if the two men above her head did... But the skiff continued on its course straight across in front of the pier, bound for the point of land down to her right. Beyond the point was the saltery.

Tom spoke again. "Them squint-eyed fuckers. They act like they own this whole goddam place. But I'll tell you, pretty goddam soon I'm gonna have some China-meat for bait on my salmon pole, and you kin *count* on that." Tom spat again and the wad made a big splash, again just a few feet from where Bonnie sat. She drew back in disgust.

"We could keep an eye out for the next time they go down to the flats there," Jimbelly kicked one foot toward the grass fields at the head of the bay, "then sneak around there and do the same thing to them they done to us."

"Naw, Jimbelly, I got something more permanent in mind, like burning that whole stinking saltery to the ground. Damn place is probably crawling with rats and bugs anyway. It'd be a service to the state if it burned down."

"Aw, you can't just go burning places down like that any more, Tom. There's laws, you know. And even if they're just Chinamen, there's women and kids over there. They'd have a state trooper out here in no time figuring out what happened." Jimbelly raised one rubber-booted foot and let a greasy fart.

"Jimbelly, if I burn them squints out don't you worry nohow, ain't nobody going to pin nothing on nobody here. Now come on, let's see what kind of trash you're fixing to serve for supper. You ain't having fish again, are you?"

Bonnie almost panicked. She'd mentioned to the cook that a crab salad would taste good... If he remembered now and looked down... "Nope," Jimbelly answered. One pair of legs was pulled up, then the other. "Tonight's spaghetti night. Meatballs too, not just tomato paste sauce."

The two men clumped off down the pier and when Bonnie was sure they'd gone she quickly tied the crab pot rope off on one of the pilings, untied her little dinghy and pulled herself along the pilings until she was out from under the pier. Only when she'd beached the boat, run up into the dispensary and flopped her back against the closed door did she feel safe. Was that just perverted macho talk? Or were they actually capable of setting a fire, burning someone's home down? She shook her head, ran her hands up along her scalp, her fingers through her hair. No, they were just talking. Mean, stupid talk, sure, but just talk – two half-literate rednecked crackers with a grudge they'd carry forever. Some drunken night in town they'd probably push an old Chinese man, or back a pickup over some Chinese kid's bicycle... Besides, there wasn't much left of the season anyway. Soon they'd be gone and the people at the saltery could continue their isolated existence in peace. "And I'll be damned," she said to herself, "if I'll let those two bigots ruin what's left of my summer." With that she set about putting things away so she could close up and go get ready for a spaghetti dinner. The crab salad was forgotten.

William came into the dispensary the next day while she was removing a wood sliver from a man's palm. "Hi, Sugar," he said to her. "Hey there, Manuel," he addressed her patient, "one of these boards reach out and grab you?" Bonnie could tell he was in a hurry. "I've got to go out and walk the flume," he told her.

Manuel looked up from his wound, perhaps interested in what William was saying but too preoccupied to concentrate.

William said, "The water's stopped again without a trickle, just like last time, so it's probably a couple of boards out of the bottom again. Just wanted to let you know where I'll be."

Bonnie kept digging at the splinter. It was big and deep and she thought she might have to cut him to get it all. It had her full attention. "OK, my man. Somebody going with you?" She kept her head down as she spoke, concentrating.

"Nope. Joe's apparently down at the Indian village for some kind of meeting and everybody else is working the catch off that big boat that's tied up at the pier. I'll just run up the flume and check it out. See you later." Ian Morgan's admonition not to travel alone away from the cannery was forgotten, or ignored.

Still without looking up Bonnie replied, "Have a good walk. Don't forget your shotgun."

"I won't."

19

The break was serious this time. William could hear it long before he reached it, water in a loud crescendo, a high-country waterfall. When he got there and saw the situation he thought he knew the whole story. An entire section of the flume had been smashed and the trestle that held it against the mountain had been crushed into kindling by an old spruce tree that toppled from its anchorage in the thin soil and slid downhill through the flume, carrying everything away. The massive tree, with its muddy clump of roots pointing uphill, had come to rest in a tangle of branches and boards on the slope below the flume. Water cascaded from the uphill end of the smashed flume, forty feet beyond where William stood.

He tested his weight gingerly as he approached the break. Where he stood on the flume he was about thirty feet above the steeply sloping ground below. Hitching his shotgun sling to a more comfortable position on his shoulder, he took out his notebook and drew a quick sketch of the damaged section, eyeballing distances, counting the number of boards they'd need to rebuild the section and the number of trestle pieces they'd need to carry up. Those things were heavy, so he decided to have a closer look below to see how many supports could be salvaged.

He had to backtrack about twenty yards to find a clear spot where he could get off the flume and onto the sloping forest floor.

There were heavy patches of ferns and mossberry and blueberry over the rocks and humus of the evergreen woods. Footing was treacherous where the ground was steepest but there were plenty of small level spots and he worked his way down among the crisscrossed trestle timbers under the flume, then into the tangled wreckage below the broken section, avoiding the new waterfall.

He was making his way around the uphill end of the tree, around the huge clump of mud and roots that had pulled out of the ground, trying to see how many useable trestle supports might have been dragged down with the tree, when he saw the ax marks. They were raw, glaring, and so entirely undoubtable. Six large exposed roots had been cut and the tree had fallen.

Suddenly William felt a shudder of fear and found himself squatting among the branches below the trunk of the tree, the shotgun held across his chest. He spent ten minutes there, nearly motionless, a soldier again, looking around for signs on the forest floor or for movement, for the blur of someone with an ax darting through the trees. The thunder of water tumbling through the flume and spilling from the break and the pounding of his heart deafened him, adding to his sudden sensation of isolation. Finally he convinced himself he was alone and stood up, feeling rational again, half silly, but still his eyes wouldn't stop moving around, scanning the forest.

He climbed back up to where the roots burst out from the muddied trunk, telling himself he was being ridiculous yet still straining his ears through the noise of the water. There must be another explanation. But there they were, the glaring insults, the irrefutable marks, at eye level, cut with an ax, clean, bleeding sap.

He looked up the slope, following the gouge the tree had made in the ground and through the flume, up to where it had stood rooted in the slope about sixty feet above the flume. Had the tree been leaning far over? He wondered. Maybe it had been and the marks he took for ax cuts weren't, but were made... no, there

246

was only one explanation. Someone had cut the exposed roots and then had stood back watching the tree complete its lean, further and further until its own weight had torn it loose, crashing down through the smaller trees onto the flume, beyond, then sliding in a spray of new water and mud and broken boards down the slope to where it now lay, its branches snarled at the bases of other trees.

William climbed up to where the tree had stood, looked at the scars of its leaving. Then he looked around for other signs. There weren't any chips but that didn't mean anything. Whoever did it may have taken them so the sabotage wouldn't be quite so blatant, or maybe they were just lost in the mud and torn earth. He looked for signs of someone walking but he wasn't a tracker and couldn't identify anything as having been pressed or disturbed by a human foot. There wasn't any need for him to be a master detective, though, because even here, where the violence of the crashing had thrown debris and soil over the evidence, there were still three root ends sticking out of the dark soil on the upper side, and the chop marks were as obvious as feathers on an arrow.

He sat for a few moments on a log near the scar, then got his notebook out again and on a clean page drew a sketch of the entire area, showing the ends of the flume, the scar, the positioning of the roots he'd found cut. He tried to be precise, adding notes about the steepness of the slope and the consistency of the ground. He couldn't help looking around through the forest as he worked, turning his head and shoulders to see behind him, trying to see through the branches and into the patches of blueberry bushes. He should have been looking for bears but that hadn't occurred to him.

When he finished he put his notebook away. Then he grabbed a handful of mud and smeared it on the cut root ends, hiding them. He worked his way back down the slope of the mountain to the tree. He covered the cut ends of the roots there also. When he was done he climbed back up onto the flume and stood looking at the whole scene for a few minutes, fixing everything in his mind. His eyes traveled beyond the waterfall up to where the flume disappeared in a gentle curve, following the contour of the slope. He knew that about half a mile further the flume ended in the ravine. He also remembered the path that ended there, the one leading up along the pipe that carried water to the saltery. He thought about going up there to see if there were signs the path had been used but he turned and started back to the cannery instead. The flush of fear he'd felt when he recognized the ax marks had come back.

****

It was mid-afternoon when William reached the bottom of the flume, climbed the stairs on the end of the main building and sat down across from Ian, who continued checking a ledger until he got to the bottom line. Then Ian pushed his papers aside, took off his reading glasses and asked, "What have we got, Engineer?" They were alone in the office.

William unbuttoned the flap on his shirt pocket and brought his notebook out. "From a construction point of view we've got a relatively straightforward case of rebuilding about forty feet of flume and trestle. I've got the measurements and a list of what we need. But that's the pretty part. Let me show you this…" He turned to the page where he'd drawn the sketch. "I hate to say it but I think somebody wrecked that flume on purpose. No, I *know* somebody did. Look…"

He went over the sketch with Ian, who studied it until he could picture the various parts in their respective places. Then Ian sat back in his chair, put his feet on one corner of his desk, laced his fingers across his ample belly. He listened quietly, nodding once in a while at William's descriptions but asking no questions until William said, "…And I'm not sure why, but I tried to cover the evidence – I did cover it, at least to the casual observer, but if it rains tonight it'll show again. It's plain as stink on a skunk – somebody cut that tree down onto our flume."

"Any sign at all who might've done it?"

William was glad Ian's question wasn't an indication of disbelief; he'd presented him with a conclusion and a description of the evidence and Ian had accepted that. Now he was going the next step. William shook his head, put his notebook away. "No," he answered, "none. I looked for sign in that area but I didn't see any. I thought about going up to the ravine to check on that trail up there but frankly the idea spooked me, so I didn't."

"Hell. Oh, I don't mean about you not going up there…no telling… No, I mean about this whole affair. That goddam Tom Archer has been hollering sabotage all along and I've been poo-pooing him. I hate to think he's been right, but now this…"

"Why would somebody want to do something like this? It's not even a very big deal – one day and a dozen guys and I'll have it fixed and the water'll be back on line. It won't even shut us down if boats come in, with the reservoir full."

Ian shook his head, like a clerk trying to figure unbalanced books. "Yeah. That gets me, too. It's petty. More like stupid vandalism than calculated sabotage. Unless it accelerates, in which case it'll be a different thing. Damn. So little time left in the season. I thought we'd make it clean through."

"Maybe we will, Ian."

Ian was thoughtful a moment, then he said, "That was a good move, you making things less obvious like that. Any chance we can keep the whole thing quiet? Call it an Act of God? Maybe it'll go away by itself."

"There's a chance, I suppose… but like I said, if it rains… Well, hell, I can go back up first thing in the morning while the crew's getting the repair stuff together and do some evidence hiding before they get there." He warmed to his own thoughts. "Yeah, I can do that."

"OK," Ian agreed, "let's do it that way. I'd like to keep this quiet, just between us. Tom Archer and a couple others around here would love to get hold of this and I'd just as soon they didn't. Let's say a tree fell on it and that's that. Agree?"

"Yeah, sure. But it's better if I can tell Bonnie. She won't blab, and she helps me think. OK with that?"

Ian nodded. "She'll keep a level head about it." Ian paused thoughtfully, then shook his head in weary exasperation and resignation. "I'll arrange with Tom to have a crew ready to go up in the morning. I'll have him check with you on what they'll need to take."

William got a surprise later that afternoon. Tom Archer approached him while he was going over the compressor coils on the ice machine, painting on a bubbly liquid, looking for pinhole leaks. William put down the snoopy-soap can and the little paint brush and came out from behind the noisy beast, wiping his hands on a big red bandanna. Tom said to him, "Ian says we got a busted flume, need a crew up there in the morning."

"Yeah, Tom, a tree came over on it, took out about forty feet altogether. I think a dozen guys can manage it. Here…" He took his notebook out and ripped out the page with the list of materials they'd need. "I think this'll do it. Most of those trestle beams are still in good shape. We'll need to carry up a couple, though."

That's when Tom surprised him by saying, "OK, Mr. Hood, I'll give this to Art Small." Small was a line supervisor. "He'll be headin' up the crew. I got other things to do but never mind, Arts's a good hand, he kin get the work done."

William had thought Tom would want to rush right up to the damage site looking for another possible entry on the sabotage log he was carrying, so this was a strange development. Instead of saying anything to complicate matters however, William agreed.

"Sure, Art's a good man, like you say. You'll give him that?" He pointed to the paper in Tom's hand.

"Yeah. I'll tell him he's got to have everything ready to go up at about... what? About eight?"

"Sounds good," said William, calculating that *he'd* have to get started about six-thirty then. The crew would move slowly, carrying tools and heavy timber. He might need a good hour and a half to get up there and figure out some way of destroying the evidence.

In bed that night, with Bonnie held against his chest in their favorite talking position, William told her everything, including his conversation with Archer. "...And it strikes me damn funny, Tom missing this opportunity to shout *Chinese*. What do you think?"

"There really was no clue about who might have done it, huh?"

"None. At least no evidence I could see. Maybe Charlie Chan would... Oops, poor choice..."

"Well," she interrupted, "of course the Chinese *are* certainly suspect, aren't they?"

"I don't know. But from what Joe's told us I just can't picture them in a conspiracy to do something like this."

"Maybe it's not a conspiracy," she argued. "Maybe it's just one of them. Maybe there's a Chinese Tom Archer over there... Oh! I almost forgot..." She sat up and folded her legs Buddha style, pulled one of the blankets around her shoulders. As he lay beside her she told him about the conversation she'd heard while she'd been crabbing. "...So maybe it's important. Do you really think Tom and Jimbelly would do something like that? Burn somebody out?"

He'd listened carefully. Now he said, "Before this flume thing I'd have said no. But I'll tell you, this has shocked the hell out of me. It's no great deal but it *is* a *big* deal and it's going to take a bunch of men at least a whole day to fix. That's serious damage. I just don't know what to think."

****

Earlier, anticipating Tom Archer's close scrutiny, William knew he'd have to be clever about destroying the evidence of sabotage. But now with Art Small leading the crew he wouldn't have to worry about it so much; the other men were just casual observers compared to Tom. William figured he could strip off the ax marks with his sheath knife, then rough the surface of the roots a bit and apply more dirt and no one would recognize the marks for what they were. In the early morning chill he looked around for Tom as the crew was assembling the gear they'd need, but he didn't see him. He stopped in at Bonnie's clinic, his slicker and a lunch in a light rucksack on his back, his shotgun slung. Bonnie and he had gotten up very early and she'd gone to the clinic as soon as she was dressed. Now she was sitting at her work table, feet up, coffee mug steaming, a Saturday Evening Post in her hands. It was almost quarter to seven. "Aha, hard at work, I see," William said to her.

"Professional reading, my dear. Are you off? Hey!" She clumped her feet down, threw down the Post. "I'm going with you! It just occurred to me. No reason I shouldn't, and if anybody's going to need a medic today it'll be up there with the construction crew, not down here."

William opened his mouth to object but just as quickly changed his mind. Why not? "Good," he said, "but you've got to speed out if you want to go with me – I just stopped by on my way to the flume – I've got to get up there *skoshi-skoshi.*"

She was throwing things into her own small backpack – a Sac Millet. "Skushi-skushi? What's that mean, oh learned engineer?"

"It means those jeans are so tight across your cute little ass…" He made a grab for her and she squealed, jumped away. "Leave me alone, you sex fiend. What about my revolver? Should I take it?"

"No need. Lots of guys up there today. And no self-respecting bear…"

"How about the walk up, just you and me?"

"…So I think you definitely should take it. Now come on, get a hustle on."

"I'm done." She took the holstered .357 he'd given her off a nail on the wall and hung it over one shoulder, flipped the pack over her other shoulder. "Let's go."

"Not so fast, Annie Oakley. You'll need both hands to get up onto the flume. Go ahead and strap up. I can wait." He looked at his watch in mock petulance. A shock of his hair hadn't been contained by his Stetson, hung down over his forehead. When she had her pack on and had buckled the revolver around her waist she tipped his hat up, brushed the hair back under it, leaned her face up under the brim and kissed him quickly on the lips. "Thanks, lover. Let's go," she said.

"That thing loaded?" He'd given her the revolver before he'd left for Seattle en route to open the cannery. She'd been pleased. Her dad had always had hunting pieces around and she wasn't intimidated by guns. William had told her, "This is because we're going to be in a wild sort of place. I don't expect you'll ever need to shoot it, but it makes one hell of a lot of noise if you do pull the trigger, and maybe that'll be useful some day." With characteristic thoroughness she'd bought several boxes of ammo and had gone to the gun club range and asked someone to teach her how to fire it. She wasn't a good shot by any means but she could hold it relatively steady and it didn't jump out of her hands when it went off. And William had been right, it did make one hell of a noise. She unholstered it now, spun the chamber slowly, looking. "Yup."

"OK, we're off," he said. They went out and followed the boardwalk until they were behind the main cannery building, from where they'd have to negotiate a steep muddy bank to reach the lower end of the flume. As she was climbing the shallow steps scooped into the slope, in front of and above William, she hesitated and turned her head back, looked down at him and said, "Oh, I've got no lunch…"

He reached up and put the palm of his hand firmly against her warm fanny, pushing her up onto the next muddy foothold. "Don't worry about that, you can live off the fat in the hand… uh, the fat of the *land*, the *land*, *the fat of the land*, I mean."

She took one hand off the edge of the flume, reached down and punched him on top of the head with her fist, caving in the crown of his Stetson. He hollered and grabbed his head and lost his handhold and slipped back down about four feet to the boardwalk. It had been an ill-considered comment, a true lapse of judgment. "I'll *fat* in the *hand* you, buddy. Come on up *here* and say that."

"OK, OK, I'm sorry," he claimed, rubbing the top of his head. The sight of her standing above him, legs braced on the flume, hands on her hips, pistol low on her right thigh and fire in her eyes made the lump worthwhile.

They made quick time up to the break, teasing and bantering all the way, their feet making hollow thumpings on the boards of the empty flume, their laughter sufficient ruckus to warn any bears of their approach. In fact they saw great footprints, very clearly, in a muddy place where a bear had overturned a rotten log next to the flume. The disturbance looked fresh and that made them apprehensive for a quarter of a mile or so, but soon their lightheartedness returned.

Tom Archer brought them crashing to seriousness again.

20

William and Bonnie had quieted as they approached the break, partly because they were winded. It had been a fast several miles, gradual but all uphill. As they reached the last solid section before the break William was leading, Bonnie right behind him. The noise of the waterfall on the other side of the break filled the forest.

A sudden flash of movement drew William's attention to his right front and in an instinctive reaction honed in muddy, bloody places in Europe he started to whip the shotgun off his shoulder as his head turned. Then he didn't know whether to put the gun into his hands or leave it slung. Tom Archer and Johnson were up on the slope above and in front of them, standing at the edge of the scar where the tree's roots had come out of the ground. William's hands made up his mind for him and the shotgun swung down into his palm, no threat to anyone, but unslung nevertheless.

Bonnie almost ran into him, stopped, also saw the two men, said, "Willie..."

"Hello," yelled Tom. Johnson waved. Johnson wore a grin, Tom Archer a leer. Tom had a light, three-quarters length ax in his hand, Johnson held a lever-action rifle, heavy bore. Both men were dressed for the woods and there was an air of competence about them.

Bonnie was visibly frightened and she put her hand on William's waist, looking past him at the intruders who were climbing down through the ferns and blueberry bushes. William and Bonnie had to move back a few yards so there'd be room for the two men to step over onto the boards of the flume top. Tom shouted over the noise of the water. "Didn't mean to startle you none, ma'am."

William suspected his wife was remembering the threats she'd heard in Tom's voice when she'd been crouched in the dinghy, but she kept her wits now. "Hi, Tom, Johnson. You did startle us. We thought we were the first ones up here."

"Yeah," William added quickly. He gestured with the shotgun back down toward the cannery, and lied, "The rest of the crew's right behind us. What're you guys doing up here? I thought you had something else going on this morning." Tom Archer had tricked him and William knew they both recognized that, and it angered him but he wasn't ready to show it yet.

Tom spoke again, settling the small ax comfortably on his shoulder. "Yeah, well, I did, but Johnson and I figured it could wait. After all, this water's mighty important. So we figured to come up and be here when the crew arrived. Thought we'd have a chance to figure out how this happened, you know? Maybe prevent it happening again. Know what I mean?" There was a clear message in the look he gave William.

William braced himself and stared back directly and now the challenge in his own eyes matched the sudden resolve in his voice. "What do you mean, Tom?"

"This weren't no accident, *Mister* Hood." Tom Archer's tone sliced any respect off his words. "Johnson and I got a real close look at things here. Somebody cut the roots holding that old tree against the hill and when they done that, over she went. Somebody done this on purpose." He swung the ax around to take in the crushed flume, the water rushing out of the shattered box. "I said

256

somebody, but we know damned well who done it and I've told you and Ian Morgan enough times so you know who done it, same as me. In fact," he peered closely at William, watching his eyes, "I'm surprised you didn't see it for yourself. You was up here yesterday. I seen some sign near that root pad, looked like footprints, maybe yours, but the rain…" He let the sentence trail off.

The void said volumes to William. Tom Archer knew William had found the evidence, but had kept it hushed up. He'd manipulated Ian and William. He'd suckered them in with a story about having other duties this morning and now confronted them with their own conspiracy to deny the obvious evidence. And the frustrating thing about Tom's insistence: he was right. The sabotage evidence was irrefutable.

"I been telling folks around here them squints want us out of this bay. They got no use for us being in here every summer. They want this place for themselves, all the way from the duck flats to where them Indians live, and now they's starting to put the squeeze on us, trying to make it too expensive for us to stay."

"That's absurd!" It was Bonnie. She shoved past William, who put his hand on her arm to restrain her. She pushed it off, went right up and stood close to Tom Archer. He scowled at her.

Tom wasn't big but he was solid and strong in spite of his hunched ways. William had seen him lift heavy equipment in his arms; he wasn't sure he could win a fight with the man. Now Tom glowered at Bonnie, who put one hand on her hip and stared right back at him. "That's so much stinking horse shit and you know it, Tom Archer. Have you ever gone over there and seen that old man, met his family? No! I thought so." She gave him no opportunity to reply and they stood toe to toe on the flume as she told him off in a loud, clear voice. "You listen to me, Mister Tom Archer. I don't know what you've got against those people but I'm telling you it's all in your prejudiced, sick mind. Those Chinese people have been living peacefully here for fifty years now and they

257

never did any of this stuff you say. And you know it." She was wound up good, her fists clenched, her jaw forward. "You listen to me and don't you *dare* scowl at me, you... you *coal miner!* I can scowl right back just as hard as you and I won't be treated this way and I won't have you treating those Chinese people this way either!" She ended with both hands near her hips and it couldn't have escaped any of them that her right one gripped her holstered revolver.

Instead of crushing her head with the ax or sweeping her off the flume, as he could have done, Tom seemed to unhunch, to straighten. He kept his look on her for a moment, then shifted it over her shoulder to William. Johnson stood behind and to one side of Tom. He had one foot on the flume, one foot up on the slope of the mountain. His forearm rested on his thrust-up knee, the rifle cradled across. He had a spruce needle between his lips, worked it like a farmer with a blade of grass.

Tom suddenly turned away, swung the ax down to his side, said, "Come on, Johnson, let's get started fixing this son of a *bitch.*" He looked at Bonnie as he said the last word.

William and Bonnie stood and watched while the two men went down to the tree, where most of the wooden trestle braces had been scattered, and began to salvage the good ones. William was still stunned at the whole confrontation. Bonnie looked a little dazed, shocked with an adrenaline rush, and after several heavy breaths to calm herself she finally plopped down on the flume, her legs dangling over the edge. William stood beside her a minute, then shucked his pack and put down the shotgun, laid his hand on her shoulder and bent over to kiss her cheek. While he was close he said, "That's telling him, Sugar. Now I'm going to do *my* thing," and he went to help move the heavy trestle timbers.

Shortly after the rest of the crew arrived, lessening the tension by spreading it out, William told Art Small, the crew foreman, he'd walk up to the gully and put the gate in the box, diverting the water from the flume so the men could work without having to contend with the waterfall. Bonnie went with him. She didn't waste any time. As soon as they were out of sight around a bend she asked, "What do you think, Willie?"

He answered with a question. "Do you think it'd be a good thing for us to pay a visit down to the saltery?"

"You read my mind, Mr. Hood. How far is it down that path you mentioned?"

"Well, Joe told me it's about three miles but you know he might be a little vague about distances. It could be more but probably that's close. Do you think the Hongs would give us a lift back to the cannery in one of their skiffs? It'd save us the walk back."

"We can ask. And we can always spend the night there if we have to, walk back in the morning."

"All right. I'd like to get this thing out in the open."

They were close to the ravine now and could hear the water cascading from the snowfields nearly a mile above them. The shadowy, dark green needles of the trees around them, the closeness of the trees, the cloud-bruised sky, all would contribute to an early darkness that day.

****

William got the gate into the flume's catchment box without problem, then he and Bonnie spent another hour and a half walking down through the forest to the saltery, following the path along the general route of the pipe, crossing and re-crossing it, sometimes veering away to skirt a thick deadfall or an especially overgrown area. Most of the way the path took them through beautiful untouched forest, the trees reaching up hundreds of feet, trunks too big for two people to reach around. Always aware of the danger of surprising a bear, they talked in strong voices to give warning of their approach, and when they tired of talking one or another of them sang. Bonnie claimed they were safest when William was singing. "Any bear would run when he hears *your* singing." William sneaked up to goose her but she heard him and raced away, squealing, down the path. As soon as they were off the side of the mountain, crossing the bench of flat land, the going was easy and it was more like a picnic outing than the serious visit William intended it to be.

Barking dogs heralded their arrival as they came out of the forest near a big wooden water tank where the pipe ended. They were at the rear of the saltery buildings, which were all oriented toward the cove in a semicircle in the gentle shape of the beach. Bonnie was afraid of the dogs and looked back at William who stepped in front of her to lead the rest of the way. He unslung his shotgun to fend them off with, and walked toward the beach. A stream led from the tank overflow down toward the cove and they followed that, wanting to approach from the openness of the bay side rather than from the surprise of the forest.

They surprised no one. The dogs beset them as they approached the rear of the buildings but it was boundingly apparent the animals were yipping and howling with pleasure, not antagonism. There were half a dozen full grown dogs and two litters of puppies, one of them very young. The puppies stumbled and tumbled in the moss and yipped and whined and fell over each other in the general melee. The noise was terrible and William turned back to look at Bonnie, who was surrounded by squealing pups and body-wagging dogs, most of them showing big toothy smiles. He laughed and she laughed with him. She scooped up a puppy in each arm, getting thoroughly licked in the process, and they picked their way toward the beach, careful not to step on the pups. The puppies in her arms smelled like warm milk.

"Hello," a young voice said from near the corner of a building. The boy was in shadow and William couldn't see his face. "Sorry about all the noise. Please come."

Going from the gloom of the forest into the saltery cove was like going from a tunnel into a wonderland. Bonnie hugged the two puppies to her cheeks and said, "Oh, Willie, it's beautiful." Her voice carried regret that she hadn't made the trip before.

They were about twenty yards from where the water washed gently against a black gravel beach fronting most of the little cove. A couple of skiffs lay on the gravel like fat sunbathers waiting for the sun to come out, and over to the left a light-duty, rather flimsy-looking walkway on stilts darted out above the shallow waters of a mud flat. Another skiff was tied to the end of the walkway. There were a number of buildings, maybe eight or ten altogether, each one different, planks and combinations of peeled log and plank, or stone and plank. All of them were painted the same pale-green color and roofed with spruce shakes, but each one had its own flavor.

"Welcome to the Hong Saltery. I'm Kai Win." William was greeted by a smiling Chinese man somewhere between forty and fifty years old with a short military-style haircut, a frugal mustache trimmed close, and a red plaid wool shirt with the sleeves rolled up to expose very muscular forearms. William shifted his shotgun and took the offered hand, expecting his own to be crushed. The man was apparently aware of his strength however, and he gave a firm but thoughtful grip as William introduced himself and Bonnie.

Kai Win next held out his hand to Bonnie, who started to take it but suddenly squealed like a schoolgirl as one of the fat puppies she held in her arms took the opportunity to leap free. Both Bonnie and Kai Win made a grab for it and while it was being juggled Kai Win quite accidentally – and even William could see it was an accident – missed the pup and thrust his meaty hand into the front of Bonnie's shirt. It all happened in a brown blur of squirming, leaping puppy, groping hands and misjudged distances.

Surprise flushed all three faces. Kai Win was flabbergasted. He whipped his hand out of Bonnie's shirt – hot iron – waved it at the ground twice like he was shaking off bugs and then slapped it several times, punishing it. The whole thing was over in seconds.

"Well there, Kai Win," Bonnie finally managed to say, wiping tears of laughter from her eyes and adjusting herself, shrugging her shoulders and rearranging herself comically, "I must say this has been quite a greeting. Is there more to come?"

"Yes, indeed," added William, "I was just hoping for a glass of water but I've already gotten the floor show."

Kai Win appeared almost too mortified to speak. A bright blush rushed up his tanned neck and face, like a thermometer rising quickly. He apologized, "Oh, I am sorry," he exclaimed, looking at the ground and shaking his head. He bowed twice, quickly, then concentrated on shooing the puppies away. While he did that William had a few seconds to observe Hong Deng Wei and Lo An as they arrived on the scene.

Deng Wei wasn't large but it was obvious he'd once been well built. There was a certain stringiness about him, mostly in his neck and hands. He wasn't robust but he didn't look feeble, either. His hair was medium length, all black. William looked at his face and thought of Eskimos. It was broad and intelligent, with a thousand wrinkles. Both his prominent cheeks had deep furrows curving through them in a smooth arc from the outside edge of his eyes to the corners of his mouth, giving him a wild man's look until he smiled, when the effect became cherubic.

Lo An, holding Deng Wei's arm tightly, was older looking, probably because her hair was entirely grey, though it was still full and luxurious. She had it pulled into a bun at the back of her neck and William wondered how long it was when she let it down. He was stunned by her beauty. Her back was as straight as a cadet's and her movements were still graceful but it was her face that enraptured him. She looked Chinese but the racial features he could identify were fine, the most delicate hints of Oriental mystery in a universal beauty. Her skin was flawless. A few wrinkles, sure, around her eyes and mouth, but those were a legacy of thoughtfulness and wisdom. Her eyes were big and she used them directly.

Kai Win introduced them.

Lo An stuck out her hand, releasing her husband's arm, and said, "Mr. Hood. I am glad you have come to visit us, and thank you for bringing your wife. We are honored by your visit."

William was star-struck and fumbled for words and Bonnie saved him. "Mrs. Hong, you honor us, and we are ashamed we haven't come to visit before this."

Lo An put back her head and laughed, a bright tinkling sound. "Ah, no, it is we who are honored. But enough of that. Soon we will all be so honored we'll be stuffy, and have no fun. Come, please."

When they were seated in well-crafted homemade furniture Lo An spoke for a minute in Chinese to Deng Wei, who nodded and said something short to Kai Win. Kai Win responded in Chinese and the old man waved his hand, acquiescing reluctantly to whatever Kai Win had suggested. Kai Win turned to the Hoods and reported, "My mother and father would be greatly honored if you would accept their invitation to stay for supper, and then remain for the night with us. We have an extra bungalow that is already being prepared for your use, and Father has asked me to send my son over to the cannery in a skiff to let them know you have safely arrived here and that we will bring you to the cannery at whatever time you wish in the morning."

Bonnie looked at William. "Honey?" she asked. "Do you think it'd be OK?"

"Sure. Why not?" he replied airily.

Bonnie rolled her eyes theatrically and said, "What my *barbarian* husband means is, 'We would love to accept your hospitality.' Are you sure…"

"It is no trouble at all, I assure you." Lo An looked at both of them when she spoke. Even Deng Wei looked pleased.

****

While the Hoods continued their conversation with the Hongs Kai Win strode down to the beach and out to the end of the walkway where his son Tako was already standing in fevered anticipation in the skiff. The boy reached toward the starter rope on the outboard motor as Kai Win got there but Kai Win said in English, "Wait a minute. Take it easy. And don't screw it up, because I had to give your grandfather my most solemn word of honor that you'd go straight over there and come straight back. With no delays. Got it?"

Tako was too excited to even pretend having much sense so Kai Win spelled it out for him. "This is no courting call, so don't go wandering around in the cannery hoping to run into her. Just deliver the message and come directly back. Got it?"

Tako responded, "Sure, sure, I know…"

"I mean it, Tako. I've told you you're going to have to have the patience of Kublai Khan or you'll find yourself nailed to a spruce tree. Know what I mean?"

"Yeah, I know." The teenager's bottom lip stuck out but Kai Win knew his son recognized that he sided with him in this matter but was powerless against Deng Wei's injunction. Tako started the outboard motor, clicked it into reverse, backed away from the walkway, turned the boat, and as he headed out of the cove Kai Win yelled at him, "Remember the wrath of the Khans!"

264

Tako raised his hand in acknowledgment and motored out of the cove with the bow high, the wake wide, and undoubtedly, all his hormonal glands at full throb.

****

The object of Tako's affections was Tina Menendez, the daughter of the worker who'd had the splinter in his hand, Manuel Menendez, and his wife Nora.

Nora was a savvy, friendly woman, half Swedish and half everything else, and at a young age she'd decided there was wisdom in the if-you-got-it-flaunt-it theory of life. She was a tall woman so she wore high heeled shoes when she went out. Her hair was bright blonde – naturally so – so she let it grow and wore it cascading down her back. She swung her hips when she walked and kept her breasts thrust out and riding high and it was no surprise when work stopped and construction gangs groaned and applauded her passage. Manuel Menendez had been just one more Mexican wolf in a hard hat when he followed her home. It hadn't even been quitting time. She'd walked by the tower building he was helping build on Ocean Boulevard, in Long Beach, California, and as usual there was a round of appreciation from the hard hats. Manuel Menendez had quite simply walked off the job. He put his gloves in the back pocket of his jeans, signaled all stop to the crane operator he'd been directing, forgot all about his lunch box – not to mention his paycheck – and followed her mindlessly to her apartment up on East Third Street. There had followed some wild scenes but in the end she'd given up and fallen in love with him. It had been good, too.

Tina took after her mother in looks and her father in disposition and got the best of both. She was lucky to have her mixed breed of parents because at fifteen she wanted the attention of boys and there was only one boy around, and he was Chinese.

Her folks thought that was fine. They certainly held no prejudice against mixed-race relationships, though almost everybody else did, it seemed. Their reaction to her antics over the Hong boy at the saltery were low-keyed, common sense.

"Nora honey, she's gonna do what girls do and he's gonna do what boys do. If she hasn't got any sense now, after all our tryin', she's never goin' to, and we can't do anything about it, no?"

"Yes, you're right, sure. I just wish..."

"Wish what, Nora honey?"

"Well... I wish there were lots of nice boys around. Oh, I think Tako's nice, but if there were lots of boys around, then she'd have to go slower, choosing. You know?"

"Si, I know what you're saying. But there's no reason to tell her no on this boy, is there?"

"No, of course not. But we'd better decide some rules, between us, so we're both telling her the same thing."

"You mean," her husband toyed with her, acting sly, twirling an imaginary mustache, "you mean how far can he go? Rules like this?"

"No, you bandito, I don't mean that. Well, yes, I do mean... Ah, Manuel..." She covered her face with her hands. "She's just my baby..."

Baby Tina was actually a well-advanced young lady, nubile, flirtatious, good to look at and in a few years anyway, trouble. But now she was just a teenaged girl with barely bridled passion and a determination not to miss out on a social life just because she happened to be in Cloud Bay, Alaska for the summer. She'd taken well to the isolation – it wasn't the family's first work in a remote camp – and her folks were proud of her.

Bonnie hadn't been completely surprised when early in the season Tina had asked her, "Bonnie, do you think that boy from the saltery is kind of cute?" She'd held her head sideways, watching Bonnie count supplies from a cardboard box.

Bonnie had looked up and smiled. "You mean the one I saw you talking with down by the skiffs the other day?"

"Yeah, him. His name's Tako and he's really intelligent and I think he's cute. Do you?"

"Well yeah, now that you mention it I do think he's kinda cute, but I'm already married and anyway, he's a bit too young for me."

Tina had gasped. "Not for you! For me! I mean…" She'd blushed, and Bonnie had laughed.

****

Tako was torn in two by his fortunes, good and bad. He'd fallen in love, right in the bay, with a beautiful girl. And now he thanked the fortune that was sending him over to the cannery to carry the message about the Hoods. Of course his father's admonition about not fooling around was clear, but maybe he'd have the opportunity to see her and talk to her. He hoped to see her, of course, even kiss her – something they'd done several times now – but just in case, he'd written her a note.

The skiff motor was at full throttle because if he hurried in transit he might have an extra moment ashore. He cut the rocky corner close where the point of land jutted out between the saltery cove and the cannery arm of the bay, then set a course that would take him past the cannery about two hundred yards out. Like an airplane pilot looking over an unfamiliar runway before he commits himself, Tako cruised past the cannery on a broad downwind leg, then turned base, and then when he could delay no more he turned final and came in toward the pier.

He hadn't seen any blonde heads among the several people outside who'd looked up at the sound of his motorboat but that didn't mean she didn't know. Maybe she was brushing her hair or something. He hoped she'd run down to meet him, and to give her more time to do that he cruised slowly past the ladder on the pier and put the skiff in on the beach in front of the little houses. There wasn't anybody about down there so he tied off the skiff and climbed the small beach up onto the boardwalk, following it slowly past the houses – one of which was hers – toward the cannery building.

He was just about to start climbing the outside stairs on the end of the factory building to go up into the loft offices when above him the door opened and the cook who looked like Friar Tuck in the Robin Hood comics came out onto the landing and started down the stairs. He had a clipboard and a bunch of papers in his hand. When he got to the lower landing he saw Tako standing at the bottom of the stairs and stopped for a second, then looked for his footing and came down, saying, "Hi, kid. You again, huh? What'cha got?"

"Hello, sir," Tako said. "Uh, I got a message from my Grandma about Mr. and Mrs. Hood, you know?"

"Oh, yeah. They went up the flume this morning with the crew. Anything wrong with them?"

"Oh, no sir. They just walked from the flume down to our place at the saltery and they're visiting with my Grandma and Grandpa."

"OK. So what's the message? I'm kind of in a hurry." He looked at papers on the clipboard.

"Well, sir, my Grandma just wanted me to tell somebody here that they're gonna spend the night at our place." Tako was craning his neck, trying to see around the corner of the building. Where was she?

The cook shuffled the papers on his clipboard, then remembered he was having a conversation and said, "I forgot your name, kid."

"Tako, sir."

268

"Oh yeah. OK, Takosar. I got the message. Is that it?" He stepped off the bottom landing onto the boardwalk.

Tako backed up a couple of paces to make room for the man's belly. "Uh, no sir, they said to tell you that somebody... uh, that *I* would bring Mr. Hood and his wife back over here in the morning." Now that Tako was further out from the building he could see down the front of it but he didn't see her flying toward him. Maybe she was working inside? Or sick or something? He felt a slight chill and realized that apart from his own personal sun setting, the Alaska sun had just dipped behind the mountains across the bay and it had become suddenly cold. He had to get a move on. If he was late getting back Kai Win would come down hard on him. And he had to face facts. He wasn't going to get to see Tina this time. The cook was walking off, down along the front of the cannery building, along the cannery edge of the pier. "Uh, sir?" Tako said to the man's back. "Could you please deliver a message for me? It's really important."

The fat man stopped, turned. "What, another message? OK, but make it quick, Takasan, 'cause I got a meal to fix."

"It's just this, sir, this note, uh, letter." He went up to the cook and handed him the message he'd written and folded and taped shut with half a roll of sealing tape. On the front he'd printed, *Tina M.* "Could you see that Tina Menendez gets this, sir? It's pretty important so if she could get it tonight..."

The man took the note out of Tako's hand, turned it over, looked at the name. "You sure you got enough tape on it?" he asked, chuckling. Then he said, "Yeah, I'll put it under her dinner plate. How's that?"

Tako grinned thankfully. "Thanks a lot, sir. Well, I got to go. Thanks, sir." He waved and ran back to his skiff, slowing to a walk as he passed the houses, giving himself one last chance to see her.

21

The crew from the flume detail was back just after full dark, about nine o'clock, so they'd had a long day. Jim Bell met them as they came off the flume behind the mess hall carrying their tools. They looked tired. "You guys take your time washing up. Shower if you want. Supper's on the stove and it ain't goin' no place so just come on in when you're ready. Pork cutlets and mashed potatoes with gravy," he told them as they passed. Manuel Menendez went past him and he had a flash of something forgotten but then Tom was down off the flume and came over to him. "Jimbelly," he said, his face darker than usual, with dirt and mud smeared over a full day's growth of heavy whiskers, "I got some real news for you. You and me's gotta' do some serious figuring."

"Why? What's up, Tom?"

"I'll tell you, but not until I've got something in my belly. I could eat a dead hog. What'd you say you got for supper?"

"Pork cutlets."

"Yeah, well, that's a dead hog, all right. After supper, you and me'll sit down and decide some things, once and for all." Tom clapped Jimbelly on his shoulder and hunched off toward his house.

After the meal, while Jim Bell was going over his menus for the next day, Tom went into the cook's office off the kitchen. He sat on a crate. "Jimbelly, whatever you're doing, put it up because there's some things goin' on that you and me's got to discuss."

Jimbelly pushed his papers aside and turned to face his visitor. "OK, what's more important than eating tomorrow?"

"That flume was sabotaged, that's what. That tree no more fell over on that water box by itself than I'm Sitting Bull. Hear what I'm saying?"

"You're saying someone chopped down a tree on purpose so it'd fall and cut off our water?"

"Give the man a brass ring. Only it weren't *chopped* down, it was cut through the roots real clever so's it'd look like a *natural* thing."

"So how come you found out?"

Tom sat back on the crate. "Because I looked. Those marks were plain to see. But there's more." He affirmed that with a fist on Jim Bell's desk. "I wasn't the only one to *notice* it, but maybe I'm the only one's going to *say* it, 'cause that engineer, Hood, and his cutesy wife know it same as I do."

"Know what, for Christ's sake?"

"When I was up there this morning he shows up early, before the crew, and get this, somebody been at them marks with mud, trying to cover up the evidence."

"Well, who…"

"I figure Hood. He's the only one who was up there before us yesterday, after the water cut off. He went up to find the trouble and I figure that's when he covered up them marks."

Jimbelly was confused and unconvinced simultaneously. "Hell, what'd he want to do that for? He's a fuckin' water engineer. You think *he* chopped that tree?"

"No, Jimbelly, he never done that. I'll tell you exactly who done it, and who he's covering up for, 'cause sure as horseflies bite it's him who put the mud on them cut marks."

"You gonna tell me, or what?"

"Yeah, but I'm surprised you ain't figured it out for yourself…"

"Jeeeesus…"

"Them squints from over to that saltery done it. No question. And Hood's covering for 'em. By the way, where in hell are they, that college boy and his bitch?" Tom Archer looked around as if he could see through the plank walls of the small office. "One minute they was there watching us work, the next minute I looked up and they was gone. I didn't see 'em at supper neither. They already eat?"

"Naw, they're over at the saltery right now. Walked down that trail. They're even gonna spend the night there. Probably gonna come back and give us all crabs and bedbugs."

"How you know that?"

"Oh, there was that Chinese kid over here with a message. Oh, shit…" He reached for his clipboard and pulled the heavily taped and folded note out. He held it up. "…And he gave me this for that blonde, the one who's got them knockers…"

"Give me that a minute. Let me see it. You say that squint kid came over here to tell you about the Hoods being over there, and they sent that to Manuel's kid?"

"Yeah. I mean yeah, he brought the message, but he didn't say nothing about this being from the Hoods." Jimbelly indicated the wadded and taped note. "He just wanted me to give it to her."

He held out the note and Tom took it from him, turned it over in his hand, then unbuttoned the flap on his shirt pocket, put the note in and folded the flap back over.

"So what are you going to do?" Jimbelly asked.

Tom thought a minute, drumming his fingers on the side of Jimbelly's desk. "I'll let you know what we're going to do about this sabotage thing. It's not the first time, you know, but Morgan wants to cover it up. Hoods are in with him too. They're trying to cover it all up but you can bet American money I ain't going to let that happen. I'll talk to you later."

****

The clouds drizzled and the outside lights, hatted with their big green metal shades, glistened the wood of the pier. Crewmen did chores on the one fishing boat tied up at the pier. The vessel had earlier unloaded fish and replenished her ice and she was about ready to head back to the fishing grounds. The sound of machinery filled the night. Tom Archer left the mess hall and went quickly to his quarters, hunched against the light rain. A short time later he came out again, snugging his slicker around himself as he walked down the boardwalk to the Mexican's place.

Manuel Menendez answered his knock and Tom exchanged a few words with him about the job they'd done on the flume. They'd put in a hard day and Tom was tired. He gave the man the note for his daughter and declined the invitation to go in for coffee. He didn't drink with Mexicans anyway, if he could help it. He said a civil goodnight and made his way back to his own bungalow.

****

Around the point in Chinaman's Cove William and Bonnie were trying to refuse a last course of food. William pushed back his chair, patted his belly and said, "No ma'am, not one more bite." He inclined his head to Lo An and said, "I'm only a mortal man, but if I eat any more you'll have to put me into the Book of the Immortals." The others could tell that old Deng Wei was beginning to tire. His eyes looked heavy and he was squirming uncomfortably on his chair, shifting his weight from one side to the other. William could see it was time for Bonnie and him to leave.

The conversation at the table had been constant, animated and friendly, even occasionally boisterous. There wasn't any alcohol served but the ambiance was tavern-like as they all sat around the Hong's table dipping their chopsticks into half a dozen dishes. Deng Wei kept leaning toward Lo An and Kai Win with comments and for translations of what the others had said in English.

When they'd said their good nights Kai Win took William and Bonnie down to the little log and plank bungalow that had been prepared for them and accepted their invitation to come in and sit a while. The supper table had been no place to raise the issue which had originally brought Bonnie and William to the cove.

When they were seated, with the stove in the corner driving out the dampness, Bonnie looked at William, who shrugged as if to say, "Yeah, might as well." Making up her mind, she folded one leg underneath her on the small couch and said, "Kai Win, that was a beautiful dinner and we really appreciate how kind you all have been. I wish we could offer you the same hospitality over at the cannery, but it's... well, it's more of a factory over there than a home."

Kai Win responded generously, "Please, no return is expected, or required."

Bonnie breathed deeply. "Actually there's a more specific reason we came over today, and I think, we both think," she indicated her husband, "you're probably the best one to talk with about it. I don't know exactly how to put it so you'll know we haven't come over here with any accusations. I think what we're trying to do is prevent some unpleasantness." She looked to William for support and he nodded agreement.

"Unpleasantness?"

"Well," she started, "I hope..." She looked in sudden word loss at her husband, who took over. "Kai Win, Bonnie and I spent today up on the flume that carries water down to the cannery."

Kai Win tilted his head. "Yes?"

274

"We were up there with a work crew doing some rather major repair where a big spruce had taken out a section of the flume, fell on it and then slid through, right on down the slope. Did a hell of a wrecking job, as you can imagine."

"Go on." Kai Win looked attentive. William could see him concentrating, as if he were picturing the newly opened gap in the forest where the big tree had stood, the red and black earth ripped by its slide, the water gushing from the broken flume. "Well, when I found it I looked around, and Kai Win, it was not an Act of God. It was no accident. Somebody *made* that tree fall on our flume."

"Cut it down?"

"No, Kai Win, it was more subtle than that, but the situation was still clear to someone who looked closely, as I did. And no mistake. Somebody cut the right exposed roots until it toppled. It was obviously already leaning over."

Kai Win sat back in his chair and put both hands on his thighs as if he were in a prisoner's dock. His dark Oriental eyes looked straight at William, then to Bonnie, who could hardly return his look, then back to William. There was no expression on his face as he said, "And you think I did it?"

Bonnie jumped in. "No, we don't. We don't have *any idea* who did it. William saw that *somebody* had made it happen and we thought we'd better let you know what's going on. Kai Win, as far as we know there's only you and us in this bay."

"You and us…"

"I didn't mean it to sound that way. I'm not setting up sides," Bonnie told him. "I mean there are people at the cannery, there are people here at the saltery…"

William cut back in. "Kai Win, somebody cut that tree so it'd fall on the cannery flume. I'm the water engineer so it's my responsibility. I'm trying…"

"You're trying to find out if there's someone here at the Hong saltery who'd do such a thing." It wasn't a question.

William thought about his answer, opted for forthrightness. "Yes," he said. "We're not accusing, we're just confused. There's got to be an answer to this. We're searching for it. That seems reasonable to me." He shrugged his shoulders. The other two were silent, waiting for him to go on. "We wanted to come talk. That's all."

Kai Win leaned back and seemed to relax again, seemed to be certain, even without thinking. "No one here did that, or anything like it."

Bonnie looked relieved. "Help us, Kai Win. This isn't a small thing, not at the cannery. It took a lot of men a long day to fix it and they're talking about it. William tried to cover it up, make it look like an accident..." Kai Win darted a sharp questioning look at William, "...so it'd go away, but that didn't work. And there's one guy over at the cannery, Tom Archer, a supervisor unfortunately, who's... well, he's just plain prejudiced."

"Against Chinese?"

William answered, his voice hard as he remembered the tone of Tom's voice and the look in his eyes up on the flume as he stood eye to eye with Bonnie. "I think against everybody, but yes, certainly against Chinese. He's saying you did it. You Chinese, that is, not you personally. He blames everything that goes wrong on you if he can and frankly, there are others who aren't all that bright..."

"So," Kai Win said. "And now this. Well, I should tell you how it is over here, but it's not going to answer your question." He settled back, began to talk. "As you said, that's a factory over there, this is a family over here. The people here, my parents, came to get away from white people, and because they didn't have anyplace else to go." Bonnie and William exchanged looks but said nothing and Kai Win continued. "They were driven like dogs out of town in the middle of winter by white men who didn't want to have to share their food with coolies. They survived though, and they came here."

"How awful," said Bonnie.

"Yes, awful. It was a long time ago but they haven't forgotten. *We* haven't forgotten. We've made a good life here, by hard work, and we have our own strong feelings, and we're not coolies any more, and this is *our* land. Someone's destroyed your flume and you think it has to be us…"

"…Because you're the only ones here…"

"…But nobody here did that. Think. Who would? My father? My mother?" Kai Win was right and William knew it. Those were ludicrous possibilities. "Me?" Kai Win smiled when he said that. "I can tell you, if I did it I'd do it *right*. But what's the *point?*" He held out the palms of his hands. "Very soon, in just a few weeks, days, really, it'll be quiet here again. You'll be gone. We'll still be here." He looked directly into William's eyes. "We'll always be here."

There was silence when he finished and William knew they'd have to think of somebody else to blame. So would Tom Archer. The Hongs were too gentle, too mature, too involved in their own life in the bay to be suspects in the sabotage of the flume, or in any other devious plot against the cannery. At least that's the way it appeared to him then and there. After a moment he sighed and said to Bonnie, "Sugar, he's right."

She agreed. "I know. And I'll bet I'm thinking the same thing you are."

He nodded. "Yeah. If they didn't do it, who the hell did?"

****

The next morning under a steel-grey sky Tako took Bonnie and William back to the cannery, handling the skiff casually, proudly, like a teenager driving his neighbors down the main street

277

of town in his parents' car. The water was choppy. They all hung on to keep from being thrown around and there wasn't any conversation. Tako managed to keep most of the water on the outside of the boat.

They'd had a light breakfast with the Hongs but the animation that warmed their supper the previous evening had slunk off during the night. There'd been a cheery stove that morning, a fine meal of clear-eyed Dolly Varden and fresh biscuits, and numerous requests for them to come back and visit again. If there was any stiffness that morning – and William felt there was – it could have been because Kai Win had told Lo An and Deng Wei the true reason for their visit.

After Tako put them on the cannery pier, holding the bow of the skiff against the rusted steel ladder with a softly putt-ing motor, he didn't turn toward home but continued on down the bay toward the duck flats. William didn't really think about that, lost in his own thoughts and not really interested enough to notice Tako hadn't brought a gun. He saw Ian Morgan on the bottom landing at the end of the cannery building, hiding from the weather, watching them walk up the boardwalk. He and Bonnie followed Ian up the stairs, talking, telling him about the hospitality they'd found.

Ian closed his office door behind them. While they were hanging up their dripping coats and hats he went over and closed the window that opened onto the cannery work floor. Then he sat down and rested his forearms on the clutter of his desk. An inventory form stuck to his arm and he brushed at it, then ignored it when it fluttered to the floor. Other papers threatened to leap off the desk after it but he ignored them also. "Well, what'd you find out?"

He hadn't spoken to them since the evening before they'd gone up onto the flume but he'd undoubtedly guessed the purpose of their visit to the saltery. He proved that by asking, "Do you think somebody over there's out to hurt us?"

278

William shook his head emphatically. "No, Ian, I don't. I can't come up with any other choices about who might have done it, but the answer stays the same, the Hongs didn't do it." Something about his conclusion nagged him, but William couldn't identify what it was.

Bonnie threw her hands up. "Yeah, I agree, but what does that leave us with?" Her comment made William realize what bothered him. In this case the obvious answer didn't seem to be the right one. Intellectually he knew the true answer was most often the obvious, uncomplicated one. But emotionally he couldn't connect the Chinese family at the saltery with the sabotage.

Ian answered Bonnie's question. "Well, I'll tell you what it leaves us with: one heck of a stinking mess and getting to the edge of ugly. That damned Tom Archer's stirring up trouble and I'll tell you, I've about had it with him. He just can't leave it alone. He's been after me twice already wanting me to get the state troopers in on it. Telling me about my responsibilities. Damn it, telling me!" His color was deepening as he spoke and William noticed it and wondered about the man's blood pressure. Ian hit the papers still lurking on his desk with his open hand, frightening small receipts into motion and driving Bonnie to comment. "Simmer down, Ian," she ordered, using her nurse's tone. "You'll bust a blood vessel." Then she asked, "So what's wrong with getting the state police involved? A lot of damage has been done, vandalism at least. Couldn't they investigate?"

Ian shrugged. "Investigate what? Sure, they could go up into the woods and look at the repaired damage, and William there," he waved his arm, "could show them the chop marks, or whatever other *evidence* we've got – some herring scales? – but then what? They going to get J. Edgar Hoover in here? No. But I'll tell you what they will do and damn it, I don't want it. They'll go over to that saltery and take names. *That's* what they'll do."

The image of government investigators arriving at the cove in a floatplane or in a chartered boat with their flat-topped hair and their flat eyes and their black notebooks shocked William. The specter was strong in the room and William could see Bonnie was affected also. Ian voiced the issue. "How many problems, just with immigration, do suppose that'll cause those apparently innocent people over there?"

Bonnie snapped her fingers. *"Exactly!* That's it. That's what Tom Archer *wants!* That's why he's pushing for the police... Oh..."

"OK," said Ian, agreeing to the obvious, "there you go. It's clear Tom Archer may have set this whole thing up himself."

"But why?" Bonnie asked. She hadn't followed her own revelation through to its end.

Ian was exasperated by the whole thing, and it showed. He shook his head. "Bonnie, I don't know. This is the first time I ever worked with Tom Archer and I don't know what motivates the man." He sighed heavily, settled back, having to deal with this thing, having to talk it out, needing to settle something. "He was transferred up here from the Whittaker factory in Monterey. I guess he worked there a couple of years and, hell, I don't know why they blessed us with him, but they did. Frankly, I think the man's a little demented..."

"A little?" Bonnie questioned.

"OK, maybe a lot. I think he's been victimized... the way he acts... the way he looks. I know he had a hard time during the war..."

"Yeah, you're right about that," William interjected. "I saw him in the shower. The man's covered with scars. Said he was in Changi..."

"What's Changi?" Bonnie asked.

"Changi was a Japanese prison camp in Singapore. Not a nice place, apparently."

"So you think he's got this thing now for Orientals? Because of the war?" She was looking at William but Ian answered. "I think that's part of it. I think they hurt him, and more than just his physical being. Hell, an experience like that…"

"So OK," Bonnie interrupted, "so he had a bad time and got victimized during the war. Lots of people did. Millions. That's still no excuse."

William said, "We're not trying to excuse him, Bonnie, we're trying to figure out why he's doing this, how to handle it."

"Why not just fire him? Get rid of him."

"Oh sure," William came back at her, "and within two days he'll be back out here with the state troopers to clear his good name and point out the guilty parties."

"Who'd be Chinese, naturally. And we have no idea what evidence he might have planted around, maybe even over there."

All three of them sat back in their chairs, thinking. The hum of compressors, generators and canning machinery joined the drum of rain on the roof in a peaceful background, like the wash of a watercolor. Voices seeped through the walls from throughout the cannery. A wet bald eagle out over the bay screeched, angry because a pair of gulls had ganged up on it to steal a fish. The clothes tree with the dripping slickers stood in the corner of Ian's office like a wounded spy in a spreading pool.

Finally Ian leaned forward again and said, "Well, I've got to do something. Archer won't let it set." He didn't come right out and ask for ideas but he obviously wanted them.

"Can we confront him?" Bonnie asked.

William shook his head. "With what? No, I think Ian's right. We want to avoid making this into the big deal that Tom wants. I think you should just keep putting him off, Ian. You can do that. Just tell him to shut up about it and tend to his work. Can't you?" William was started, went on. "Hell, Ian, in just a little while we're done and gone from here anyway. Can't you hold him off until he realizes it isn't going to work? He'll quit it then."

Ian gave a great sigh and William saw how really tired the man was. The old guy should retire, he thought. Ian swiveled his chair around, saw the paper on the floor and picked it up, flipped it onto the mess of his desk. "Yeah, I suppose I can do that. But I'll tell you, I just might blow off instead. Christ… Maybe he'll get tired of it."

William encouraged him. "Yeah, I think he will. Maybe you can keep him busy on other things, too. What's the boat schedule look like…"

Together they sat for another thirty minutes discussing their strategy. Before they were finished they recognized there were sides: them against Tom Archer, Jim Bell, Johnson, maybe a couple others as well.

"But I warn both of you," Ian said. "If this gets in the way of canning fish, if I can't get the job done because of this stupid thing, then I'm going to do whatever's necessary no matter how many innocent Chinese get their papers scrutinized. Clear?"

William answered. "Ian, I don't think it'll come to that."

"I hope not. Now you two get to work and leave me to fight this paper. I think it's winning." He stirred the white mess on his desk as they left.

****

Ian's heart wasn't in his work and after William and Bonnie left he quit pretending to work on the papers and sat quietly, rubbing his temples with both hands. He was tired, felt he'd worked a full day even though it was only mid-morning. More than tired, Ian knew he was weary. It was time for him to quit this business, take his retirement money and reduce the load on his head, which was attached directly to his heart. The doctor had told him during his annual checkup in the spring, "Ian, you're in good shape for a man your age, considering the shape you're in, which is only fair. Cut down on your workload..." and he'd continued with the usual stuff. But he was right and Ian knew it. It was time to devote himself to other things, like the magnificent flies he tied for his fishing friends.

This damn business with Tom Archer... There was a knock on his door. "Come," he said. The door opened to admit a worried Manuel Menendez. He walked in and stopped against the front of Ian's desk. His fingers touched the papers, began poking them, nervous, distracted. "Ian," he said, "I'm worried about Tina, and so is Nora. She went out early this morning and we haven't seen her since. Nora says she's looked everywhere. I've been working on getting that south drain unclogged. Is it OK if I take off long enough to look around the place? Nora's really worried, si?"

Ian stood immediately and came around from behind his desk. He took Manuel's arm and led him back toward the door, saying, "Manuel, if you're worried, I'm worried. You bet. Get someone else to look at that drain. Better yet, forget the drain, it can wait. You go with Nora and look around again. Tina's got to be here someplace. Take whatever time you need. And if you don't find her let me know right away. I'll be here."

Manuel went out and Ian went back to his desk and sat down but he was too restless to work. After fidgeting a few minutes he got up and went down to the main floor where he could move around, pretending to inspect the equipment. The people on the floor, in long shiny aprons and yellow, elbow-length rubber gloves, were cleaning up from working a boat that had come in early that morning. Ian walked around talking to people and the activity felt good, helped him get Tom Archer off his mind.

As he was finishing his lunch in the mess hall, a canned ham sandwich with thin-sliced canned pineapple in place of lettuce, Manuel Menendez came back to him. He had Nora with him and they were both plainly worried. "Mr. Morgan," Manuel said, "we've looked everywhere…"

Nora said, "She's nowhere here, Ian, nobody's seen her. I'm worried sick. What if…"

"Wait a minute, Nora, Manuel. Here, come here, sit down."

He patted chairs next to him. They sat down, concern pinching their faces, making their hands wring and their voices tight. Ian mentioned all the places they should have checked and they nodded or shook their heads at each one, confirmed having looked there. "OK, then it's clear she's taken a walk, because she's not on the cannery grounds, right?" He stopped one of the workers passing by his table and asked him if he'd go to the dispensary and ask Bonnie to come to the mess hall. He kept his voice light, his tone confident. He would not yet consider the cold waters beneath the pier or the dark, dripping forest.

While they waited for Bonnie Ian pressed Manuel and Nora, calmly, to think about what Tina was wearing. Did she look dressed for a walk along the coast? Did she have her raincoat? The screen door slammed shut behind Bonnie, who hurried over to their table. "Hi, Nora, Manuel. Ian?"

"Bonnie, Manuel and Nora have been looking around for Tina, but she's apparently gone off by herself without saying where, and they're starting to worry. She's not on the cannery grounds. She didn't mention anything to you, did she?"

"No, she didn't say anything to me. In fact I haven't seen her at all this morning since we've been back from the saltery…" Her mind flashed pictures of their skiff ride that morning, the drizzle against her face, the sound of the outboard motor as Tako steered through the chop… Tako! Was it possible? She put her hand on Nora's shoulder, asked, "Did Tina mention anything to you about meeting Tako this morning?" She looked at Ian and explained, "I just remembered about the boy bringing us over in the skiff this morning and…"

284

Manuel broke in. "Oh, carumba!" He pounded once with his fist against his forehead. "Tom Archer brings over a note last night for Tina, said the saltery kid he's give it to Jimbelly for her. Maybe these two kids figured out how to get together this morning, and she didn't tell us." He balled his fist. "I'll…"

"You won't either, Manuel Menendez," Nora told him with Teutonic force. Then she relented. "I'll just be so glad to see her safe and sound… But where could they be?"

Ian asked, "Bonnie, which way did Tako go after he dropped you off?"

"Toward the duck flats, I think… let me think… yes, he did. I can remember seeing him hit the rougher water just out a bit from the point, going up toward the head of the bay."

"OK, that's our best guess, then. Manuel, why don't you just get one of the guys to go along with you…"

Nora butted in, "I'm going."

Ian tried again, "OK, Manuel, why don't you and Nora…"

Bonnie interrupted. "Can I go too, Nora?"

"Jesus Christ. If I can finish…" Ian complained, "Manuel, you and everybody…" he rolled his eyes around the mess hall to encompass the rest of the world, making the situation lighter with the gesture, as if the girl were already found, "…jump in the skiff with the Evinrude – I think it's in the best shape – and cruise on down toward the flats. You'll probably see the kid's boat on the beach. Let me know when you get back. And don't forget your life preservers and a gun. Company policy."

22

Manuel had pictured it right. Tako's note hadn't said anything about concealing the meeting from her parents; Tina had decided that on her own, undoubtedly thinking she wouldn't be gone long enough to be missed, if she thought about it at all. She was generally a thinking person but she was a teenager and there were times when it seemed her head was hollow and all her thoughts were secreted from glands. She and Tako were alone on the planet and when they heard the motorboat come around the bend that sick feeling of trouble washed over them and fouled the sweetness of their day.

Their meeting had been innocent and lovely. They'd kissed, twice, after Tako was out of the boat and Tina had helped pull the bow up onto the pebbly little beach, dancing to keep their feet dry, light, happy, forgetful. They were just around the curve of trees from the cannery and had found a dry spot under a heavily branched tree where they'd forgotten time, talking, spooning.

Tina's parents were both silent, watching the horizons and the dark water until they got her home and inside, where Nora finally broke into hand-covered tears and Manuel took the muzzle off his anger. A small buzzing, Tako's motor, slunk around the point, was suddenly gone, erased.

"We didn't do anything, Poppa," Tina wailed.

"Si, you didn't! Your madre and I are worried sick because you didn't let us know where you was. Don't you think we got some worried? Huh? You think maybe that's Long Beach out there? Huh? Chica? You think we just let the lifeguard worry about you, no?"

The result was prison for a week, Tina forbidden to set foot beyond the boardwalks running throughout the cannery complex. In effect it was house arrest.

****

On the far side of the point in Chinaman's Cove the gavel wouldn't fall so cleanly. Tako had ignored the restrictions inherent in his orders and had seriously misjudged the attention he was lately drawing. When he arrived back at the cove, righteous, the sides of his pride and the tops of his ears still burning from his run-in with Tina's parents, he faced an angry Kai Win on the beach.

When the skiff had been tied and they were topping off the gas tank Kai Win said, "Tako, I'm not mad because you snuck in a visit with that girl. I'm upset because you were supposed to come right back here and you didn't. It might seem like the whole world's conspiring to keep you from enjoying your life and maybe they are, I don't know, but from now on you're on notice, got it? You take one of those skiffs out, you better damn well have my permission. You got that?"

"Yes, I got it." Tako snarled, surly. Then he whined. "There's no good reason I can't date Tina. It's just because she's not Chinese." He looked at his father, suddenly defiant again. "Well, that's true, ain't it?"

"*Isn't* it, Tako, *isn't* it. Yeah, probably. But you understand we're talking about two different things, right? I mean, I personally don't care if you date young grizzly sows but I do care about where people are around here…"

"I know, I shouldn't have taken so long. But it's true, isn't it? That's the only reason Grandfather won't let me go over there and it ain't... it *isn't* fair." He pouted, kicked at the drum of gas in its angle-iron cradle. The sun had finally busted through the clouds and the bay was sparkling, choppy, topped with caps bleached white in the sunlight.

"Well, what I think," Kai Win told him, "doesn't matter too much. Your grandfather says he doesn't want us over there at that cannery, so that includes you."

"But that's dumb. Just because..."

"Careful, Tai Co." He used the Chinese pronunciation of the boy's name. "Maybe it's not fair, but that's the way it is. And aside from that, you don't know everything that's going on..."

Tako was a strong puppy, pulling, twisting, fighting a tight collar and a short leash. "Well it's not right. Can't you talk to him? He'll *listen* to you. *Nobody* listens to anything *I* say around here."

Kai Win sided with Tako. At the beginning of the season when Deng Wei said he didn't want anybody spending time at the cannery it had been a casual statement recognizing that nobody had reason to go there. It hadn't caused any stir then. But that was before Tako had first seen the blonde girl and before he'd first manipulated a visit so he could meet her. When Deng Wei had become aware, finally, that Tako was spending an inordinate amount of time there, he had clamped down, restated his injunction and charged Kai Win to enforce it. Kai Win was caught in the claw between the old man's conservative rule and the boy's natural, innocent need for social experience with a girl his own age. "I'll tell you what, Tako." The boy cocked his head over, face still grouched, but an eye showing suspicious hope. "I'll talk to your grandfather. I don't promise anything, but I'll try."

And he had, but his father wouldn't budge, setting his lips and delivering a history lesson to Kai Win. Kai Win was able to avoid catching the old coolie's bitterness, but still he had to tell

Tako, after the boy had hounded him hourly for a report, "Tako, your grandfather says those people are going to be gone from here in a short while…"

"Awww…" Tako said, already hearing the answer.

"…And he says he doesn't want you over there hanging around. He says they've got work they're trying to do over there…"

"Well, I could help, you know. I could apply for a job over there. I'm old enough to work in a cannery."

"And you've got work to do over here. We've got firewood to get in."

"Ah… Father, you know that's just so much dog shit. That old man's just prejudiced. I hate him. Damn old coolie anyway."

Kai Win couldn't get out of the middle. It was a tough one and he realized there wasn't any simple answer. Searching for honesty at this moment, he knew there was no answer at all. He wanted to lash out at the boy for his remark but he held himself back. He put an arm around his son's shoulders and said, "Just be patient, Tako. Maybe in a while…"

Tako shrugged from under his father's arm, drew away defiantly. "I haven't *got* a while! She's going to leave and I'll never get to see her again, so don't tell me…" Suddenly the tears flooded and Tako turned and ran, pushing himself around the corner of the building.

Kai Win didn't follow. He didn't know what he could say to his son. Worse, he knew there was nothing that *could* be said. Everything would have to take its own course.

******

Across the bay, near the meadowy crest of a ridge, a four-point blacktailed buck stood at the edge of the tree line vigorously swiping its antlers against the branches of a stout bush, making loud clacking noises, trying to rid itself of the last shreds of velvet

289

still clinging in tatters, and strengthening its neck muscles for the occasional combat to be faced when the rut started. The deer was concentrating on one flapping pennant of velvet hanging off a sharp forward tine… a brown blur of motion flashed and the buck turned to meet it, bunched muscles already tensing to leap away, bounding to safety…

The bear was too close, had come up quietly, hidden behind the deer's concentration and the noise of the antlers against the bush. As the bear made its killing rush, raising a paw to swipe down its prey, the deer whirled and as the great paw came slashing down with its raking four-inch claws and terrible power the deer presented its antlers. The bear's rush was too momentous to alter, the swing of the paw too furious to stop, and as the bear clubbed through with its killing slam one sharp spine of the deer's rack was driven up between the toe pads of the bear's paw, right up through the palm just in front of the heel pad, tearing through the soft, furry skin fold, jamming its way up between the bones, puncturing its way through the flesh and skin on top of the paw.

The bear screamed and jerked back even as the shock of its blow snapped the deer's neck. The buck dropped, already dead, and as the bear pulled back, the antler snapped just above its fork, leaving a six-inch studded spike protruding on both sides of the paw. The bear was wild with pain and rage and swiped with its other paw at the deer, slashing great bloody gashes down the flank of the dead animal, disemboweling it, spilling its steaming entrails into the grass. The smell of the deer's viscera infuriated the bear and it began to bound in circles, trampling the grasses and bushes, screaming and roaring, sending other deer scurrying for a radius of a mile and scaring flocks of ptarmigan into the air with panicky whooshes of wing. And every time the terrible impaling spike touched the ground great red spasms of pain flashed up the bear's arm into its shoulder, through its brain.

290

The bear kept up its ranting, the dead deer forgotten and lost in the distance, until it found itself rolling on a patch of wet snow in a shallow gully, which seemed to soothe the paw. The bear calmed, lying on its belly, back legs stretched out behind, the injury cradled in the snow under the animal's jaw. It licked the wound, worried the spike with its rough tongue, even took it once in the side of its mouth and chewed at it, not with the sense to pull it out but to disintegrate it. The chewing renewed the pain though, so the bear contented itself with licking.

Finally, well into the night, the bear's belly rumbled so it moved off, looking for something to eat. Limping on three legs made the wounded arm throb but the creature had to answer hunger. Eventually it found a rotten log and managed to roll it out of place and smash it into pieces with its one good paw and its strong muzzle but the reward was small, a few white grubs. They made no impression on the beast's hunger. The bear worked its way painfully back to where the deer had died but the carcass had been carried off, nothing left for the bear but a spiral of drying entrails and the smell of blood. The injured animal ate the cold guts and licked the blood off the grass. Every few minutes it raised its face and howled, a bewildered sound in the quiet night.

Over the following days the bear grew progressively weaker, starving to death as deer and marmots easily eluded it and its body used the fat stored for winter. The wound had become foul and infected around the spike and the pain had moved all the way up into the bear's shoulder and was starting to effect its back. Its movements weren't coordinated and its instincts were slowed. The bear found a few old berries but they couldn't make up for its losses. Then the smell of fish came up the slope and the animal began to work its way painfully down through the forest to where a few salmon were still running through the duck hunting channel, into the small lagoon.

****

In the cove at the saltery Tako struggled against his own wounds. Since the affair with Tina's folks he'd been a caged martin, pacing around the cove, doing his chores haphazardly, sitting for long hours chunking his sheath knife into a piece of firewood. His drives tortured him and his mind was no help. He imagined her touch on his cheek and was instantly erect. He masturbated twice, three times a day. He cried, he sulked. He badgered Kai Win to press the old man again but he was afraid to do that himself, and he couldn't talk to his mother, Gwen Do.

****

Tako's mother knew. She knew how her son was feeling, what he was going through. Her heart broke for him. She'd even argued with her father-in-law about letting the boy go over to see the girl but Deng Wei was adamant, and forbade it. Entreaties to Lo An, who could usually make the old man see the sense in something, were futile.

"Grandfather isn't right in this matter, Gwen Do," Lo An told her. "But he's still your father-in-law and my husband and we live in his house and his mind's made up. I can't change his mind and I won't permit disobedience to him. Be patient, Gwen Do," she counseled, putting her arms around her daughter-in-law and reaching up to stroke her hair. "They'll be gone soon and then at least the pain will diminish."

"Mama, it's time for Tai Co to go outside, you know. He's never going to be happy here. Especially not now. He can't accept this just because it's the Chinese way. You know that?"

"Yes, I know. And I knew it long before. When he came back from school I knew it had rooted in him, the restlessness. Woman-child, it's the legacy his grandfather has left him."

292

****

Tako made up his mind the morning after his aborted visit with Tina. His night had been torture, pictures racing by from one agony of imagination to another, his body wracked with the tossings of his teenaged desires. He was going to have her. She was his woman. The obstacles looming between his sweated bed and a vague future of blessed togetherness faded into insignificance. He couldn't plan more than one or two steps ahead, confronting then the dark chasms of the unknown, but planning even one motion was enough to invigorate him. He'd just go, and everything would fall into place.

His first steps in the days following his decision involved the making of a plan and the gathering of his resolve. It wasn't easy, but one by one the obstacles to his intentions confronted his enthusiasm and were put aside. By the end of that week he was ready to make his move and though he knew what that move should be – communicating with Tina – he wasn't sure how he was going to do it without his parents knowing.

The answer chugged into the cove on a flat-sky morning when the tops of the mountains across the water were just visible under the clouds, like pointed knees beneath a table. During the night it had snowed up there, the sign people in the North watched for as summer waned, the terminal dust that ended all seasonal activities and sent frail scurriers south. Of course the Hongs never left the bay during the winter. They were used to the seasons, all of them. To Tako, however, it was irrefutable confirmation that his plan had to proceed rapidly.

He went quickly out to the end of the mud flat walkway as the fishing boat tied up. The skipper was a red-bearded acquaintance who stopped at the saltery several times each summer. He had established trade relations with the Hongs, bringing them supplies they ordered from town, occasionally buying some of their home-made smoked salmon. This dull grey day he greeted Tako. "Hello, my man. Looks like summer's over." He turned to thrust the ends of his jaw-hair at the small crack between the clouds and the snowy mountain tops. "You ready for another winter, or are you going outside this one?"

Tako said, "Hi, Mr. Tally. Yeah, I *wish.*" They both laughed, partners in the knowledge that Tako would rather live someplace else.

Ignorant providence smiled on Tako then. The boatman said, "Tell you what. I've got some stuff for you folks but it's on the bottom. I've got to take some groceries over to the cannery. How about you ride over there with me and help unload, then we'll come back here and unload your stuff. It'll be a bunch easier to get at..."

Tako could barely believe his ears and turned to look over his shoulder at the saltery, wondering if he just dare get aboard without saying anything. They'd probably only be gone a couple of hours... But then he remembered his last run-in with his father and better judgment won out. At that moment he saw his mother start out toward the boat along the walkway, pushing one of their big two-wheeled carts. He quickly told the boatman, "Great idea, Mr. Tally. You hold on. I'll just run and tell my mother I'm going." It was the perfect setup. He'd been requested to go. He hadn't even come up with the idea in the first place, so it wouldn't look like he'd planned it. And his mother was easy, she'd let him do it, especially since they were just going over and coming right back. Probably she wouldn't even tell the old man...

Tako bounded down the boards and met his mother, took the cart from her, almost knocked her off the walkway in his enthusiasm. "Mom, Mr. Tally says he needs me real bad to help unload some stuff at the cannery and then we'll be right back to unload our stuff. That's OK, isn't it? It'll just be a quick trip. We'll be back in no time..." He pecked her quickly on the cheek and started off with the cart, just gaining speed when her voice halted him.

"Tai Co!"

He stopped, stood still a moment, straightened his back, still faced out toward the boat, collected himself for the disappointment. Slowly he turned back to face her.

She said, "Tako, you be careful. Don't get yourself into any trouble. I'll tell anybody who asks that you're not even going ashore, just helping Mr. Tally move some supplies. OK?" Her eyes said she hoped it would all work out.

He wanted to run back to her, to hug her and thank her, but he was afraid she'd change her mind or somebody else from the saltery would come out and his chance would vanish. "Thanks, Mom," was all he was able to say, then he turned and ran back to the boat. In a minute they were chugging out of the cove.

When they rounded the point and had gone along the coast to where they could look into that part of the bay where the cannery stood they could see more than the usual amount of activity there. Several big fishing boats were in, one of them tied alongside the pier, two others hanging off the big Norwegian buoy in front of the cannery. Milton Trent's boat was tied up behind the fishing boat at the pier and there were several people standing there, talking to Milt. Tako used Mr. Tally's binoculars to scan the pier. She was there.

They tied up just in front of Milt's boat as the other vessel vacated the spot. The tide was high and as Tako stood on the bow rail his face was almost level with Tina's as she sat on the edge of the pier, her blue-jeaned legs dangling. Tako wanted to go ashore, to take her behind one of the buildings and feel her body and her lips against him but knew he didn't have time. If they were going to make plans it'd have to be now, here. But it was just right. They were under observation by anyone who wanted to see so nobody would suspect anything. They could talk while Mr. Tally was over gabbing with the others on the pier.

She told him Milt was planning to come back to take out the cannery workers in less than two weeks.

The plan they made was simple and Tina seemed to go along, not disagreeing with Tako's dream or Tako's plan. He'd leave the saltery early on the morning Milton was due to take the work crews back to Juneau, or maybe the night before, and he'd hide around the cannery someplace. Then in the general melee and hauling of baggage as everybody loaded aboard Milton's boat, he'd slip aboard and stow away...

It was a good plan, Tako thought, and he was committed to it with every clamoring cell. He didn't have the perception to see how far Tina was willing to go along. It didn't occur to him that her romantic response to his visions might stop short of actual participation. When it appeared nobody was watching Tina leaned over and they sealed it with a quick kiss.

Tako and Tally unloaded the supplies for the cannery, then untied and set out for the saltery again. Tina waved from the pier, Tako watching the curves of her through the binoculars until she was out of sight. Back at the saltery Kai Win met them at the end of their walkway. He looked directly at Tako, who whined, "I didn't even go ashore so don't get on me. All I did was help unload the stuff."

Kai Win looked to Tally, who knew nothing about the restrictions on Tako. Finding no broken rules aboard, Kai Win said, "OK. Let's get our stuff ashore. How are you, Mr. Tally..."

****

Ian Morgan was one of those visiting on the pier with Milton Trent. He'd walked out of his office and down the stairs on the end of the building when he saw Milt's boat pulling in. They talked briefly about Milt's trip out from town, standing there on the pier, then they moved to the mess hall where they sat holding coffee mugs and eating Jimbelly's cinnamon rolls, talking about the season and the logistics of backhauling the cannery workers at season's end. "You can take everybody but the closing-up crew to town, then come back for us. Did you see that terminal dust on the mountains?"

"See it? By damn I felt it. We anchored up last night at the top of the island and before it got dark I could see the mountains over around Sitka taking a full load. We may have an early winter this year." They finished making their plans and Milton said, "I'd better get back, Ian. Those boys will have unloaded and I want to catch the tide running out. I see Tally's brought you some stuff too…" The two men said goodbye and Milt went out, catching the screen door with his heel to prevent it slamming. Ian rinsed out their cups, poked his nose into the oven to see what was for supper, then went outside and started up the stairs to his office.

He got about halfway to the first landing when he felt his breath go, his energy quit. He was holding onto the rail with his left hand. When the pain shattered his arm and raced to his wrist he tried to move his hand from the rail to cradle it against his chest, but his grip was locked. Sweat chilled his forehead and the small of his back, fear made his legs shake. He tried to catch his breath, couldn't. He went down on one knee on the stairs, still holding the banister. In a moment the pain eased and he was able to move. He turned around, sat on one of the stairs, held one of the rail supports.

"So this is how it starts,' he said to himself. He hoped no one would see him. He made up a story if they did. "…Just sitting here in the sunshine thinking about the season." Never mind that it was cloudy and turning cold now, a strange time to be sitting on the stairs, a strange place to be sitting now. "God, just let me finish this and get home again…"

******

At the head of the bay dark clouds of holiday-bound geese and ducks flocked, crowding each other from the tidal ponds, exchanging stories, honking hurry-ups and goodbyes. Snow quilted the great alpine meadows above the tree line, driving fat nervous deer into the trees.

Across from the cannery the bear limped along the shoreline, picking its way toward the mud flats at the head of the bay. The wound was horrible. The paw was swollen now to almost twice its normal size and it was hot and tight with infection. Fever reddened the bear's world and stole its balance, made the big animal swoon, swaying back and forth, three legs splayed among the sharp rocks of the coast, one burning spiked paw held where nothing would touch it. When the beast stumbled it howled agonies, a sick, drooling monster living on grubs and old grass and offal on the beach. The bear hugged the tide-lines, cooling the fire in the cold water, finding mussels and pieces of rotten fish and other inadequate sustenance.

******

Tako was in the forest just inside the tree line about a hundred yards down the beach from the saltery. There was a leaning tree there caught between two others, a tangle of branches making a perfect place about eight feet above the ground where he was caching little sacks of supplies and belongings. He'd been through his meager wardrobe, selected his finer clothes, wrapped a bundle of them in a piece of canvas, now stashed them among the branches. He had food there too, a few canned goods, smoked meat, some cool-smoked salmon wrapped in wax paper and bound into a package.

298

23

At the cannery Ian Morgan tried to take it easy. He did more of his work in the front room of the bungalow he shared with William, dreading the climb to his second story office. Once when a small flash of pain passed his face, Bonnie asked him if he was feeling all right. He considered telling her about the attack he'd had and asking for some medicine to make the now constant, dull, discomforting pressure go away, but then he didn't, knowing he could tough it out until he got to Seattle. It was only a few days away now.

Indian summer blessed the bay. Racy high clouds zoomed across the green-framed window of sky above the water. But the nights were cold and the breeze carried the scent of snow. A few more boats chugged around the point but when they'd unloaded paltry catches their skippers said goodbye. "…Our last trip in and we're headed south." Then there was only tomorrow, and the season was over. Tako's mother hugged Kai Win as if she'd never see him again, and left the saltery on Mr. Tally's boat for Juneau to buy winter supplies.

****

Throughout the forest stood dead trees which provided the saltery's winter firewood. Each time Kai Win cut down a dead tree he selected a living replacement somewhere near the tide-line and banded it with his ax, cutting through the cambium and dooming it. In several years the tree would be dry, ready to be cut and split, full of crackles and heat. Though most of their heating was now done by oil brought from town in fifty-five gallon drums on the deck of Tally's boat, the wood stoves were still used and each winter the saltery devoured about fifteen cords of wood. Tako and Kai Win were the woodcutters.

****

At the tidal flats the dying bear found the stinking carcass of a dolphin rolling in the mud as the tide receded. Gulls and sea lice and other pickers had eaten most of it but there were bones with putrid flesh between them and it was almost a meal to the bear, giving him some small strength. The animal was weaker every day, unable to sleep but sometimes falling unconscious. In its fevered stumble along the water's edge it often stopped, turning in a confused, spinning daze on three legs, tripping and falling, snapping with foamed jaws at the pain. Everything was blurry and hazed red, the hunger just one more burning pain. The bear finished eating the rotten bones of the dolphin, licked the last black stain from the mud and hobbled on around the head of the bay, toward the cannery.

****

Kai Win wanted to make a late-afternoon run down the coast to a tree he and Tako had felled the day before and bring back a skiff-load of wood before dark, but he couldn't find the boy. He was just getting mad and ready to start hunting for him in earnest... *"Kai Win!"* There was fright and desperation in his mother's voice and he put the Swedish saw he was carrying into the skiff and quickly went to where she stood on the front porch of the house. She was wringing her hands, shaking her head, disheveled, distracted.

"What's wrong, Mother?"

She wailed, her normally strong voice broken and old, "It's your father, and I think he… Oh, Deng Wei…" She covered her face with her hands and began to sob.

Kai Win moved up the stairs onto the porch beside her, patted her shoulder as he edged by, looking past her, peering into the relative darkness of their house. "Where is he, Mother?" He leaned into the house with his head and shoulders but his feet stayed outside as if they didn't want to step on the floor. Deng Wei, his father, might be lying on that floor. His mother couldn't stop sobbing into her hands. Her shoulders shook and he didn't know whether to stay with her or go inside. Finally his need to know the facts moved him. He guided her to the chair on the porch where Deng Wei used to sit and pushed her gently into it, consoling her with small useless words. Then he went inside.

The old man of the venerable, honorable, pig-eating Hong family was sitting slumped in an upholstered chair in the living room. His head was forward on his chest. His position was relaxed, like an old man sleeping in the sun on a warm summer afternoon. He'd followed the rivers of a continent to the sea and the sea had brought him to his fortune, and his fortune wasn't much but it was his, and it was rooted in the land, and the land was his. He hadn't found the gold, but only because he'd never bothered to look. The land had been enough.

Kai Win stopped when he saw him, held his hands clasped, said gently, "Hong Deng Wei, my father."

There was no response. Kai Win did not expect one. He went to Deng Wei and touched his hair, a mother's touch, felt the slack in the old man's neck. He went down on his knees before the chair, turning his head so he could look up into his father's face. Deng Wei's eyes were closed.

Again Kai Win reached up and touched him, on the cheek this time, putting the palm of his hand against Deng Wei's face as a lover touches his beloved. Deng Wei was warm against his palm and it was hard for Kai Win to believe him dead. He heard a noise behind him and turned, pulling his hand away, rising to his feet. When he did, Deng Wei started to fall forward slowly in the chair but Kai Win didn't see him because he was turning to Lo An. She gasped and pointed at Deng Wei and Kai Win turned back just in time to catch him before he fell out of the chair. He positioned the body back in the chair but Deng Wei's head lolled back and the sight of his face made Lo An break into tears again.

In the late afternoon air above, a vee of geese talked about the mud flats at the head of the bay and about the Willamette Valley grain fields waiting at the end of their long journey. Elsewhere a river swirled where it met another in an eddy, then moved on.

Kai Win couldn't bear seeing his dignified father with his head thrown back and his mouth open. He put one arm under Deng Wei's knees and worked the other behind his back and lifted him from the chair, stumbling a little as he straightened and took the old man's weight, but recovering, turning. Lo An was sobbing, her face down, covered with her hands. She was standing between him, with his awesome burden, and the bedroom.

Kai Win had to speak. It was hard for him. All the sounds of his being were in his throat. But he had to speak now, not think. "Mother, let me take him into the bedroom."

Still Lo An stood there, smaller now that Deng Wei was gone. Her back had always been straight and firm. Now it was bent. She trembled as she sobbed. She kept her face covered as if not seeing would hide her from the loneliness, from missing her beloved old companion. Oh, the bitter days of the mines, the stumbling through the snow, the Indian camp days and the long, laughing years of building… Kai Win had to speak again, "Mother…" and touched her on the elbow with Deng Wei's knee.

The touch reached her, as if Deng Wei himself had touched her, and she pulled her hands down from her face, wiped the full stream of tears from her eyes with the backs of both hands, reached with one hand to touch Kai Win and said, 'Yes, in the bedroom. Thank you, our son." She stood aside so he could take the body of her husband into their bedroom.

He laid the old man's body on the bed, straightened him. He arranged his hands across his chest, folded, but they wouldn't stay there, kept flopping down, so he placed them gently alongside his waist, straight down, as if that's the way Deng Wei wanted it.

Lo An stood beside him, watching. "So many years, so fast…" she said. "He was such a fine coolie…"

Kai Win backed away, leaving her alone in the room with Deng Wei. He also wanted to stay by Deng Wei's side, to remember the times, one after another, but Deng Wei was dead and there were things… First he had to find Tako. Time and thought seemed compressed. His temples throbbed. Frustration clouded into his mind as he wandered from house to house and back again, aimless, tears welling in his eyes, overflowing when he thought about the loneliness of Lo An…

He looked back into the room at his beautiful mother and the body of his father. Lo An was sobbing quietly now, her old hand resting, still, against her husband's cheek. "Mother," he said, quietly, then louder. He had to make her understand he was leaving her alone. There was nobody else at the saltery. "Mother, I am going to look for Tako. Stay here, Mother. I'll be back soon. Stay here with Father."

She looked up at him and he thought she understood. He gave her one last glance. Then he left the house. The sun was gone beyond the mountains on the other side of the water and a little thin film of clouds had gathered, purple sheets wrinkled by the setting rays. The bay was absolutely calm, licking at the stones of the beach with the gentle slack of tide.

Kai Win turned quickly in all directions as soon as he was out of the house, saw nobody, saw nothing. He turned toward the path behind the house. Where else could Tako be?

He was so distracted he forgot to arm himself.

****

In the forested gloom Kai Win ran for a quarter of a mile along the path before he found Tako's tracks. He stopped briefly, examined them, then started again, still running, following. Soon the path was climbing the face of the mountain alongside the water pipe and he was breathing hard. He had to slow to a walk, pushing his knees with his hands as he strained to make as much speed as he could. Sweat beaded on his forehead and he wiped it, swiped the wet edge of his hand against his pants. He expected to see Tako coming back down the trail toward him at any moment. There was no sound in the forest except his own.

He got to the top of the path, saw the water gushing into the box at the lip of the pipe and peered into the shadowed darkness among the trees for a glimpse of Tako. He saw nothing but the dark pillars and black holes of the forest and continued on, across the ravine, onto the top of the flume. There he saw some sign: Tako's boot had picked up mud in the ravine and had left light smears on the side of the flume as he'd climbed up. Kai Win touched it. Yes, it was fresh. Tako had come this way.

What was the boy doing? Why was he headed toward the cannery? And with night coming on… Kai Win paused, looking back the way he'd come, running his hand across the top of his head, turning toward the cannery, listening, visualizing his mother alone with Deng Wei. Where lay his duty? Should he run back to be with her, wait for Tako to return on his own accord? Or find him?

He'd come this far... he should find the boy. He took two deep breaths and began walking down the flume, his heart pounding, his head racing ahead, his feet picking up the spacing between the wooden braces. He wanted to think about his father lying on the bed at home, and about his mother, but in the settling dark he had to think about his footing on top of the flume. He walked quickly, head down, concentrating. To slip and fall off could be fatal in several ways, in several unthinkable ways.

****

Milton Trent was making a wide swing through the bay on his approach to the cannery when he saw the bear on the shoreline. It was about half a mile north of the cannery and he could see it was moving unnaturally even before he put the glasses on it. He throttled to idle, put the boat into neutral and raised his field glasses. As soon as he was focused he could see the bear was in serious trouble. The beast was thin and staggering, its head lolling, its balance gone. It looked as if it wouldn't last the night, much less be able to survive the coming winter, but it was still a formidable creature. Milton put the boat into forward gear and idled, gliding quietly closer until he was about a quarter of a mile away, then he slipped into neutral again and let her drift while he glassed the animal.

Although he couldn't tell what it was, he could see that something had injured the bear's paw or arm. A trap? A wound from some hunter? The beast was already nearly dead, struggling among the rocks on the beach, trying not to touch the swollen club of its paw to the ground, staggering, swaying.

Milton quickly made up his mind to shoot it and was reaching for his rifle when some slight sound of the boat reached the bear, striking though the red haze of its pain. The grizzly raised its head and looked toward the water. Squinting against the closing curtain of the day's light, it saw the intruder out on the calm water.

Before, it would have stood to face anything, might have strutted back and forth on the beach snuffing at the boat, rolling its back muscles until its shag danced, roaring its ownership of the world. But not now. Now it was hurt and distracted and had no mind for anything so it turned and before Milton could sight his Winchester it disappeared into the trees.

Milton thought briefly about going ashore to hunt the bear, except he was alone on the boat, and it was nearly dark, and the prospect was too terrible to consider seriously. In its agony and desperation this bear was a grotesque peril to all life in the bay but there wasn't anything Milt could do except tell them at the cannery about the bear, warn them of its approach, though most of the people there would be leaving with him tomorrow anyway. And he'd have someone go over to the saltery in one of the cannery skiffs to warn the Chinese and they could be on the lookout for it. Even though it looked very sick it was still powerful… ah, probably the saltery dogs would run it to ground and Kai Win would kill it.

Milton continued on to the cannery. The plan was for him to take most of the workers out the following morning to Wrengoon, where they'd catch the small bi-monthly ferry to Juneau that afternoon. He'd then come back and complete the lift, giving the shutdown crew a day to close things up for the winter.

He tied up the boat and was just climbing the ladder to the pier when he heard a woman scream. The quick, thoughtless sound, an unconscious vent of surprise suddenly chopped off by frantic concern, speared from the main building and Milton stopped, focused, then hurried. On the pier, slapping the rust of the ladder from his palms, he was just starting to follow the track of the scream when Bonnie Hood hurried around the far corner of the building, careful of her hasty footing on the boardwalk. She clutched a medical bag. "What's wrong?" she asked. "Who screamed?"

Milton was just about to respond when the upstairs door opened on the end of the factory building and one of the women workers rushed onto the landing, put both hands on the railing, saw them down on the pier and yelled, "Help! Come quick! Mr. Morgan's down!"

Bonnie and Milton cut the corner of the boardwalk and sprinted up the stairs onto the landing and through the door the woman held open.

Ian Morgan was crumpled on the floor next to his overturned swivel chair. His coffee mug leaked its dregs across the planks next to his feet. Bonnie and Milt both threw themselves to their knees and put their hands on him. His skin was clammy and sweat slicked his forehead. He clutched at his chest, held his shoulders shrugged forward to take the tension from the searing band across his lungs. "Hurts. One before…" he croaked, "didn't want to tell you. Should have. It's my heart." His eyelids squeezed shut and he struggled against the ripping in his chest.

Bonnie went right to work while Milton sent the other woman for blankets. She pulled her stethoscope from the bag and pried gently at Ian's hands so she could listen, but he didn't want it and she didn't want to force the stress. She was able to lay the stethoscope against the edge of his chest, enough to hear the irregularity, the sounds of fluid scraping. Rummaging quickly in her bag she brought out a small vial. Tiny white pills spilled into her palm.

"Ian, I'm going to give you a pill. Have you had these attacks before?" She leaned close to him and studied his face as he tried to answer. He moved his head in tiny abrupt nods, grimaced, said, "Last week, same thing, weaker, thought I'd make it."

"You'll make it. I'm going to put this pill under your tongue. It'll make the pain stop. Open." Louder, in his face. "Open your mouth, Ian." She pushed the pill under his tongue, held her palm gently under his jaw. She stroked his forehead and almost immediately she and Milton could see relief on his face. Two women arrived carrying blankets and a pillow and other people were stomping noisily up the stairs to the landing. In minutes people who liked him had made him comfortable, tucking the blankets around him to keep the gathering chill off and warming him with their concerned hands.

Bonnie and Milton were drawn aside, talking quietly about what to do when William arrived. Tom Archer was just behind him. Bonnie said, "We've got to get him out of here now, Milt. I know you were going to take us all out tomorrow but I can't do anything for him here. He needs to get to a hospital or we might lose him. Can we get a plane in here?"

"Maybe. I'll get on my radio and see what I can do." He went out and scurried down the stairs and over the side of the pier, down the ladder to his boat.

Upstairs they watched Ian and spoke in hushes. Ian was soon trying to un-tuck the blankets, pushing his elbows out and trying to sit up, but Bonnie and William restrained him with pressing hands and soothing talk, making him relax. In a few minutes Milton was back. "I talked to the Coast Guard dispatcher on the radio. They've got a rescue going outside Sitka and that's got the cutter tied up. I also talked to Sea-Air Flights but they say it's too close to dark for them to get in now. They said to get him to Wrengoon tonight and they'll have an ambulance plane on floats come in there first thing in the morning."

Bonnie spoke up. "Why can't they just come directly in here with that floatplane in the morning. It'd save Ian a boat ride."

"They're worried about the weather. They say it's usually easier to get through the pass over the island to Wrengoon but it might not be possible to get down the channel to the bay here, if the weather's closed in. Sometimes that cloud cover sits right down on the water for days. They're right, Bonnie."

William was the senior company man now and he took charge. "OK, then, that's what we've got to do. You might as well take everybody on this trip, Milton. No telling what's going to happen once you get Ian to the village. If the weather does get bad tonight and that plane can't even get off the water in the morning you may have to take him all the way into town yourself. Sound right?"

"Right."

William turned to Tom Archer, who'd been standing silently throughout by the door. "Tom, make the rounds. Tell everybody the boat's leaving right now. Have them stow all their stuff and get right aboard. Tell 'em not to fool around, that we want to pull out in about fifteen minutes, just as soon as we get Ian's stuff gathered up and he's aboard."

Milton piped up. "Tell them to leave my cabin free for Ian, Tom, but they can put their stuff anyplace else they can find room. On deck is fine. It'll be a bit crowded but with this calm water it'll be no problem as far as Wrengoon."

"Right, Mr. Trent. I'll get right on it." Tom looked at William. "You goin' out on this trip?"

William said, "Bonnie's going out with him." She nodded, most of her attention still on Ian. Her arms were crossed tightly across her chest in an unconscious statement of concern. William added, "I'll stay and make sure the place gets shut down."

Milton was sitting on Ian's desk. William said to him, "What time do you figure you'll be back here tomorrow if you get Ian off at first light in the plane?"

"It's about three hours with the water like this. If it stays calm I should be back about... say about eleven."

William nodded and turned again to Tom Archer. If he'd been talking to Manuel or one of the foremen on an engineering

309

crew it would have been a natural gesture for him to touch the man, put his hand on a shoulder or fix a grip on his arm to inspire his best, but Tom's fortress of dour never permitted such connection. William said curtly, "OK, Tom, that's it then. Take a quick trip up the flume and put the gate in after you've got everybody rousted onto the boat. We sure as hell aren't going to need more water than we've got in the tank tonight. You can help close the place up and go out tomorrow."

Tom nodded, agreeing, and left on his chores. Soon he'd made the rounds and people were streaming from their abandoned quarters down the boardwalks to the pier, lowering sacks and suitcases and bundles over the edge and onto the deck of Milton's boat. Sea gulls were streaming in from all distant directions, notified by excited pulses that there'd be scrounging opportunities in the wake of this annual vacating.

Within minutes the boat was loaded.

A few people were staying. Jimbelly and Tom Archer would go out on the next trip, as would Manuel and Nora, who were staying to do any last minute cleaning. Tina was going out with Milton and Bonnie and the rest and would meet her parents in Wrengoon. William would be responsible for the final locking of the facility.

Ian was brought down on a stretcher, well wrapped in blankets for the chilly voyage along the dark and rocky shores. Bonnie had supervised his transfer while William went through Ian's house stuffing his belongings into suitcases with the finesse of a second-story burglar hearing the front gate open. Shortly, men at the pier had handed the stretcher carefully over the edge onto the boat.

Bonnie reappeared on deck just as Milton was throwing the stern line off. William was standing on the pier. "You'll get all our stuff, won't you?" she said.

310

"Everything except that old green sweater of yours. I'm giving that to Tom Archer for a valve packing."

Milton was backing the boat, getting his stern out, yelling for a helper to let go the bow line.

"You better not, Engineer, that's my security sweater. I'll see you tomorrow." She tossed him a kiss but the boat was away and a swooping gull got it.

"I miss you already," he said, louder now over the engine noise. "I hope Ian's OK. Take good care of him, Sugar."

Almost yelling now. "Take care of yourself. See you tomorrow…"

The parting was too sudden, wholly unplanned, and neither of them wanted it or was ready, but it was done. William watched, squatting on the edge of the pier, playing idly with a splinter in a plank as the boat turned and chugged toward the point, its deck covered with people and their stuff, dots and dashes of diesel smoke at the top of her stack. He watched until she was around the point, then in the suddenly loud silence he went off to begin his last chore

24

Tom Archer put on a light jacket, grabbed his shotgun, checked its load and headed up the flume, his boots a fast cadence above the rush of the water. The double-barreled gun was chambered with two duck loads, not slugs, but he didn't take time to reload it. He'd need an hour and a half to the end of the flume where he'd put in the forbidding gate which would slap the ravine's stream back into its own steep, rocky bed until the next season. As he walked, the shotgun slung on his shoulder, he thought about where he was and what he was abut to do, shutting the flume, and he realized it was over, the season. He hadn't really thought about that fact before now. It had gone so quickly. The thumping of his boots on the boards and the rush of the water through the flume worked together to block out the rest of the world and he walked with his own melancholic thoughts now, lost in the deep forest of his thinking.

He'd felt tired when he'd left Monterey but this summer had been good for him. Others had complained about the isolation once in a while but he never had. He liked it, liked knowing they were all alone up here...

Except for the squints.

At once other images tried to crowd their way out of his mind but as he almost always did he pushed them back, drew a quick black curtain across the leering face of Anthony – *No!* – and across the dim memories of what they'd done. Other images flashed forward but he was able to block them also – stabbing, stabbing, slashing, *NO!* – until his eyes squeezed shut and he stumbled on a cross brace, almost fell but found his footing and now had the full, impersonal, Oriental face of all Chinese across the lens of his mind. It was his filter against the other things he wouldn't let himself think about and he gave himself to it completely, hating.

****

Half a mile in front of Tom Archer Tako felt the beat of someone coming up the flume and almost panicked. Or were they coming down? He stopped, started, stopped, started, looked both ways, a rabbit between holes. It could be somebody coming quickly behind him, hurrying to catch him and drag him back… No! When that boat left the cannery tomorrow with all those people aboard, he and Tina would be among them, snuggled safe in some warm hidden corner, on the way away from this place.

Quickly he went forward, keeping his tread light, taking his weight with his ankles and knees until he came to a place where he could get off the flume and onto the slope of the mountain. He tossed his bundle down, then jumped and landed on springy legs, hoping his own sounds were muffled by the dusk. Snatching his small burden, he shrugged into the bushes under the trestle.

His ears told him of a small rubbing noise, close. He turned his head to it, realized it was a branch jostled into sound by his own trembling. He put one hand on a trestle beam to give himself balance, waiting. His hand could feel the coming pulse.

In a short while the man thumped around the nearest bend, passed overhead and continued on up the flume, footsteps thudding nearer, then away. The whistle of his breathing silenced a tiny cricket. Tako peeked at his hunching, retreating back.

His father had told him, after the Hood's visit, "Tako, there are some low-life people in that cannery. One of them's a man named Tom Archer, and you stay away from him. He's not right in the head. Maybe he's even dangerous. He's kind of crippled up, walks..." Tako had thought his father was just giving him a boogyman story... It was him! He ducked back down.

When the pounding was gone he backed carefully from the bushes, his chest a resounding drum. He hoisted himself and his few possessions onto the flume. His bundle clunked quietly when it hit the boards – his grandfather's old revolver, stashed in the bottom of the sack – and he waited, listening to ensure only he had heard it, then he went on his toes toward the cannery.

****

Kai Win had walked about two miles along the flume when he felt the small vibrations disharmonic with his own that told of someone else on the flume with him. He stopped and could feel the rhythm and was fair in presuming it announced the approach of Tako. A small breeze moved past him as the cold air from the snowfields moved down to the low ground for the night, and the thick-needled branches of the trees clinging to the slope of the mountain on his left sighed. He needed to rest while he waited for Tako. He picked a place, sat on the side of the flume, his legs dangling. He looked around, pensive, thankful to have these few quiet moments alone with the memories of his father. He could feel the vibrations of approaching feet.

Within a few moments a figure came around the curve of the flume a hundred yards away but it wasn't Tako, it was Tom Archer and he was armed with a shotgun or a rifle – Kai Win couldn't tell at this distance in the poor light. Kai Win had never met Tom but he recognized him clearly from the description William and Bonnie had given him the night of their visit. He also remembered what

314

they'd told him about Tom, and about the revenges he'd sworn. Kai Win had no personal knowledge of the depth of Tom's prejudice and hate, but he knew the Hoods believed it to be full and abiding.

What should he do now? And – wait a minute – *where was Tako?* Had anything happened to him? He must have run into Tom Archer. A chill went through him. What if Tako *had* met Tom Archer on the flume? Then where was he now? Had he continued on toward the cannery? Had Tom *let* him continue on? Would he? Would Tom have hurt him? Kai Win had no way of knowing.

Suddenly he realized Tom hadn't seen him! Where he sat, the shadows and darker backdrops of the forest camouflaged him from Tom's direction. In a few moments Tom would see him but so far he hadn't. Kai Win made a reactive decision. Quickly, like a seal off an ice floe, he slipped over the edge using a trestle brace as footing for a heel, ducked under, then swiftly came up on the other side where the bank was steep and close to the side of the flume. He felt more secure on the ground, less exposed. The feeling an infantryman knows. He was in the deep forest, alone, facing a hateful man. The man was armed. What might happen? Kai Win had no idea and acted again in response to that vacuum. Near his foot was the chunky part of a broken limb about three feet long and he picked it up, hefted it lightly, moved it so it leaned next to his hand against the trestle. It wasn't much comfort, but some. Ducking down, he was out of sight.

He waited until Tom was just one step beyond him, then stood. In a voice he made friendly, he said, "Hello there."

Tom's reaction was surprisingly cool. He stopped and turned as if voices from the belly of the forest were the most natural thing. The shotgun remained slung on his shoulder, and small facts like that make big differences in the instantaneous confrontations of armed men among trees. It would have been a natural reaction for a trained, surprised man to unsling his weapon in a smooth movement as he turned to face the surprise, but Tom hadn't, having heard a voice without threat.

Kai Win would have had to allow him that reactive move, the flowing of the gun from the shoulder to the hand, because that would have been the natural motion under the circumstances, carrying no threat in and of itself.

But Tom Archer did not take the gun off his shoulder in an instinctive move. He didn't move the gun to his hand *until he saw Kai Win's face.*

****

When he turned in surprise and saw the Chinaman grinning up at him all the blocked images in his mind broke through at once, a ghastly kaleidoscope of sensations and pains and tortured denials, and flashes spotted in his head behind his eyes, and then the shotgun was swinging around off his shoulder and his stiff finger was going to the triggers and he was blasting the filthy squint-eyed son of a bitch with both barrels at once.

25

Kai Win had the split second granted him by the very decisiveness of Tom's actions. He recognized deliberateness as the shotgun swung, leveling, from Tom's shoulder, and his own taut fear hauled him down into a crouch of protection. The horrible double charge blasted barely over his head, exploding chunks of wood from the edge of the flume and sending slivers of spruce into the skin at the top of his shoulder. One heavy lead pellet glanced under his scalp just behind his left ear.

As the booming echo crashed off through the trees Kai Win heard the distinct click of the shotgun's breech opening and the pop of the two spent shells being ejected. Before the smoking cardboard and brass tubes had hit the wooden top of the flume, Kai Win had his club in his hand. He took three quick steps alongside the flume in Tom's direction, bent over so the man couldn't see him, and at the place he hoped Tom stood he popped upright, his chest at the height of the top of the flume, swinging the piece of wood with both hands, catching Tom at the backs of his calves.

The blow swept Tom's feet out from under him and he fell heavily on his back, thumping the water box with an expulsion of breath and surprise. Kai Win heard a brittle cracking at the moment of strike and hoped it was Tom's legs but knew instead it was only his club. Tom's back slammed the flume and the air whooshed from his lungs and the shotgun shells in his fingers pitched into the forest below. Tom's grip was firm on the gun but it was a stone age weapon now.

In the forest the wind shuddered the trees and in the combat beginning on the flume the odds were evened.

Kai Win dropped his broken branch and reached, on his tiptoes, groping, got his fingers in Tom's trousers cuffs and jerked, frantic to keep him from using the advantage of the gun, tugging him, throwing his bleeding head back for momentum, pulling as violently as his balance would allow. Kai Win was a roiling cloud bursting to light, his whole being shrieking with the power of this sudden combat. In a span of seconds the pace of his universe had raged from contemplative to frantic. His cells and his blood were electric charges bursting his skin. His brain raced to make sense of his reactions and the differential stretched his nerves to screams. He hadn't yet set himself to combat, hadn't yet had the opportunity to think, to be even one thought ahead of violence...

****

Tom's center of gravity had blown from under him, the black tree tops flashing past his thoughts just as he was realizing what had happened. He thought he had gotten two full loads into the squint and the air was slamming back into the rent of blast and his fingers had already started to reload the gun, and in the edge of his eye he saw motion and his legs were blown from his body with a tremendous crush of pain and sound. His head and back smashed the flume and as he saw himself slipping through the fogs of shock he struggled to focus, felt himself pulled toward the forest, a living prize being dragged to a lair and his thinking disintegrated and he was wild, lashing with his feet, twisting and throwing himself against the terror.

****

Kai Win had him almost at the edge and shifted his grip to Tom's ankle, was trying to pull him off the flume and onto the ground where he could kill him when Tom's boot lashed out, catching him high on the forehead, flaying through his scalp in a burst of stunning light. Kai Win's eyes rolled with the flashings and blood gushed across his vision but his grip was locked to Tom's leg and as he was thrown back from the blow he managed to pull Tom screaming from the flume. The man's head smashed against the trestle beams as he fell and as he threw his arms to protect his head the gun was flung from his hand. It caromed off a tree trunk, slithered under the flume through the blueberry bushes among the trestle supports, clattering against rocks on the steep slope. The two men were alone with their strengths now.

****

Tom Archer was dazed, landed hard and was addled again, and again the breath pounded from his lungs as he was thumped to the ground. A sharp spine of bedrock pierced his back above his kidney, and his weak elbow smashed against a trestle piece. Lightning shot up his arm, through his wrist, set the fingers of his hand afire. His head shook itself against the stabs of pain and confusion and his body twisted, thrashed against the ground and the grip on his leg and the imbalance, trying to swim through the pains and close with his adversary.

****

Now Kai Win had the advantage but he realized only mortal frenzy would sustain it. One of them would die this night under the trestle. He groped for a weapon, anything, still locked with one

319

hand to Tom's leg, fighting to keep his struggling opponent down and off balance. His other hand, clutching, groping and clawing in the forest trash for a weapon, for support on the hillside, closed on the broken half of the branch he'd used to knock Tom down. He seized it and it came up in his hand a dagger, jagged splinters of half-rotten wood, and he stabbed, stabbed, stabbed, yelling, throwing himself behind the blows, frenzied to kill.

****

Tom was a thrashing shark, throwing himself to escape, flailing with his arms and legs, kicking again and again, finally knocking the hand off his leg, freeing himself just as the squint's weapon slashed down. Red hot splinters pierced into his thigh just above his knee, ripping through his pants and lancing into his skin. The pain was overpowering and he screamed, kicking again, throwing himself to get away.

The other man took a powerful blow just below his knee and his leg caved and he went down, losing his weapon, grabbing at the trestle for support.

Tom threw himself over backward, away, away from the trestle, down the slope, and the other man heaved himself to follow. The shotgun was there, somewhere. Tom rolled and pushed up to his feet but their battleground was steep and his feet went from under him again and he flopped back against the slope. He was just to his knees, lifting his head, raising his face to confront his opponent when a fist smashed into his cheek.

The sound of bones crushing was like sticks breaking. The side of Tom's face caved in, his cheek shattered, white gristle and bone flashing before the blood spurted.

Gouts of pain gushed up Kai Win's arm. His knuckles were shattered and his wrist broken.

Both men writhed, fighting themselves now, refusing the demands of agony, trying to get their feet under them so the killing could continue.

Half of Tom's face was swelling fast and blood poured down his neck and across his shirt from the gaping wound on his cheek. His eye had turned black instantly, the eyeball itself a red orb, sightless. He thought for a second his neck had been broken by the blow to his face but he pushed the fears aside, tried to ignore the shock, turned his head to put his only eye on his opponent and as the man struggled to regain his feet, cradling his broken hand, Tom looked once around quickly, to find the shotgun.

It was nowhere. Almost totally dark. The flume above them was a stark silhouette.

****

Both men struggled for position now, Kai Win trying to keep Tom on his left side so he could grab at him with his only hand, trying to keep the blood from his forehead out of both eyes, almost blind. Tom's leg throbbed where it was stabbed and he hobbled, a crab, clutching at the mountain, trying to get into position to hit or kick. Neither of them wanted to close and wrestle, both too badly hurt to survive the biting and tearing of a grapple.

Tom found some footing and struggled against the slope, got one foot set, found some leverage, caught his balance and as Kai Win lunged for his legs, he lashed out with his foot. It caught Kai Win on the shoulder, rocking him back in a spin and twisting his feet from under him. He tumbled and slid down into the bushes below.

****

Tom was presented now with his first opportunity to charge, to take the advantage of momentum and plunge into battle from the heights, hoping for a killing blow, but he could barely see. His eyes were clouded with blood and with the swelling and the pain of his wounds, and night had come. The next blows would be struck in the dark.

Still wondering where the shotgun was and whether the Chinaman now had it, unsure of the extent of the other man's wounds, unwilling to commit himself to close fighting in the dark, Tom took the opportunity to escape. He used the footing he'd found to launch himself toward the trestle and was just crawling through the cross beams to get on the other side, from where he could crawl up onto the flume itself, when he was struck a tremendous blow on his right shoulder blade that sent fire rushing across his back and down his arm. He was driven nearly unconscious by the pain, and was saved from falling down the slope only by his embrace of the trestle beam.

****

Kai Win managed to stop his slide down through the small bushes and found himself with a large sharp rock clutched in his hand and in the last film of light he heaved it with all his remaining strength, hoping to brain Tom Archer. It struck the blade of the man's shoulder, probably breaking bone, putting his right arm nearly out of commission. Both men, gladiators, had hurt the other in a fast, grunting, killing lust.

Kai Win struggled to his knees and began pulling himself, clawing his way up the slope toward the flume and Tom, who was almost lost in the darkness.

****

Tom forced himself from the pain in his back and in his face and leg, his whole body burning, and pulled himself through the trestle braces, grimaced against the screaming his mind craved. His leg throbbed where huge splinters grated in his flesh. His face pounded in time with his heart, the eye closed entirely now, and his right arm hung, almost useless. He fought his way through the cross beams and turned to crawl onto the flume just as Kai Win got to the other side of the trestle.

Separated by five feet of cross braces, it was a stand-off. Neither man could make the next move. If Tom tried to get to the top of the flume he'd be exposed long enough for the other man to body-blow him, and that would end it. If Kai Win started through the trestle toward Tom he'd be tied up among the braces and cross beams, helpless to defend himself. Both men stood gasping, hauling air into their lungs, watching the other in the darkness and thinking no further than the agony of the moment. Both struggled to gain firm footing, preparing to fight more or flee.

Tom moved then, down along the trestle about three feet, crabbing sideways, watching his footing, keeping a wary eye on Kai Win, who took the opportunity to start through the trestle, cradling his broken hand, carefully watching for Tom to reverse himself.

Tom reached his goal, a stream of water jetting out from holes made in the flume by his shotgun blast. Quickly, using his good arm, he dashed water against his face and the snow-chill revived him, braced him, made him feel he could finish this thing. The shock of the cold water cleared his head and at that same moment he realized his footing was solid and with no reflection he threw himself up onto the flume, full length, rolled onto his knees, staggered to his feet. Pain swept through him in sickening waves and he felt himself blacking out, gave up his hopes to finish it here and now. He rubbed the nausea quickly from his mind, shifted his balance, turned and began stumbling down the flume toward the cannery.

****

Tako slowed as he felt the flume leveling out just above the cannery. The night was shallower here, the forest getting thinner as he neared the shore of the bay. Finally he could hear the flume water splashing into the reservoir tank and could see the shapes of the buildings against the lighter background of the open bay. He stopped then, out of plans and out of momentum, not sure what to do. The forest was a bouquet of needles and snow smells, pungent among his breaths. He spent many minutes sitting on the flume in the heavy shadow of a large tree trying to decide what his next step should be, resting on the stairs of a decision.

He couldn't spend the night there on the flume, for sure. It was getting cold and he'd have to find shelter for the night. But more important than a night spent shivering was his knowledge that Tom Archer was somewhere behind him and would be coming back soon. He reasoned the man had gone up to shut off the water in preparation for the next day's abandonment of the cannery and he knew the change in the water flow would give him plenty of warning that the man was on his way back.

Then suddenly he felt the approach of heavy, uneven treads. Hurrying, stumbling footsteps on the flume. He could feel the vibrations in his buttocks, up along his spine, and each *thud, thud* pounded a chill nail into his soul. He jumped to his feet and glanced up hastily into the dark potential of the forest, then peered in the direction out of which Tom Archer would come from the blackness. The vibration in the boards beneath him shoved him out of his indecision and he turned to start off the flume, to go down among the cannery buildings to hide… He was taking a step when the door at the lower landing of the cannery building opened. A

324

yellow cone of exposure was thrown out into the night, past him, missing him but floodlighting the flume behind him. He glanced toward the light and saw a man come through the door, saw him turning, starting to close the door...

Then Tako felt Tom Archer's nearness. He turned, and looked, and saw in a strobe the hideous apparition, froth at his mouth, half his face torn, his single eye a red hole of terror, grotesque. Blackened blood was streaming through the coats of mud on his face, gushing with the throb of his exertions from his gaping cheek, across his throat, down into the mat of his chest. His clothes were tattered and flapping with the head-jerking shuffle of his coming. Toward Tako.

In the freeze of Tako's sight Tom Archer was a monster hobbling at him along the flume, making no attempt at silence, huffing, his breath a putrid cloud before his ruined face, his horrible eye leading through the dark and into the light like a penetrating, evil bulb.

For a lifetime Tako was petrified, then he was hurled into motion by the explosion of his fright. As blackness crashed in with the closing of the door he whirled and hurtled toward the end of the flume, threw himself onto the side of the mountain, flung himself down the muddy embankment to the base of the water tank and darted for the concealing depths of the shadowed buildings beyond the factory...

Praying in a silent blabber that Tom hadn't seen him.

26

Tom *did* see him. He saw a small abandoned bundle and the movement, a figure, dashing away, leaping, wide-spread arms and legs flying. He saw him through a red and black haze in silhouette, but loathing focused the lens of his hates and he recognized the Chinese boy. A silent enraged roar shattered the tortured cells of his brain. His pains were blanked, the wounded man behind him forgotten, his mind locked on the holiness of stamping out *this* one, this *it* that filled his mind.

Where did it go?

There, darting around the tank... He would trap it, clutch it, bludgeon the filthy life... stab and slash...

****

Tako's soul heard the pitiless roar behind him and convulsions churned the coils of his guts. He plunged through the dark, arms thrown in a cross before his face, rebounding, looking for a crack, a hole among the shacks, trying locked doors, pushing at windows, turning to see behind him, dreading to see the ghoul on his heels.

Another door. A knob. It squealed, opened. He shoved against it, pushed it open, darted inside, closed it behind himself, leaning against it to keep from shaking to death. Absolute darkness.

He had to hide!

Reaching, groping with his hands, straining with useless eyes, he felt his way forward, kneed into something. Piles of gunnysacks. He felt his way along them, seeing with trembling hands. He found an opening and shouldered sideways, pushed himself into a hole. Crouched down, feeling, touching cardboard cases, cans, pieces of cloth and discarded trash. Dust floated into his nose and he fought the sneeze.

Something ugly scurried in the lair and he shrank back, clutching himself, his teeth chattering, images of tortured death… Oh, God…

The door *crashed* open.

Tom Archer stood hunched in the dark rectangle of the doorway, slobbering, ragged breath wheezing through a slime of snot and blood, his arm spread to the frame, an executioner from the devil at the door of a dungeon.

Tako shuddered, cold stinking vapors rising from his body, steam burning through the cloth of his pants as the acid urine poured from his bladder. Breath trapped in his throat. He willed himself from existence, to the edge of death, tried to shrink, feared the pounding of his heart would give him away, sounding drums pointing, pointing, POINTING!

The monster lurched in the doorway, stumbling forward in the litter, searching with the holes of his ears for his prey. His voice, thick and wet, filled the small shack like a low growl from the clay of a grave. "You're here, Anthony. I'll gut you with my bare hands. I can feel your eyes… I'm gonna cut 'em… you can't hide…"

Tom turned, reached at the wall.

Tako heard the glassy rattle of a lamp chimney. He saw his own steaming guts being torn from their roots and spilled into the filth on the floor, felt the black nails ripping through his skin and the horrid teeth on his throat…

Tom lifted the chimney and Tako's imploding mind showed the glimpse he'd had, the swollen eye, the smashed grotesque face, the blood pouring from the open cheek...

A match flared, a sun, an instant before blindness.

Tom Archer's three teeth were cruel fangs in the hideousness of his face.

The match moved to the lamp and the shed grew features as the wick caught.

Tako cringed from the advancing wave of light, wracked with shakes. In an instant the monster would see him and would rip his limbs from his body... Tako's hands clutched at themselves and at the sacks, trembling, seconds left to his life. His right hand closed on a can. It was smooth and cool and heavy against his palm and his fingers embraced it.

Tom Archer raised the lantern high, angling his head so his eye could follow the light, hunting the corners of the cave.

Tako threw the can at the horrible face with all his strength. He heard the sickening crushing of flesh and saw the lantern flung in a streaming arc against the wall. There was a crash and a flash of darkness thickened with terrible groans and the heavy smell of fuel, then a flicker, then a growing *whoosh* as the fire drank in the spreading kerosene.

In an instant the flames had trapped a stack of paper, spread to a rumpled pile of rags, were reaching for cartons and the wall. Tako drew back from the heat, saw Tom Archer writhing on the floor. In the bounding shadows he saw Tom Archer struggle to his knees, his hands covering his face, his elbows held in tight against the agonies. New blood poured between his fingers and a creening sound filled the shed. The crackling...

Now! Tako lunged past the creature on the floor, twisting his legs away from a blind grab, jerking himself away, a shrew cringing from the talons. His wits curdled at the animal wail that filled the shed when the groping claw closed on air and the tortured body collided again with the floor.

The flames climbed as Tako raced through the door, spinning out onto the boardwalk, deciding, deciding this way, toward the far end of the cannery. Away from Tom Archer.

****

In the shed Tom Archer felt the heat of the flames against his shattered face, tried to focus but couldn't. He stood, staggering, tottering back and forth, both hands holding his head, cradling his face where the sharp-edged can had struck. It had slammed into him just beneath his nose, had caved in his upper gum and split his lip from one side of his mouth to the other. His face throbbed and burned as if the fire were already licking its flesh. "The fire! Got to get out…" He groped, felt the flames, felt the wall, tried to see through his pain, tried to hold his eye open against the smoke, finally touched the cold air being sucked through the door, knew the heat of the flames was behind him, and was outside.

The back wall of the factory loomed in front of him close enough to lean against, supporting him, but the heat grew behind him, made him move. He turned the same way Tako had gone, away from the end of the flume, struggling along the boardwalk in the darkness behind the factory, fleeing now, not chasing.

****

From the flume Kai Win saw the flames shooting through the roof of the shed, saw the fire reaching toward the main building. In the dancing light he saw the figure of Tom Archer stumbling down the boardwalk behind the factory building, away from him. He reached the end of the flume and jumped as easily as he could onto the embankment, sliding under the flume. The shock of the movement drove a groan from his throat and he clutched his wounded hand to his chest, raised his eye to divert the flowing blood from his forehead, yelled weakly, croaked, "Tako…"

He struggled to his feet on the muddy slope, then slid down to the boardwalk. The pain shot through his arm as his broken hand jammed into the bank. The heat was already on his face. Flames were crawling up the back of the main building, licking at the old paint, climbing higher, stretching up onto the roof. Soon the whole building would be ablaze.

A muddy bundle on the ground caught his eye. He recognized things, knew it was Tako's, picked it up, held it in his hands, immediately felt the shape of his father's old revolver, the one Kevin Aspin had given to him when he and Lo An fled Canyon of Gold. He quickly dug into the bundle, cradling it at his elbow to protect his broken hand, digging, caught the trigger guard and pulled and jerked the gun out of the bundle, looked quickly to see it was loaded, threw the bundle back to the ground and looked around, finding his direction, moving…

He ran, gasping Tako's name, following the boardwalk to where it turned through the flames between the sheds and the factory building. Colored light jumped from the painted walls. Steam jetted from between the boards of the walk and climbed into the gases and smoke clogging his way. There was too much heat against his shielded face and he backed away from the chute of fire in the alley, turned along the end of the building, lurched across a muddy patch of ground to another boardwalk, staggered across the end of the building past the stairs and around the corner.

27

Tako mindlessly raced for his life. He reached the far end of the factory building and turned its corner, ignoring the boardwalk, one hand on the wall to whip speed into his turn, pounded back up onto the boardwalk, his feet thundering in cadence with his heart. In his ravaged mind Tom Archer was close on his heels, reaching for him. He charged through the darkness and ran full speed into a railing, nearly knocked himself out. The breath was smacked from his lungs.

Flickers of light shot out toward the bay from the rising flames. Tako stood trembling for just an instant, gasping, trying to get his wind back, willing himself to move again, knowing Tom Archer was just around the corner and coming for him. From where he stood shaking and sucking the air into his lungs he could go into the black of the forest or along the pier in front of the cannery. Quickly he decided for the pier and he lurched in that direction, was just starting to run when a crouched man stumbled around the far corner of the factory.

The distance was too great and the light too confused for Tako to make out who it was but in his fevered imagination it could only be Tom Archer. He skidded to a stop and turned where he stood, looking back in the direction from which he'd just come, was just shifting his weight to move toward the forest when Tom

Archer thrust himself around the corner in front of him, a hideous ghoul. Then who…

Tom Archer stopped. Then he started to move, bent forward, one arm already reaching, the claw of his hand dripping blood.

Tako backed up along the pier, feet groping on the uneven planks, his eyes frozen on the slow advance of his own horrible death. He chanced a quick look over his shoulder at the man who'd come around the far corner of the factory and was still lurching slowly toward Tako, supporting himself against the building as he moved. Who… Kai Win, *his father!*

At that moment Tom Archer also saw the approaching figure and without a reflective second or hint of hesitation he turned and lurched off, back through the bouncing shadows and light of the flames, into the blackness of the forest beyond the end of the pier.

Tako watched him disappear and turned around again just as Kai Win reached him.

Kai Win stopped, looking in the direction Tom Archer had taken. His words were broken by the ragged breath he clutched and drew into his lungs. "Tako…" He leaned over, retching. The sound of the growing inferno nearly drowned the sound of his gasps. "We have to. Make sure everybody. Out. It's gone. Everything will be. On fire. Tako, you stay here, on the pier. Go out there. Next to the water." He pointed to a place." Don't move. Do not move, no matter what."

"But that man…" Tako pointed, both hands extended toward the wall of the forest.

"Don't worry. He's finished." Kai Win looked up at the blazing cannery building. "I'll go through, make sure they're all out…" He suddenly realized something, turned and looked in all directions, up and down the boardwalk. "Where *is* everybody? There should be people…"

At that moment people did start to appear. Manuel and Nora hurried around the far corner of the building, coming from their place. Behind them there was shouting, then William and Jimbelly ran around the corner. They'd all been in their own bungalows down above the dark gravel beach, and the sound of the flames and the light bouncing off the bay had just reached them.

William rushed up to Kai Win, took one close look at his face, saw the revolver in his hand, said, "My God, Kai Win, what happened?"

Kai Win answered, "No time now. Is anybody left inside?" He pointed with the gun toward the building, which had become a silhouette against the flames. Soon the pier itself would be blazing, no safe place except the deep forest away from the cannery, and the water.

William shouted against the noise of the flames. "No. Nobody left here! They all went out today. We've got to get out of here!"

Tako pointed, shouted, "Look!"

At the beach below the bungalows Jimbelly was pushing a skiff into the water, throwing himself in, pulling the motor rope. William started to run there, to stop him, but after only a few steps he halted. It was useless. The motor was already started. The man had too much of a head start, was panicked, was deserting them, taking the skiff... Without a backward glance Jim Bell headed out into the empty bay and was soon swallowed by the night. Even the sound of the receding motor was quickly lost in the growing roar of the flames.

William yelled, "Never mind! There's another skiff! Come on, it should be at the other end of the pier, by the trees. We'll use it..." The heat on the pier was becoming intolerable as the factory building fed itself to the flames. Soon the front wall would collapse and the entire pier would be engulfed, even the bungalows and the near edges of the forest would go. The whole area around the cannery would be a pyre.

When they reached the forest at the end of the pier where the other skiff should have been, William yelled, "What the hell? It's gone!"

Kai Win yelled back, "Tom Archer went in there. He's got it."

****

William began to recognize the depths of his own confusion. What? What was Kai win doing here anyway? Here, at night, at the cannery? Why was his face so battered, his hand, the gun... Why would Tom Archer... And Tako? What the hell was going on here? And the fire... He started to confront Kai Win with his confusion.

Kai Win stopped him, yelled over the noise behind them, "Tom Archer tried to kill me up on the flume. He ran into the forest here. If he's got the skiff he's somewhere out there now." He pointed toward the bay. There was no time now. "We can take care of him later. Right now we've got to get out of here." The heat slammed against them. William pointed to the flame-brightened wall of trees. "Come on, we've got to get off this pier, into the forest, away from here. We can make it down the shore until we're safe..."

Tako held up his hands, backing up toward the heat, palms out. "*No!* That man's in there. He tried to kill me. I'm not going there!"

William started to say something when Nora yelled, "Wait, there's another boat! Under the pier! Bonnie's crab dinghy!"

They all raced down to the center of the pier, looked over the edge, down the ladder. Manuel was the first to see it tied below the pier. "But wait. It's too small for all of us. It'll take three people, maybe four."

William shouted against the noise of the night, "Manuel, you go down and pull it up next to the ladder. Nora, you follow, then you, Tako. You three get in. If there's room, Kai Win, you go. Hurry! Be careful!" Allowing no argument, he shoved Manuel toward the ladder, then Nora. "Go on, Manuel, hurry!"

Manuel disappeared over the edge of the pier, down the ladder. Nora followed. The others leaned over the edge, watched Manuel pull the dingy around, saw him get in, grabbing at the gunwales with both hands to still its rock. He pulled the dinghy next to the ladder and helped Nora in. "Come on! One more!"

Kai Win pushed Tako toward the ladder. "Go on, boy."

Tako stood for a second looking at the two men, then went over the edge. When he'd eased himself in, fitting himself against Nora in the bottom of the little boat, Manuel yelled up, One more! We can do it! Come on, but be careful."

William said, "Go, Kai Win!"

Kai Win held up his broken hand and shouted, "I can't get down the ladder. Quickly, you go. I'll go to the forest."

William started to argue but Kai Win had already turned and was fighting his way past the heat toward the forest where Tom Archer had disappeared. William went quickly down the ladder and when he'd squeezed himself into the dinghy Manuel carefully paddled it away from the steaming pier.

****

Kai Win was just inside the forest, pushing carefully through the branches to get down to the shore when he heard a pitiful scream and the sounds of thrashing in the shallows ahead of him. He knew it was Tom Archer and went to finish things.

****

Tom Archer had remembered the skiff at the end of the pier and knew he needed it. He was too badly hurt to make it far through the woods. In the skiff he could get out. He could make it to the Indian village, drifting on the night tide past the saltery and then motoring out of the bay through the dark night. Then? He shook his head, trying to clear it. He reached the water and turned toward the cannery, following the high water mark in the prancing shadows along the trees toward the fire-lighted outline of the pier. The skiff was where it should be. He got in, found the paddle, unclipped the rope, then pushed off with the paddle, staying close in to the shore where the trees shielded him from the light of the fire. His entire body burned with his pains and a continuous low groaning burbled past his ruined, bleeding lips. Still he moved, paddling with his one arm, slowly dragging the yawing boat through the tensions on top of the water.

He hadn't gone far along the shore when he heard the others, loud, yelling about the missing skiff, but by then he'd gone far enough to feel safe starting the motor. He was beyond their reach. Let them burn. He shipped the paddle, almost blacking out, and turned to the outboard, struggling to see through all the darknesses.

There was no gas can! The motor was useless.

Overwhelmed, fighting waves of nausea, shuddering with the throbbing bolts in his face and shoulders and leg, he got the paddle again, saw the tide was taking him away from the shore and panicked, forgot any plan, just knew he had to get ashore, to think, to decide what to do. He paddled as frantically as he could toward the shore. He would pull the boat up, tie it, rest until he could decide what to do...

Finally he heard the bow scrape against the rocky shore. He moved carefully forward and stepped over the side onto the rocks. He had no more thoughts for the others, or for the unknown night.

336

As he shifted his weight onto a water-slick stone his foot went out from under him and the shifting momentum of his changing balance hurled him down onto the jagged rocks. He heard his thigh break and as his gasp of a scream surged through the froths in his throat he knew he was a dead man.

****

Fifty feet further down the shoreline the grizzly heard the pain and picked up its lolling head. Trying to keep its balance, it limped forward on failing legs to investigate the watery, thrashing sounds of a large animal in agony.

28

In the village down the coast the meeting went on, as it always had and as it always would, continuing even when there was only one old Indian talking to himself in the meeting house. This day there were half a dozen men there, talking about one of their company. That one limped to the water bucket, took a drink, replaced the dipper on its nail and turned back to face the others who were all sitting on the floor against the unpainted walls. Stinking kinnikinick glowed in a pipe and unfiltered cigarette smoke blended with the acrid tendrils leaking from the old wood stove. Rheumy eyes watched the one who stood by the water bucket.

One of the men spoke. "You did well. You made trouble for the intruders that they could not understand." There were nods of agreement. "There was no simple answer." Heads nodded. "This old man is still sad those others had to be killed long ago. But the one who sold our land in the bay without the approval of this council, the one whose bones rest in the crab-shaped cove, he betrayed his people and called retribution on himself. And the white man who brought the Chinese coolies to Canyon of Gold would have told others what he found in the ravine above, in time, if he had been allowed to live. It was unfortunate that he used his white man's law to give the land to the Chinese." Silent nods again, all around the perimeter of the room. "Maybe it was a mistake, when they first came here, to sell the Chinese man and his woman

338

the supplies they needed. We could have made them leave our island those many years ago, perhaps. But it was good that we were able to discover what they knew, and what they did not know.

"Now this old man is happy. It has all turned out to our advantage." He looked up at the one who was standing and accepting his due. "It was very clever of you to stir up the whites at the cannery, to set them against the Chinese. Now the saltery is deserted, and the cannery is in ashes, and the secret of the gold nuggets in the ravine is safe again. If they had stayed, someday they would surely have found the gold and then, soon, all our land would be gone, as the Black Hills were taken from our brothers in the time of our grandfathers."

There were more nods of agreement among the men, and Joe Badhand silently accepted their regards. He was sorry the old Chinese coolie was dead, but it was his time. And the other two, the ugly white man with shame in his eyes and the strong Chinese son… Well, there have always been the bears, and one must beware of them. He lifted his chin to get attention and when he had it, said, "But we must always be vigilant. The white men are not patient. But the Chinese people are very patient. Perhaps even more patient than Indian people."

****

In another hut of the Indian village the old Chinese woman hugged the shawl tighter and rocked in her chair, back and forth, remembering the sounds and the sights. She could still smell the deer skins thawing in Kevin Aspin's shed, heated by the bodies of the coolies. Deng Wei and her son were often on the edge of her hearing and sometimes she spoke, answering them. And she cried for them.

Later, after word was passed in Juneau, a young man came to stand in front of her, waiting silently until the Indian who had shown him to the hut had closed the door, leaving them alone.

"Hong tai-tai." He bowed deeply to a revered grandmother of the Family. "I am Hong Gwo Dau. My old grandfather said you are to come with me. He says you will spend your days with us in Ju-no until some nephews and nieces are ready to come and salt the herring fish in the summer. He says the saltery is on the land of Hongs and he tells me to say that land must never again be a wilderness. My old grandfather says to remind you of the day of the deer skins. He says to remind you of the words you spoke to the men that day. He says he was one of those men.

"We are Chinese. We are Hongs. We are your *family*. Come."

Cover photo by the author.
Author photo by the mailman.
Bear painting by Alicia.

Made in United States
Troutdale, OR
05/18/2025

31359343R10208